...Til was very attractive, but it had been Harp's initial impression that he was straight. Nonetheless, Doug had purposely left the house, allegedly on an errand, leaving Harp and Til alone. After he excused himself to go to the bathroom, Til returned, stark naked, his cock erect. "I figured this might look good to you guys."

In fact, it looked extremely good to Harp. The fat seven-plus inches of smooth, nicely circumcised meat standing straight out from Til's muscular body looked very good indeed, but Harp played his cards fairly close to his chest. "Well, you've got a great body and a nice big cock, but why do you think that either Doug or I would be interested?"

Til leered as he approached the seated Harp, stroking the shaft of his delicious cock, "C'mon, I'm not stupid. Two guys livin' alone like this, both really good-lookin' guys, askin' me out here. I know what you want!" He stepped in front of Harp, the mushroom head of his throbbing cock only inches from his mouth. "This looks good to you, don't it? C'mon, check it out!"

And it did look good to Harp, and as Til took the back of his head in his hand and pulled it inward, he opened his mouth and accepted the offering. As Harp fondled Til's balls and savored the delicious mouthful, Til drove himself deep into his throat with savage thrusts for some time, but then unceremoniously pulled out and led Harp to the bedroom, where he flopped on his back and smirked, "Make love to this big cock!" As Harp stripped off his clothes, knelt over the supine Til, and again began to suck and lick the exciting shaft, Til purred, "Yeah, suck me off!" and moaned encouragement to Harp in ever-increasing passion as his thrusts grew faster and deeper. Holding Harp's hair tightly in both hands and forcing his head up and down the lengthy shaft, Til was fucking his mouth with real ferocity and obviously nearing orgasm. Harp barely managed to pull his head away before Til's massive emission spattered them both with his violent discharge....

Model/Escort

An erotic novel by
JOHN BUTLER

FLF/STARbooks Press
Sarasota, Florida

This book made possible in part by a grant from
the Florida Literary Foundation.

First edition published in the U.S. December 1998

Library of Congress No.98-074232
ISBN No. 1-891855-07-7

"This novel hymns the joys of
sex between men, often in quite explicit
terms. If you don't enjoy singing along with
hymns of that nature, this book is not for you.

If that is the case, find something else to
read, turn on the TV, have a nice day.

If the reader perceives a slight
deviation from reality here and there,
if at times this seems to be a
paean to penile plenitude,
bear in mind that we always sing
hymns louder and lustier when the
organ is big!"
—John Butler

DEDICATION

In the course of my life, I was fortunate enough to enjoy sexual liaisons with many, many attractive and exciting young men, some of whom appear in the following pages somewhat changed, and under different names, but interacting with fictional characters in the story as they interacted (or as I had hoped they would) with me. Although I had unforgettable sexual experiences with a gratifyingly large number of partners, I was blessed with only three lovers—two of them my partners in long-term relationships, and who both tragically left this world far too many years before their time here should have been up.

My first lover, Richard, with whom I lived for only a few months, and who initiated me into the thrill of complete sex does not appear in these pages, but our actual experiences together are lovingly remembered as I recreate them here under the guise of fiction. Richard is very much alive, I am happy to say, but he is doing very well without me, I am sad to report! Still, I continue to love him.

Of my two major lovers, one lived to be only forty-nine, and died as the indirect result of a terrible physical disease. The other died as the indirect result of a terrible mental disease, and was only in his thirty-first year. One was my lover for a far-too-short period of only six months. One was my lover for a far-too-short period of only twenty-four years. After reading the following pages, some might think that the lover who died at thirty-one was the one I enjoyed the twenty-four year relationship with; such is not the case!

I thrilled to the wonderful kind of love celebrated herein with those two men. The first was the sweetest and kindest man I ever knew—and I was the only person in the world to know fully how sweet and kind he was. The second was quite simply the most astonishingly beautiful human being in the world, and literally millions of gay men the world over knew how beautiful he was. One I knew to be completely honest and moral; one seemed to share those qualities, but I later learned he was dishonest, self-centered to a dangerous degree, and almost completely amoral—and maybe even beyond that! Yet I loved them both. I still love them both.

One of those two unforgettable men is actually mentioned several times in the pages that follow, but neither appears in the story in any real or fictionalized form. But this book is nonetheless dedicated to them:

For Mike, and for Rommel

Rest in Peace, my wonderful Mike, my glorious Rommel— I shall always love both of you. I hope by now you have met and discovered the common bond you share in me, and lie together regularly, anticipating the heavenly, eternal threesome we will someday celebrate together.

BRAD

1.

For a long time now, he had felt guilty about not feeling guilty. No, really guilty! I mean, what the hell was the matter with him? He apparently had everything a reasonable man could want—a beautiful wife, a son that any man would be proud of, a successful business, and until fairly recently a happy (if a bit dull) home life. But one day in the spring of 1995 he announced to his wife that the present that would most please him for his impending forty-fifth birthday was a divorce.

Perhaps one of the reasons he thought he should feel guilty was the way that Gwen had reacted. She couldn't have been nicer. (That, incidentally, had pissed him off—she should have caused a scene, at least.) She was, in fact, so calm and understanding that he couldn't help feeling that she might have been preparing a little separation announcement of her own, but she had not needed to play that particular card, and had thus let him assume the role of home-wrecker. After the fact (of course, it's always 20/20 hindsight) he realized that there had been no lack of clues that her interest in sustaining their union had begun to fade even before his had completely eroded two years earlier.

They both came from stable, well-to-do families (his probably better described as wealthy) back East—families who did not regard divorce as the natural concomitant of marriage that it was rapidly becoming. Had they stayed back East, and had Brad gone into the family investment business, they might have continued to lead the narrow, prescribed existence their families would have expected from on-site offspring and siblings. But, there was no use in crying over spilled blue blood; they had emigrated to California for both their education and their adulthood.

It took Gwen Andrews three years before she headed West to be with her future husband and long-time sweetheart—she as a sophomore transfer student, he in grad school by then. Her parents had categorically refused to allow her to follow Bradley Thornton to Stanford University when, two years after he departed for Leland Stanford Jr.'s former farm, she had graduated from an institution which was something between a "ladies' finishing school" and a nunnery. They insisted she matriculate at Vassar or Radcliffe, or some other civilized institution, and so she dutifully put in a year at Wellesley before her father capitulated to her ever-more-shrill protestations and shipped her off to Palo Alto. At least it was in the Bay area, he rationalized, far removed from the moral cesspool of Los Angeles.

As fate would have it, Brad had arrived in California in 1968, but in spite of the free-wheeling sexual background soon to be chronicled here, and armed with cordovan wingtips and a budding fraternity mentality, he had resisted the siren song of the bizarre denizens of the Haight-Asbury district forty miles to the North. By the time Gwen showed up, the "Summer of Love" was showing signs of an approaching, and perhaps even encroaching Autumn. They were married in Gwen's senior year, and both received degrees on the same Spring morning: his a Master's of Business Administration, hers a double-major B.A. in English Literature and Journalism. Brad's father reluctantly set him up in business, a travel agency, which occasioned considerable head-shaking and eye-rolling on the part of both the Andrews and the Thornton clans.

In 1974, they settled in San Francisco—at that time indisputably the most beautiful and enjoyable city in the world. Gwen attended classes at San Francisco State while she learned and polished her skills as a homemaker and hostess in their modest three-bedroom house in the Richmond district, only a few blocks from the esthetic and recreational attractions of either Golden Gate Park or Lincoln Park.

By the time Gwen's Graduate degree was due, so was she—and their son, who was to be their only child, was born just three days after her M.A. was conferred in 1977. Joshua Andrew Thornton was, to their way of thinking, the most beautiful child ever born, and as the golden-haired, tanned, athletic, sweet and cheerful boy grew, their families, their friends, their neighbors, their acquaintances, and even casual passers-by seemed to come around to their way of thinking. Josh came by his stunning good looks honestly: Gwen was a strikingly beautiful woman, and the golden-haired, muscular

Brad was generally considered one of the most handsome men in San Francisco—a city which was attracting more and more handsome men every year. It was, incidentally, becoming increasingly obvious to the country that it was the presence of those handsome men which was perhaps as great a factor in attracting even greater numbers of handsome men to the city as the famous landmarks and enviable climate.

Brad and Gwen's parenthood further convinced their families that they had made a serious mistake in relocating to the West Coast. "The Land of fruit and nuts," as Gwen's father had grumbled in a characteristically cliched pronouncement, "is no place to raise a child. And a son, too—my God, can you imagine what lies in store for him?" No one was quite sure what logical train-of-thought led to the conclusion that a boy was more prone to corruption in the California sun than a girl, but no one ever much challenged Mr. Andrews' assertions anyway; his self-certified *ex cathedra* pronouncements were, in fact, frequently vulnerable to challenge, but it just seemed easier for everyone to let him have his say, and, basically, ignore him.

By the time Josh was old enough to attend school, Gwen put her education to use as an assistant editor for a struggling feminist magazine. Her journalistic skills and business acumen qualified her for the top editorial position within a fairly brief period of time, and shortly thereafter the magazine was re-named *Bitch*; under Gwen's direction its readership grew exponentially in both size and dedication, and *Bitch* became a sort of hip, sassy, chic *Ms*.

Brad's business thrived as well, and he was fortunate enough to find staff sufficiently loyal and capable, and whom he recompensed sufficiently, that he had to devote little time to the actual operation of the several Thornton Trips and Tours outlets in the Bay area. He also granted virtually all of the travel perks to his administrative staff (strangely, neither he nor Gwen was especially fond of traveling), which further cemented loyalty and provided incentive for excellence. Gwen actually worked much harder than he, and devoted far longer hours to her work. As a result, Josh was more often with his father than with his mother, which was an arrangement that all three of them found ideal.

Brad guided his much-loved son through the usual Little

League, Cub Scout and Boy Scout activities, and high school soccer (mercifully, Josh was not interested in football), and the two presented the perfect picture of The All-American Boy and his Dad—Norman Rockwellian to be sure, but not sickeningly so. Josh was an uncommonly beautiful boy (and, later, young man), but he was occasionally a pain in the ass, and Brad was an equally handsome, supportive father who occasionally screwed up and failed to understand his son. Still, they were much closer than most father-son pairs, and even when puberty set in and his classmates decided their parents were actually sub-cretinous ogres, Josh continued to respect and venerate his dad. He also loved Gwen; she was his mother, after all, and she was a good and loving mother—if a little more preoccupied than his friends' mothers seemed to be. He also *liked* his parents—perhaps more important than loving them, actually.

Two years earlier, Brad had set the occasion of Josh's high school graduation and anticipated enrollment at Gwen's grad-school alma mater, San Francisco State, as the time to announce his desire for a divorce. His son would be more or less on his own, his wife was ever busier with her own pursuits, and he would have reached an age where if he was to effect sea changes in his life, he needed to act.

The sea change Brad particularly sought was one which would have been fairly unthinkable only a few years earlier, but in the nineties was becoming relatively commonplace. It could be viewed as a step toward self-realization, or as emancipation from socially enforced sublimation, or as an assertion of independence. His family (and, in spades, Gwen's family) would no doubt view it as an act of madness, or satanic possession, or perhaps (worst of all) even the act of a latent Democrat (if they ever learned of it—he was beginning to wonder if he even gave a damn if they did). However it might be viewed, it was something he had long contemplated and had refused to consider until recently. And it was very simple to explain: he wanted to come out of the closet as a gay man.

Bradley David Thornton—fraternity man, occasional jock, husband, father, something of a poster boy for all-American values—had known for thirty years he was gay, but until two years ago had refused to accept the concept (no—the fact) that although he lived a heterosexual life, in his sexual fantasies (where his true nature manifested itself) he really preferred boys to girls, men to women. For eighteen years he had completely sublimated his desires, and even in the last two years had only occasionally indulged them. Even the thirty-year window of sexual awareness was conservative; he'd found men's and boys' bodies more attractive than their feminine counterparts as far back as he could remember, but he hadn't worried about it until he entered prep school at age fourteen. Before that he regarded it as a "stage" he was going through—normal "hero worship" or one of the other typical subterfuges under which incipient gay men delay or deny acceptance of their budding nature.

It happened there had been an almost universal participation in some form of homosexual horseplay at his Connecticut prep school, Darby. There could not have been more than a half-dozen of his classmates who had not at least tried sucking a cock, or kissing and fondling another boy—especially in their first few years there. By their final year, most of those who had not just tried sucking a cock, but who had realized that ambition countless times had become firmly interested in girls; the same was true for the surprisingly large number who reportedly had also enjoyed taking one 'up the butt' or burying their own in a willing ass. Except for the occasional instance of mutual masturbation or the "boy was I drunk last night" slip-up, most seniors had abandoned their brief flirtation with homosexuality, leaving it to those few who might want lengthier dalliance with confirmed sodomites. Brad was almost sure he was part of this latter class, but until his senior year only one other person was equally sure—his roommate of three years' duration, Roy Saunders.

Roy, a sophomore, and he, a freshman, had been rooming together not more than three weeks when Brad walked in on him one afternoon and found him busily "flogging the dog." Rather than hiding himself and acting embarrassed, Roy had simply grinned and said, "Sorry about this, Thornton—I've just gotta relieve a little pressure!"

Brad grinned weakly back at him and tried to hide his sudden erection. "No, that's okay."

"Of course if you'd lock that door you could help me, if

you'd like."

Brad was presented with a dilemma. He was afraid to give in to his initial impulse here, but the young man lying before him was not only someone he had really come to like and admire, he was also one of the few boys in the school who might be even more handsome than he—and he was stroking an organ of such tempting beauty, such undeniable rigidity, and of such an enviable and (to Brad) stupefying size, that every instinct told him to go for it.

After locking the door, indicating how he had resolved his dilemma, Brad demonstrated that he would, indeed like to help Roy with his predicament, and Roy quickly discovered that Brad himself needed (or at any rate wanted) help with the identical problem. They had a difficult time even finding all their clothes after the intensely passionate hour that followed—the first of hundreds upon hundreds of such sessions over the next three years. And in the course of their first hour as sexual playmates, Brad realized a number of ambitions that had hitherto been only fantasies. He had not only kissed another boy passionately and fondled his body with equal fervor, he had provided the oral worship he had dreamed of, and had discovered the corollary delight of being on the receiving end of that brand of worship! What he had not really thought much about doing proved to be the most exciting thing that happened that afternoon. The thrill of sharing orgasms with another boy had certainly occurred to him, but to have his discharge actually sucked from his cock at the moment of ejaculation—and swallowed as greedily and joyously as Roy did his—so stimulated him that he was more than ready to return the favor a few minutes later. The taste? Nectar, ambrosia, excitement ... love. By the time their 'first anniversary' rolled around (the next afternoon, one whole day as ... whatever they had become) they had celebrated that same thrilling communion service three more times—and (most exciting of all) they had shared it simultaneously each time.

It was not more than a week later that Roy lay on his back with his legs spread wide and raised high, and invited Brad to learn what real love-making between two boys could be like. Brad learned quickly—and, thereafter, demonstrated his new-found skill often! The sensation? Excitement, pleasure, thrill ... ecstasy! ... LOVE! When he succumbed a few days later to Roy's pleading, and knelt on all fours to offer himself to the eager lover who knelt behind him, he doubted he could make good on his offer. But he put forth special effort, wanting to provide Roy with the same thrill the older boy had provided him. The feeling? Discomfort, pain, greater pain, unbelievable warmth and thrill, followed by utter, complete, blinding rapture!

It would no doubt have been easier on Brad had he made his "debut" as a sexual bottom with a boy less spectacularly endowed than Roy, but it would have been somewhat less thrilling. He could not have known it at the time, but he later came to appreciate how naturally suited his first lover was to providing him the thrills he sought. Aside from the excellent and admirable equipment he employed so masterfully in his love-making, Roy was also affectionate, considerate, and good-natured. Brad could not have been more fortunate in finding those qualities in a first love.

For almost three full years Brad and Roy were, in effect, lovers as well as roommates, but no one apparently much suspected their true relationship—or, if they did, they said nothing about it. There was a very active and not-at-all kind or subtle rumor mill at Darby, but Roy and Brad were not mentioned as a team when—as must inevitably happen—one or the other of them had done something to stir up the interest of the gossipmongers. They were careful about their love-making, eschewing the practice of it in the woods, the locker room, or any other places where they frequently found themselves tempted, and containing it in their dormitory room when they were in residence—and always locking their door. No matter how frenzied or athletic their often extremely passionate pursuits became, they allowed themselves to be as vocally excited as they wanted to be only when they were able to insulate their activities from others—in their own rooms when they were visiting each other during breaks and holidays, or in hotel or motel rooms when they were on trips.

If both were in residence, it was a very rare day that each did not bring to his partner at least one or two orgasms, and three and even four climaxes were not uncommon, although normally not in the same session (two- or three-session days were usual).

Brad's record with Roy was five orgasms in one twenty-four hour period, but Roy topped that record quite a number of times, and often while he was topping the beautiful, blond runner-up! Youth!

It was only after Roy graduated that Brad began to wonder if there might not have been some suspicion of the nature of their relationship after all, for during his entire senior year he was besieged with an unusually large number of apparent propositions to share sexual favors with a schoolmate. No doubt many were proffered because it suddenly seemed he was more available, but he did not realize how stunningly attractive he had become: a vision of his face and body fueled the production of thousands of manually-produced ejaculations, and only a few of those engaged in producing them were brave enough to seek live contact with their inspiration. Most of the overtures he received were subtle and tentative—although some were relatively blatant, and quite a few were out-and-out propositions—but Brad turned a deaf ear and a firmly zipped fly to most of them. Only a half-dozen or so of the most unusually attractive or well-endowed were taken up on their offers.

The fact that his new roommate during his senior year was an unimaginative troll was helpful. "Mook" Dawson was two years younger than Brad, and probably owing to his inferior class standing, agreed (and, surprisingly, kept his promise) that anything which occurred on Brad's side of the room was none of his business, and was not to be related to anyone! Brad entertained various handsome and horny callers a number of times when his roommate was on site, and entertained his super-endowed classmate Dan ("Whopper") Toole rather frequently.

Dan Toole's nickname was granted in honor of his possessing the most admired and envied cock in the dormitory—more imposing than even the departed Roy's by a good (no, a great) inch-and-a-half. His family name was simply a fortuitous, delightful coincidence. Even those not disposed toward homosexual play of any kind commented on how superbly hung Whopper was. Almost everyone in the dormitory had at some time or other handled the stunning dick and brought it to full and magnificent erection, and almost all of those had gone on to coax from it an emission of a such a copious and explosive nature that Whopper gained the additional nickname "Shooter"! An impressive percentage of those checking out Whopper's equipment had gone on in private to further accord it far more serious and gratifying attention. Although he was completely masculine and athletic as well, Whopper was by nature disposed to offer himself in such a way that those who worshipped at his 'shrine' found their idol more than willing to return in kind any acts of adoration they performed. Put more plainly and succinctly, Whopper was happy to return a blowjob, or to take anyone up the butt who'd offered his own ass to his monster cock's pleasure.

The last two months of Brad's senior year found him in another relationship, this time with Chris Drake, a diminutive, blond, very handsome, but also slightly effeminate boy, two years younger than he. It had begun dramatically one Friday night, in what proved to be by far the most complicated and emotional sexual experience Brad had ever known.

Following a shower Brad was coming out of the bathroom on the dormitory hall, naked but for a towel draped over his shoulder. He was surprised to see one of his classmates coming out of a room across the hall from the bathroom—also naked, and not even with a towel—and (he couldn't help but notice) with a cock not only mostly erect, but obviously moist and even glistening! Nudity was not unusual in the dorm, but aside from trips to the bathroom or shower (and the housemaster did his best to curtail even that limited display of naked flesh), it was normally contained in one's room—and walking around with an almost-dripping hard-on like the one Randy was sporting was certainly not usual! The door to the room stood open, and Brad could see several guys inside—also naked.

He asked, "What's going on?"

Randy grinned and said "You'd better get in there, Thornton!" Then he headed down the hall.

Brad put his head in the door and gasped. The large two-man desk in the room had been cleared, and young Chris Drake lay on his back on it, naked, his raised legs widely spread, and moaning in ecstasy. Holding Chris' legs apart, and standing between them, one of Brad's classmates was violently driving his cock into the young blond's ass! There were three other naked boys in the room, watching intently and stroking themselves as they did. One of them was Whopper Toole.

"Whopper, what in hell is going on?"

"Jesus, Thornton, this is unbelievable! Drake kinda went crazy a little while ago. Jerry and some other guys were teasing him and he yanked off his clothes, shoved everything off his desk and lay down on it, and told Jerry to fuck him! Then he said that when Jerry was through he wanted every one of them to fuck him. So far, four guys have blown their loads inside him, and look at him—he's enjoying the holy hell out of it! Shit, he jacked himself off twice while he's been getting it!"

Brad could see spatters and a sizable puddle of white fluid on Chris' stomach.

Brad was well aware that Chris Drake liked to get fucked. He had made it very clear to Brad that he wanted sex with him, and on three different occasions the younger boy had joined Brad in bed—where the two had done just about everything imaginable. It had been Brad's impalement of him on his impressive cock that Chris had been especially enthusiastic about, however, and even though Chris was still only around sixteen, Brad found him to be an extremely satisfying sex partner. But this! My god, they were gang-banging the kid.

"Damn, Whopper, why didn't somebody stop them?"

"Does it look like he wants to stop? Hell, the kids eating it up! Darryl and Andy are next in line after Brent is through, and then I get to fuck him! Shit, man, look how horny we all are!"

Brad had to admit that Chris seemed to be in heaven. He was moaning in pleasure, and eagerly meeting the thrusts entering him. In a few minutes Brent fell over Chris, and began to kiss him noisily. His driving buttocks sped up and he shortened his stroke. Both participants panted and though their cries were muffled by their mouths, it was obvious they were ecstatic while Chris took another orgasm into his body.

Darryl positioned himself behind Brent and began to caress his ass. "C'mon Brent, I get it next!" Brent stood, grinned over his shoulder at Darryl, and moved aside. Darryl stepped in, and with one lunge buried himself deep into Chris, who again began to moan in pleasure and counter the violent thrusts of the new cock entering him.

Brad's own cock was fiercely hard now, and he and Whopper

watched Darryl, and then Andy both deliver their loads. Andy had been one of those classmates who had approached Brad for sex after Roy's departure, but had been turned down. He was nice-looking, but not especially handsome, and of only slightly more than ordinary endowment. Watching Andy now, however, Brad was surprised to see how uncommonly beautiful his ass looked—undulating, and writhing as he drove himself in—and wondered if he might enjoy receiving from Brad the same thing he was now giving Chris. Furthermore, Andy was demonstrating such considerable skill at what he was doing that Brad suspected he would himself enjoy submitting his own body to that expertise! He made a mental note to reopen negotiations with Andy soon.

After Andy finished, he withdrew, cupped Whopper's obviously ready equipment for a moment (quite a long moment, if the truth be told), and told his magnificently endowed classmate to "go for it." He also groped Brad (equally 'at the ready') for quite a few seconds longer than he had afforded even Whopper, and gave him a sexy smile on his way out. Brad felt sure opened negotiations with Andy were going to prove productive and quite interesting!

Whopper raised Chris' legs as he positioned himself behind. "Here's the biggest cock around, Drake!" Chris closed his eyes and licked his lips as he panted, "Give it to me hard, Whopper!"

Whopper and Brad were alone in the room with Chris now, and Brad fondled Whopper's ass as he fucked, and inserted the tip of his finger into it. Whopper was feverish with excitement as he pounded Chris, but he turned his head slightly and commanded Brad, "Deeper, Thornton, finger-fuck it!" He continued his merciless pounding of the writhing youngster, and soon his anal sphincter clamped Brad's invading finger tightly while he drove his cock as far into Chris as he could, until his body grew rigid and he froze in position. Brad could feel the spasms of Whopper's orgasm transmitted to his finger—seven or eight spurts, apparently, each accompanied by a wild grunt.

Chris' legs rested on Whopper's shoulders; he smiled up at him and whispered, "You're always the best, Whopper! God, what a dick!"

Whopper's hands played over Chris' chest. "You want Thornton now?" Without waiting for a reply, he stepped back, withdrawing from Chris as he did so, and yielded the place of honor to Brad.

Chris held his hands out toward Thornton. "Fuck me, Brad! Kiss me and fuck me hard!"

Brad turned to Whopper. "For God's sake Whopper, stay and watch if you want, but close the door—if the housemaster wandered up here and found this we'd all be out on our butts!"

By the time Whopper had closed the door, Brad was lying on top of Chris and the two were kissing passionately as Brad gradually entered the youngster. Chris' sphincter was distended, and his chamber was full of the orgasms of the eight guys who had already screwed him, but even though the tightness Brad usually enjoyed in Chris was not there that night, the presence of eight different loads bathing his cock in a soup of passion was incredibly stimulating.

Chris murmured his appreciation of Brad's love-making, and while his participation in his gang-bang had been eager before, it became almost savage now.

"Fuck me, Brad! It's always you I want!"

Whopper's finger entered Brad from behind, and stimulated him even further, and soon he was discharging an enormous load into the writhing receptacle so eager for it. He held Chris in his arms and their kisses went from wildly passionate to very tender.

Brad raised his head and looked into Chris' eyes. "Chris, I...."

Chris suddenly burst into tears and his arms went around Brad's neck and pulled him down. "Oh God, Brad, it's just you I want. Take me to your room and keep fucking me. Make love to me. I don't want anyone but you!" He was now racked with sobs.

Brad put his arms around Chris and began to lift him; Chris tightened his arms around Brad's neck and his legs around his waist. With Chris riding him, Brad stood all the way up, so that their chests were pressed together. Brad looked at Whopper. "Open the door for us, and get Chris' bathrobe from the closet." And he cradled Chris to him while he carried him down the hall, still impaling the youngster on his erect shaft—and given Chris' tears and sobs, to say nothing of his own recent violent orgasm, Brad's cock remained amazingly rock-hard!

As he carried Chris in a kind of obscene and mobile *Pieta*, the nine orgasms flooding the boy began to leak out around the shaft still inside him and dripped over Brad's testicles and down his legs.

Whopper followed, carrying the bathrobe, and opening Brad's door. He began to follow Brad and Chris into the room. "No, Whopper. Throw the bathrobe on Mook's bed and leave us alone. I'll talk to you tomorrow." Mook, fortunately, had gone home for the weekend.

Brad gradually eased Chris down onto the bed; miraculously, he still remained buried inside him. Chris whispered. "I got fucked nine times, Brad. Please make love to me now."

And Brad stayed inside Chris and very slowly and affectionately gave him what he wanted. His second climax inside the boy arrived only after an extended, very tender time. His love-making becoming violent and fierce only as another orgasm approached and erupted.

They both slept as if exhausted. They both were. Their arms were around each other all night as though they were in love—they both were, Chris head-over-heels, and Brad in a kind of protective way.

The next morning Chris was sore, but demonstrated his head-over-heels love for Brad in a heels-over-head position several times during the day—a position Brad himself joyously assumed to further satisfy the sweet young blond who obviously adored him, and who was himself a very satisfying top.

For the two months remaining in the school year, Brad and Chris kept mostly together sexually. Brad squelched comments about the gang-bang, and Chris did not again evidence the wild hunger that had apparently brought it on. Brad did check out the unusually callipygian Andy, and found on the six or eight occasions when they made love he was a very *taking* young man as well as a *giving* one, and a very talented bed partner. There were also an even larger number of times when he himself yielded, rather easily, it must be admitted, to Whopper's pleas for some more time together with him in bed.

Aside from those diversions, Brad kept himself for Chris, and was the older-brother/protector/lover that his young admirer apparently craved. He suspected that Chris also spent a little time in bed with Whopper, but that was fair enough—and who could blame him, given Whopper's very special qualifications.

Leaving a tearful Chris at the end of his tenure as a Darby student was the most difficult thing Brad had encountered at that institution. They promised to keep in touch, and be together again soon, but although Brad wrote a number of letters, Chris never replied. Had Chris' family learned of the relationship? Was he okay? He never found out.

. . .

During the summer following his graduation from Darby, as he prepared to go to Stanford, Brad had managed to sublimate his desire for what he so exuberantly shared with Roy (and Whopper, and Andy, and four or five others), and had so lovingly known with Chris, and convinced himself he could find the same love and joy—or at least an acceptable substitute for them—in the arms of Gwen. He had successfully seduced a number of other young ladies before he and his future wife first made love, and he was delighted (and more than a little surprised) to find that he had actually enjoyed the experience. If the occasional thought of Whopper's dick, or Andy's ass, or the physical attractions of Roy or Chris or another of his senior-year handsome or well-endowed young men crossed his mind at the sexual "moment of truth" with a girl (or during the heated moments just preceding it), what harm was there in that? And later—after marriage—when those thoughts cropped up far more than just occasionally, Brad chalked it up to nostalgia, and determined to be a faithful husband.

At Stanford he joined SAE fraternity, and found there almost none of the innocent or frequently serious homosexual horseplay that had characterized his life at Darby. He had any number of fraternity brothers who were unbelievably attractive, but who seemed irredeemably straight. He dated some of the girls in his "sister" sorority, and visited whore houses in San Francisco on a few occasions with his fraternity brothers, but for the most part he considered himself engaged to Gwen, and kept himself true to her ("after his fashion," to be sure). His social life was almost completely limited to his fraternity, so except for a few drunken binges which resulted in shared beds and an extension of the "boy was I drunk last night" explanation to "boy I was so drunk last night I don't remember what I did!", he didn't screw around with guys any more.

Well, except for Geoff, the tall high school kid with the huge basket who worked on his car, and ... well, that was a fluke, and doesn't really count—and Geoff was really asking for it, anyway. He really was ... asking for it. And he had asked for it so politely, Brad hadn't have the heart to turn him down, so he didn't. But he did turn him over, and the kid had enjoyed that a lot ("a lot" both in the sense of 'very much' and 'frequently'), and the kid turned him over, and Brad had enjoyed it enormously ("enormously" in the sense of 'a great deal' and also—even more importantly—as it referred to the stupendous equipment Geoff had brought to the task).

When the talented young man graduated high school a couple of years after he began entertaining Brad in the back room of the garage, and moved to Los Angeles to seek similar activities on a wider scale, Brad decided he would turn over a new leaf, rather than turning over a new school boy.

So as he approached his forty-fifth birthday he wasn't exactly considering coming out of the closet for the first time. If he hadn't fully emerged from it during his Darby days, he had certainly kept the closet door open to receive callers—and at least ajar when he had later received service (and responded in kind) well beyond the automotive variety originally supposed to be provided by Geoff.

2.

Brad had seen his first lover only once since his graduation from Darby. On the occasion of his Twenty-Fifth Class Reunion, in 1993, he had gone back East and found Roy Saunders in attendance also. He might have assumed his former roommate had disappeared from the planet following his graduation had it not been for the occasional reference to him in *The Darby Ranger,* a semi-annual-or-so fund-raising publication. This newsletter somehow managed to follow graduates to their homes no matter how far flung they might be, nor how assiduously the 'old Darby boy' might attempt to fade into the landscape. Brad's own educational progress, his marriage, his fatherhood, and his business accomplishments—and financial contributions to Darby, or course—had been dutifully reported in the newsletter. But he had read almost nothing there about Roy's post-Darby life; he knew that there had been no reference to marriage or fatherhood, however, and he could not help but wonder if his former roommate had found another 'roommate' (or perhaps a series of such?) to share the special kind of relationship they had enjoyed together.

Checking the registration lists for the Reunion as soon as he arrived, Brad was excited to see that Roy was supposed to be there, and that even Andy and Whopper were scheduled to appear, but no mention of Chris Drake. Mook Dawson, his only roommate aside from Roy, was apparently not going to attend the Reunion. Who cared? Whopper's and Andy's names had occasionally appeared in the Ranger, but he had heard absolutely nothing about Chris since he had graduated.

He encountered Andy, who still looked very good. Society had now evolved a name for what had first attracted Brad to Andy: "bubble butt." And Andy's butt looked as enticing as it had so many years ago (when Brad had first observed it in action servicing Chris), but he ignored any oblique references to their sex play during their senior year. It seemed fairly obvious that Andy was no longer offering his most attractive feature for the delectation of his fellow man. It is an imperfect world, and tragedy abounds.

He was on the lookout for both Roy and Whopper, but it was Whopper who saw him first. It was a good thing he did, since Brad wasn't sure he would have recognized him, clothed at least.

Whopper was in his early forties, but could have easily passed for his late fifties. He had not been gorgeous as a student, but (aside from the extremely attractive appendage which lent him his nickname) he'd been reasonably good-looking. No longer could he be described as attractive—overweight and balding were adjectives more rightly applied. He was friendly, and he and Brad had a good visit, but there was little point to it. He had been married for fifteen years, was the proud father, with endless pictures in his wallet, of four children, and owned a reasonably successful Chevrolet agency. Any oblique references Brad made to their former sexual relationship were met with nervous laughs. "We were crazy kids, weren't we?" He knew nothing about where Chris Drake was: "He didn't come back to Darby after you graduated, and I never heard what happened to him."

Brad was forced to share family pictures and reminiscences with Whopper, but he was delighted to find an excuse to get away from him. His heart leaped into his throat, however, when he caught sight of Roy on the lawn in front of the administration building.

Roy had been somewhere between unusually and spectacularly handsome when he had been a student; Brad was pleased, and even excited to find that he still belonged comfortably in that range. True, he was now in his forties, but he could easily have passed for a thirty-year old—and not even "in the dusk with the light behind him" as W.S. Gilbert had stated it in *Trial by Jury*, an operetta he and Roy had shared an enthusiasm for. Brad regularly considered that he himself could easily pass for a much younger man, and he was quite right. He had always been a good judge of masculine beauty, and he recognized it when he saw it every day in the mirror. Roy and he had been a pair of dreamboats the first time they had jumped into bed together, and time had been unusually kind to both of them. They still had their basic good looks, of course, but they also had all their hair (and still all it's original color). They had retained their waistlines, and, thanks to a combination of the vanity they both shared and the enthusiasm for fitness which had arisen in recent years, their bodies were actually in better condition than ever.

As Brad approached his former sexual playmate (his former lover?), Roy happened to turn his head toward him, and a huge grin split his face.

"Thornton! My God!" He started for him, and stretched out his hand in greeting. "Jesus Christ but it's good to see you!" He abandoned the idea of a handshake and crushed Brad in a bear hug.

Brad's arms went around Roy, and he hugged back with equal enthusiasm. "I can't believe you're here! This is fantastic!" He released him, stepped back, and looked him up and down. "My God, Roy—you look spectacular! You look just as good as you did twenty-five years ago!"

"Well, twenty-six, but who's counting?" He threw his arms around Brad again. "And you look even better than you did twenty-six years ago!" And this time, unless Brad was much mistaken, his hug was tighter, and his lower body pressed into his much more tightly than before ... and could that have been the suggestion of a pelvic grind on Roy's part? Surely not, but ... yes, there it was again, and ... Jesus, was Roy's cock getting hard as he pressed himself to Brad? He had to admit his own cock was taking up a lot more space in his shorts than it had only a couple of minutes earlier!

"Really, Thornton, you ... "

"'Brad,' please, Roy! You may look great and I may look okay, but we're not still prep-school mates!"

Roy laughed lightly. "Of course, Brad. But, really ... Brad ... people always spread the most arrant bullshit at reunions about everyone looking just like he did back in the Ice Age, but you really do look even better! And, at the risk of embarrassing you, I might add that I thought you looked very, very good back then!"

Brad was pleased and a bit embarrassed, but he was also more than a bit excited—sexually excited, thinking about their life together at this school. He blushed for a moment before he grinned, "God, Roy, do you have any idea how very, very good you looked to me back then?"

"I have a complete grasp of how you felt, and how I felt,

and, well...."

"How we felt?"

"Look, Thornton, if ... Brad. If you'd rather not talk about what we really felt for each other back then, we won't. You can tell me about your wife and son, whose names I have seen in the unrelenting columns of *The Darby Ranger,* and how your business is going, and all that, and I can bore you with the same sort of drivel. Is that what we're going to talk about after all these years?"

"No! Well, yes! I do want to get caught up on what you've been doing, and I want to show you pictures of my wife and son and all, but that's not anything near all that I want to talk about with you. My God, Roy, you were the most important person in my life for three years, and then you disappeared from the face of the earth. Where can we go to really visit?"

"All right, I have to sit with the class of '67 at this god-awful luncheon, and you'll be with the class of '68, but as soon as it's over, come to Room 219 at the Darby Inn, and whether the sun is over the yardarm or not, we're going to have a drink and continue telling each other how absolutely wonderful we look!"

"Great! I can hardly wait. I'm in 304 at the Inn, so you can get me drunk and I won't have to drive home!"

"Done! I may get you drunk enough that you might not want to go home. How would you feel about that?"

"Roy, I ... "

"Sorry, Brad, I shouldn't be quite so forward I guess, but I think I want to declare my intentions before we get together. Don't even answer my question, but don't be surprised if I start to put the make on you, and you can brush me aside and tell me how unredeemably heterosexual you've become if you want. I won't get angry, I promise. I'll be disappointed, I also promise you that, but we'll still have a wonderful visit."

"I think I know how I feel about our having a real reunion." He smiled crookedly.

"Well, are you going to tell me in advance?"

"No. Where's the mystery in that? I'll see you right after the luncheon." Another close hug, and Brad started off, but turned back. "And Roy, it's irredeemably not unredeemably!"

"Roy laughed and grinned. "Right ... Bitch!"

Brad returned the grin and went back to join Roy. "And I've

been an irredeemably unredeemed heterosexual for quite a long time, but ... Jesus, Roy, you do look extremely tempting!"

"Christ, Brad, if you don't fall off the wagon, I'll get you off it some other way!"

"Fair enough!" He glanced around to be sure he could not be overheard. "As long as you get me off! And you can bet your sweet ass—your *very sweet* ass, as best I remember—I'll get you off, too!" He wondered what Roy's expression looked like as he turned to leave, but it had been too good an exit line to resist!

Jesus! After almost twenty years of denying himself what he wanted, if not always exactly denying what he wanted, was he going to jump back in bed with his former homosexual lover just like that? He answered his own question: "You're goddamned right I am!" And the luncheon seemed endless.

It was close to three o'clock when he rapped on the door to the room. Hearing "It's open!" from within, he entered and found Roy mixing a drink. "Scotch okay?" Brad agreed, and as Roy began making his drink, he said, "I was tempted to greet you lying naked on the bed beating off—I recall that was how I first got your interest a long time ago—but I wasn't completely sure what you'd say today. I know I told you to lock the door that time if you wanted to join me." He handed Brad his drink, they touched glasses and sipped, and he put his hand on Brad's shoulder. ""You can lock the door again, if you want to."

Brad smiled, cupped Roy's neck in one hand and pulled his mouth in to give him a long kiss. He returned to the door and locked it with obvious ceremony. "I definitely think we should have the door locked! I want to at least try to catch up on twenty-five years of not being in bed with you! But sit down, and let's talk first. I also want to hear how you are and what you've been up to." They sat and filled each other in on the course of their lives since they had last been together.

Roy had gone on to Yale, and then entered business with his father. It had worked out well for a while, but eventually his family began to wonder why he didn't date more frequently, and to subtly pressure him about the engagement-marriage-family route they wanted (read: expected) him to follow. He had dated one girl for a couple of years, and they had been seriously talking about marriage—he with considerable reservations and trepidation—but she came to his apartment unexpectedly one afternoon to find her 17-year-old brother in bed with her future husband, and in a position which was not only compromising, but was almost gymnastic. Once her brother sat her down and explained that he was there because he wanted to be, that it had been he who seduced Roy the first time, not the other way around, and that there had been a long string of such sessions with her intended partner which had begun when he (the brother) was only sixteen, she calmed down and agreed to a quiet and unexplained parting of the ways with her flawed marriage prospect.

"Of course her brother didn't have to do much seducing, as you can imagine. And he and I carried on for another year after that until he went off to college as an unbelievably attractive, talented, and (I am proud to report) sexually experienced freshman. My family never heard about that, but eventually when I stopped dating girls entirely and seemed almost always to be in the company of attractive young men, they gave up. I say 'seemed to be' around attractive young men; what I mean is I was around them all the time, although usually I was paying court, for want of a better word, to only one at a time. I've had a half-dozen or so long-term relationships over the years. Hundreds of quick, meaningless, and wonderful one-or two-night affairs. You'll meet Paul tomorrow. He's the current boyfriend, and looking to become a long-term one. And he is a hunk! He's coming by for dinner and to spend the night tomorrow, and then he's going to continue on upstate to see his family when I go home. At any rate, my family probably know that Paul, and the ones before him, were more than friends or roommates, but we just don't talk about it. I took over the business when dad retired about ten years ago, and it seems to be prospering in spite of the fact that it's being run by a confirmed faggot. And you, my married friend, whose bones I am going to jump if you take as long in telling his story as I took telling mine, what is with Brad Thornton, and why is he apparently so willing to have me jump those still very, very sexy bones?"

Brad related the developments of his life to Roy. He was honest about the affairs with Chris and Geoff, and he told Roy all about Gwen and Josh. Josh's picture elicited an unsettling response from Roy: "My God, he's beautiful! He might only be sixteen, but I'd go to bed with him in a heart beat! Is he gay?"

Brad was taken aback: "No! No!" He paused, then added, "Well, I don't think so!" He was obviously flustered.

Roy apologized: "Sorry, Brad, out of line, and all that, but you must admit he truly is gorgeous."

Brad admitted he was anxious to renew, or at any rate to relive for at least a day or two, his sexual relationship with Roy because, in the first place, he had never really stopped wanting to have sex with him, and besides, he was extremely horny. But he was cautious: " But I have to admit it's been around twenty years since I've been to bed with a guy, and I'd love to feel a cock inside me again. Geoff left my life one morning twenty years ago, after giving me something like the fuck of my life, but it apparently didn't last. I've squelched that desire all these years, but I see you, and I remember how wonderful you felt when you were inside me, and how I loved being inside you, and ... well, I want you again. Simple as that, I guess."

Roy said, "You've got me ... simple as that. Because I want you, too, almost as much as I did that day you first walked in the door and told me you were my new roommate. It took me about three weeks to work up the nerve to put a move on you back then, it's only going to take me about three minutes this time! Now get out of those clothes!"

Brad stood, finished the remainder of his drink, and began to pull off his tie. Staring into Roy's eyes, he finished undressing without a word while Roy's eyes locked on his as he stood and accomplished his own silent disrobing. The two continued to stare for a long moment, and then the gaze broke as their eyes ranged in appreciation over their naked bodies. Both by now were fully erect, and Roy's cock, whose dimensions Brad remembered as having been ample, thrilling, and filling during his student days, now looked even bigger! In a whisper, he said, "My God, Roy, you look good enough to eat!"

"If you don't eat me, Thornton, I'm going to be very, very disappointed." He approached and took him in his arms as he said "And if you're not by all odds the most edible man I've seen at this wretched Reunion, I'll eat my hat."

Brad's arms went around Roy and he whispered into his ear, "You're not wearing a hat. Just eat my cock!"

Roy's lips found Brad's, and the two kissed very chastely. Then the tip of his tongue began to gently lick the entire surface of Brad's lips, whose own tongue then began to lick Roy's. Their tongues started a slow, sensuous intertwining and alternated deep penetration of each other's mouths as they performed a ballet of ever-growing passion, their lips now firmly locked together. Their hands had begun a gentle, sensuous exploration as they first kissed, and their sweet fondling grew in excitement along with their kissing. Soon each held the other's now-undulating ass firmly in his hands and pulled him in tightly, so that their now painfully erect cocks ground together.

Roy began to sink to his knees, transferring his kisses to Brad's neck, lingering quite a while to suck on each nipple, licking his chest and stomach, nuzzling in the thatch of golden pubic hair surmounting the throbbing cock now pressing against his chin, and finally licking and sucking the sack that hung below it. He sat back on his feet and looked up at Brad. "My God, you are a beautiful man!"

Brad smiled down at him and leaned over to kiss him. "No more beautiful than you." Another kiss—longer. "I don't think anyone will ever be as beautiful to me as you!" As he straightened up, he gently took Roy's head in his hands and pulled it in to his groin.

Roy's hands grasped Brad's hips and just before he opened his mouth wide to take him inside, he murmured, "Your cock is just as beautiful as you are, Brad, and it's grown. God, you're going to be a helluva mouthful!" With that Brad felt the heat of Roy's mouth consume him as the tongue which had so recently danced with his own began to massage his cock, and the tight ring of lips traveled up and down its entire length, sealing him inside the wonderful vacuum Roy brought to bear. His hands now held Roy's head tightly, and pulled it in to match each deep thrust as he drove himself deeply inside.

It had been a long time since Brad had experienced a sensation this intense. Gwen was not averse to servicing him this way, but her ministrations had never provided the thrill he had experienced when it had been a man's mouth he filled. He had long ago concluded that it took a man to understand what really turned another man on, but he also had to admit he just enjoyed this more with a man, because he knew his partner would no doubt be invading his own mouth this wonderful way, and he not only found that incredibly exciting and satisfying, but it was something he most certainly could not share with a woman. Besides, it had been a long time since he had enjoyed even the lesser satisfaction of Gwen's oral service. Six months? A year, probably. But it had been twenty years since he had known this thrill, and it was Roy's expert ability, combined with the fact that he had not had an orgasm in several days that inspired an unusual ferocity in his drive into this hot, voracious mouth.

As his plunging grew deeper and more rapid, Brad began to pull back as he cried out, "I'm going to come, Roy!" But Roy's hands only held him tighter, and drew him even closer, until finally, with Roy's lips firmly buried in his pubic hair and every inch of driving cock embedded deep in his throat, Brad began to grunt and exclaim as his orgasm burst. Roy only sucked harder, and murmured in excitement while spurt after spurt of Brad's emission erupted inside his worshipping mouth.

Roy barely managed to avoid gagging as he received Brad's orgasm. Rather, he opened his throat as much as possible to allow for the thrilling liquid explosion inside him. As Brad's hoarse cries and violent panting died down, and as the huge shaft filling his throat shrank somewhat and grew less rigid, Roy's hands caressed Brad's buttocks and he murmured his delight in the gift he had just received. He also savored the taste, the warmth, and the slick consistency of that gift, and before he swallowed it, he used it to bathe the organ that had delivered it to him so forcefully.

Brad's hands were now fondling Roy's head gently as he cooed his contentment and appreciation. "God in heaven, Roy, nothing ever felt that good!" He withdrew himself from Roy's mouth and fell to his knees, where he replaced his cock with his tongue, which Roy proceeded to suck with equal enthusiasm, and Brad could taste his own semen in Roy's mouth. Their hands were so busy caressing each other, and their kissing so passionate, they weren't aware when they fell to the carpet, where they writhed together in a transport of lust.

Eventually, they rested in each other's arms. Roy outlined Brad's jaw with his finger and smiled at him, "That was the first time I've let anyone come in my mouth in seven or eight years, and I'd almost forgotten how exciting it is to do that, but I've never forgotten how very, very wonderful yours tastes!"

"But I tried to warn you, Roy. I know it's dangerous to suck anybody off any more. I tried to pull out."

"I knew what I was doing. You told me you and your wife have kept to yourselves all these years, and I believe you. I wanted to feel you bursting inside me the way you used to, and, if possible, it was even more wonderful than I remember." He grinned broadly. "And that means it had to be abso-fucking-lutely magnificent!" Look, I swear to you that I'm safe; I practice safe sex, but I still monitor my HIV status regularly, just to be sure. But all that aside, even if I beg you, don't let me come inside you without protection. Promise?"

"I promise, as long as you come inside me with protection!"

"You can count on that!" He stood and moved to the bed, where he lay down in the middle and held out his hand. "Come here, Brad." Brad stood and joined him, and they spent a time rolling around on the bed, caressing each other and kissing. With Brad on his back, Roy knelt over his head with his knees nestled in his armpits. His throbbing shaft filled Brad's vision, and he leaned forward to position himself on all fours over Brad, as the latter opened his mouth to admit him.

As thrilling as Roy's oral ministrations had felt to Brad after all these years, he was even more excited to again practice this form of love-making as the passive partner. Here was something he had not known since the very exciting and well-endowed Geoff had fucked his mouth so often, so endlessly, and so enthusiastically, and for which Gwen had been able to offer no acceptable alternative during that twenty-year hiatus. Even as he began to make love this way to Roy, his mind was racing ahead to the kind of sexual congress he most enjoyed, and which again his wife had not been able to provide him, with him as a 'bottom', or willing to provide him, with him as a 'top'. But those thoughts receded as he began to feast on the bulk of the exciting shaft now driving into his throat; he had thought it huge when he had first swallowed it at age fourteen, but today it struck him (wonderfully) as the gigantic equal of Geoff's prodigious cock, and almost as colossal as the legendary Whopper's! This last thought was an example of faulty memory at work, no one Brad had met up until that time ever had a cock even almost as titanic as Whopper's.

Caressing Roy's buttocks and pulling him in tightly, Brad feasted with almost delirious rapture. In spite of the years it had been since he had practiced this, he had no trouble whatever in relaxing his throat to the point he was able to fully accept this massive invasion. After a far-too-short period of time, Roy's plunging grew very rapid and his gasping indicated an imminent orgasm, but at the last split second he withdrew, and a violently-propelled cascade of his hot emission covered Brad's face and hair, and even spurted well past his head! Roy cradled Brad's head tightly in his arms and he pulled them onto their sides, with his rigid cock now pressed against his face. Brad held him tightly also, and they lay there for a considerable time as their ecstasy faded into a warm, delicious glow.

Finally, Roy murmured, "Jesus Christ, Thornton, you're better than ever!" They released each other and re-positioned themselves in an embrace. Roy looked at Brad and snickered, "And I believe you've got something on your face," before he began to slowly and methodically use his tongue to clean up after himself!

They freshened their drinks, and decided, in the interest of efficiency, to shower separately. At dinner they ran into a number of former classmates, and enjoyed the idle kind of reminiscences that Brad had thought would probably be the most he would get from this reunion. He had not, he was almost sure, come back to Darby with the idea of re-experiencing any of his sexual liaisons, but the memory of his activities here made the very air seem aphrodisiac. A few comments which passed between Andy and Roy over dinner suggested to Brad that his former roommate had sampled the delights of the other's body during their school days, as he himself had, and Roy later confirmed his suspicion, but Andy seemed no more interested in even admitting to, much less repeating, sexual congress with Roy than he had with Brad.

After dinner and a boring reception following it, the former lovers retired again to Roy's hotel room. Brad had anticipated that if the kind of sex he and Roy had shared that afternoon had been magnificent (and it had been!), the re-experience of love-making of the kind he and Roy most enjoyed would be stupendous, sublime, *epic*.

They had not been in the room ten minutes before Brad knelt on all fours at the side of the bed, naked, and almost trembling with anticipation as he panted, "Fuck me, Roy!"

Roy stood behind Brad, donned a condom and lubricated himself, and brought as much fervor to his compliance with the request as it had been tendered with. His hands held Brad's waist and he looked in appreciation at the stunning backside presented for his enjoyment: over forty years in age, and as smooth, as rounded and succulent, as beautiful as that of an eighteen-year old. He watched his rigid flesh enter between the two perfect globes and sink into the hot chamber which gripped him deliciously.

It is seldom that expectation as keen as what Brad had felt is realized in practice; this time the actuality even exceeded the expectation, and by an exponential factor. He re-experienced the pain he had first known when Roy penetrated him. After all, for two decades only his doctor's finger (and, if the truth be known, his own finger far, far more frequently) had entered him there, but the pain was soon past, and was replaced with the rapture, the pervasive delicious heat, the unbelievably erotic stimulation, and the satiety of the presence deep inside him of this insistent organ upon which he so joyously impaled himself.

["Satiety: The condition of being full or gratified beyond the point of satisfaction." The word could have been coined just to enable Brad to describe his feeling at that moment, but had he been doing the coining, he would have used a much stronger term than satisfaction.]

Roy used his hands to pull Brad violently back toward him to meet his brutal forward thrusts. For an ecstatic ten or fifteen minutes Brad's head rolled, he groaned loudly in the throes of unparalleled rapture, and he drove his body backward and forward with ever-increasing rapidity and savagery. It was so wonderful it seemed like only seconds, far, far too short a time, before this unthinkably perfect fuck ended. It was also so wonderful that it completely absorbed him, and might have been going on as long as he could remember! Like all good things must—and, alas even such glorious things as this—it finally came to an end.

With a loud cry, Roy 's hands seized Brad's waist so tightly he would have cried out in pain if he not been in such ecstasy, and he buried himself as far inside as he could. He grew rigid, and his body shook with the spasms of his massive orgasm; a series of appeals not really directed anywhere, much less to heaven ("Oh God! Oh God!") seemed to match each spurt he delivered into the condom. The heaving of his chest finally subsided, and he fell over Brad, pinning him to the bed on his stomach.

"Thornton, you are the best fuck in the land! You can't imagine how really, truly good you are."

"Jesus, Roy, I wish you hadn't been wearing a rubber. That is absolutely the only way that could have been the least bit better! You are still the master fucker of all time!"

Roy laughed. "First is usually best, you know. And, if I remember right, I was the guy who plucked your cherry."

Brad laughed and rolled over beneath Roy. "Yeah, and you're the master plucker of all time, too!" He kissed him for a long time. "And happily you showed me this afternoon you are also the master sucker of all time."

Roy stood. "Guilty on all counts! But, we are going to have another drink and relax for a few minutes. I am exhausted, but nobody leaves this room until I get screwed—at least once."

Toasting with their fresh drinks, Brad said, "I look forward to screwing your still incredibly attractive butt, my very good friend."

"Thanks for the compliment. I return it in spades, and hearts and diamonds and clubs for that matter! You look about as good as you did when you were seventeen and I was nineteen, and the world was our oyster."

"Don't oysters make you horny? That's what happened!"

Roy laughed. "Well, whatever it was, I've stayed horny all these years. And I was afraid you were going to turn out to be one of these guys who plays around at taking it up the butt and down the throat when he's young, and then gets married and forgets he ever did—or ever even wanted to."

"Yeah, I've seen a few cases of that today."

"Haven't we both? And speaking of them, I thought Andy

still looked damn good."

"I thought I caught a few nuances in your comments to him at the restaurant; so you did screw around with him."

"Guilty, I'm afraid. I have to admit I wasn't exactly true to you those years we were together. Does that break your heart?"

Brad smiled. "No, not really." He laughed-but his heart was not completely in it. "No, of course not. Oh, it probably would have if I'd learned about it back then. I'm afraid I was pretty much in love with you, you know."

"I know ... I knew! And I really loved you too, Brad. Hell, I'll always love you, you know. But I wasn't any good at being especially faithful, I'm afraid. Hell, I'm still not. You'll meet Paul tomorrow, and I expect he'll bend your ear about that! And I shouldn't be too surprised if he doesn't try to get you to bend your body over his, and then bend over a table, or a chair, or the bed. He's a horny little devil, and I think he may be even less naturally disposed to fidelity than I." He stood and came over to the chair where Brad sat and kissed him tenderly. "But I did love you, and I do love you."

Brad held Roy's face for a minute after he finished kissing him. "And I feel the same way about you, in spades, and in all those other suits you mentioned."

Roy sat again and said, "Well anyway, Andy and I got in the sack together quite a lot in my last year or so here. He was truly talented, and he had one of the most fuckable little asses I'd ever seen. And, I'm happy to say, he loved getting it plugged."

Brad told him about the night of Chris' gang-bang, how he had observed Andy's ass in action and had arrived at the same conclusion about the beauty of his fundament, and made the same discovery about his appetite.

"I only vaguely remember Chris Drake," Roy said. "Small and too sensitive for his own good, as I recall. I was never tempted to put the make on him, but I didn't feel the need to seduce everyone in sight then. I had you, didn't I?"

Brad laughed harshly. "Yeah, but you also had Andy."

"Well, if the truth be known, Andy and several others. And speaking of that, did you see Whopper Toole? My God, he's a wreck!"

"So you were fucking with Whopper too?"

"My God, Thornton, you know what kind of dick that boy had. Of course I was fucking with him! If you didn't sample that, you were nuts! God, Whopper the Shooter, what an unbelievably well-equipped and talented lad he was! Jesus, I almost get a hard-on thinking of him every time I go into Burger King and order a 'Whopper!' And he showed me pictures of his brood—like you did."

Brad erupted in a bark of laughter. "Yeah, his *brood* is bigger than mine, too."

Roy echoed his laughter, and went on. "And he has a 14-year-old kid who looks just like he did at that age. And the kid either has his towel rolled up in the crotch of his bathing suit, or he takes after his daddy! I'll have to get Whopper's address and get in touch with little Whopper in a few years!" He himself burst out in a loud laugh. "Shit, do you suppose I'll start getting a hard-on when I order a "Whopper Junior?"

Brad stood, walked over to the open window, and called out (not too loudly), "Men and women of America: lock up your sons!" He walked back to his chair and grinned. "Jesus, nobody's son is safe from you, is he?"

Roy smiled devilishly, but perhaps a bit wistfully as well, "They never were, Brad. But out of deference to you, and in honor of our undying love, I promise you that you won't need to buy a chastity belt for your son ... ah ...."

"Josh."

"Right ... Josh. But seeing young Josh's picture, it might be a good idea to put one on him for the next few years anyway. I'm not the only one out there, you know! Well, anyway ... back to Chris Drake."

"Well, after you left, and before I took Chris under my wing ...."

"Yeah, well under your something!"

Brad chuckled. "Right! Anyway, I suddenly found there were all sorts of guys who wanted to get me in the sack. And I couldn't very well turn them all down, just because my true love had graduated AND NEVER EVEN WROTE A GODDAMNED LETTER!. (Roy raised a hand, "Sorry!") Whopper was one of them. Like you say, who could resist that? So I didn't, and I guess I must have not resisted fifteen or twenty times. Like you said, he was as talented as he was hung!"

"Well, it may seem unkind, but I wouldn't fuck him with your dick now."

"Well, yeah, but maybe if he came at you in the dark with that thing ... "

"Well, if it were pitch black, it could be kinda fun, couldn't it?" They both laughed. "But to get back to the point, Thornton, I was really glad to learn that in your years out there with your ever-so-stunning wife and your even-more-stunning son, you hadn't, like Whopper and Andy and a few others I've talked to today, conveniently forgotten that in addition to the joys of learning Latin declensions we had a helluva lot of good extra-curricular times together!"

"I've never forgotten, Roy, but when I got married, I decided I had to put that aside. I didn't come out here planning to get laid, believe it or not."

"But you just couldn't resist my charms!"

"I couldn't resist your dick!"

"Well, my charms and my dick! So ... what happens when you go back home?"

"You know, Roy, I can't say. After today, I'm not sure I can keep denying what I really want. I'm afraid you've planted the seeds of doubt in my mind."

Roy stood and approached him, raised him to his feet, and took him in his arms. "I love planting any kind of seed I can in you, Brad. Unfortunately, the times being what they are, I have to plant my seed in that fucking latex prison we just flushed down the john. But I'm really excited to think that you can plant your seed in me without that kind of restriction. I haven't felt that wonderful rush of orgasm inside me in a long time. What I'm trying to say, my friend, my lover still, that is, I'm *dying* for you to screw me!"

Next to the screwing he himself had experienced only shortly before, satisfying Roy's wishes thrilled him as nothing had since his last meeting with Geoff. It was apparent that Roy was, and had been all these years, practicing what he was now experiencing. Still, the grip of his ass on Brad's dick was unbelievably exciting. His former lover was tight, hot, and thrilling beyond words, and the sensation as Roy's entire body drove backward violently, and gripped him tightly while he moved forward, working in perfect synchronization to counter his thrusts as he knelt behind him, filled him with a sensation of power and a feeling of animal lust that turned him into a savage fucking machine! Roy's groans of passion and Brad's guttural, feverish litany of sexual verbalization ("Gonna fuck that hot ass!" "Take my big cock!") continued until Roy almost screamed, "Throw me on my back. I want to see you fuck me, I want you to kiss me when you shoot your load in me!"

Brad withdrew, seized Roy's body and flipped him over quickly, raised his legs, and immediately drove his cock back into him in one fierce thrust. His thrusting became frenzied. Roy's legs rested on Brad's shoulders, and he raised himself well off the bed for the 'home stretch' which Brad's panting and moaning presaged. Finally, with a particularly violent lunge, he exploded inside Roy, whose cries indicated it had been a palpable eruption. "God, that feels so great! Shit, I haven't felt that in so long. Oh God, Thornton, don't stop! Don't stop!"

Roy seized himself and began to frantically masturbate as Brad remained buried inside him; in just a minute or two, he climaxed on his own stomach.

Brad fell on top of Roy, whose arms cradled his neck, and whose legs circled his waist. They kissed passionately, and murmured wordlessly around their busy tongues. Eventually, as Brad became dead weight on his chest, Roy whispered to him, "Don't stop, stay inside me and fuck me again!" The resumption a few minutes later of both the undulation of his buttocks and his penetration of the tight chamber still encasing his shaft indicated Brad intended to honor this last request. Although it took much, much longer, he continued his assault on Roy's voracious bottom until he delivered another forceful and much-appreciated offering.

Brad grinned happily and proudly, "I don't think I've had three orgasms in that short a time, about nine hours, really, since the day I got married. You inspire me, Roy."

"We used to get off three and four times, and even five once or twice, if memory serves!"

"Yeah, but we were kids!"

Roy kissed Brad and held him tight. "You make me feel like a kid again, Brad. This has been very, very special."

"And I've got to get to my room, because Gwen is going to call me when she gets in this evening. Come and sleep with me."

"I can't. Paul is going to call here pretty soon. Your wife ... Gwen? Yeah, Gwen, might not be suspicious if you're not in, but Paul will know I'm screwing around if I'm not here. Come back after Gwen calls." They separated, Gwen called, and Brad returned to spend the night locked in Roy's arms, as happy and content as he could remember being in a long, long time.

They made love again in the morning, before going to the theatre at Darby for a special performance of the Drama Club's production of *The Odd Couple*, given in honor of the old grads.

While they strolled over to the theatre they exchanged rather hilarious stories of their experiences when they had been students and dragooned into various theatrical enterprises, and not always in male roles.

Roy laughed, "I wonder how many drag queens were created by having to play girls in boys' prep school productions, and finding they liked the experience! Wait! Chris Drake! I remember him now. He was a really beautiful Maid Marian in some Robin Hood show we all suffered through. Mercifully I only had to suffer through that one as a spectator, but ... yeah, I remember. Jesus, he was disturbingly beautiful in that!"

"And I'll bet you would have loved to be playing Robin Hood and unloading that enormous quiver of yours into him!"

"Right on target!" Brad uttered a grunt in appreciation of Roy's humor. "And weren't those Merry Men cute in their tights? Jesus, I would have loved to rob their riches and give them to poor me!"

"Well anyway, if I remember correctly there are only a couple of small women's roles in this one. Do you suppose they're doing *The Odd Couple* in honor of our getting together again?" "I'll bet they are, the smart asses!"

The show, Roy and Brad agreed, was actually rather good. They thought that the two youngsters playing "Gwendolyn" and "Cecily" were reasonably decent actors, and "Cecily" was uncommonly attractive: "fuckable" was Brad's exact word. They attended yet another luncheon, and this time, Brad got to see the pictures of Whopper's children. He readily agreed with

Roy's assessment of the enormously bulging 'Speedos' which "Whopper Junior" sported. "Probably hiding a ten-inch chip off the old block!" he joked.

Back at the hotel, they went to Brad's room for a short drink and a quick blow-job delivered by Roy to the more-than-willing recipient. Brad wanted more, Roy wanted more, but Paul was due to arrive soon.

As Roy prepared to go down to his room, he told Roy, "I'll call you when Paul arrives, and you have to come down and have a drink and go out to dinner with us. Paul is gonna knock your socks off!"

If getting one's socks knocked off meant experiencing a sudden pounding in the chest and a concomitant stirring in the crotch, Brad felt that Roy's description was exactly on the mark: Paul Stavros proved to be gorgeous. The word Roy had used when he first mentioned him was "hunk"—another bull's eye.

Let's just suppose for a moment here that Brad Thornton—not Brad Thornton the model husband and father, but the Brad Thornton whose true character is perhaps becoming evident as this narrative progresses—was going to send off a special order to "The Guy Store" for his custom-built ideal man, the "man of his wet dreams," so to speak. Here are the specifications that would probably appear in the blanks on the order form:

Dark hair, preferably black, not too long, and in curly ringlets all over his head. But the rest of the body almost completely hairless, except for a nice generous thatch above the juicy, fat and lengthy item specified below.

Not too tall—only average height, say five-ten. A muscular, well-developed body (not overly muscular, like a hard-core body builder, but just short of that); extremely broad shoulders and big arm muscles (but in proportion); flat waist with washboard stomach; narrow waist; l-o-n-g legs; very muscular thighs and calves (but again, in proportion—not exaggerated); big hands with long fingers. Ass specification included separately. Extra points for a subtle "outie" navel.

A bubble butt. But not a little one, an ample one—two rounded, smooth hemispheres of solid, muscular flesh opening onto a small, pink orifice guarded by a tight sphincter muscle fully capable of seizing and holding, but also fully capable of expanding to meet demands made upon it.

A BIG penis, fat and lengthy even when flaccid; circumcised preferred but not required; optimum length of eight inches when erect; large, fairly light-colored "helmet" (glans penis); girth negotiable (but tending toward a five inch circumference); a smooth, light-colored, only lightly veined shaft, capable of sustaining maximum rigidity for long periods, and minimum "down time" between erections.

Broad forehead, prominent cheekbones, square jaw with chiseled profile, brilliantly white teeth (and lots of them—thirty-two a bare minimum), deep dimples that appear when those brilliant teeth flash a smile, slightly pouty mouth and generous lips to form said smile, something a bit more than a suggestion of a dimpled cleft chin, generous eyebrows in the shape of a flattened "V," and coal black eyes which especially sparkle and are parenthesized by generous smile lines when a grin appears.

Experienced, but not jaded. Age negotiable; maturity a must, but within that framework, young, ranging perhaps from an experienced and mature 17- or 18-year old, if that is possible, to a youthful early thirties.

Roy had called at six o'clock to say that Paul had arrived, and told Brad to come down and join them in a half-hour. Brad knocked on Roy's door at the appointed hour, was ushered into the room, and when Roy said, "Brad, meet Paul Stavros" he extended his hand to shake that of a man who seemed to be the very incarnation of his "Guy Store" wish list. To be sure some of the qualities could not be judged, since he was fully dressed, but the extremely tight polo shirt and the even tighter trousers outlined the concealed features in such a way that they also promised to live up to specifications.

As Paul and Brad exchanged pleasantries, Roy grinned and rested his arm casually, but protectively (or was it possessively?) on his lover's shoulders. Paul was, in Brad's estimation, so achingly beautiful, that for a moment his temples throbbed, and it was somewhat difficult for him to keep his mind on even this simple conversation. He actually had to exercise his will consciously to overcome his initial strong reaction to Paul, but in a few minutes the three were seated, sharing drinks and small talk.

Paul was a twenty-three year old native of Philadelphia who had come to Roy's attention when he began working in the mail-room of his concern. His personnel file revealed that he had only a high-school education, and lived at home with his family, who had moved to Hartford, where Roy's business was located, when his father was reassigned there. Within days Roy suddenly decided he needed special help moving and re-organizing things in his office, and this black-headed Greek god (he actually was Greek) agreed to work overtime and help out. Somehow, they didn't get much done that first night, since Roy evidenced so much fascination with Paul's background, his interests, his goals in life, etc., that they sat around and chatted until it was too late to really accomplish anything. Paul agreed to come back the next evening and help, and Roy was so appreciative he took him to a late dinner.

The next evening, for some inexplicable reason, they didn't get much accomplished either, and a bottle of scotch was located, the consumption of which militated against working efficiency, and another late dinner led to Paul's agreeing to drop by Roy's apartment for a nightcap. Slightly woozy after drinking the nightcap, Paul decided to accept Roy's invitation to spend the night.

Roy rested his hand on Paul's knee (they had been sitting ever closer together on the sofa as they chatted) and said, "You can have the guest room if you like. There are pajamas in the dresser in there."

Paul smiled and began unbuttoning his shirt. "I never wear anything to sleep in, Mr. Saunders, I...."

"Roy! Please, I asked you to call me Roy when I'm not at the office."

"Right. Roy. Well, I'll be glad to sleep in the guest room if you want, but I'd rather sleep with you if that's what you'd like." Before the stunned Roy could reply, he added, "And if you do, I sure as hell hope you like to sleep naked too! One of the guys at the office said he thought you'd like me; I hope you do"

Roy stood, and his erection was already bulging obscenely in his slacks. He held out his hands to Paul. "I do like to sleep naked. And I do like you, Paul, and frankly I've wanted to sleep naked with you since I first laid eyes on you."

Paul reached forward and began to stroke Roy's erection. "God, your cock is hard! And it's so big! Will you fuck me, Roy?"

Pulling Paul to his feet and enfolding him in his arms, he kissed his upturned lips and murmured, "I'll fuck you Paul." He led him into his bedroom, and they began an all-night cuddling, kissing, sucking, fucking marathon which left neither of them in any shape to work the next day. Paul proved to be a voracious bottom, who could not get enough of Roy's massive shaft inside him, and a very capable cocksucker as well. He was so inspired by Roy's virtuoso ability as a glorious buttfucker that he demonstrated he was almost as tireless and dedicated a top as he was a bottom.

The astonishing thing about the beautiful young man was that he turned out to be as sweet and affectionate in bed as he was savage and insatiable. Wonderfully, his sweetness and affection were evident out of bed as well. Roy anxiously courted Paul, who seemed genuinely interested in a relationship with him, not just a few quick fucks with the boss.

Their relationship developed rapidly, in fact, and within a month Paul had moved in with Roy and the two were lovers. Paul had expressed his discomfort at being accorded special attention at work, so he left the firm and became manager of the apartment complex where Roy lived, and where Roy owned not only the unit he occupied, but the entire group of four buildings the complex comprised. It was an actual job, which had needed filling for a while, and which Paul did well—and for which Roy paid him well, of course.

Paul had no fewer than six older brothers, all but two of whom had at one time or another developed a serious interest in fucking their younger sibling. By the time he entered high school, he had developed an equally serious interest in getting fucked by them—and not only bestowed on a number of his schoolmates what his brothers took, but also developed a keen interest in, and considerable talent for doing the honors as the donor, rather than the recipient. His perfect beauty meant he always had a number of attractive young men, including several of his teachers, interested in sharing his developing sexual appetites and abilities. Girls literally drooled over him, and he was polite, but showed no interest in dating them. His natural athletic ability and gym-built body were sufficiently impressive that he was never labeled a "faggot," as were most of his schoolmates with either an epicene manner or a similar lack of apparent interest in girls.

After high school he spent four years as an enlisted man in the Navy, and found an even broader and more exciting time there for a little over a year. In a typical week he had sex with five or six different shipmates, and sailors or civilians who picked him up in bars or on the street. Then he met an older man, a recently separated, forty-year old Lieutenant Commander, who fell completely in love with him, and with whom he shared a relationship for the duration of his service. The relationship was not a completely monogamous one on his part. He was often out to sea, and yielded readily to the temptations and inducements offered by his horny shipmates. When it was time for him to re-enlist or return to civilian life, he opted for the latter, left his lover, and moved back East, initially living in his family home. He had been there only a few weeks when he took the job in the mailroom at Roy's firm. The rest, as they say, is history.

When Roy went to the bathroom, Paul told Brad, "I can sure see why Roy used to be in love with you."

"Thanks, Paul. And I can see why Roy, or absolutely any sane gay man in the world, would be attracted to you."

"Look, Brad, I'm driving upstate tomorrow morning to visit one of my brothers and his family, so I'm going to get an early start, but I'd like to see you some time, and get to know you better. If I can get back to California, can I call you? And would you see me—alone?"

"Yes, Paul. God, yes! I'd like that. But, you know I'm married, so it might be hard to explain, and ... oh hell, we'll work it out, I want to see you again." He looked deep into the beautiful black eyes and spoke slowly, "I almost feel like I've got to see you again—alone—and get to know you really well." Paul grinned. Pulling a business card from his wallet, Brad gave it to Paul. "My phone numbers are on this, but you'd better get in touch with me through the travel agency."

"Look, please don't say anything to Roy, okay? You know why. I'm happy with Roy, but ... I think you and I could have a lot of fun together too, couldn't we? And, I dunno, Brad, but something about you ... when I saw you, my stomach did flips. And I knew if there was any way, I ... I really need to see you again, okay?"

"I promise you, Paul, if you can come out, somehow we'll get together, and we'll have a lot of fun, okay?" Paul grinned and pocketed the card as Roy returned, and they went out to dinner.

Brad's mind was racing. "Jesus Christ! What am I thinking of? I have a wife and a wonderful son at home and I've been straight for twenty years, but in the last twenty-four hours I have had sex twice with my former lover, and have just all but promised to have sex with another man I met only minutes ago!"

Over the years he had, of course, seen other men he found attractive, and had been obliquely approached, sometimes overtly, by other men interested in having sex with him. Still, he had remained faithful to his marriage vows, and refrained from appeasing the sexual appetite which had all but completely occupied him from before puberty to his engagement and marriage. If he had not come to this Reunion and seen Roy again, and been naturally led to a renewal of their old relationship, however temporary, would he have succumbed to expressing what he had hitherto believed to be his former sexual nature?

Brad was not self-deluded; he had thought often in the day or so since he fell into bed so easily and joyfully with Roy again, that this had probably been long overdue. In truth, he had not been "naturally led to a renewal of their old relationship" because he could have resisted. But he had wanted it as much as Roy had. The appearance of the astonishingly attractive Paul had perhaps, he feared, drove the final nail in the coffin of his denial of a homosexual nature. He could not remember ever having seen someone as exciting or desirable as Paul, not even the accommodating Geoff, whose hot teenager's body had proven irresistible to him so many years ago. Whopper's dick, Andy's ass, Chris' vulnerability,

Geoff's youth and ravenous appetite for sex had all proven irresistible to him in the past as well, but that was in the past for God's sake! Why now, after twenty years, was he lusting (the only word for it) after a man's body so strongly that he was willing to endanger his marriage? He answered the last question himself. "I'm gay, for Christ's sake! I want to be doing again what Roy and I enjoyed all those years. I want to kiss someone and hold a loving body in my arms and feel his own hard-on pressing into mine. I want to feel someone inside me the way Roy and Geoff and Whopper felt. I want to sink my dick into a man, not a woman any longer! And most of all, right at this point, I want to do all those things with Paul, maybe the sexiest man I've ever seen. I can't pass up the opportunity to have sex with anyone as attractive to me as he is, even if it endangers my marriage, and even if he is my friend's lover!"

The seeds of doubt that Roy had allegedly sewn in Brad's mind had matured very, very quickly with the appearance of Paul!

During dinner Paul and Roy sat together opposite Brad in a booth, but Paul's lower leg sought Brad's, and pressed against him frequently. And when it did, Brad invariably found Paul's eyes looking very intensely at him. After dinner he had to excuse himself and retire early, leaving Roy and Paul to themselves. The sexual electricity he felt emanating from Paul was all but disorienting him.

The plan the next morning was for Roy to drive back to his office in Hartford very early, leaving Paul to drive to his brother's house when he was ready; Brad's plane back to San Francisco did not leave until early afternoon, and he planned to check out of the hotel and return his rental car at the airport around lunch time.

At the hotel elevator, as Paul and Roy prepared to get out, Paul shook Brad's hand and expressed his pleasure in having met him. He looked deep into Brad's eyes, and his handshake was especially tight. Electricity flowed and Paul's heart beat fast.

Roy gave Paul a quick kiss and said, "I'll look in on you as I leave in the morning and say goodbye then."

Brad went to bed, but slept very little.

The phone rang shortly after eight the next morning, shattering the fitful sleep that had finally come to Brad. "Brad, Roy. Getting ready to leave. Get your lazy, but sexy, ass out of bed and say goodbye to me. I'll be right up."

Brad threw water on his face, brushed his hair, and barely had time to take a few desultory passes with a toothbrush and gargle with mouthwash before there was a knock on the door. He opened it to admit Roy, carrying his suitcase.

Roy put his arms around Brad and kissed him warmly, and for a long time. Brad was glad he had caught at least a moment with a toothbrush and the Listerine. They hugged each other and their kiss began to turn passionate. Roy laughed and stepped back. "Whoa! If I get started, we'll be in the bed again, and as much as I'd like that, I have to get back to the office. Brad, this has been an even more wonderful get-together than I could have hoped for, and you're just as attractive and just as sexy as you ever were. And *please,* don't let it be another twenty-five years before we get together. And the next time we get together, please fuck me just the way you did, and let me fuck you just the way I did. It couldn't have been better, and I love you, and I always will."

"I think you know how much I enjoyed our being together, Roy. Do you realize I have had more orgasms in the last two days than I normally would in two weeks? And half of those would have been self induced! The only problem is, I don't know how to feel when I get back home!

"You'll figure it out, baby. Let me know what happens, okay?"

"I will. I love you too, you know. And let me know if anything happens with Whopper Junior!"

Roy laughed. "I'm off. And Brad, in case you didn't notice, Paul was mighty taken with you. I think you did notice, though, and unless I'm seriously mistaken, you were pretty taken with him."

"Roy, I ... "

"It's okay. He's upstairs getting ready to leave, and my guess is that he'll want to see you before he leaves. Whatever happens, if anything happens, Paul doesn't belong to me, and I don't belong to him. If you two wind up in bed, I don't need to know about it, and in fact, I don't want to know about it. I'm pretty much in love with him. God damn he's gorgeous, isn't he? But I know I'm not going to stop looking around, why should he? But I don't think Whopper Junior's the one for me." He held Brad at arms length and looked into his eyes for a long moment before he smiled, kissed him quickly, turned, and left.

Brad watched him walk down the hall to the elevator, then returned to the room, shaved, and got in the shower. He had been out of the shower only a few minutes when the phone rang again. It was Paul.

"Do you want to see me?"

"Yes, I do. How long can you stay?"

"I'm going to check out and come back up to your room. How long *can* I stay? How long do you *want* me to stay?"

"I think I want you to stay for a lot longer than you can. I know it's way too early and too complicated for me to say I want you to stay for a lifetime yet. I'm supposed to leave around noon. Hurry!" He hung up and brushed his teeth much more thoroughly. He did not get dressed, answering the door when Paul knocked a few minutes later clad only in a towel knotted around his waist.

It was obvious Paul was as hungry for Brad as he was for him. As soon as Brad closed the door behind him, he was in his arms, and the two embraced and kissed hungrily for a long time, a very long time. Paul's hands roamed Brad's all-but-nude body, and the towel soon dropped and they explored even further. He panted in Brad's ear, "I couldn't keep my eyes off you last night, and all the time Roy was fucking me after we got back to the room I was pretending I was really with you. This morning he was riding my cock and he stopped and looked at me and said, 'Brad's really hot, isn't he?' and then he started riding me even harder. I guess he could tell how much I liked you. He beat off while he was riding me, and just when he started to shoot his load all over me, he said 'You and Brad are both really hot!' I figured you two guys fucked each other before I got here."

"How do you feel about that, Paul?"

Paul pulled back and smiled at Brad. "I'm sorry I wasn't here to share in the fun! Anyway, after Roy shot his load this morning, he stopped riding my cock before I got mine—which he almost never does. I think he knew I was going to come and see you."

"I'm almost sure you're right, Paul. How do you feel about that?"

"I don't care, Brad, I'm here now, and I want you to make love to me!" He sank to his knees and murmured in admiration. "You're so fucking beautiful, and your prick is even bigger than I had hoped."

He took Brad's cock, hugely erect and throbbing by now, deep in his throat and his lips held it tightly as they began to travel back and forth, first nestling in his pubic hair, then withdrawing until only his cock-head was still enclosed, and repeating the cycle deliriously, over and over. Brad looked down at the head of curly black ringlets and the perfect face accepting the thrusts of his organ, which he drove ever harder and harder into the worshipping younger man. Paul's hands pulled his buttocks in to him, but as Brad's cock began to drive more and more violently, one of Paul's fingers sought entrance. Soon the finger was invading him even more rapidly and fiercely than Brad was invading Paul's mouth.

Suddenly Paul stopped and released Brad's cock. He caught his breath, and then began to lick the shaft and the balls feverishly. After a few moments, he looked at Brad and gushed, "God, I wish you could come in my mouth."

Brad seized Paul's head in both hands and drove his cock back in roughly. "I'm safe! Take my load!" Paul's hands held his buttocks almost painfully tight for a few minutes while Brad renewed and redoubled the assault on the hot, sucking mouth. After only a few minutes of violent plunging, his orgasm began to spurt into Paul's mouth, which sucked even more hungrily while he cried out passionately and continued his invasion long after his climax had ended. Paul's hands explored his ass as he murmured his profound satisfaction, and Brad murmured endearments and ecstatic expressions of appreciation for the masterful love-making he had just experienced.

Paul released his cock, and he looked up and smiled happily. "I haven't taken a load in my mouth in years, and I can't remember a load I wanted more, or enjoyed more!" He stood and they kissed again, tenderly this time.

Brad began to unbutton Paul's shirt, and Paul took over his own undressing. As he stripped he told Brad, "When I first got big enough to have sex, four of my brothers used to fuck me all the time. I guess the oldest two would have too, but they were out of the house by then. Ari, the oldest one at home, fucked me first when I was only twelve, and he was nineteen. They all used to make me eat their loads, too. Only Andros—Andy—he's only two years older than me, he was the only one who would let me fuck him. And we used to suck each other off too, and he was the only one who was nice to me when he fucked me, and he never brought his buddies around and let them fuck me like my older brothers did."

"God, what a childhood!"

"Yeah, I know, but by the time I was fourteen or fifteen, I wanted to get fucked all the time. I used to get it at least ten or fifteen times a week. By the time I was a senior in high school it wasn't just my brothers and their buddies any more, I was also finding guys I wanted to get screwed by, and some that liked to get fucked back." By now he was seated and was removing his shoes, still wearing only his briefs. He stopped and looked up at Brad. "I shouldn't have done you first thing; I wanna get fucked by you, I really want to. Can you come again?" His shoes hit the floor and he stood. Brad knelt and his hands began to tug at the elastic on Paul's briefs.

"I'll come again for your Paul. You can't believe how much I want to fuck you. You're unbelievably desirable and exciting!" He pulled the shorts down, and Paul's cock sprang out. It wasn't as large as Roy's or his own, and it missed the optimum specifications of his Guy Store wish list perhaps, but it was still of a generous size, certainly above average, and fully as beautiful as the other specs would have called for.

Paul stepped out of his briefs, closed his eyes, and murmured his satisfaction as Brad began a comprehensive exploration with his hands, his eyes, his lips and his tongue, encompassing every part of the truly glorious body. A Greek god indeed, fully deserving of worship! Paul's ass, when he first saw it, literally took Brad's breath away. Perfection. Aside from the slight deficiency in cock size, only the fact that his navel was not an "outie" and there was no trace of a cleft chin kept Paul from being the absolute ideal of masculine perfection in Brad estimation.

Kissing and worshipping the magnificent ass inspired Brad

to do something he had done only once or twice before, with Andy of the beautiful fundament. He had kissed and licked all over Roy and Chris and Whopper and others, and had actually kissed their sphincters often—usually immediately prior to challenging those muscles to open and admit his shaft—but with Andy he had at least once been so inspired by the beauty of his ass that he invaded the anus with his tongue, and, in effect, fucked him that way. Both Chris and Geoff had regularly enjoyed doing it to him. It was a uniquely exciting sensation, which he adored, but he had not been moved to return the favor with either of them no matter how attractive and satisfying they were otherwise. But the sheer perfection of Paul's backside was irresistible. Brad quite literally buried his face between the ample, rounded globes of smooth, muscular flesh and drove his tongue as deeply as he could, in and out of the ecstatic young man, whose appreciation was fully evident. Paul's hands reached behind to pull Brad in even more closely, and he panted and moaned in ecstasy as the darting, dancing tongue thrilled him completely. "God, Brad, I could almost come just from you doing that. That feels so fuckin' good!"

Breathless, Brad stopped his oral worship for a moment, and Paul turned around. His rigid cock slapped the side of Brad's face, but almost immediately disappeared into the depths of Brad's throat. As he fondled Paul's buttocks with one hand, and with the other drove two fingers deep inside him, Brad devoured the very exciting shaft until, with cries of animal lust, Paul suddenly jerked it from his mouth and sprayed his emission all over him. Paul quickly fell to his knees, licked Brad's face and shoulders clean, and kissed him passionately.

They retired to the bed, where they caressed and embraced each other as they continued to kiss, until Brad suddenly said, "My Plane!"

Paul kissed him feverishly and said, "Get a later flight. Stay with me."

In less than fifteen minutes, Brad had re-scheduled his flight for one day later, had extended his rental car and his stay in the hotel for a day, and had left a message on his own answering machine in San Francisco, telling Gwen he would be delayed.

Paul reached his sister-in-law. "Andrea, is Andros there?"

She went to get him as Paul whispered "Andy and Andy," referring to Andrea and Andros, and giggled. "Andy? Paul. Listen, I'm gonna be a day late getting there. Any problem? ... Great. And Andy, do me a favor. If for any reason Roy calls, tell him I've gone out for a few minutes or something, and call me at this number right away and tell me [he read him the phone number of the hotel and Brad's room extension], and I'll return his call from here. I'll owe you big, okay? ... Yeah, Andy, right ... yeah, I got lucky, and he's gorgeous, and ... yeah, he's definitely worth it! Thanks, bro ... I love you too, and I owe you really, really big! ... "

He looked at Brad and grinned. "Yeah, it's really big, too! ... . . Andros, I'd give you that for old time's sake, anyway, you know that. Don't I always? ... yeah, and that would make it even better!" He hung up and smiled at Brad. "All set, we've got twenty-four hours!"

They used their twenty-four hour reprieve productively.

Paul proved to be an unbelievably exciting and appreciative passive partner in anal sex, if not as frenzied as Chris had sometimes been, he did not miss it by a great deal, and he gloried in the feel of Brad's eruption inside his chamber, something he had not permitted other partners in a long time. After their first such bout, Brad expressed the hope that Paul would service him the same way. Paul went to his suitcase, returned with a "butt plug," and asked that Brad put it in him.

Butt plugs, for the uninitiated, are cones of hard latex, produced in varying sizes, and with a flange of sorts which prevents the entire device from disappearing into the body of someone taking it into his rectum. The plug Brad put inside Paul was seven inches in circumference at its base—a large one, by any standard.

Brad had seen not only butt plugs, but also an increasingly diverse assortment of dildos and other accoutrements of sex play in shops in San Francisco, but he invariably only looked around and left when he entered one of them. The dizzying variety of gay pornographic magazines and videos was enormously tempting to him, but he resisted the temptation to buy any of them; he had no idea where he could hide porn from his wife. He had obliquely suggested to Gwen that they buy some dildos for use on her in their love-making, but she had rejected even the suggestion out-of-hand. Brad had, of course, thought he might use the dildos on himself when he was alone, but like the porn, he could not hide a dildo from Gwen. He had buried his interest as he had continued to deny his homosexual urges.

As Brad was putting the butt plug in, Paul's dick grew to maximum rigidity, and he told Brad to lie on his back. "I don't top a lot, but when I do, I always use something like this. I pretend it's somebody's big cock up my ass while I fuck and it makes me so fuckin' horny I could screw for an hour!" Brad raised and spread his legs, and if it was the butt plug providing the inspiration for Paul's to perform, it was wonderfully effective. Paul fucked Brad like a raging stud, kissing him and whispering passionate endearments and encouragement in his ear. He had not put on a condom, and although Brad had intended to caution him to do so, he was soon so completely delirious with the sustained, savage, expert screwing the magnificent boy was giving him that he forgot all about it until Paul unceremoniously pulled himself out at the height of his passion and began to spray his emission over Brad. Paul's orgasm was huge, and felt incredibly hot as Brad received it on his face, his chest, his shoulders, and even in his hair. It was six or eight copious spurts, accompanied by droplets shooting willy-nilly all over his body. The massive explosion of passion that Brad had coaxed from Paul only an hour or so earlier before did not seem to have affected his sperm production in any way!

They rested, they cuddled, they explored each other's bodies lazily and sensuously, exchanged endearments, and Paul learned the details of Brad's life, including his questioning his ability to continue to hide his sexual appetites any longer. "So are you going to come out to your wife when you get back home?"

"I honestly don't know what I'll do, Paul. More importantly, there's my son to consider. He's not even seventeen; how would he react if he found out his dad was gay? He's very tolerant and understanding about other people. I've heard him jump with both feet on his friends who have used names like 'nigger' and 'faggot', but ... I don't know, I just don't know how he'd react, and I love him too much to let my wanting to fuck a guy endanger our relationship."

"Brad, I don't think you just want to fuck guys, do you? It looks to me like you *need* to fuck guys." He put his arms around Brad and kissed him tenderly. "I need for you to fuck me again, soon."

Brad obliged him. They went out and ate a late lunch and returned to the room and slept in each other's arms for a time, waking to Paul's urgent desire to be serviced again. Brad smiled at him, " I may have one more good fuck left in me today. You want it now or later?"

Paul left the bed and again went to his suitcase. This time he returned with a very formidable dildo, which he presented to Brad. "Here's a good friend of mine that Roy bought for us. Use this for now." The device was not only flesh-colored, it even felt like actual flesh, yielding like real flesh, but with ample rigidity to make it effective. It had large balls attached, with spherical inserts deep inside them that moved freely when massaged, and made them feel like actual testicles. The suction cup at the base was not going to be needed here. The awesome feature of this dildo, however, was its size. Brad had seen outrageously large dildos on display, but this was not so large that it seemed unreal. In fact, it was probably an inch shorter than the fabled Whopper's mighty organ.

Later, Brad measured it. He discovered that the shaft was just over nine inches in length, and six-and-a-half inches in girth. And, Brad thought, it was stunningly beautiful even though only a reproduction.

"God, Paul, this looks like fun. Does it have a name?"

"Meet the Jeff Stryker model!"

"I've seen pictures of Jeff, and I know he's a porn star, but I've never seen any of his videos. Is this really the same size as he is?"

"It's supposed to be modeled directly from his dick."

"Jesus, I'd like to meet Jeff Stryker!"

Paul laughed. "You and probably nine out of ten gay men in the world! This is gonna have to do for now."

And it did, and it did so splendidly. Brad enjoyed wielding it on the dark Adonis who cried aloud in his enjoyment of it, and seemed to be insatiable in taking it. Paul's enjoyment seemed so intense, in fact, that Brad could not help but try it himself, and he spent a delicious half-hour with Paul providing the 'engine' to drive Mr. Stryker's ample and beautiful endowment into him. So great was his enjoyment that he later had Paul ride his cock while facing his feet, so that Paul could employ "the Stryker alternative" to service him simultaneously, which seemed like such a good idea to Paul, that he forewent his butt plug in honor of the larger prosthesis when he screwed Brad much later that night.

By the time Brad and Paul drifted off to sleep, they were both exhausted and sexually spent. Brad had experienced at least five climaxes during this full day—certainly a record he had not attained in many, many years. But the younger, and seemingly tireless satyr in his arms had delivered at least two or three more orgasms than he had, mostly joyously and forcefully spewed and sprayed over Brad's back or stomach in wonderfully hot profusion. As he held Paul in his arms, and listened to the gentle whisper of his breath while he slept, Brad considered how sweet and innocent this sexually insatiable, perfect young man seemed.

"Roy is an unbelievably lucky guy! If it weren't for Gwen and Josh back home, I'd do everything in my power to make him fall in love with me instead."

He sensed that to an uneasy extent he had already accomplished that goal he knew he could not set for himself.

Their love-making the next morning was passionate and ultimately satisfying, and when they parted shortly before noon, Paul promised to keep in touch and somehow get out to San Francisco to be with Brad again; Brad again urged utmost discretion in calling.

Gwen was uncharacteristically warm and friendly when he returned home. Josh was particularly glad to see him because five days without his father was an unusual event, and he could not remember them having been apart that long except for times when he had been off to summer camp.

Brad dreaded the subtle signs from Gwen that signaled she wanted to have sex. They were not even subtle the night he returned, and he surprised himself by performing creditably in spite of his having had two orgasms that same morning, and more orgasms during the time he had been away than he had experienced in at least two, or possibly three months. And he knew he was *performing* for Gwen; almost all the time he was making love to her his mind was back in Connecticut, engaged in meaningful sex with Roy, and experiencing rapture with Paul at a level he could not remember having achieved since Geoff left him and his life turned toward heterosexuality. In his mind it was Roy and Geoff and Paul he was having sex with.

As he drifted off to sleep, he knew without question that his marriage was doomed, and that he had to find a way out of it without hurting Gwen or losing Josh. How? His dreams, however pleasant, provided no answers:

"The Academy is pleased to present the 1993 Best Actor award, for his portrayal of a husband who is not only straight, but continues to enjoy fucking his wife, to ... Bradley Thornton." Brad kisses Roy and Paul and Chris and Andy and Whopper and Geoff, all seated in the same row with him, and stumbles to the stage to accept his well-deserved reward as the tears stream down his face and the orchestra plays an appropriate song. Not surprisingly, it's 'Send in the Clowns.'"

Almost three thousand miles away, Paul lay in the guest room of his brother's house, where his brother had visited him after his wife went to sleep, and as much as he had enjoyed sex with Andros (he always had), he had imagined it was Brad inside him, making love to him, not his brother. His thoughts were less fanciful: "Shit, why does he have to be married! I love Roy, and I know I've got it good here with him, but I'd throw it all away for a chance to be with Brad. I'm gonna be sure he always knows where I am. I think he feels the same way about me, and he said himself he didn't know what was gonna happen with his marriage."

3.

Brad knew he had to maintain the facade of marriage and heterosexuality for another two years. After that, Josh would be in college and, for all practical purposes, on his own. Brad did not honestly feel Josh would have any trouble accepting his parents' divorce, but he was concerned about how his son would react if he discovered his father was gay.

Emotionally, Brad knew maintaining the facade was going to be extremely difficult after his experiences at the Darby reunion. Still, he loved his son completely, and knew his emotions were going to have to bow to his intellect for at least two years. He still loved Gwen too, but he now realized that he loved her as the mother of his son, his friend and companion of nineteen years, and as a nice person; in the last few years, however, she had been displaying a kind of anti-male feminism that he had not observed in her before, inspired, he felt sure, by several of the women she worked with on her magazine. Any one of them could have been a namesake for the magazine's new title.

He had already begun to sense she was exercising wifely duty to him rather than interest in sex during their love-making in the last year or two. He had not given it a great deal of thought, surprisingly enough, and had assumed it was normal for couples who approached two decades of inhabiting the same bed. He wondered if Gwen would even be especially upset at the prospect of a divorce. Still, he knew he was consciously planning to abandon his marriage vow, and it bothered him far less than he knew it should.

He was already starting to feel guilty about not feeling guilty.

For the next two years his home life basically changed little, on the surface reflecting almost nothing of the turmoil of his inner self. Gwen seemed ever busier with her duties at *Bitch*, and was more frequently absent for meetings and interviews evenings and weekends. Given his decision to ask for a divorce, this suited Brad admirably. Josh's final two years in high school found him more than ever wrapped up in the activities of his soccer team, the several clubs he belonged to, and his gang of close friends. As a result, he was also gone more than he had been. Brad did regret this situation with Josh, but he knew that his son was growing up and growing away from him. He accepted that Josh's school life and friends were now more important to him than his relationship with his parents.

Brad found he had more time to himself than he ever had before. Between his return from the epiphany he had experienced with Roy and Paul, and the date of Josh's graduation, he used that free time to explore his homosexual nature, without often indulging it.

Acknowledging again that he found men sexually desirable, Brad began to look at them differently, and much, much more closely. There were very attractive, sexy men everywhere, and he also reluctantly admitted that he found a great many very young men equally desirable, many of them no older than his own son!

Remembering Roy's reaction to Josh's photograph, Brad had also considered his son in a new light when he returned from the Reunion. He had always known his son was uncommonly handsome and well-built. He even knew he was hung, but he had never considered Josh's unusually large penis and testicles as anything but simply one of the many things that made him who he was (in truth, however, he had perhaps felt a bit of pride in this manifestation of paternal heritage!). Roy had looked at his son's picture and declared he would like to have sex with him. As much as it had shocked Brad, it had also forced him to consider thinking of Josh as a possible sex object for another man, and he had to admit that his son was not only physically very attractive, he was also sexy as the devil, and even—as Roy had so succinctly put it—gorgeous!

Brad had never thought much about Josh's sex life, strangely enough. He had tried explaining the facts of life to him a few years ago, but had been laughed down. "For God's sake, Dad, they tell us about the birds and the bees in school you know, and we talk about contraception and AIDS and all that stuff." He knew Josh was fully developed physically, and had even inadvertently caught him masturbating on two occasions. Mercifully, Josh had not realized either time he had been observed. He also had to accept the fact that by the time he himself had been ready to graduate high school he had experienced a passionate three-year love affair with one schoolmate, and another shorter love affair with a younger schoolmate that grew out of a gang-bang in which he himself had participated. Moreover, in addition to a few one-time liaisons with schoolmates, he had thrilled to both the magnificent ass of Andy and the prodigious cock of Whopper over and over again, and his parents had probably entertained no inkling he was even sexually active. Was Josh having experiences like these? As close as he was to his son, he knew they couldn't discuss it. All he could do was to be there if his son ever needed to talk about it.

Maybe Josh was gay. After all, he seldom dated; mostly he escorted girls to major school functions where his friends also had female companions, but probably no more than once or twice a semester. For the most part, he hung out with his friends. Brad told himself it wouldn't bother him if his son were homosexual, but he knew how he himself had struggled to suppress his true nature for so many years, and didn't want Josh to endure that. Certainly there were no outward signs of homosexuality, he thought, but then he had to admit he had no idea what those signs might be. He himself exhibited no "outward signs", and with the exception of the overly-sensitive Chris, all his sex partners had been very masculine, and he probably would have had no idea any of them were interested in homosexual sex if he had not watched his own cock penetrating them over and over, and felt theirs inside him.

Brad was masculine, he was handsome, he was athletic, he was even married. Yet, he was gay. Most of Josh's friends were very good-looking—was he screwing around with them as his father had been at his age? If Josh were gay, would he "come out" to his family? Brad had to accept the possibility that his son could be a practicing homosexual, and he might never know it.

Equally disturbing was the fact that lately Josh's friends had begun to look unusually handsome to Brad. In truth, many of them seemed quite mature, and were beginning to seem sexually attractive to him. Given their ages now, and his increasing willingness to explore his homosexual nature, it was understandable that he found them so, still he could not help but feel guilty about it, and he tried to put it from his mind.

They had to be off limits to him under any circumstances.

About a year following his Reunion, Brad got a message at his office to call Paul Stavros at a Connecticut number, but he delayed returning the call for a day or so. He half hoped that Paul wanted to come out and be with him again, but he also wanted to discipline his sex drive until he could ask for a divorce. He certainly did not want to take any chance that Gwen would discover him in a compromising situation before they had at least separated. Remembering how indescribably attractive Paul was, and how thrilling his encounter with him had been, Brad did what any red-blooded (albeit homosexual) American male would have done. He returned the call.

Paul's voice and his words sent the blood racing through Brad's veins. He was coming to the West coast to visit another brother (not Andros) in Seattle, and wanted to swing back through San Francisco to see Brad on his way home.

Did Brad want to see him? Assuredly. Did he see him? One might question the Catholic orientation of the Holy Father in the Vatican and receive the same answer!

Paul stayed only two nights, in a hotel on Union Square, and Brad found time to spend several hours with him each day and evening, although spending the night with him was out of the question. Paul was still in his relationship with Roy, and was still happy to be, but he told Brad he had thought about the wonderful night they had shared thousands of times, and had often picked up the phone to call him, but had always backed out.

Their love-making was intense and hungry, but they shared a lot of tender cuddling and kissing as well. Paul had brought no "toys" with him, of course, so they went to a sex shop and bought the same Jeff Stryker dildo they had both enjoyed their first time together, and employed it on each other enthusiastically, and with considerable satisfaction! Brad planned to discard the object when Paul left, but he managed to sneak it into his house and hid it carefully for occasional use when he was alone (better than nothing, he reasoned).

Brad explained that he was contemplating asking for a divorce fairly soon, and that once he was free he would let Paul know, so they could get together again if he was still interested.

Although he was tempted to visit some of the city's many gay bars, Brad resisted the temptation. He thought there would be time enough to seek sex partners when he was divorced, when his son was no longer at home, when he was free to do so. But he did find himself visiting some of the sex shops along Polk Street, however. While before he had only very rarely dropped in on one or more of them—and even then just for a brief moment or two—now he often perused the magazines featuring nude men, and began to become familiar with some of the current icons of gay porn.

He readily succumbed to the temptation to watch some of the pornographic videos shown in the quarter booths in these shops. He was astonished at the sexual prowess of porn stars like Jeff Stryker, whose films he sought out especially because of his memory of Paul's dildo. He often sat in the booths and watched the stud Stryker masterfully plying his huge tool, and he marveled at other super-hung studs like Rick Donovan and Tom Steele doing the same. Cute "bottoms" like Kevin Williams, or Joey Stefano, or the unbelievably built and gorgeous blond Adonis Steve Fox turned him on equally, but it was the versatile ones like Erik Houston, Mike Henson, or Matt Ramsey that especially appealed to Brad.

In the viewing booths, Brad discovered that he frequently was propositioned for sex, and he actually had to fend off passes from other men who were interested in giving him blowjobs (or more!). He found politeness in refusing them often proved insufficient, and he occasionally had to resort to surliness. As he watched the videos, he usually masturbated, often having to ignore erect penises being offered to him through "glory holes" in the walls.

On only one occasion was he recognized at a sex shop, shortly before Josh's graduation. That he had not encountered anyone he knew in his visits before that was fortuitous, but sooner or later his luck was due to run out; that it "ran out" with one of his own son's best friends was frightening—but, as it turned out, rewarding.

Brad had entered a sex shop late one afternoon, and had started toward a viewing booth in the back, carrying a favorite video, when he spotted a familiar face looking at the gay magazine rack: Eric (he was so shocked he could not even recall his last name for a moment), one of Josh's buddies. He quickly ducked into a booth and sat there with his heart pounding, not really interested in watching a video at the moment. He heard someone enter the booth next to his, and instead of a hard cock coming through the "glory hole," he heard Eric's voice, and saw his lips speaking at the opening. "Mr. Thornton, open the door. I know it's you, and I have to talk with you." Brad squeezed his eyes shut and said nothing, hoping this wasn't really happening. "Come on, Mr. Thornton, we need to talk. I'm coming over there, open the door." His gentle rap was heard only a few seconds later. Brad resignedly admitted him.

Eric stepped inside. "It's Eric Neeley, Mr. Thornton. I saw you come in, and I saw that you recognized me. I think we need to talk."

"Yes, I saw you, Eric. Sit down."

"Look, Mr. Thornton, I guess you know why I'm here. And I guess I have a pretty good idea why you're here."

"Eric, I...."

"Look, I would never tell anyone I saw you here, and I know you won't tell anyone you saw me here. We're here for the same reason, right?"

"Eric, look, I don't think I can deal with this. God, you're my son's friend, you're only seventeen years old, and...."

"No, Mr. Thornton, I was eighteen last month, and I can be in here. Actually I started coming in here long before I was eighteen, though, and I come here because I like to watch these movies, and I sometimes get in the booths with guys. You know what I'm saying?"

"Okay, you're eighteen, Eric, but ... "

Eric put his hand on Brad's shoulder and gently pushed him down onto the bench. "Sit down, Mr. Thornton, Let's look at the video you got here together. I'd like to watch it with you." Brad sat, Eric took the video and put it in the VCR.

The video Brad had taken with him into the booth was *The Bigger the Better*, not at all recent, but the most exciting one he had so far encountered. It featured the enormously hung Rick Donovan driving his cock into the perfect ass of the handsome, magnificently hung and built Matt Ramsey in just about every way possible, and whether he was riding up and down on it, or lying on his back or kneeling to receive it, Ramsey hungrily took every inch of Donovan's monster and gloried in it!

As the video began to play, Eric said, "Oh yeah! This is a great one!" and he sat on the bench next to Brad; after a moment he stood briefly to fast-forward the tape to the part where Rick Donovan and Matt Ramsey are left alone in the classroom where the opening sex scene, the one that qualified it for Brad's favorite, is played out. As the action got hotter, Eric's leg pressed against Brad's; Brad held his breath as they watched, but soon the torrid scene won him over, and he was fully erect when Eric stood, dropped his pants and shorts, and began to stroke his own erect cock. "God this makes me hot, Mr. Thornton!"

Brad tried not to look as Eric masturbated, but he was incapable. As he looked, Eric turned to face him, his busy fist exercising his sizable and (to Brad) beautiful shaft almost in his face. Torn between the voice of conscience ("This is your son's friend! He's a child. He's off limits!") and his demanding sex drive ("Go for it! This kid's got a hot cock and he's ready to give it to you. And probably a lot more than just that!") Brad yielded to the latter, sank to his knees, and opened his mouth to admit Eric, who seized his head and began to thrust himself deeply and violently into the hot, moist vacuum provided for his gratification. "Suck it, Mr. Thornton! That is so fuckin' hot!"

While he feasted on the young man, Brad's hand caressed the undulating buttocks as they drove Eric into him. Soon Eric reached behind himself, took hold of Brad's forefinger, and guided it into him. As the finger penetrated all the way, Eric began to hump it enthusiastically and his hands again held Brad's head tightly while he renewed his oral assault.

Eric grasped Brad's shoulders and pulled him to his feet; he embraced the older man and whispered in his ear, "I'm really close, but I don't want to come yet!"

As Eric sank to his knees and began to unbuckle his belt, Brad yielded to his urgings and helped drop his pants and shorts to the floor. He had not had sex with a man in almost two years, and while his conscience screamed to him "This is your son's friend; you can't do this!" his sex drive answered "Fuck you! This kid is cute, he's hot, he wants me! I want his cock, I want his ass!" The voice of his libido clearly won out, and Eric demonstrated he was as accomplished a cocksucker at age eighteen as Roy had recently proven to be, with some thirty years of practice!

Brad could not hold out long, and soon he was driving himself savagely into Eric, whose moans of pleasure indicated he was enjoying the occasion as intensely as he. He pulled out from Eric barely in time, and his emission began to erupt from him in huge spurts, coating the upturned, smiling face. When he had finally discharged his enormous offering, he pulled Eric's head into him and hoarsely expressed his thanks. Eric rubbed his face into Brad and caressed his buttocks as he tendered his appreciation with equal fervor.

Standing and embracing, Eric and Brad began kissing passionately, both ignoring the discharge still coating the former's face. Around his busy tongue, Eric panted, "I wanted you to fuck me, Mr. Thornton!"

In spite of his orgasm, Brad was still delirious with passion. "You fuck me, Eric. Then I'll fuck you. I promise!" With that, he turned around and bent over, bracing his arms on the bench and offering himself to Eric.

Eric's hands began to explore Brad's ass. "God, I want to fuck you, Mr. Thornton. You look so fuckin' hot!"

On the TV screen, the astonishingly sexy Matt Ramsey was in a complete transport of lust as he bent over while the incredible Rick Donovan cock plowed him brutally. "Do that to me, Eric. I want you!"

"I've only got one rubber, Mr. Thornton!"

"Put it on and fuck me, Eric. I'll pull out before I come in you later! And for God's sake, quit calling me Mr. Thornton. For now just fuck my ass!"

Eric took a condom and a bottle of lubricant from his pants, where they puddled around his ankles. Brad rewound the video to the beginning of the Rick Donovan scene while Eric lubricated both his cock and Brad's ass. In only a minute Eric was pressing against Brad, was soon inside, and the fierceness of his forward thrusts met the reverse thrusts of his ecstatic partner. They both watched as Matt again bent over the desk to receive Rick Donovan's stupendous prick, as Rick lay on his back and invited Matt to ride the enormous pole, as Matt bobbed up and down in complete thrill for some time, and then as he lay on his back while Donovan penetrated him 'missionary style' and brought himself to climax with absolute, complete sexual mastery over his insatiable bottom, who then used his hand to coax an enormous, explosive orgasm out of his own prodigious cock.

Throughout the twenty-minute scene they watched on the screen, the passion of the two viewers grew along with the actors, and by the time Ramsey blew his regular huge explosion of come, Eric was ready, and his violent thrusts and grunts signaled his own arrival at orgasm. Eric fell over Brad, and stayed buried deep inside as he kissed Brad's neck and ear. "Jesus, Mr. Thorn ... Jesus, that was fantastic! You are such a great fuck!"

Eric turned his head and looked back. "You're a great fucker, Eric! You can't imagine how much I enjoyed that!"

"Show me how much you did. Do me the same way! Can you come again?"

Brad stood, and took Eric in his arms. "I can come again, Eric, I assure you. I want that hot ass of yours!"

Turning around and leaning over the bench, Eric smiled over his shoulder. "You want it this way?"

Brad knelt on the floor. "Get down here on your knees, Eric." Eric positioned himself on all fours, and proved to be as expert a bottom as he was a top! He vocally encouraged Brad with ever-increasing passion as he accepted the older man first on all fours, then rode him as he lay on his back, and wound up on his back with his arms around Brad's neck and his legs on his shoulders. Unconsciously, they had emulated the events of the Donovan-Ramsey fuck, but while they shared their own fuck Matt Ramsey and a young brunette were now doing the same thing on an exercise bench. As Brad watched Ramsey's perfect ass driving his massive cock into the younger man, he matched him stroke for stroke, and again pulled himself out barely in time, spewing another offering on Eric, this time on his chest and stomach, at the very same time that Matt Ramsey shot his famous, enormous wad explosively all over his partner.

He collapsed over Eric, and the two spent a long time on the floor, caressing and kissing. "You're fantastic! I've never been fucked better than that! And I've never fucked anyone as hot as you. I've gotta see you again, Mr. Thornton. When we can find a bed and do it right and do it all night!"

Brad's mind was whirling. This is Josh's friend; it's obvious he's well experienced. Have he and Josh been having sex? Could he have learned to fuck this way with my own son? What if Josh found out about this? I can't take the chance he might. How would he react? What if he and Eric are lovers, and he learned his own father screwed with his lover. What if Gwen found out! My God, she'd crucify me! No, I can't do this again, it's too risky. But damn, I enjoyed this so much! "Eric, I can't tell you how much I enjoyed this, and how very, very attractive you are, but we can't do this again. I ... there are all sorts of reasons, okay? I want to ... I really do want to, but I just can't."

"Think about it, Mr. Thornton ... think about it Brad." Eric kissed Brad long and tenderly.

Smiling wistfully down and stroking the face of the attractive young man lying below him, Brad said, "We can't Eric. And I guess it had better be Mr. Thornton."

"Just promise me you'll at least think about it ... Mr. Thornton."

Again they kissed, even longer, and more passionately. "I'll never say anything about this to anyone, I promise you, but you promise me you will at least think about seeing me again, okay?" A huge grin lit up Eric's face. "Okay, Brad?"

"I promise you, I'll think about it, Eric. But I don't think it can happen again, no matter how much I want it to ... and I do want it to."

After they were both dressed, and preparing to abandon the booth, Eric sank to his knees, unzipped Brad's pants and again took his cock in his mouth. He brought him almost to the brink of orgasm again, before standing, kissing him on the lips, and whispering in his ear, "Make it happen, Brad!"

Eric turned and left, and Brad used his fist to achieve yet another explosive climax. As his discharge splattered on the door Eric had just closed behind himself, Brad panted, "I'll make it happen again, Eric!"

Before his forty-fifth birthday, a week after Josh's graduation and he announced his desire for a divorce, Brad had sex three more times. Actually, he had it four more times, if you wanted to count the time he actually (*mirabile dictu*) had sex with Gwen. He had been somewhat surprised to find that he could still perform with his wife following his return from the Reunion, but increasingly it had been just that: a performance on his part. He did not find sex with Gwen unpleasant. It had simply become uninteresting to him, so he avoided it as patronizing on his part and demeaning to her. Only a week after his encounter with Eric, she had instigated sex, but he sensed that it was *pro forma* for her. There had certainly been no great joy in it. Still, he functioned.

His other three sexual trysts did not involve partners of the opposite sex. The first had been fairly brief, totally unanticipated, and vaguely disturbing. He had been walking along the trails in Lincoln Park, on the bluff overlooking the Golden Gate when a naked, twenty-ish man had stepped from behind a tree and propositioned him. Although he had frequently been approached for sex with others along these trails, he was always been slightly shocked and alarmed, and uninterested. But he had never been solicited by a really attractive man before, and this one was extremely handsome and in a state of quite impressive arousal! Brad took him up on his offer; he might still have been shocked and alarmed, but he was not one to pass up what seemed to be a good opportunity.

Retiring to a blanket spread in a secluded glade, the young man, whose name Brad never caught, was fully equipped with a supply of the necessities of safer sex, and both participants slaked their various thirsts and hungers quite well indeed. The young man was not only quite handsome, he was a splendid sex partner (something of an insatiable stud when "on top" and wildly voracious when "on the bottom"), but he was obviously not interested in a repeat performance, so when Brad left the glade less than an hour after he entered it he felt equidistant between frustrated on the North and soiled on the South. Still at the same time he had found the experience unusually exciting—perhaps due to the element of danger—and, strange to say since he also felt frustrated, quite satisfying. Mulling it over in his mind as he cut his walk short and headed straight for his house, he decided he was satisfied sexually, but frustrated emotionally.

Had he been asked before if a strictly meaningless, impersonal sexual encounter would have proven satisfactory, he would have rejected the idea out of hand. Still, as Roy had almost two years earlier planted the seed of reversion to his homosexual nature inside him, this anonymous stranger had planted another seed in Brad. Brad now felt an appreciation, if not yet an appetite, for anonymous sex. In any case Brad had immediately appreciated the young man's expertise at seed-planting and the depth of his plowshare, and however troubled he might have felt over the encounter at first, he certainly felt well plowed, and smugly felt he had himself plowed just as expertly and deeply as his anonymous partner. Certainly he had done much more than just functioned as he had with Gwen.

Did he feel guilt over having brought more passion and interest to sex in the bushes with an anonymous stranger than he had with his wife?

No.

As fate would have it, the other two sexual encounters he experienced occurred on consecutive nights, only a few days after Josh's graduation.

Although Brad's parents declined to make the trip because his father was not in the best of health, Gwen's mother and father both came to San Francisco for their grandson's graduation. Mercifully they opted to stay in a hotel near Fisherman's Wharf, renting a car to transport themselves around the city and out to the Richmond District, where their daughter and her family lived. Although they were both in their seventies now, they were quite active, and Mr. Andrews was still quite sure sin lurked around ever corner in California. Given his experience in the park and what happened to him a few days later, Brad felt the old man might be on to something!

Josh's graduation was joyful. He was a class officer and salutatorian of his class, and it was apparent both at the ceremony and at all the attendant functions that his family witnessed in any degree, that he was a popular student. He planned to attend San Francisco State, beginning in the summer term; given the impressive AP (advanced placement) scores he had attained, he would be well on his way to sophomore status as the regular school year began. Although his closest friends clamored for his attention, Josh made it a point to spend time with his visiting grandparents.

Eric Neeley was one of those clamoring for Josh's attention, of course. He was, after all, one of his closest friends. Brad now felt uneasy seeing Josh with Eric, and he had seen them together frequently following the encounter at the Polk Street sex store. There was nothing unusual in that, however; Eric had visited Josh at home countless times over the last several years, and had often slept over, in one of the two beds in Josh's bedroom. There was nothing unusual in that either, a number of Josh's buddies often spent the night there. Now when Brad saw Eric, though, he felt somewhat disturbed, vaguely worrying about the relationship between him and his son, and the secret he himself now shared with him. Still, Eric was, as he always had been, friendly and polite with Brad. To be sure, some long and very fraught looks passed between them when no one else was observing, and the few times Eric slept over, Brad had been as nervous as the proverbial cat on a hot tin roof, but there had been no repercussions.

On only one occasion had Eric made any actual allusion to their encounter. A few days following it, he was visiting, and when Josh left to go to the bathroom, Eric said very tightly to Brad, "Mr. Thornton, I really need to see you some time!" Brad had gently, but firmly discouraged him.

Immediately following Josh's graduation, Mr. And Mrs. Andrews wanted to take three or four days to drive up to see the Napa Valley wineries and vineyards, the redwoods, Mendocino, and the coastal scenery before flying back East. They urged Gwen, Brad and Josh to accompany them. Gwen seemed pleased at the prospect, and readily agreed to go. Brad was really not interested in the trip at all, and managed to bow out gracefully by pointing out how crowded the car would be with five people. No one but Josh was disappointed in that arrangement. Josh was not excited at the prospect, but he nonetheless dutifully acceded to his grandparents' wishes, on condition that he be allowed to drive. "Thank God!" Brad thought.

With a plethora of remarks about the "non-traveling travel agent" and injunctions to "hold down the fort," the Andrews' rental car drove away and Brad breathed a sight of relief. Three nights and almost four days on his own: practice for what he hoped to begin seeking in a week's time.

His first night alone he treated himself to a couple of rented porn video tapes: a just-released Steve Fox film (*All American*) and a classic Jeff Stryker (*Stryker Force*). Paul Stavros was the most beautiful man he had ever had sex with, but Steve Fox had to be the most beautiful man he had ever seen (albeit only on video). In this latest movie Steve finally demonstrated he could be a very satisfactory top as well as a voracious and expert bottom! Jeff Stryker was, well, Jeff Stryker (arguably the hottest man he had ever seen). As he watched the climactic moments of the Stryker film, Brad rode the dildo molded from the stud's amazing endowment suction-cupped to the floor, and fancied himself enjoying the delights of the original being employed so very, very masterfully on the screen, also remembering how the incredible Steve Fox had employed an even much larger one on himself so gratifyingly in his next-most-recent film, *Flashpoint*.

Returning the videos to the store the next morning, Brad picked up a copy of *The Golden Gate Nation*. Although he invariably discarded it before he got home, he read it regularly, keeping up with events, but also poring with fascination over the classified advertisements. At least three or four pages of each issue were devoted to men who were offering themselves as "Models/Escorts," but it was obvious they were not really offering to model for anyone, or escort their clients anywhere but to bed! Whatever euphemisms they might employ, these young men were offering their bodies for sale, and they were almost exclusively young men, if the ad copy was at all accurate.

The picture ads were especially intriguing to Brad. Many of these young men had fabulous bodies and apparently very impressive endowments. Few faces were ever shown. The copy in the text-only ads, such as "Greek God," "yummy ass," "super hung," "ten inches and a bubble butt" *ad erectus*, promised even greater attractions, but Brad wondered how much of that was true. He had often been tempted to call one of the "escorts" and sample his wares, but decided he would wait until he was free to do so. He well knew there were those who considered prostitutes and their clients as morally reprehensible, but he saw nothing inherently wrong with adults doing what they wanted with their bodies, as long as all parties were agreeable and no one was hurt. Not rationalization, he truly believed that, and always had.

There were three or four theatres in the city which featured male porn stars, performing between showings of videos on the screen. He had also followed their ads in the bar rags and occasionally one of Brad's favorites had appeared at one or the other of them, but he had never yet succumbed to the temptation to attend. He learned that while Gwen and Josh were away Race Rivera was appearing at the Top 'n Bottom, one of the male porno theatres in a better section of town. Most of them were in the shady Tenderloin district.

The young Race Rivera, a handsome Latino (Mexican, he guessed, given the surname, although it was probably not his actual name) with a great build and a cock which seemed to hang to his knee, was a relative newcomer on the scene, but was already one of Brad's favorites. The heavily muscled Race, nineteen or maybe twenty at most, had copper-hued skin, with a sexy blend of Hispanic and Indian facial features. His medium length, coal-black, straight hair was parted in the middle, and his body was otherwise almost completely hairless, except for a mild growth under his arms and a generous thatch over what was probably his second most attractive feature. But to Brad his most attractive feature was an ample, perfectly rounded, velvet-smooth ass of absolutely succulent quality, mounted high on his long legs. Many would have argued that alleged second most attractive feature prominent beneath that thatch of pubic hair, should receive top billing. To be sure the cock was more than just impressive: uncircumcised, long and fat and dangerous looking even when flaccid, but perfectly proportioned and as velvety smooth in appearance as its owner's perfect rear end. When erect, Race's cock was a behemoth almost without parallel in the porn world, probably an actual ten inches in length (porn publications called it twelve, of course) and almost as fat at its tip as it was at its base (and its girth was proportional to its startling length). It was seemingly hard as steel, capable of long-sustained erection, and during orgasm produced a prodigious quantity of his discharge with such force that he frequently coated his partners with it.

In almost all of his on-screen appearances Race had topped his partners, but there had been two films Brad had seen where he had proven himself to be a hungry and apparently insatiable bottom as well. Stryker's Brad-bestowed title of Sexiest Man in the World might very well be up for grabs soon by this truly awesome newcomer.

One of the "trademarks" of Race's performance had become his violent discharge shooting straight up in the air as he lay on his back immediately following a very rapid 'dismount' by his partner. His emission often seemed to reach a height of five or six feet, earning him the nickname "The Latin Vesuvius". Brad determined that he was going to go see Vesuvius erupt in person.

Brad found out that Race was appearing on stage three times each day, at one, five and ten o'clock. Assuming that the earliest show would be the least crowded, Brad asked for a ticket for that, but learned that the twenty-five dollar ticket allowed him to enter or leave for the entire day. Seated toward the back of the darkened auditorium, with only another ten or twelve patrons in attendance, he waited through the last few minutes of a mediocre porn video badly reproduced on the theatre screen, nervously watching men shuffle furtively in and out of the curtained side entrance. The film suddenly stopped, and Race appeared on stage in a bright spotlight, fully clothed. He danced to the deafeningly loud disco music, gradually removing his shirt and tank-top undershirt. His chest looked almost as magnificent in the tight undershirt as it did when bared. Then he dropped his breakaway pants, leaving him clad in only a G-string.

It didn't seem possible to Brad, but Race looked more appetizing and exciting in person than he did in his videos. He circulated around the darkened auditorium, visiting each patron and waving the impressively full crotch of the G-string in his face, then facing away as he straddled each pair of legs and bending over to give each horny man there a really close-up view of his magnificent undulating ass. It had apparently been obvious to the ticket seller out front that Brad had not been here before, so he had instructed him that he was expected, assuming he was pleased, to slip dollars bills into the G-string or the stockings of the dancer when he came around to him. He had provided him with a supply of them, which Brad later happily put into the tiny, but extremely well-filled pouch of Race's G-string. He was more than pleased.

An announcement had been made just before Race's appearance cautioning patrons that they must not touch the genitals or backsides of the performers, and signs were posted to that effect as well. The rest was, apparently, fair game, however, so all, Brad included, generously caressed Race's broad, muscular chest and arms, the hard washboard of his stomach, and his mighty thighs.

As he danced in front of Brad, Race's hands held his shoulders and he leaned over to whisper, "Look good?"

Brad, busily embracing the massive chest panted, "Shit, yes!" One of Race's hands left Brad's shoulder, and soon found its way to his crotch, cupping his painfully erect cock. Race again whispered, "Get it out for me before I come back!"

The Latin Adonis returned to the stage and gradually—and very sensuously—removed his G-string, leaving himself clad in only boots and socks. His cock was already semi-erect, and as he danced around the stage, he massaged it until by the time he returned to the audience, it was throbbing and bobbing in full erection. Going out into the house again, he frequently had to discourage audience members whose hands eagerly sought the monster dick dancing so temptingly in front of their faces, and a few even tried to take it in their mouths, but Race gently dissuaded them.

It seemed to Brad that when Race had his back turned to several patrons, presenting them with another view of his now completely bare and luscious ass, he could see their hands reaching around and playing with the impressive cock; he couldn't be sure.

When Race returned to him, he straddled his legs, and began swaying back and forth in front of him, which caused his beautiful huge shaft to swing temptingly in front of Brad, actually grazing his lips with his cock-head. Brad felt he was close to orgasm. As Race had suggested, Brad had opened his fly, and his erect cock was exposed. With his cock tantalizing

Brad's lips, Race reached down and took Brad's cock in his hand and began to stroke it. He panted in Brad's ear, "Yeah man, nice cock! Feels really hot!"

He sat down heavily and squirmed, almost permitting Brad's cock to penetrate his undulating, muscular ass, but then he stood and shifted his legs so that he was now straddling Brad, facing away from him. He bent over, so that Brad's face was only a couple of inches away from his asshole. Brad's hands traveled up the side of Race's legs and reached around his body to seek his fabulous cock. Race made no move to stop him, and soon both of Brad's hands were stroking the hot, unbelievably huge and hard prick. Race's hand reached back between his legs and continued to stroke Brad's cock as he looked back at him and said, "You like my cock too?"

Brad was about to reply when Race moved backward so that Brad's face was actually buried between the cheeks of his perfect ass. For just a few moments, Brad was masturbating Race Rivera's gargantuan cock and kissing his asshole.

If Race had continued to stroke his cock for even fifteen seconds longer Brad would have ejaculated, but Race released him and returned to the stage, but not before he turned back and whispered in Brad's ear. "I enjoyed that, man. Damn, you're hot!"

As soon as he returned to the stage, Race squirted some lubricant into his hand from a dispenser on a table placed there and obviously and tantalizingly worked it into his ass. He knelt on all fours, facing away from the audience, and clearly fucked himself with his forefinger while he smiled back over his shoulder. He then stood and began moving around the apron downstage, masturbating in earnest, often turning around to treat his audience to the beautiful sight of his magnificent ass driving his cock into his fist. After a few minutes he backed up to the table and lay his back on it, his feet still on the floor. A few more frantic strokes along his stupendous shaft, and it shot several enormous spurts skyward as several patrons called out "Vesuvius!"

Race quickly stood, and several more less-furiously propelled spurts shot straight out from him. He shook his mighty cock and coaxed a few slighter emissions and a few final drops from it, grinned at the audience and flipped them a quick salute, grabbed his clothes from the stage, and exited quickly.

It was one thirty, but the past half-hour had passed far too quickly for Brad. As he stood to leave a few of the men in the theatre headed for the side entrance, and a few were obviously masturbating and "finishing themselves off" after Race's thrilling performance. Brad himself felt like getting off, but he was damned if he was going to do it here!

After calming down and walking for a bit, Brad decided he would return to the Top 'n Bottom for the five o'clock show, and another close look at the fabulous Latino stud. He went to his office for a few hours, and was back in the theatre shortly before five. He had noticed earlier than no one sat in the first few rows, and he wondered why. He himself had sat fairly far back because he hadn't known what to expect. He knew now what to expect, and he expected that if he sat in the very first row he could see the legendary Race Rivera eruption from up close, and it was there that he positioned himself, only two feet from the edge of the stage.

Shortly after five the spotlight again picked out Race, and he duplicated his dance and strip, starting out into the auditorium in his g-string and boots. As he straddled Brad's legs he said, "Hey, you're back! Couldn't see you from the stage." He ground his pelvis about two inches from Brad's face, then leaned over and whispered into his ear, "Liked what you saw, huh?" He reached down and discovered that Brad had not only unzipped his trousers, but had pulled them down to expose himself completely. Race's hand cupped his balls and stroked his erect cock. "Hmmmn. I can tell you still like it. That really feels nice. Keep it that way for me, I'll be back!" He turned around and treated Brad to the sight of his glorious behind before moving on to the others. There were a few more than there had been at the one o'clock show, but not many.

After completing the circuit and returning to the stage to strip completely and bring himself to another breath-taking erection, Race again positioned himself directly in front of Brad. He whispered, "Take it!" and he put both arms around Brad's head, completely shielding it from view for the rest of the audience, and pressed his cock against Brad's mouth. Brad opened his lips and he thrilled to the salty taste and vast bulk of Race's huge cock-head entering his mouth. His tongue immediately began to worship the magnificent shaft as it filled his mouth and stretched his lips before starting a thrilling series of deep penetrations and near withdrawals. He could not see it, of course, but Race was grinning at the audience, only his head and shoulders lit by the follow spotlight. He did hear him saying to the audience, "I think he likes me!"

At the same time Race was fucking his mouth hard and deep, and Brad cupped and caressed the splendid, smooth ass driving the monster organ into him. It only lasted a minute, but it was thrilling.

Not since Whopper had last invaded him had he taken a cock of this dimension into him. *It feels wonderful,* he thought. He wanted it to go on forever, and to feel this incredible cock shooting a hot load in the deepest recesses of his throat!

For a moment he was back at Darby with Whopper plunging the biggest prick he had ever seen into him as prelude to burying it where he most loved to receive it; the sinuous, smooth ass he fondled felt like....

Race unceremoniously yanked his cock out of Brad's mouth and lay back on the stage apron, with his gargantuan organ standing straight up. Brad wanted to stand, bend over this hot stud's body, and take his matchless dick back inside where it belonged, but he had returned to reality when Race pulled himself out, and so he restrained himself.

Race humped upward into the air, his muscular ass clearing the stage by several inches with each upward thrust, and his cock bobbing temptingly as scattered applause rewarded his efforts. Brad was too busy applying his right hand to his own cock to applaud! Race stood and sat in Brad's lap. Again his cock almost penetrated the Latin Adonis's ass as he wriggled it. Race kissed him lightly, whispered, "I'll be back!" and went on to the other patrons.

After completing the circuit, Race returned to the stage, bypassing a return visit to Brad's lap. He continued as he had in the earlier show, lubricating his ass and finger fucking himself, but suddenly he jumped down from the stage, and again stood before Brad. With his hands on Brad's shoulders, Race wriggled his ass as he lowered himself onto the throbbing shaft he found in Brad's lap. This time he continued to sink down, and having been lubricated, Brad's cock slipped easily inside. Race bobbed up and down the full extent of Brad's cock and whispered, "Shit man, you feel great!" Then he looked up and again grinned at the audience. "I know he likes me!" He continued his ride. But whispered in Brad's ear as he leaned over to kiss him, "If you get close to coming, pull out, okay?" Brad nodded.

After a few minutes, feeling that orgasm was unavoidable if this kept up much longer, Brad reluctantly put his hands on Race's thighs and lifted him up away from his cock. "I'm too close—better stop!"

Race stood, leaned over and kissed Brad for a long time while their tongues explored their respective mouths. Race leaped back on the stage, and continued his show. Parading the apron as he masturbated enthusiastically, he grinned broadly, frequently winking at Brad. Soon he was ready, and again with his feet still on the floor, he lay his upper body back on the table and his massive orgasm shot from him in a glorious fountain before he stood and continued. This time only one patron called out "Vesuvius!," but all were applauding!

Brad marveled that Race was able to produce such a copious discharge, having seen a similar eruption only four hours earlier. Race stood abruptly, and time seemed to slow almost to a crawl for Brad as he watched, frozen with fascination while another huge jet of semen shot from Race's magnificent organ, came nearer and nearer to him, growing in size ... growing huge, obliterating the scene on stage ... engulfing the world in a flying, shifting, amorphous mass of opalescent liquid ... and landing directly on his eyebrow and flooding his right eye before he could react! He squeezed both eyes shut in reflex, and felt another huge spurt hit his forehead a split second later, with even greater force. He heard Race mutter, "Oh shit!"

He pulled his handkerchief out and was wiping his eye, as he looked up to watch Race shake the last few drops of his discharge onto the stage, grab his clothes, salute, and begin to exit.

Instead of going off into the wings as he had earlier, Race jumped down to the auditorium floor and came over to Brad. "Man, I'm sorry! Come with me and let me clean that up for you. I really didn't mean to do that!"

Brad said, "No, that's okay, really."

Race took his hand and pulled him up. "Come on, it's all over your hair and everything." He went through the curtained side exit, still gripping Brad's hand, and they went backstage into a dressing room.

Locking the door, Race turned to Brad. "I really am sorry, man. I didn't mean to shot all over your face!" He grabbed a towel from a chair and wet it in the sink. "Sit down and let me clean you up." Brad sat on the only chair, and Race began to sponge his forehead and hair. "I think you better take off your shirt and run some water into that eye." He giggled. "Man, that was some load of come, huh?"

Brad was stripping off his shirt and tee-shirt. "I was so surprised I couldn't even close my eyes! But to answer your question, that was some load of come. Jesus, you shot a load like that just a couple of hours ago. I don't see how you can do it." He leaned over the sink and bathed the discharge from his eye.

Race laughed, "Shit, give me an hour I can do it again. I gotta lotta come, man! I'm the horniest sonofabitch you ever saw."

Brad stood and wiped his eye, "You make me the horniest sonofabitch you ever saw!"

"Yeah, I did kinda turn you on, didn't I? I was trying to!"

"Why me? I'm not complaining, you understand. I think you're the hottest guy in videos. I sat there and sucked your cock and fucked your ass! Hell, I was in heaven!"

"Hey, I enjoyed it too, you know. I almost never do that during a show, but you're the hottest guy I've seen in this place, by far. There've been a couple of pretty cute young dudes, but I like older men, and you're definitely one hot-looking older man!" He ran his hands over Brad's naked chest and shoulders as he said this. "Here, give me that towel and sit down again." Brad sat again, trying not to stare at the beautiful pendulous cock, huge even though no longer erect. "You live here? What's your name?"

"I'm Brad Thornton." He held out his hand and Race shook it. "And yes, I live here in the city."

"I'm Gundo Lopez, Brad. Good to meet ya," and he leaned over and kissed him lightly on the lips.

As Brad closed his eyes while Race was dabbing at his hair

and face, he said "I never heard the name 'Gundo' before. Of course I've never heard of anybody named 'Race' before either."

"Well, my pop's ex-lover picked out Race Rivera for me. My real name is Tony Lopez, but I'm a 'junior', Antonio Lopez, Jr.—El Segundo, the second, you know? I hated being called 'Junior,' and the guys my pop hung out with started calling me 'Segundo' for a while, but it finally got shortened to just Gundo. So, that's me. I'm from L.A."

"Your dad's lover was—"

"A guy. Yeah, my pop, Tony Lopez Primero, is gay. Somehow he got my mother pregnant and they got married, said he wanted to prove he was a man or something, but he knew all the time he was gay. There's no question he's my pop, though—we look just alike."

Brad touched Race's ... Gundo's fat cock. "Even here?"

"Oh yeah, Pop's dick is big, but that's one way I think maybe I'm more like my other dad, Tom Hunt, my Pop's lover all the time I was growing up. His dick is really huge. I've felt it a lot of times when it was even bigger than mine. He was a porn star for a long time, but then he got into making movies instead of being in them. Anyway, the short story is, my mother and pop never really lived together, and she took off when I was about ten, leaving me with my pop and Tom. I grew up around horny naked men, I hadda turn out gay, but I knew I was even before that."

"So how did you get in porn?"

"Tom used to let me hang around the set. Pop helped out, but he wasn't in any of the videos. I don't know why, he looks great. Shit, I'd go to bed with him in a minute if he'd let me! Of course, Tom did take me to bed after I got to be about sixteen or so. That's probably what broke them up. Anyway I loved seeing all those hot guys, and I used to let some of them feel me up and play with me to get hard. I used to really like playing with them, too. Pop and Tom didn't know it, but by the time I was thirteen, I was suckin' a lot of dick behind the sets, and by the time I was fifteen, I was takin' 'em up the butt, too. And my dick was gettin' so big, I was givin' it to a lot of 'em up the butt. By the time I hit sixteen they all loved my big dick down their throats or up their butts, and we didn't hide behind the sets any more; I was usually on the set, and my dick and my ass and my mouth got a lot of famous porn stars hard for the camera.

"There were a lot of times they'd watch me jackin' off or fuckin' some other guy at the side of the set so they could stay hard enough, and a lot of times some famous cocks went directly from my mouth into some other very famous mouth or butt. So anyway, Tom started putting me in the films as soon as I was legal."

"Does it pay enough to live on?"

"Nah, but it means I can get a helluva lot of money from guys who want to have sex with me. That's where the money is. When I'm dancing like here I've usually got somebody lined up after every show for anywhere from three hundred to five hundred dollars, and after the last show I usually go for an all-nighter for a thousand or more."

"So I'm keeping you from something. Let me get my shirt back on and get out of here."

"No, I don't have anybody lined up now. I've got a guy pickin' me up for an all-night after the ten o'clock show, but that's it."

"Well look, I don't have that much money with me, but we could stop at an ATM and ... "

"Hey, Brad. I'd go to bed with you just for fun, but I wanna make up to you for shootin' my load in your eye. Do you wanna fuck with me?"

"Yeah, Gundo, hell yes. I really want to fuck with you. I've wanted to fuck with you since I saw your first film. You wouldn't believe how many times I've beat off watching you and thinking about that very thing."

Gundo moved in and put his arms around Brad, with their lips almost touching, he asked, "I wanna fuck you; can you take me? A lotta guys can't."

"Gundo, I promise you we'll get every inch of that monster cock of yours inside me, or I'll die trying."

"Hey, I don't wanna kill you! I just wanna fuck you!" He kissed him, tenderly at first, but soon they were locked together in real passion, tongues invading each other's mouths and hands exploring feverishly. "C'mon, get your shirt on, Brad, and let's go to my hotel room; I wanna feel that hot cock of yours inside me again."

"Uh, Gundo...?"

"Yeah?"

"I think maybe you ought to get dressed too!"

He laughed, retrieved a sheaf of bills from his socks, threw them in his gym bag, and quickly dressed. By that time Brad was also ready, and they went to Gundo's room nearby, in a hotel which was surprisingly nice, given the fact that the Top 'n Bottom was footing the bill.

Gundo's private performance for Brad in his hotel room was more than just an encore; it was a real sexual duet between the two, with Gundo taking from Brad as well as Brad taking from Gundo. Brad's experience with Whopper and his recent practice with "Jeff Stryker" (although Jeff himself had not been present!) prepared him well for his repeated impalement on Gundo's astonishing organ, and the Latin beauty expressed his admiration for both the extent of Brad's receipt of it as well as his enthusiasm. Brad, while not quite as formidably equipped as Gundo, was still a strong contender in the "big meat" sweepstakes, and Gundo expressed his appreciation excitedly as Brad penetrated him again and again.

Gundo had another show to do at ten, and an all-night customer after that, so he limited himself to one truly spectacular demonstration of his special "Vesuvian" ability, which was directed not into the air this time, but calculated to cover his partner's body. Still, he would not let Brad go until he had enjoyed no fewer than three such eruptions on Brad's part, only one visible, which was like Gundo's, designed to coat the eager recipient, and two deep inside him.

Orally, they shared each other mutually and at great, great length, and each provided an eager hot chamber, intense vacuum, expert lingual stimulation, and a voracious and apparently bottomless throat for the other. Alas, the times being what they were, neither could consume, as each wanted to, the product such wondrous activity produced.

The two lovingly explored each other's bodies, both manually and orally, and enjoyed such tender caressing and kissing that they opted for room service over going out to eat, and Gundo barely had time to get back to the theatre for his ten o'clock show. Brad watched again, sitting once more in the front row and enjoying Gundo's cock down his throat and his own up Gundo's butt, more-or-less in full view of an audience! The final eruption that concluded Gundo's performance missed Brad this time, although he would have sworn it had been intentionally aimed at him.

A brief chat and some impassioned kissing and petting with Gundo in his dressing room before the two had to separate elicited a promise from Brad to come to West Hollywood (Gundo's home) for at least an all-night bout some time fairly soon, and a promise from Gundo that he would let Brad know if he were going to be in the Bay area again.

"You're a hot man, Brad. I want to see you again soon. Yeah, I want you again!"

"I promise you I'm going to be able to be with you again very soon, and I'll come down to L.A. to see you as quickly as I can." Brad had explained his planned divorce to Gundo, and had even shown him Josh's picture. Gundo's reaction to Josh had been almost identical to Roy's: "Damn, I'd like to go to bed with that one!" Brad decided he had better keep Josh's picture out of the equation in upcoming encounters.

Brad left, stopped by the video store on the way home, and rented two Race Rivera videos for the night. He sat up late watching the beautiful, sexy man he had fucked and been fucked by that day, raising the tally of orgasms for the day, which was already unnaturally high, to an even more impressive number.

The next night Brad planned a quiet evening at home. He had returned the Race Rivera videos to the store. He still felt the glow of yesterday's sexual excitement so vividly that he intended a completely asexual evening, even if it were the last one before his family returned.

He roamed Castro Street for an hour or so, enjoying the sight of so many good-looking young men, and the freedom of so many of those young men to walk hand-in-hand and display mutual affection. He looked forward to what he was increasingly thinking of as his own freedom to become a part of this society soon. He had dinner alone at a Chinese restaurant, and returned home around nine, planning to start reading the latest John Grisham thriller and turning in early. No more than fifty pages into the book, the doorbell rang.

He opened he door to Eric Neeley. "Can I come in, Mr. Thornton?"

"Eric! Ah ... Josh is out of town."

"I know. I know he and everybody else isn't due back until tomorrow night. That's why I came. I want to see you!"

"I ... Eric, I don't know what to say. I really don't think we ... Eric, this isn't a good idea."

Eric stepped inside and closed the door behind him. "Mr. Thornton, I told my folks I was staying with another friend tonight, and they don't expect me home. Let me spend the night with you." Brad began to speak, but Eric stepped in and put one hand over his mouth, with the other one on his shoulder. "Don't tell me you don't want to see me. I know you enjoyed what we did in the video booth that afternoon as much as I did, and I know you told me it couldn't happen again, but I keep thinking about how wonderful it was that day, and how much I wanted to do it again with you." His hand had left Brad's shoulder, and was caressing the stiffening bulge of his pants. He squeezed it, "This says you want it, too, doesn't it?"

Brad had often thought of the encounter with Eric, and although he knew it was both dangerous and unseemly, he wanted a repeat as much as Eric obviously did. There was certainly no denying he grew fully erect in Eric's hand! Eric had slept over with Josh a couple of times since he had fucked with Brad, and each time Brad had lain awake, torn by the desire to go to his son's room to make love with his sexy overnight guest, and frustrated by the impossibility of doing so.

Apparently Eric had felt the same way. "The times I've been over here since that time we fucked each other were really difficult for me. It was all I could do to lie in there, knowing you were only a few feet away from me, and I couldn't have you." He took Brad in his arms and the older man's resistance melted as he kissed him tenderly. "I want you again, Brad. Don't you want me?"

Brad kissed back passionately and began to fondle Eric's ass. "God yes, I want you Eric. Get your clothes off!"

Looking intensely into each other's eyes, the two stripped completely as they stood there in the vestibule. Both were fully erect as they embraced again, and their cocks ground together and their hands explored each other's bodies as passionately as their tongues explored each other's mouths. Eric was kissing Brad's neck as he panted, "Fuck me, Brad. I want to feel you inside me again!"

Eric got his wish that night. Over and over and over! Brad was surprised at his own stamina. He had, after all, experienced wild sex the night before with Gundo, had ended the night by masturbating to a Race Rivera video, and had begun this day the same way. Eric was eighteen. It was no great surprise he was capable of slaking his apparently insatiable appetite—but Brad was forty-five, yet he matched Eric orgasm-for-orgasm.

They sucked in "69" and screwed each other to orgasm on the floor in the vestibule before they ever made it to a bed, and in bed they repeated their performance with many variations during the course of the evening. They slept in each other's arms, and in the morning greeted the day by sharing orgasms again, after which they showered together and wound up sharing yet another round of discharges under the spray. Brad fixed Eric breakfast preparatory to his departure, but before it was half consumed, they were again naked and inside each other on the bed.

The question which was bothering Brad vanished each time they made love, but invariably surfaced again in the afterglow of orgasm: Was Eric having sex with Josh? Finally, before Eric left, Brad broached the subject.

"Look Eric, it's certainly not necessary for me to say I enjoyed this. It was dangerous. It was ill-advised. I'm old enough to be your father. I am the father of one of your best friends. All of that, but, god, I had a wonderful time, and I think you're one helluva fine ... I don't know, a ..."

Eric giggled, "How about a fine piece of ass, Mr. Thornton!"

Brad grinned at him and kissed him. "Okay, Eric, you are one helluva fine piece of ass."

"And I think you're the best piece of ass I've ever even thought of, much less had, Brad! I want you again right now, and I'm gonna want you again tonight, and ... "

"Whoa! I don't see how this can happen again, Eric, no matter how much we want it to. And I do want it, too. But then, I wouldn't have thought last night would have been possible, so ...we're just going to have to play it by ear, Eric. If you stay over with Josh, you can't be with me, and I can't be with you. So it can only happen if we're absolutely sure of being alone together. Right?"

"Right! And I'm happy knowing that you want to be with me again. It will happen. I'll make it happen!"

"Before you go, Eric, there's something I wanted to ask you before, and have wanted to ask ever since you showed up last night. Will you answer me truthfully?"

"Sure I will!"

"Okay. Have you and Josh ever ... well, fooled around? Do you think Josh is gay? Do you think he suspects that I am gay? I guess you suspect I'm gay, don't you?"

Eric laughed. "I started to think you might be gay the first time you sucked my cock! I guess you figured out the same thing about me when I chowed down on yours! Anyway, no, Josh and I have never fooled around, and no, I don't think Josh is gay. And ... what else? Oh, yeah. No, I doubt seriously that he suspects you're gay. He would have at least hinted at it, I know. I sure as hell never suspected you were gay!"

"Thanks Eric. I hope you're telling me the truth, but I also know you would probably lie to me if the answers were 'yes' to any of those questions. I know I would if the shoe were on the other foot. You know, don't you, that I'm trusting you completely not to say anything to anybody, especially Josh, about what we've done together, even if...."

He again took Brad in his arms. "Not about what we've done together, but about what we do together! Okay? It's not over! And don't worry, I'm not telling anybody anything, but I am telling you that if you want it, we'll be together again, and as often as we can work it out!"

"Thanks for everything Eric—for being a good friend to Josh, for keeping our secret, for being...."

"A good piece of ass! Thanks for all the same things, Brad. Oh, I guess I'd better start calling you 'Mr. Thornton' again until the next time. It sure seems odd to call you that knowing what we've done. How about if I called you 'Mr. T?'"

"Oh shit, no Eric. Mr. T was that big black guy with all the gold chains on that television show."

Eric laughed, "Right, *The A Team*; I'd forgotten. I used to watch that when I was a kid. Yeah, that's just not you, is it? Gotta go," he kissed him, "Brad. And Mr. Thornton, please tell Josh I called him, and that he should call me when he gets in. I've got a lot to tell him!" He started out the door, then turned briefly and laughed, "No, not about this. About school stuff!"

Brad was alone, virtually sated after two consecutive nights of utter sexual abandon, but happy as hell and eagerly anticipating the gay bachelor existence he envisioned for the near future. He set about washing bedding and preparing for the return of his family, including his non-gay son (if-IF-Eric were telling him the truth).

4.

Gwen's parents returned East and Josh started school at San Francisco State University. Although his home was only about three miles north of the school, he moved into a dormitory on campus. The 'empty nest' syndrome might have set in for Gwen and Brad, but there was no time. When Gwen asked him what he wanted for his forty-fifth birthday a few days after Josh moved, Brad "screwed his courage to the sticking point" (as Lady Macbeth had once encouraged her husband to do), and told her he wanted a divorce.

He was actually spared having to come right out and ask for a divorce. Answering Gwen's query about a possible birthday present, he told her he was going to ask for something very unusual, and something only she could give him. He piqued her curiosity with that statement, but immediately regretted it as sounding somewhat facetious. Beating about the bush, talking about how they had each been going their separate ways lately, and how there seemed to be little intimacy between them any more, and ... Gwen's foot was tapping faster all the time as he stirred in the factors of Josh's majority and his absence from the home ... Gwen's fingers were now tapping in rhythm with her foot.

Finally, she said, "Brad, are you trying to say you want a separation, or your freedom, or you want to go your own way, or, after twenty-one years, you want a divorce? Is it 'A' or 'B' or 'all the above'? Come out with it! What do you want?"

Brad pussyfooted his way through all the possibilities Gwen had enumerated, but finally admitted a divorce was what he sought. "I know this comes as a shock, and you're probably very hurt, and you have every reason to be furious with me, but ... "

"But I'm actually not, Brad. And in fact, I don't think I'm terribly surprised. We've been growing away from each other lately, and now that Josh is more or less on his own, this is probably a good time to reassess our relationship. After all, we're one of the last couples we know who haven't split up! At least let's be friends, no matter what. I think that's important for Josh, especially."

Brad had anticipated tears, recriminations, and general high drama, followed by acrimonious negotiations between their attorneys. And he was (he hoped) prepared to deal with all that if Gwen acceded to his wishes; God knows what he expected if she dug in her heels and refused. He was not at all disappointed to find that his expectations were far removed from the reality of the situation as it developed. As noted at the beginning of this narrative, Gwen was so cool and, for want of a better word, organized about dealing with a separation and divorce, that he could not help wondering if she had not also been considering the prospect. Subsequent developments seemed to suggest she had been.

Brad's offer to move out and leave the house to Gwen was rejected. He was to pay rent on an apartment for her while divorce arrangements were being made and carried out. He was to remain in the house himself, to continue to provide a home for Josh, who would no doubt still be around his home for weekends, vacations, study breaks, etc. Gwen's salary at the magazine was more than adequate for her needs of the moment; nor was transportation a problem. She thought her BMW far preferable to Brad's vintage Corvette, anyway. Ownership of the house, insurance, wills, and so on, could all be sorted out and dealt with as negotiations proceeded. In any event, she moved out of the house and into a new, expensive two-bedroom apartment on Russian Hill within a week.

One condition she was firm about: it was up to Brad to explain everything to Josh. The unstated subtext was that Brad would explain to their son if he could.

Josh was remarkably understanding, even telling Brad he had been a little surprised that he and Gwen had stayed together as long as they had. "It's not like you guys fight, or anything, but it's seemed to me like you've been separated for the last couple of years, you've just been living in the same house! We'll be fine; this is still my house, and I'll visit Mom in her apartment, but I'm really not going to be seeing either one of you that much any more, Dad. Anyway, for the last few years, it's seemed like it was pretty much just you and me. Mom hasn't seemed to be aware that I was around most of the time, but naturally I still love her. She's my mother, after all. And I love you of course," Josh stepped in and put his arms around Brad. "And I really do love you, Dad, but I'm pretty much on my own now."

Brad held his son in his arms and had to take just a moment before he could reply. Josh's affectionate gesture had moved him considerably. "Thanks for being so understanding, Josh. I know you're on your own now, but I'll always have a bedroom for you, whether it's here, or somewhere else. Where I live will always be your home, understand?"

"Of course I do, Dad."

"But there's one thing I hope you'll still do for me, even though you are completely on your own now."

"Sure, Dad, what is it?"

"I hope you'll let me continue to pay your tuition and fees, and support you in the manner to which you have become accustomed until you get a good paying job!"

Josh kept a perfectly straight face as he shook Brad's hand, put his other hand on his shoulder, looked squarely into his eyes and said, "Okay, Dad, I'll permit you do that for me if you behave yourself!"

"Why, you ..." They began to wrestle playfully until Josh suggested they go get a pizza, after which they did go get a pizza, and the new arrangement was a *fait accompli* as far as Josh was concerned.

Surprisingly, Brad did not go on a sexual rampage once he became a free man, although he began to enjoy (perhaps far too mild a word) a considerably increased scope in his activities.

He felt he had to exercise maximum caution in lining up sexual partners, and he usually did. For one thing the ease of his separation from Gwen had been far too simple. It aroused his suspicion. Was she going to spy on him and try to catch him in some sexual situation that would give her ammunition for a more favorable divorce settlement? It didn't seem likely, but on the other hand, he felt he had understood his wife less and less recently. The Gwen he married would not have sought revenge, but neither had that Gwen been the editor of a strident feminist magazine. In fairness, he also had to admit that the Brad she married had not been ready to leave her to seek comfort in the arms of other men! She could be looking for something—it needed to be kept in mind.

Furthermore, he discovered that Josh was around home a lot more frequently than he had anticipated, often popping in without warning (which was his right, after all, this was his home), so Brad had to be careful, he certainly didn't want his son to discover him *in flagrante delictu* with some stud. He doubted Josh would be as understanding about that as he had been about his parents' separation.

Over the course of the next six months his situation with Gwen simplified considerably. She announced that the publisher of her magazine (and of quite a number of others as well) had asked her to marry him once she was free, and she had accepted. She would become the new Mrs. Quentin Turley, and both she and her husband-to-be sought the speediest divorce possible for her. A Nevada legal arrangement brought the whole thing to a close by New Year's Day, 1996. It was all very polite and antiseptic, and Brad even attended his ex-wife's simple wedding ceremony with his son.

The one complication that ensued as a result of Gwen's remarriage was that Josh was around the house even more frequently. He had (out of a sense of duty, Brad thought) visited his mother at her Russian Hill apartment often, where she maintained a bedroom for him. Even though there was a room ostensibly called "Josh's room" in the rather palatial digs of the Quentin Turleys across the Golden Gate in Sausalito, the alleged occupant almost never used it. Josh felt uncomfortable around his new stepfather. Indeed he didn't really like him (nor did Brad), and preferred to limit his meetings with his mother to lunch or dinner when she was in the city, and an occasional ceremonial visit to her new home. Which meant he was home more often than Brad had expected.

During the first few months after Josh moved to campus to begin Summer school, Eric was still in town—he was due to enter Pepperdine University down the coast in Malibu for the fall semester. Knowing Josh's class schedule made it easy for Eric to arrange short trysts with a now more-than-willing Brad, and on the occasion of a four-day week-end Josh and two of his other friends used to take a trip to Mexico, Eric spent three whole days and two nights in languorous, near non-stop love-making with his friend's father, mostly in the very bed where his friend had been conceived.

By the time Eric was ready to leave for Malibu, Brad welcomed the separation. He was not tiring of Eric; quite the contrary, he was becoming far too fond of the boy, and it was obvious Eric was beginning to fall seriously in love with him. Eric had admitted all along he had been at least a little in love with Brad from the moment he first met him, and considerably more so since the afternoon he had fallen to his knees in front of him in the sex shop on Polk Street.

Brad continued his walks along the bluffs of Lincoln Park, and he continued to rebuff the advances of most of the men who obviously offered themselves for clandestine sex in the bushes. He never again encountered the same man he had first had sex with in this park, but remembering how exciting and attractive that man had been, he began carrying condoms and lubricant with him on his walks, just in case. Once or twice a month he might see a really attractive man apparently making himself available, and on most of those occasions he shared furtive and fairly fleeting sex with him. But he usually felt mildly ashamed and somewhat soiled following the encounter.

On only one occasion was sex in the bushes as memorable as his first encounter there had been, and that was with a beautiful, sexy, hung young man who proved to be only sixteen years old. Brad had no idea of his age, of course, or he would no doubt have passed up the opportunity obviously being offered when the slim young man stepped from behind a tree and confronted him, totally naked, stroking a very impressive erection, and smiling sexily. "You got any ideas about what I can do with this?" Brad had a number of ideas, and they found a particularly secluded location to explore them.

It was fortunate the young man, Tommy, had brought a blanket to the park with him, because within minutes he was lying face down on it with Brad buried to the hilt in him, and his ass welcoming the deep thrusts as eagerly as they were being rendered. Brad's first orgasm was copious, and Tommy removed the condom carefully from him, so that when he knelt over Brad, who lay on his back, as requested, with his legs raised high to accept Tommy's massive cock, he used its contents to lubricate his own condom-sheathed cock and that part of Brad's anatomy he proceeded to enter both enthusiastically and deeply. Although he was fairly epicene, once inside Brad he certainly fucked like a man.

Tommy was obviously quite young, so Brad was not only thrilled by, but was also equally surprised by the absolute mastery the boy brought to fucking! Seldom had he felt so completely and thoroughly fucked as he did when Tommy's gasps and spasms finally signaled his orgasm. The youngster's huge cock remained erect and buried deep inside him as they kissed and caressed for a very long time. Following an even longer period of exchanged cocksucking and hugely exciting "69," Tommy mounted Brad's cock as he lay on his back and brought himself to another orgasm, which splashed over Brad's face and chest. Staying inside Tommy, Brad managed to roll him on his back, and the eager boy's legs locked tightly around his waist while he continued to make love to the insatiable youngster. As he came close to emission, Tommy begged, "Let me see your load," so he pulled out at the last minute and bathed Tommy's face and chest in his hot discharge as thoroughly as his own had just been coated.

Lying together in each other's arms, their mutual emissions sticky on their chests, they kissed tenderly, and Tommy admitted having seen Brad in the park several times, and had wanted to approach him earlier. "I really like older guys, and I've never seen an older guy here with a cuter ass or a bigger basket." He kissed him again, and undulated his hips, grinding his still-erect cock into Brad's. "And your ass is a lot cuter when you're naked, and there was even more in that huge basket than I had even hoped for!"

It was then that Brad discovered Tommy was only sixteen, but the deed was done, so he continued to enjoy the youngster's magnificent love-making technique. Before they left the glade where the blanket had been spread, they had spent considerably more time locked in "69," and Tommy had come in Brad once while he knelt behind him, and yet another time as he bucked and drove wildly up into Brad while the latter rode his apparently indefatigable shaft.

They had been in the bushes almost three hours when Brad finally declared he had to go, but at the pleading of Tommy, knelt behind him and fucked him once again. He had not expected to be able to ejaculate again, but Tommy was such an eager and appreciative bottom, that eventually he delivered another orgasm, following which he collapsed over Tommy, still buried inside. Tommy's ass continued to work Brad's cock busily, and soon the two rolled over and in only a few strokes Brad brought Tommy's throbbing cock to another climax, which completely covered his fist. Tommy disengaged from Brad and knelt next to him to lick all his own emission from his hand, the fruits of his fifth orgasm! If Tommy seemed to be something of a come machine, Brad was not terribly surprised. He well remembered when he was able to (and frequently did) do that with Roy when he had been sixteen; hell, he'd had three orgasms himself this afternoon, pretty good for a forty-five year old.

Despite Brad's reservations about Tommy's age, they both agreed they would be looking forward to repeat encounters. Tommy finished dressing and disappeared into the bushes after a long kiss and a hoarse whisper, "You're the best fuck in the world, Brad. I can't wait until next time!"

And there were several "next time" encounters with Tommy in the park. Between encounters with the sixteen-year old and visits by the eighteen-year old Eric, Brad was getting a lot of teen-age cock! After Eric began college, however, visits with him became very rare, limited to his vacation times, and then almost impossible to schedule because of the coincidence of Josh's being at home on vacation at almost exactly the same times.

Eric continued to 'sleep over' occasionally in the spare bed in Josh's room when the latter was home, and Brad felt frustrated to think that Eric lay there only a few feet from him, probably as eager to make love as he was. Once Eric crept into Brad's bed in the middle of the night, and they made very quiet, very careful love with Josh asleep in the next room. Brad was so nervous about the proximity of his son, however, that they never repeated it.

Although he had never enjoyed hanging out in bars, Brad did from time to time visit some of the city's many gay bars, and connected with a number of attractive men for occasional sexual experiences. Nothing lasting developed as a result of those experiences, but at least they were mostly with men of a more mature age than Tommy or Eric. Of course, neither

Tommy nor Eric could have legally entered a bar, but Brad did once spot Eric in a popular bar on Castro Street, accompanied by another man, and the two were obviously in the latter stages of seducing each other! It hurt Brad and made him jealous to see Eric there under those circumstances, but he knew he couldn't enter a relationship with Eric anyway, so he had to accept that he was going to be active with other men; he just wished he hadn't seen the evidence. Fortunately Eric did not see him that night, and nothing was ever said about it.

On a number of occasions Brad revisited the Top 'n Bottom theatre or one of the other two where live porn stars 'danced.' Nothing remotely resembling the excitement of his visit there with Race Rivera marked any of those visits—even when Gundo himself appeared on one occasion. "Race Rivera" was becoming increasingly popular, and all his post-appearance time slots were filled by paying suitors on that occasion. He and Brad did get together for dinner and coffee, and twice during the week he was in town Gundo managed to get away from his 'all-nighter' early enough to take a cab to Brad's house and share his splendid body and matchless cock for a couple of hours, leaving time for the stud to build up a sufficient head of steam for his first show of the day.

Gundo himself felt frustrated at not seeing Brad under better circumstances, and made him promise to come down to West Hollywood and spend some time alone with him soon, so in the spring Brad flew to L.A. and spent an incredible weekend in Gundo's bed, in Gundo's arms, to say nothing of in his mouth and in his bottom! Gundo spent just as much time on that occasion in Brad's arms and various eager orifices.

One evening Brad lingered at a Castro Street bar and talked for a long time with an extremely sexy young man, who was obviously ready to go to bed with him. Unfortunately, there was no way the two could go to the young man's apartment, and Josh was in residence at home, studying for an exam. Frustrated at the situation, and keenly desiring the horny and admittedly ready stud in the bar, Brad rented a motel room on Market Street, which the two kept hot and busy for several hours. When a similar situation developed only a few weeks later, it became apparent to Brad that he had to provide himself some alternative location for sexual activity if Josh's frequent and usually unannounced visits home were not to limit his freedom. He decided he would simply rent a studio apartment somewhere, stock it with the accoutrements of sex, and use it as his secret sexual hideaway. By installing a separate phone line there, he could even be free to call or accept calls or messages from potential bed partners.

Nothing appealed to him in the Castro Street area, but down near the Embarcadero, on Townsend Street, he found a place consisting of one large living-sleeping room with a partitioned small kitchen and a generous bathroom. It was new and very well appointed. Within a few days Brad had put a relatively modest entertainment center in place (TV, VCR, CD system), installed a new telephone and answering machine, moved several stored pieces of furniture from his garage, and had stocked the kitchen with plenty of beer, liquor, mixers, and even some snacks.

For the serious business of sex, he liberated his Jeff Stryker dildo from hiding and relocated it to Townsend Street, along with a generous supply of condoms, lubricants, poppers, and linens. He budgeted a thousand dollars to stock porn magazines and movies, and a few other toys like cock rings and, hoping to lure Paul there, butt plugs. He worked out a deal with a sex store operator, and was given an extremely attractive price on magazines and videotapes.

By spring he felt he was ready to look for the first visitor. He had a sizzling collection of videos now, starring such luminaries as Jeff Stryker, Ryan Idol, Adam Hart, Jason Andrews, Johan Paulik and, his favorite, the unbelievably handsome and sexy Lukas Ridgeston. The scene with these last two making love to each other at the end of *Lukas' Story* was far more than just fucking; it was one of the most stimulating things he had ever seen, and certainly one of the most achingly beautiful. Furthermore, he felt Lukas was the only possible competition in the "most beautiful man in the world" race with the absolutely god-like Steve Fox.

Naturally, he acquired complete sets of both Race Rivera's and Fox's work. He added a sampling of favorites from an earlier time: Tom Steele, Erik Houston, Mike Henson, Matt Ramsey.

A number of youths he met in bars yielded readily to his invitation to visit his new apartment, and once there and with Brad stripped, yielded even more readily to his beautiful body and generous endowment. He gave several of these his new telephone number, and many of them left messages for him to arrange repeat visits. He entertained Gundo there for two incredible days just preceding a return engagement at the Top 'n Bottom—even for a few hours twice during that engagement. He called Paul Stavros back in Connecticut and got him to promise to visit soon. He gave Eric Neeley his new telephone number, and they were able to arrange to be together rather regularly when Eric was home from school.

In October, during his second trip to Los Angeles for sex with Gundo, he enjoyed the closest thing he had seen to an orgy since he had been the last participant in the gang-bang of Chris Drake back in prep school.

The first two nights with Gundo had been similar to others he had spent with the Latin Adonis (extended, joyous, and ultimately satisfying sex on an epic scale), but the night before he left, Gundo took him to the house of his mentor, Tom Hunt, a former lover of Tony Lopez Primero and something of a second father, known in his porndays as "Tom Fox", who now both managed his protege Race Rivera's career and featured him in many of the porn videos his company, Fox Hunt Productions produced.

Tom was slightly older than Brad, but he was still in extremely good shape, and ruggedly handsome, and who, at Gundo's insistence, proved to Brad that he was even more stunningly hung than his magnificent protege. A pair of absolutely identical twins—tall, blond and drop-dead gorgeous—lived with Tom; the three had been lovers for years. In their bedroom Brad knelt on all fours at the edge of the bed while both Tom and Gundo took turns standing behind him and providing the kind of breath-taking thrills only men with such stupendous endowment could generate, and at the same time the twins took turns kneeling in front of him to accept his oral worship. Following the fuckings he received from Tom and Gundo, he was stunned to find he was able to accept the cocks of both twins at the same time.

Brad and Gundo had a wonderful time taking turns at

servicing Tom as he knelt for them, and later the twins held each other and kissed while Tom and Brad lay side-by-side on their backs and the pair rode their cocks. Tom demonstrated his incredible rapacity at the end of the evening when Brad, Gundo, and both twins knelt next to each other at the side of his bed. Each of them spent considerable time enjoying the invasion of Tom's stupendous cock as he stalked behind them driving it in savagely, taking turns on the four eager backsides waiting his pleasure.

As Brad and Gundo were preparing to leave, Tom presented Brad with a "Tom Fox Dildo" as a souvenir of his visit. Like the Jeff Stryker model, the huge latex penis was supposedly molded directly from Tom's, and was marketed under the name he used in his pornography work. Laughing, Tom agreed to an on-site comparison, and the dildo indeed proved to be an exact replica once Brad had brought the original to full erection with his mouth. The twins insisted that Brad take care of what he had instigated ("If you don't suck that thing off, we're gonna get fucked again tonight!"), so they and Gundo stood and made bawdy comments while Brad knelt before Tom and used his mouth and (only at the last moment) his fist to bring yet another gusher from the magnificent prototype for the souvenir. Tom's hands held Brad's head so tightly as he delivered his offering that there was no way he could have avoided the facial bath he received even if he had wanted to— which was highly unlikely. Tom knelt before Brad and licked his guest's face clean of his own emission before giving him a very passionate goodbye kiss. The nutty taste of Tom's semen on his own tongue lingered in Brad's mouth as the twins used their tongues to stimulate him and share its delightful flavor in their goodbye kisses.

Late that night, back in Gundo's apartment in West Hollywood, Brad was actually so completely drained of sexual energy that he hardly responded when his host took him enthusiastically and at length while he lay on his stomach—all but exhausted. He was refreshed the next morning, however, and he and Gundo shared a couple of rounds of enthusiastic fucks, even at one point each happily riding his own Tom Fox dildo as they embraced and kissed! In addition to the Tom Fox dildo, Brad took with him on his return to San Francisco the memory of the most deliriously abandoned sexual experience of his life.

Brad regularly found classified ads in *The Golden Gate Nation* offering the escort services of minor porn stars. He had arranged to meet in his apartment with a few of those he found particularly attractive, and while he had found them wonderfully uninhibited and accomplished masters in the art of love-making, he found they tended to be less satisfying than he expected. He sensed a kind of narcissism in them that kept them from really sharing sex. He didn't object to the body worship they seemed to desire most (and a couple of them were quite worthy of worship), but he felt the experiences were too one-sided to provide complete enjoyment.

Porn stars advertising as escorts were, moreover, relatively expensive. For the money he had to pay even a second-tier porn 'name,' Brad knew he could hire three other bed partners from the same classified ad pages. Judging by some of the photos in *The Nation* classifieds, a number of these independent sexual entrepreneurs offering their expertise for appreciative gentlemen were extremely attractive.

His first two experiences with local escorts had not been particularly gratifying. His first had been with a very muscular and handsome young man, who welcomed Brad's equipment enthusiastically in every orifice he could offer, but whose own rather disappointing endowment, to say nothing of his inability to keep even that in a very useable state of rigidity, did not make his reciprocal offerings very satisfactory. He had, instead, wielded the latex substitutes for Jeff Stryker and Tom Hunt, which Brad could have done for himself. The second one was fairly well built, and hung like a mule. The bulge in his jockey shorts pictured in his classified ad had been as exciting as it promised, but he balked at taking from Brad what Brad had so enthusiastically and satisfyingly taken from him. Nevertheless, he considered the encounter a success.

About a month after he had last been with Gundo, right after Josh returned to his dorm following the Thanksgiving holiday, Brad visited a few bars and found nothing promising, and he was horny enough to call another escort. This was his third try, and this time he hit pay dirt.

Opening to the last pages of *The Nation*, an escort ad which had previously offered promise caught his eye: a photograph of a naked young man, shown from the top of his head to just below the upper limit of his pubic hair. The face looked attractive, but since much of it was obscured by a black bar he could not be sure; the body was undoubtedly attractive, slim waist, broad shoulders, muscular arms, flat 'washboard' stomach, and fantastic tits. The ad read: "ANGEL! 25, five-eight, 160 lbs,, guaranteed eight inches of fat, iron-hard meat, to-die-for ass, handsome, hot, and versatile. This angel may not have wings, but I'll sure spread 'em for you anyway. Or, would you rather spread 'em for me? Let Angel usher you into heaven. Out calls only." The text was followed by a pager number.

Brad called Angel's pager from his apartment, and punched in his own number. It was not uncommon to have pager numbers unreturned, or returned only after a very long time, so Brad was pleasantly surprised when only about ten minutes later his phone rang.

A deep and very sultry voice said, "This is Angel, returning your call."

Brad, also speaking in an unnaturally deep and breathless voice, as for some reason he always seemed to do instinctively when he talked on the phone concerning a possible sexual liaison, said, "Yeah, Angel, this is Brad. I was calling about your ad. You really sound hot, and I was wondering if we could get together."

"Sure. What did you have in mind?"

"Well, you said you were versatile. I love topping a hot guy, but I love being on the bottom too."

"Okay. We can get together tonight if you want. I only do out calls, so I'd come to you. $150 if it's in the city."

"Yeah, I'm down near the Embracadero, and tonight's fine, and $150 sounds good. How long?"

"Well, that depends on how things go, frankly. Probably no more than an hour, though. What's your name?"

"My name's Brad, and I'm forty-five, but I'm good-looking, I guess, and I'm in good shape. One thing, Angel, if things go well, you know, if we like each other, do you enjoy kissing and cuddling?"

"You sound great, Brad, and if things are right, I love kissing and cuddling. So what do you think ... do we get together?"

Brad affirmed his desire to have Angel come to see him. He gave him the address, and a half-hour later, the doorbell rang. Fresh from the shower, clad only in a towel around his waist, Brad looked through the peep-hole and saw a fairly short, dark-haired man waiting. Even given the extremely limiting viewing possibilities a peep-hole offers, "Angel" promised to be cute as hell.

Brad opened the door and looked at Angel.

Bingo!

HARP

1.

At almost exactly the same moment that Brad Thornton's Delta flight departed the San Francisco International Airport in October 1996, bound for LAX and his memorable tryst with Gundo, Tom Hunt and the twins, a United flight arrived there from Atlanta, carrying Mark David Harper as one of its passengers.

By the time Brad had been met at the airport in Los Angeles by a Gundo Lopez eager to share his body at the earliest possible moment, Mark David Harper's cab was depositing him at the Travelodge on Market at Valencia, but no one was waiting there to share his body—not yet, at any rate.

Within five hours, however, he returned to the motel with another young man, who was as avid to discover the exciting possibilities of his body as Gundo had been to revisit Brad's. Gundo's reconnaissance was well under way by this time, of course, and he and Brad were no doubt going over familiar territory a second or third time, but it could have been no more thorough or mutually rewarding than the excited exploration Mark David Harper's body was subjected to by the feeling, kissing, licking, sucking, and penetration of his new-found admirer.

The name by which Mark David Harper was generally addressed had undergone a number of changes over the years. Growing up he had been called "David" by his family—to distinguish between him and his father Mark Gordon Harper; in spite of the coincidence of his and his father's first name, he wasn't technically eligible to be called "junior," thank God, so he was spared the possibility of being saddled with that. And he was even more thankful to be spared the equal indignity of "Little Mark."

By the time he entered high school, many of his friends began to call him "Doc," taking their cue from his initials. One of his best friends had begun calling him that when he made the connection between M.D. Harper and his doctor, who was an "M.D." The name stuck for a time, until his football teammates in High School began calling him "Harp." It was the first name he had been known by that he liked, and he conducted a quiet campaign to make the latest moniker stick. By the time he was ready to graduate from Oconee High School, outside of the small town of Oconee, South Carolina (which was not, strangely enough, in Oconee County, although such a territory existed in the upstate), everyone called him "Harp". Even his family had gradually absorbed the new name.

So at the very moment when Brad Thornton lay beneath the famous stud Gundo Lopez in West Hollywood and offered his ass as sanctuary to one of the porn world's biggest, hardest, and hottest pricks, the twenty-four year old South Carolina expatriate, whose soon-to-be universally-admired ass was at that very moment gratefully and joyously welcoming the same savage invasion from the stranger who knelt behind his naked body in the San Francisco motel, was called, and will henceforth be referred to in these pages as "Harp." The happiest man in that particular Travelodge that night—and the luckiest, considering the beauty and expertise of the muscular blond who welcomed him to his new home town with deep, savage thrusts—had traveled a road much longer, figuratively, than the actual distance between upstate South Carolina and "Baghdad by the Bay." The road was long because it was only straight at its beginning; after that it may have been direct, but it was far, far from *straight*.

Considering how important sex became to Harp, it was surprising how late he came to it (no pun intended). Considering that once he reached sexual maturity his appetites were unfailingly homosexual, it is even stranger that his first experiences were with partners of the opposite sex. He was raised on a farm, and since conventional wisdom seems to hold that most rural boys are likely to be initiated into sex at a very early age when they are 'cornholed' by their older cousins, the fact that Harp's first homosexual experience did not occur until he was almost eighteen seems particularly surprising.

For Harp, like most farm boys, the facts of life were a part of growing up (although he was not called 'Harp' until later, for purposes of clarity he will always be referred to by that name here). By the time his pubic hair began to sprout and he accidentally discovered the thrill of orgasm one night while he played with himself in bed, he was already thirteen. Still, sexual activity involving more than his own hand was several years away, possibly because of the fairly doctrinaire Christian atmosphere in his home, perhaps due to his early personal shyness (which completely disappeared later in life), or it might have been that he realized, and felt embarrassed about how much larger his cock was than those of his friends (this attitude not only disappeared in later life, but turned 180 degrees around when he began showering with other boys in high school and realized they both admired and envied his impressive superior endowment).

Whatever the reason for Harp's delayed maturity, it was more than halfway through his tenure as a student at Oconee High that he first experienced sexual congress, and by then most of his friends were bragging of their own conquests, and it is possible, but probably unlikely, that a number of them were actually telling the truth. He had certainly by this time begun dreaming of satisfying his sexual urges, and he realized that while he fantasized about sex with girls, it didn't excite him nearly as much as the thought of doing something sexual with some of his football teammates. He assumed his homosexual curiosity—he did not yet have a name for it—was both natural and only temporary. His friends certainly had a name for those who put that kind of curiosity into action, though, he heard them refer to other, usually effeminate boys and men as 'fairies', 'faggots,' or 'queers,' but he was certainly not a queer or a faggot!

By his junior year, he was already the first-string quarterback for the Oconee High football team, the Polecats—the students apparently took a perverse pride in having an offensive animal as their nominal mascot. As such, he was something of a local hero, and his ever-more-stunning good looks made him the object of many of his female schoolmates' fantasies. He learned later of a few cases, out of a surprisingly large number, of his status as a sexual fantasy-object for some of his male schoolmates as well. Halfway during the football season, one of the cheerleaders, Maria (pronounced ma-RYE-ah) Jenks, hinted so often to Harp that she wanted to date him, and with such little success, that she finally gave up and asked him.

Harp had dated quite a number of girls, of course, but had until then only held hands with them and shared a fairly chaste kiss or two with some. He did not feel any great urge to seek further intimacy, and he was beginning to wonder why that was. When he went out on his first date with Maria, however, she had a clear-cut agenda in mind.

It is a sad commentary on the moral state of today's youth to note that some high school girls are not virgins; such was the case with Maria. She had, in fact, screwed with almost all of her classmates on the football and basketball teams, and quite a number of those in the class below her. She'd even tried a few things with some of her female fellow-cheerleaders, but she hadn't much enjoyed it. It was time to "nail" the unbearably cute, sexy Harp Harper, and his perceived beauty was enhanced in Maria's imagination when she learned inadvertently from a young man who labored over her one night on a blanket in the woods that Harp was blessed with the biggest cock on the football team.

Maria had long since decided that the larger the organ that filled her, the greater the pleasure. She decided to ascertain the validity of the report concerning the cute junior quarterback.

Parenthetically, the young man who informed her of the spectacular size of Harp's cock was in error; there were several football players better endowed than Harp, although that situation would change in a year or so as he attained his full growth. It is amusing to note that the informer secretly would much rather have been lying naked over Harp's body than Maria's. Actually, *under* would have been even better. He thought Harp the sexiest guy he'd ever seen, and he knew that the most beautiful and desirable thing in the entire world was Harp's rounded, succulent, breath-taking, completely perfect ass! As he informed her of the superiority of Harp's cock, he was fantasizing that the superior object in question was doing to him what he was now doing to Maria, something that he himself desperately wanted to do also to the aforementioned most beautiful and desirable thing in the entire world! He was, incidentally, only one of the first in a very long line of boys and men to take note of the magnificent beauty of Harp's ass and declare it to be, quite simply, perfect.

Harp got his first piece of ass, as they say, under the

bleachers at the high school football field. He performed rather well, especially given the nature of his still undiscovered lusty appetite for sex partners of his own gender, and Maria was well-pleased, although she realized that her information on the ultimately superior dimensions of the cock he employed had been a bit erroneous.

Harp was less thrilled by the experience, and might have found Maria's further attentions onerous had she not decided the exalted senior who captained the football squad was the prey she sought for a lifetime of marital bliss. Maria knew that Harp filled her with greater pleasure (so to speak) than her new mate-to-be, but the latter's equipment was at least better than most, and he wanted her so badly that he both went out of his way to perform splendidly with her, and was also perfectly willing to do almost anything else she wanted for the opportunity to continue doing so. Harp had not only done little to ensure Maria's satisfaction on the occasion of their sole experience together (she had to do most of the work), he hadn't actually enjoyed it any more than he did his solitary, fantasy-fueled sexual exercises.

Apparently Maria put the word out that Harp was not an especially satisfying partner, and in spite of his good looks his sexually active female schoolmates sought greener fields, but only after a few of them propositioned Harp and tested the validity of Maria's claim. Harp was polite, and performed adequately in those further experiments, but was beginning to think that fucking was going to occupy a rather low place on his list of priorities.

Since the so-called 'nice' girls didn't push to be noticed, Harp basically coasted along without further shared sexual activities until his senior year. Strange, since he was becoming a particularly horny young man. By his senior year he was usually masturbating at least three or four times daily, and not just fondling his now very impressive tool, but coaxing prodigious eruptions from it on each occasion. He was not openly admitting to himself yet that more and more his teammates' and other guys' bodies were assuming a large place in his masturbatory fantasies, but, subliminally, he knew that he was becoming aroused by male bodies, not the female ones he was expected to think about.

Harp was helping his father in a field next to the highway one summer afternoon before his senior year, stripped to the waist, tanned, and sweating—handsome as the devil now that he had attained his growth. A young college professor who had just finished building a lake house a mile down the road from the Harper farm drove by and spotted him, and resisted the temptation to slam on the brakes to get a better look at what appeared to be the modern manifestation of Adonis on a farm in South Carolina. He brought his car to a more dignified stop.

The young man working in the field who caught Doug Truax's attention that summer afternoon in 1989 was indeed impressive. The now near-adult Harp Harper (he was seventeen) was not imposing in stature, only five-eight, but he did not at first appear to be unusually short, since his body was perfectly proportioned; it was only when one stood next to him that his below-average height was noticeable. He had been fairly scrawny as a youngster, but thanks to good genes and work with weights in the high school training room, his body was now an absolute knockout! He had a V-shaped torso, with broad shoulders tapering to a narrow waist; his stomach was flat and muscular, and his legs and arms were gym-built-muscular also, but not unduly so. Except for his pubic and underarm areas, his golden-tan, velvet-smooth body was almost hairless.

Pendant below that flat, washboard stomach was an unusually large and smooth circumcised cock which was quite impressive to look at even when flaccid, but when attaining its full erection was formidable indeed: over six inches in circumference, and a good solid eight inches in length. It was very good, and unbelievably solid, as a number of men and boys were to discover fairly soon. Nestled behind this quite beautiful organ—when flaccid—or hanging pendulously below it when in its prodigious glory, was a brace of testicles of equally impressive size and apparent potency. The two elements of his sexual equipment complemented each other perfectly not only in appearance, but in performance as well: the testicles produced an extraordinary amount of semen, and the impressive penis to which they supplied this ammunition delivered it with maximum velocity and force, and the recuperative powers of both were equally remarkable. In short, and in earthier parlance, Harp had a monster set of balls, and he could shoot a huge load, and quite often, out of his stupendous hard cock.

The assessment of his ass by the teammate who had fantasized about it even while screwing Maria Jenks was accurate: Harp's ample, rounded, firm and muscular ass was perfection. The roundness and beauty of his buttocks was subtly enhanced by a very sexy tan line which resulted from Harp's enjoyment of sunbathing while clad only in a thong bikini, a very narrow band of white low around his waist, with a triangle disappearing downward into the crevice between the sublime globes of his luscious posterior. Few were treated to the bare sight of this magnificence, mostly just his teammates in the locker room, and while it played a significant part in the erotic dreaming of several of them, several more whose sexual fantasies did not normally extend beyond the strictly heterosexual were so moved by its beauty that they at least contemplated a slight deviation from their normal appetites in order to do more than just admire it.

Truth was, all but a few of the Oconee High football team would, under the right circumstances, have been quite thrilled to fuck Mark David Harper's glorious ass.

It would be a shame if such a superb body were crowned by facial features of lesser beauty; mercifully, such was not the case. Harp was as attractive facially as he was bodily. He had dark, almost black hair, quite straight and long enough so that when combed straight back it provided a frame for a high forehead, a broad face with wide-set black eyes, high cheek bones, and a strong, square jaw. His lips were generous, and his large teeth were brilliantly white when he smiled. When, better yet, he grinned, which he often did, the target of his grin invariably felt better somehow. Harp's grin was captivating, engaging, infectious, and an accurate manifestation of his sweet, generous nature, and if tested could probably have melted a candle at fifty paces.

Harp's only imperfection was his nose. Put simply, it was too large; put another way it was the slight exception to the ideal that made him look real, instead of "Ken Doll" perfect. In no way did his somewhat outsized nose detract from his features. Instead, it provided effective contrast to underscore the seeming perfection of the rest of the package, and succeeded in making him even cuter and sexier.

It was no wonder that Doug Truax was moved to stop when he spotted Harp stripped to the waist in the field. To a man who appreciated masculine beauty as much as Doug did, he could have done no less. If Harp had been naked, and Doug could have seen the glories concealed at that moment by his very tight Levi's, the car would no doubt have ended up in the ditch.

As it was, Doug emerged from his car and introduced himself to Harp's father, whom he had seen on any number of occasions as he drove by, and at whom he had regularly waved. Even had he not spotted the younger Harper, Doug would have stopped to introduce himself to his new neighbor sooner or later; sooner seemed a good idea with an introduction to this hot young beauty as a possible additional bonus.

"I'm Doug Truax. I just built a house on the lake down the road, and thought I'd better finally stop and introduce myself."

Shaking the hand offered to him, the older man replied, "I'm Mark Harper, Doug. Nice to meet you. I've driven by your new house a few times while they were building it. It looks nice. What do you do?"

"I teach Spanish and Latin at Farrar. This is actually my fourth year here; I've been living in faculty housing, but I decided I'd like to live on the lake, so I built a house. Is this your boy?"

"Yeah." He called out. "Come over here, son."

As Harp approached, Doug's heart skipped the proverbial beat on seeing the tempting, apparently very well-filled 'basket' in the crotch of the worn, tight, sexy jeans. Up close, the upper body looked every bit as tempting as it had seemed from the road, and Harp's mirrored sunglasses added a cocky, sexy element to what Doug now realized was a face to match the body.

"This is my son. Real name Mark, like mine, but we all call him Harp. Meet our new neighbor, Doug ... I'm sorry...."

"Truax. Doug Truax." Harp pulled off his sunglasses with his left hand as he extended his right; the grin he flashed Doug as they shook hands racked up several more of those proverbial heart-beat skips.

"Nice to meet you, Mr. Truax." It was a firm handshake, but not so firm that it seemed to bespeak excess teenage *machismo*. Doug would have happily kept holding the hand indefinitely.

"Please, we're going to be neighbors. I'm Doug. So, are you a student at Farrar, or are you just home for the summer?"

Harp laughed and again flashed his killer smile. "Gosh no, I'm just starting my senior year here at Oconee High."

"Hunh! I figured you were a few years older than that." For a senior in high school to be mistaken for a college student is a compliment; Doug knew full well what he was doing.

"Nah, I'll be eighteen in a few weeks."

Doug chatted with Harp and his father, trying not to appear to be more interested in visiting with the son than he should be! Fortuitously, Harp's mother called from the farmhouse, summoning the older man to the telephone, and Doug bid him goodbye, but lingered to talk further with Harp, who walked with him as he went back to his car.

"Do you ski, Harp? I've got a ski boat and my own dock; I'd be glad to pull you around the lake, if you want, and I'm always looking for someone to drive while I ski."

"That sounds great. Just tell me when we can go!"

Doug laughed, "Well, you're working, and I'm on my way in to teach a class, but how does this evening sound? Six o'clock or so?"

The killer smile broke, and Doug melted completely into the ground. No, wait ... it just seemed that way!

"Six o'clock is great. I'll be there!"

They bid each other goodbye, Doug started the engine, and watched as Harp turned and went back to the field. This was his first view of Harp's crowning glory, and even though it was concealed, the worn, tight jeans displayed it to magnificent advantage. Doug's thought as he drove away was something of a prayer of thanksgiving: Jesus Christ in heaven—what an ass! His second thought was more a prayer of supplication: God, I'd like to get in his pants!

The thirty-six year old professor who drove away from the Harper farm at that moment, filled with profound appreciation for the beauty of the apparent heir to it, often managed to surround himself with masculine beauty, but seldom of that degree. He himself was attractive, in an average sort of way. He was five-ten, weighed 150 pounds, and exercised and watched his diet enough so that he was in good shape.

He taught at Farrar University, a private college located at Oconee. Originally a Methodist school, Farrar had long since severed its ties with that church, and was now independent, with an on-campus student body of some five thousand in 1989. Doug had joined the faculty in 1985, while he was in the final throes of his doctoral dissertation from the University of Georgia. He was a good teacher, and his Spanish classes were popular. Fortunately, since there was usually a bare minimum of students interested in pursuing Latin.

Doug enjoyed teaching and enjoyed the company of young people, but especially enjoyed the company of young men. And if those young men were physically attractive he particularly sought their company, and more, after class hours if at all possible. If not quite preoccupied with sex, he was certainly very actively occupied with it. Women held no interest for him at all, and he was sufficiently personable and handsome that he was not only successful in winning the sexual favors of a great many of the young men he went after, he also regularly had sex with others who sought him out, and whom he found attractive. Once in bed, he was a very satisfying partner, capable by endowment and by nature of being an extremely gratifying "top," but also greatly appreciative of the delights of being on the receiving end of a deftly-exercised hard cock well placed in either of his principal orifices.

Given the provincial and fairly conservative nature of both the town and the campus, he had to exercise considerable caution and discretion in his liaisons. Still, he managed to find a plentiful supply of sex partners, including usually a few of his former students (he tried to avoid going to bed with students currently enrolled in his classes, for obvious ethical reasons) as well as fellow college employees and townspeople of similar appetites. Atlanta was only a two-hour drive away, and offered a wealth of interesting, and interested, young studs.

His new house on the lake near Oconee promised greater freedom for sexual sports than had been possible before. It was very secluded, and he need no longer worry about neighbors questioning the frequent and often late-night visits by attractive young men, nor worry about excess noise at the height of passion. Although he had occupied the house only a month or so, his new bedroom was thoroughly broken in—only the night before he first met Harp he had simultaneously entertained two students there who had taken a class under him that spring, and both of whom he had enjoyed sex with earlier that summer. Both were gorgeous, both were hot, both adored screwing and being screwed. When Doug had encountered them together in the local movie theatre the night before, he had asked them to come out for a drink and a late swim with him. The drink and swim had quickly turned into a very exciting and satisfying "threesome" of an exuberance he could never have permitted in his former housing.

Since he was relatively satisfied sexually, following the many hours of his exhaustive romp the night before, Doug was able to restrain his natural desire to jump the gorgeous young Harp's bones as soon as he showed up to ski, promptly at six. There was no question that sooner or later he was going to look into getting Harp into bed. He was certainly one of the sexiest guys he had ever seen, and quite possibly the most beautiful as well! Harp was not yet eighteen, but that did not especially bother Doug. He had been to bed with several sixteen-and seventeen-year olds of enormous sexual ability—and even one very talented and precocious fourteen-year old. Whatever the age, he knew the greatest caution needed to be exercised so as to avoid those factors he especially did not want to find in a prospective sex partner: unwillingness to participate freely in at least some homosexual activities, inability to keep shared experiences secret, and guilt. He was well experienced in sensing whether a young man he was making a play for wanted to have sex with him, and was persuasive and eloquent about convincing him to keep quiet and feel good about it afterward if he succeeded in seducing him.

The process of (1) sounding out the willingness of the possible sex partner, (2) setting up the proper relationship, and (3) moving in for the seduction, was often a long one (especially with such a young prospect as Harp), but Doug determined to set the wheels in motion immediately, and work toward finding if (1) was sufficiently positive to begin moving on to (2) and (3).

Stripped down to his skimpy bathing suit, Harp was unbelievably attractive to Doug. The large 'basket' he had displayed in his Levi's appeared huge in the confines of the tiny silken pouch, and the material was tightly stretched over the rounded buttocks to reveal what Doug thought was probably the most perfect ass he'd ever seen. He longed to drag Harp's bathing suit down to his ankles and bury his face between the cheeks of that ass. Amazingly, Doug succeeded in concealing his seemingly perpetual erection, and in keeping Harp from being aware of his fascination with his physical beauty.

They skied until there was no light left, and Harp had a wonderful time, not just in the physical exercise, but in what he had perceived as the easy camaraderie of the experience. In truth, although they had both enjoyed their afternoon together, he alone was relaxed. Doug was virtually drunk with desire and at the same time sobered by the need to pursue this young man slowly and cautiously.

Prior to leaving for home, Harp stripped out of his trunks before putting his Levi's on, and he was unaware of Doug's reaction. Harp had faced away as he pulled the bathing suit down, giving Doug his first unobstructed view of the matchless beauty of his ass with its tan line; then he turned around and demonstrated unwittingly that the obviously impressive organs that had been concealed by his pouch were even larger when freed of their restraint, and were of a degree of beauty almost on a level with his ass! Doug had to conceal his erection with his towel as he watched Harp strip out of his trunks and prepare to get dressed.

"You've really got a great body, Harp!"

"Thanks! Just lucky, I guess. I sure don't work real hard at it."

Doug was emboldened to make his first real contact with this ultimately desirable body. He pressed a hand on Harp's washboard stomach. "You had to work to develop this!"

Harp laughed, "Yeah, well, I work out some. But you've got a good body too." And as he said this, the totally nude and totally desirable youngster put his hands on Doug's waist. Doug was thankful Harp was by then looking into his eyes, so that he did not see how full and throbbingly erect the sight of him and his touch had made his cock.

Uncharacteristically, Doug was so impressed with Harp that as soon as he dropped him off at his house that evening, he pulled his cock out and masturbated while he drove back home, then went inside and continued to masturbate as he fantasized about the magnificent boy while he buried his face in the towel Harp had just used. He wrapped the damp towel around his aching cock as he brought himself to a demanding climax in the moisture that had recently been blotted from the magnificent body, the stunning cock, and the incomparable ass. After going to bed, Doug could not stop thinking about Harp, and finally found sleep only after he coaxed another explosive orgasm from his cock. In his imagination, it was buried deep inside his new young friend's ass.

By the beginning of the fall semester of his senior year at Oconee High, Harp felt right at home at Doug's house. He and his new friend swam and skied every other day or so, and often even more frequently than that. It was not unusual for them to share an impromptu dinner or watch television together before Harp went home. Although Doug was almost twice his age, Harp felt no real gap between them because of that. His father was only ten years older than Doug, but Harp felt that Doug was of his own generation.

He was becoming aware of the fact that Doug touched him a great deal, but it didn't bother him at all. If anything, it made him feel warm, and he enjoyed the contact, and often returned it. They talked about everything, and Harp was also becoming aware that Doug larded his conversation with an unusually large number of sexual innuendoes; again, it did not bother him at all. He somehow felt closer to Doug when they were kidding about masturbating, or talking about hard-ons or getting laid. He had, however, admitted his dalliance with Maria Jenks to Doug.

Harp began to wonder if Doug was interested in him sexually. He also began to wonder if he himself might be mutually interested. By this time he was admitting to himself that he was fantasizing about sex with guys, and that Doug was very nice looking and well-built. He had done nothing at all yet to satisfy his curiosity about his attraction to guys. He was, however, beginning to accept that he was possibly gay, and was beginning to ache to satisfy his mounting desires. Ironically, long before Doug decided Harp might welcome sexual overtures, Harp had admitted to himself he wanted them—he just didn't know how to broach the subject, nor was he at all sure Doug was interested in sex with him.

At the same time, Doug was getting hornier and hornier. Harp looked better to him all the time, and he could not stop getting more and more demonstrative with him. Finally, he decided he could wait no longer to see if Harp was amenable to exploring mutual sex play. Harp's eighteenth birthday was right around the corner, and it seemed like a good time to determine if anything was going to happen.

Doug had quite a number of porn videos. Most were exclusively male, but he had several heterosexual and bisexual ones as well, which he often showed to prospective "tricks" as ice-breakers for exploring their sexual appetites. He had saved himself from embarrassment and possible repercussions several times by observing that a young man he was hoping to seduce reacted very negatively as he watched the bisexual element gradually turn to the homosexual. Progressing from the heterosexual to the bisexual, and then, if things looked promising, to the hardcore homosexual had often established the proper mood for successful seduction. It was time to check Harp's reactions.

The night after his eighteenth birthday (Doug had called it "Your first full day as an adult!") Harp went to Doug's house for Sunday night dinner, and when Doug asked if he wanted to watch a porn videotape he had borrowed, he readily agreed. Although he had little experience with drinking, and although he was still not old enough to drink legally, Harp readily accepted a beer before they put the tape in the VCR.

The tape was one Doug had himself assembled, by dubbing from a variety of sources. There was about a half-hour of heterosexual sex, followed by a heterosexual episode that led to a homosexual one in a brand-new bisexual video he had just found. This was followed by another homosexual episode with a female standing by, but not participating, and then two hard-core gay scenes.

Watching for any negative reaction, and occasionally getting him another beer, Doug observed Harp carefully as he played the tape. He paid special attention to Harp's crotch, and saw a very clear hard-on develop during the heterosexual opening scenes. He was not especially happy to see this, but since the male partner in both scenes was really hot, he was not discouraged. He himself was pretty horny watching the handsome man with the huge cock in action, even if he was seeking the wrong sort of target.

Harp's hard-on not only remained in the second set of excerpts. It obviously grew as he watched the stud Jeff Stryker first fucking a woman, then fucking another woman before he turns to her muscular husband and shoves his monster cock all the way up his butt for an even more exciting fuck.

By the time the star performs a solo dance in the shower, with his cute butt pumping and his stupendous cock bobbing tantalizingly, Doug was more than pleased to note that his young guest was beginning to massage his crotch.

Harp stood up abruptly and said, "Excuse me, I've got to go to the bathroom," and then left the room. Doug didn't know if Harp actually needed to use the bathroom, or if the video had offended him.

Locking the bathroom door behind him, Harp dragged his pants down below his crotch and began to masturbate almost uncontrollably. He was so excited by what he had just watched that his cock was actually aching. It had been the most stimulating thing he had ever imagined, much less seen, and there was no doubt in his mind that it had been the guys in the videos that he had enjoyed watching. He also knew now that he was eager to at least try to have sex with a guy, and he was pretty sure Doug was interested, but he was scared to think he might be wrong. In his mind he conjured up the pictures of Jeff Stryker fucking the husband and performing his unbelievably sexy dance in the scene they had been watching, and with his eyes closed tightly and his head thrown back, he played with his ass with one hand while with the other he clasped his shaft tightly, and savagely brought himself to a truly gigantic orgasm, violently propelled all over the commode.

It took him some time before he could get control of his cock and get it back in his Levi's. He used that time to clean up the evidence of his orgasm, and when he rejoined Doug, he was almost calm again.

"Are you okay, Harp?" Doug had stopped the videotape.

"Yeah, I'm fine, but look ... I think I'd better get on home."

"Shit! Those movies ... I shouldn't have showed them to you. I didn't know what all was on them! We won't watch the rest."

"No, that's okay. They were fine, but ... it's late, and I'd better go."

"I'll drive you home."

Harp was already edging out of the door. "No, that's okay. I think I'll walk. Look, I'll call you tomorrow, okay?"

Doug apologized again for showing him the videos, and watched Harp walk up the driveway and head for home. He felt disappointed, of course. He wanted Harp so badly he could scream. But also frustrated. He could have sworn Harp had been getting horny watching Stryker's monster tool in action, but he was also a little worried: Had he gone too far? Would Harp say something to someone about him trying to seduce him? There was nothing he could do about it that point, so he went to bed, but did not get to sleep for several hours.

Walking the mile or so to his house, Harp could not decide if Doug had shown him the videos to get him horny and put a move on him. Doug had never said anything that really indicated he was interested in more than just friendship, and even though he did bring up sex a lot in their conversations and frequently put his hands on his body, he couldn't be sure it meant anything. He knew one thing, though, after watching the videos tonight, that he was ready to go to bed with Doug if he wanted, and he would just see what might happen. He cursed himself for "chickening out." He should have stayed to watch the rest of the videotape and allowed Doug to make a move if he was going to. He was still so excited at the parts of the tape that he had watched that his cock grew impossibly hard again long before he got home, and he stepped off the road and spent another fifteen minutes fantasizing and producing another frenzied and thrilling orgasm—clearly visible in the moonlight, with its first few jets propelled so violently they shot a good ten feet into the warm night air!

Early the next morning, as Doug was just getting ready to step in the shower, Harp called.

"I want to apologize for leaving so fast last night. I had to think about some things."

"That's okay. I was sorry you had to leave. Look, I shouldn't have shown you that video."

"No! I enjoyed it, I really did, and I want to watch the whole thing. If you're not mad at me, can I can come back soon and see it all?"

"Sure Harp, any time. Tonight if you want."

"That's fine, but it will be eight o'clock or so. I've got football practice this afternoon."

They agreed that Harp would come over at eight for a re-viewing, and Doug began to think that his groundwork might pay off after all.

There was a slight bit of awkwardness when Harp showed up that evening, but when they sat down in front of the television and he asked Doug to "fast forward" through the first part of the tape (the heterosexual scenes), hope began to dawn in Doug's mind. It was not until the part where Jeff Stryker begins to fuck the husband that Harp wanted to resume watching, and Doug was pleased to note Harp began surreptitiously massaging his groin almost immediately. By the time Stryker had begun his sexy dance in the shower, it was clear he was now fingering an impressive erection.

In the film, a man and a woman had watched Stryker's ecstatically erotic dance, and as it ends, the stud fucks the man while the woman watches. At that point it was clear Harp was quite excited, and Doug decided it was "now or never" time. He stood and began to unbutton his pants. He said, "I'm sorry, Harp, I've just gotta beat off a little!" He dropped his pants and shorts to his ankles, and began to stroke his hard dick.

Harp murmured, "No, go ahead. This is really hot!" and continued to grope and play with himself. He watched Doug peripherally, and, without saying anything, soon unbuttoned his own Levi's and tried to get his cock out. It was too hard to manage, so he stood and pulled his Levis' and shorts down as Doug had, exposing his own cock, throbbing with full erection, and apparently hard as steel.

Doug gasped quietly. Harp's cock was both huge and breathtakingly beautiful, and he longed to fall to his knees and take it in his mouth, but he forced himself to proceed cautiously. "Damn, you've got a big prick, Harp!"

Harp snickered and began to stroke himself as he sat and said, "You've got a pretty nice one yourself!"

Harp's heart was beating wildly. He, too wanted to sink to his knees and do something with Doug's cock! Suck it? Probably so. He'd certainly heard the term 'cocksucker' used enough to know what it was, and that guys did that to other guys, and although he knew that usually when someone used the term he was insulting someone else, in his fantasies he had often taken a dick in his mouth and down his throat, just like these hot guys in the movie had been doing. Instead of moving toward Doug's cock, he watched in fascination as the scene with the fantastic Stryker ended, and was replaced by one in which an incredibly cute guy (Mike Henson) seduced a young blond (Kevin Williams) and fucked him like an absolute master while another well-built, really sexy guy (John Davenport) watched by means of a video camera as he beat off.

For ten or fifteen minutes Harp watched the next, and final, scene on the tape. It was so unbelievably stimulating that he was completely lost in it, and forgot that Doug was even there. This one brought together the hot dark guy with the huge cock who danced in the shower room (Stryker) with the cute guy who seduced the young blond in the scene just past (Mike Henson). The cute guy proved to be a completely unbelievable cocksucker (How could he get all that thing in his mouth?) and he took the gigantic cock up his butt in just about every possible way. By the time the dark guy shot a second huge load all over the cute guy, Harp thought he was not going to be able to delay getting his own much longer. He looked at Doug. "I've gotta get my load! Should I go to the bathroom, or can I have a towel?"

Doug had been stroking his own cock, of course. He was just as excited as Harp was, but he had been watching Harp, not Jeff Stryker and Mike Henson. "If you want to, we could take our clothes off and work on each other. I'm ready too! What do you think?"

Harp stood and stepped out of his pants and grinned. "I think that would be fun!"

Both divested themselves completely of their clothes. Doug

took Harp's hand and led him to his bedroom, where once inside he put his arms around him and their two rigid cocks ground together. At long last, Doug held this gorgeous, hot young man in his arms, and his hands played almost reverently over the delicious roundness of the smooth ass.

After a few minutes of bliss, during which he was thrilled to find that Harp was returning his embrace, Doug pulled away. "God, I'm sorry, Harp, I shouldn't be doing this! But I'm so fuckin' horny!"

Harp pulled him back in and embraced him. "I'm just as horny!" He released him and lay down on the bed, holding a hand out toward him.

Doug needed no further invitation, and joined Harp on the bed. He still wasn't sure how far he could go, so he continued to resist the temptation to give Harp the blowjob he had so long wanted to deliver. Instead, he fell next to him, and the two began to masturbate each other. "Jesus, what an incredible handful of prick!" Doug panted.

"Man, that feels so good!" Harp said, and after a moment stopped stroking Doug and rolled over on top of him. Their cocks were pressed together as Harp's body completely covered Doug. Doug's arms encircled the young man's body and Harp cradled his head in his hands and smiled down. Without saying anything, Harp began to slowly hump, and his huge cock was sliding up and down Doug's stomach as their lips came closer and closer together. Doug's hands again began to worship the magnificent ass which was thrashing over him, driving the precious cock against his own. Soon Harp closed his eyes and his mouth sank to Doug's, and they began to kiss—sweetly, and affectionately for a long time, but then as Harp's humping became more frenzied, and as Doug's hands began to stroke and explore his ass more and more excitedly, their kissing became extremely passionate. Each was driving his tongue deep into the other's mouth, and Harp began to pant and grunt with passion. In a moment, Doug felt the gush of a huge orgasm spilling out onto his stomach, ejected with great force from the still-driving gigantic tube of hard flesh. The heat and slickness of Harp's discharge stimulated them both, and rather than slackening, the intensity and passion of their kissing only increased, and continued for a long time, only very gradually abating to a point where they were kissing sweetly and tenderly again.

They lay locked together for a very long time, kissing each other affectionately now, murmuring their satisfaction. Harp's cock had lost its stunning rigidity, but Doug's still poked into him as he continually explored the glorious territory of Harp's now slowly and sensuously undulating ass. Very gradually, Doug felt the massive prick which had delivered such a stunning orgasm only ten or fifteen minutes earlier stir to life again, and its return to full rigidity was accompanied by a parallel growth in the ecstasy of their kissing.

Doug's hands took Harp's head and he pulled him away from his lips and smiled up at him. "I've gotta get my load!"

Harp rolled off him and lay on his stomach. "Come on my ass like that guy did in the movie. That would be hot!" Doug straddled him, and in only a few minutes was discharging his own copious orgasm on the rolling, humping ass below him. He was almost screaming with passion as he coated the young Adonis, "God, Harp, you've got the hottest ass I've ever seen!" As Doug gradually calmed down, Harp said "God, that felt good!" and his hands came back and played over his own ass, spreading the hot, viscous fluid all over the rounded buttocks, and massaging it into his velvet skin.

Harp rolled over between Doug's legs and he grinned up at him. "I'm still hard. You want me to come on you?"

Doug leaned down and kissed the smiling lips. "Come on my face!"

They changed positions, and the magnificent younger man knelt over Doug's torso, frantically masturbating his prodigious cock. Doug took over for a while. "My god your cock's the hardest one I've ever felt!" And it truly was. Doug, a man who had held many hard and very impressive cocks in his hands, had rarely held one as big and fat as this one, and never one so thrillingly rigid before. As he squeezed it, he could feel the blood throbbing inside the huge, supremely firm shaft.

Presently Harp seized himself again, and after only a minute or two said, "Here I come!" Doug's hands again pressed the beautiful ass of his partner, who exploded another massive discharge, using his hand to distribute it all over the adoring face and mouth. With Doug's face completely covered by Harp's come, the two again embraced and kissed for an ecstatic eternity.

Ultimately, they simply lay there, holding each other, Harp's massive second orgasm now dried on their two faces. After a long period of complete silence, Harp giggled.

"What's so funny?" asked Doug.

"Do you really think my ass is the hottest one you've ever seen?"

Doug propped himself up on one elbow and looked directly into Harp's eyes. "I don't know what you think of me for saying that. But, yes, your ass is not only the hottest one I've ever seen, I think it's the most beautiful thing I've ever seen in my life. I can't believe how exciting it was when you wanted me to shoot my load on it. Whatever that means to you, Harp, your ass turns me on like nothing I've ever seen. And your cock is the hardest one I've ever felt."

Harp grinned, "Oh, have you felt a lot of 'em?"

Doug bit his lip, thought for a long moment, then nodded. "Confession time, I guess. Again, I don't know what you think of me for saying this, but yeah, I've felt a lot of hard cocks, and yours is not only the hardest, by far, it's one of the biggest I've ever felt, too. It's damned near as exciting to me as your ass is, okay? And I think you're more attractive and hotter than any of those guys in the movies we watched tonight. So ... what do you think of that?"

Harp smiled slowly and raised his head to kiss Doug gently. "Well, I think that's really nice."

"So, where do we go from here, Harp?"

"I really don't know. This is the first time I've ever done anything with a guy. I've thought about it quite a bit lately, but I wasn't sure if that was what I wanted."

"And what do you think now?"

"I know I enjoyed this a lot, and ... well, I don't know about the rest of that stuff we saw in the movies. Can we do this some more and just kinda see where it goes?"

"Harp, we'll do this as often as you want, and we can take it as far as you want, or just stop it right where we are now."

"I want to do it again soon, okay? And I'm pretty sure I want to see where else we'll go. Be patient with me?"

A very long, very sweet and affectionate kiss. "As patient as you want me to be. You're terrific, Harp!"

"So are you, Doug. Shit! Look at the time. I've gotta get home!"

Harp took a very quick shower, and as he was drying off, he dropped his towel and extended his cock to Doug. "Kiss it?" Doug knelt and placed a very chaste kiss on the head of the flaccid, but still impressive, cock, as Harp said, "We can start there next time, okay?"

"I can't wait! Turn around." Harp turned around, And Doug planted a series of equally chaste kisses all over the glorious ass, ending with one fairly deep between the cheeks. Then he stood, Harp turned around, and they shared another kiss before the younger man dropped to his knees and kissed the head of Doug's cock. They both dressed and Doug delivered the young Adonis to his home.

Lying awake in bed that night, reliving the last several ecstatic hours in his mind, Harp knew that the sexual experience he had just shared with Doug was immeasurably more satisfying and exciting than those he had shared with Maria Jenks and the girls after her. He reassessed his thinking about the importance of fucking in his life. After watching the fantastic men in Doug's videos, and after feeling the thrills he had shared that night with Doug and the promise of the next time, he felt now that fucking was perhaps going to prove a major factor in his life. He knew now, however, that it wasn't going to be with girls! Eighteen years old, poised on the threshold of his senior year in high school, he could not have known how very important fucking was going to become in his life in the very near future. For now, however, he looked forward to meeting with Doug again to explore his sexuality further, and hopefully extending that exploration to include several friends from school who had been lingering on the very edges of his conscious desire for the last several months.

2.

In spite of his eagerness to explore his emerging true sexuality, Harp proceeded slowly, partially out of caution, but largely due to his lack of confidence in his own ability to perform at a level of potency and assurance that he felt Doug, and others he now admitted he found attractive as possible sex partners, might expect. Although he did not know even their video names, he wanted to be every bit as aggressive and forceful in love-making as Jeff Stryker and Mike Henson had been, but he also hoped he could be as receptive as Kevin Williams had been to Mike Henson, and as the latter had been to the ferocious invasion of Jeff Stryker's incredible tool. He was almost sure Doug wanted to suck his cock, and he knew he would enjoy that. Maria Jenks had done a very enjoyable job of 'warming him' up that way before he screwed her. In fact, that appetizer had been far more enjoyable than the main course, and by way of dessert she had coaxed a second orgasm from him that way before he took her home. He was equally positive he wanted at least to try returning the favor for Doug, and felt fairly confident he was going to enjoy that as well.

Fucking was another matter entirely. If it turned out that Doug wanted him to fuck his ass, he certainly wanted to try it. Jeff and Mike had both obviously been in heaven while they fucked butt in the video he had seen. Whether he himself could enjoy getting fucked was far more doubtful, but remembering how totally delirious with joy Kevin had seemed with Mike buried deep inside him, and how Mike had seemed equally rapturous with the biggest prick Harp had ever seen disappearing unbelievably into him, he felt he was probably going to experiment with it at least. Doug had a nice-sized cock, about the size of Mike Henson's he calculated, and it would sure be a lot better one to experiment with than one the size of Jeff Stryker's, or, he could not help but think proudly, one as big as his own.

Although he was eager to begin sexual exploration with Doug, it was a busy time of the year, the beginning of both the semester and football season, so Harp was not able to meet with his prospective lover again until late in the week. Even then, their meeting had to be fairly short, as he had a football game the next night, and the coach expected them to be in bed by ten at the latest. As with the more conscientious of his teammates, that meant he usually retired by eleven.

Their meeting may have been short, but it proved to be every bit as thrilling as both Harp and Doug had hoped it might be. Harp no longer needed to be picked up, since his grandfather had presented him with his old car as an eighteenth-birthday present (as an alternative to trading it in on his new one), so he parked at Doug's house right after supper. As soon as he got through the door, Harp threw his arms around Doug and began to kiss him passionately. A delighted, and somewhat surprised Doug responded eagerly, and as they ground their pelvises together, it became obvious each was fully erect and ready for action.

Standing in the living room, they watched each other strip completely, without a word. They moved together and embraced again, and the thrill of naked skin against naked skin, hard cock against hard cock, tripled the excitement of their initial embrace. Their kiss was unthinkably long, alternating between tender affection and naked lust. Still nothing had been said; nothing really needed saying, both knew they were going to make love to each other that night. Both knew also that this was to be something of a maiden voyage of exploration for Harp, who was as eager to set sail on this voyage as Doug was to steer the course for him.

Doug sank to his knees, and taking Harp's fiercely hard, throbbing cock in his hand and looking up at the young Adonis, he finally broke the silence. "You told me the other night you wanted to start here the next time. Do you still feel that way?"

Harp sank to his knees, and again enfolded Doug in his arms and kissed him passionately, and whispered into his mouth, "I want it even more now than I did then!" He stood, with his hugely erect throbbing magnificence bare inches from Doug's mouth. Doug's hands went behind and cradled Harp's rounded, velvet buttocks as his own head was seized and he felt the head of Harp's cock at his lips. "Suck me, Doug!"

Doug opened his mouth and very slowly Harp penetrated him, inch by inch, until the entire length of his splendid endowment was engulfed by hot, moist welcome. He began slowly to fuck as Doug provided intense vacuum (Maria Jenks' efforts had been nothing like this!). The feel of Doug's hands eagerly fondling his humping ass, the sensation of the tight ring of lips traveling the entire length of his throbbing cock as he countered its action by driving himself as deeply into the hot throat as he possibly could after each near-retraction, the excited murmurs of ecstasy Doug uttered, all combined to take him to a height of rapture he had previously only imagined.

"Oh God, Doug! God ... Oh God! That is the most wonderful feeling I've ever had. Suck me! Don't ever stop!"

And Doug didn't stop. Harp continued to drive into his mouth, alternating between periods of slow and very sensuous love making, and fast, deep, and savage face-fuck. Although he was inexperienced, Harp paced himself perfectly to make the experience last as long as he could, using the loving to postpone imminent orgasm, after which he fucked again until he once more sensed he needed to return to making love or erupt inside Doug's hungry mouth. Eventually he knew he could hold off no longer, and after an especially long, fierce period of burying his cock as deep into Doug as he could, he shouted, "Here it is!" and the orgasm that burst into Doug's throat was as totally satisfying to the recipient as it was to the donor.

Doug swallowed enough of the copious ejaculate filling his mouth to make room for the further jets of the hot liquid that seemed to continue exploding from the huge, delicious organ he was, to use the appropriate term, worshipping. No prick had ever felt more exciting in his mouth. He could not remember ever having completely taken a cock of this huge size so completely into his mouth and throat. No blowjob he had ever administered had been quite so perfectly balanced between the sensuous and the savage (Harp was obviously a natural master!). He could not remember ever receiving an offering of semen in such quantity, delivered in such a seemingly endless series of copious jets, or as forcefully propelled as that he had just taken, nor one as sweet, as fresh, as delicious. Kneeling before the teenaged beauty, Doug realized he had just administered the supreme blowjob of his life. And he had administered a great many of them. He was well aware that it had been inspired by a great talent on the part of its recipient.

As for Harp, he was well aware that nothing in his entire life's experience was anywhere near as exciting, as satisfying, as wonderful! He remained buried inside Doug while he voiced his happiness, his gratitude, and his admiration for the perfect technique that had brought him to this level of ecstasy. At the same time, Doug continued to murmur his satisfaction, unable to do more than murmur, because his mouth was still very much filled by Harp's formidable cock. Doug continued to suck until every possible drop of the wonderful liquid was drained from the magnificent treasure, which he laved with his eager tongue where it rested inside, and simultaneously bathed in an unswallowed portion of the epic orgasm.

As he had been sucking Harp, Doug decided he would swallow that load. He told himself Harp had to be safe. The thrill of taking a load either orally or anally was something he had missed a great deal, and the slightly salty, nutty taste of this sweet young stud's emission lingered deliciously on his tongue, as satisfying to his discriminating palate as the finest wine ever produced.

Harp had been pressing Doug's head in to his belly, where his lips nestled in his pubic hair. With his orgasm finally exhausted, and with his cock now flaccid, Harp raised Doug to his feet, and they stood there and kissed and embraced until Harp was led into the bedroom. Falling onto the bed, their kissing began to extend to all parts of their bodies. After Harp's slow, intensely erotic sucking and licking of his nipples and stomach as he lay on his back, Doug thrilled to the feel of the busy mouth taking his painfully hard erection inside.

Harp took to cocksucking as naturally as he had to face-fucking. He had some trouble getting all of Doug inside, but he responded to the suggestion that he relax and open his throat, and soon he was enjoying the entire shaft inside him. He had expected to enjoy this, but he found he loved the sensation of a hard cock driving into his mouth, and everything about it: Doug's hands holding his head tightly as he plunged inside, the weight of Doug's legs on his shoulders, the play of muscles in Doug's busy, driving ass as he played with it, the taste of a prick, stimulated him to try to give as satisfying a blowjob as he had received.

Taking his tip from Harp's actions, Doug paced himself similarly, and when he felt that orgasm could not be delayed much longer, he made Harp stop for a moment, and he explained to him that he could not come in his mouth.

"But I want to eat your load, the way you did mine."

"Harp, you can't! We'll talk about it, but right now keep sucking. You're fantastic! When I tell you I'm going to come, stop sucking, and I'll shoot my load on your face, okay?"

Harp grinned, promised, and engulfed the hard cock again in one dive. His renewed efforts soon brought Doug to the brink, and Harp barely stopped in time following the warning of approaching orgasm. No sooner had Doug's cock left his mouth than it began to spurt its load all over Harp's face and neck. Harp's hand eagerly worked it, and once he had completely drained it, he knelt over Doug's face, come dripping from his nose and chin, and grinned down. "That was unbelievable! Guess what?"

"What?"

"I just love to suck dick!"

They giggled and rolled around together like two kids, taking time to kiss and caress like two adults, and to exchange sweet endearments of post-coital euphoria like two lovers. There is an old Latin adage: *Omne animal post coitum triste es.* (All animals are sad after intercourse.) Anyone watching Harp and Doug at that moment would have clearly understood some ancient Roman didn't know what the hell he was talking about.

Doug explained the danger of transmitting the HIV virus, and made Harp solemnly promise he would never take semen inside his body unless there was some reason to be sure his sex partner was HIV-negative. "If there is ever the tiniest bit of doubt, play it safe. Promise me."

"I promise. I really do. I knew something about that, and I was kinda surprised when you let me shoot in your mouth, but Jesus, I loved doin' it!"

"Not one tenth as much as I loved taking it, believe me! I know you're safe, you'd have to be, but when you start getting sexually active, you just don't know. It sounds weird to say it, but I'm almost positive I'm negative. But you're not sure I am, and I wouldn't do anything to worry you or endanger you."

Harp smiled and kissed him affectionately. "Thanks, Doug.

You're a nice guy. The other night and tonight with you have been the most wonderful times of my life." Then his beautiful face broke into a huge grin as he raised himself to kneel over Doug's face. his huge prick once again throbbing in full erection. "But it ain't over, is it?"

Doug grinned back and put his hands around Harp's waist to draw his body in. "By no means!" He stretched his lips wide and relaxed his throat to initiate another round of bliss.

Harp did not actually discover "69". He had imagined it before, and, of late, rather frequently, but he did discover how incredibly satisfying mutual cocksucking could be. They managed to prolong this round endlessly, deliriously, thrillingly, and their almost simultaneous orgasms were a near match for their earlier ones, with Doug lying on his back and receiving another copious flow in his throat while his own jetted straight up into Harp's face.

Although Harp had to get home soon, they snuggled and kissed and talked as long as they could. Although Doug wasn't "up" for another ejaculation so soon, he did want to fill Harp's request for another blowjob "for the road." It seemed unbelievable to Doug that he could have swallowed three such enormous emissions in only a few hours, but the force and the obvious joy of the deliverer made it clear he had given him three of the very best.

Before dressing, Doug began to tease Harp, gently insinuating just the very tip of his forefinger into his ass. Harp had played with his own ass quite a bit in the last few days, remembering how excited Kevin Williams and Mike Henson had been to take so much more into theirs, but the feeling of Doug's finger felt much more exciting than his own had, and promised even greater thrills than those they had shared tonight. He began to play with Doug in the same way, and Doug pushed against his finger so that it entered him completely.

Nothing was said as they fingered each other and kissed. Finally Doug said, "The other night we ended up with you saying, 'We can start here next time.' I think that would be a great final line right now, too, if you want to come back!"

Harp's finger gently plunged in and out of Doug, and Doug was emboldened to penetrate a bit farther; Harp said "We won't start here next time." There was a long silence as Harp watched Doug's face fall, and then he snickered. "But we will start there right after you give me a blowjob!"

Doug's face burst into a grin and they exchanged a playful kiss before Harp dressed and prepared to leave. At the door they exchanged final kisses, expressing mutual appreciation and admiration for what had been for both of them an unforgettably hot, and yet very sweet evening of love-making and lust.

The experience he had shared with Doug seemed to strip away the haze from the fantasies Harp had entertained regarding friends and classmates he found sexually attractive. Instead of thinking warmly of some kind of sex play with them, he now visualized himself very specifically either kneeling before them or lying beneath them to service them orally, and he could almost feel the heat and moisture of their mouths and throats accepting the gushers of semen his busy hand produced as he contemplated it.

It was more than a week before he could set up a date with Doug to pick up where they had left off. He was frustrated by the delay, as he was especially eager to sample the lusty joys of anal sex he had seen in the videos. Before that period was over, however, he had seized an opportunity to act out one of the fantasies he had been entertaining, hazily for some time, but quite clearly during the last week.

The teammate he found most attractive was Dodge Venturi, a tall, dark, and handsome boy who lately had seemed inordinately friendly when he and Harp had showered together. Dodge's actual first name was Diogenes (his parents had been "hippies" when he was born. He was lucky they hadn't saddled him with "Earth" or something along those lines). But he had been called Dodge almost from birth. He was also a senior, and had been a fairly close friend of Harp's since grade school. Lately, however, Dodge had been unusually friendly, often putting his hands on Harp when they were alone together, talking about sex much more frequently than they ever had, and standing unusually close to Harp as they showered together. Frequently he and Dodge were the last to shower after football practice that fall, just the two of them together, and Harp had the distinct feeling Dodge was engineering that arrangement by means of the conversational delays he instituted and sustained. As they showered together, Dodge seemed to have a perpetual semi-erection, which usually turned into a full blown hard-on when he toweled off and invariably asked Harp to dry his back.

It had very gradually begun to dawn on Harp that it was his naked body that was stimulating Dodge. After the experience with Doug, dawn broke clearly over the horizon of his perception: Harp realized that Dodge wanted to have sex with him!

The prospect of sex with Dodge was decidedly appealing to Harp. He not only liked him a lot, but he was handsome, with a good body, and the post-shower erection he regularly sported lately was generous and quite stimulating to his imagination. In fact, ever since Harp had watched Kevin Williams and Mike Henson and the others 'going down' in the videos, he had viewed Dodge's cock as good enough to eat. Sensing that Dodge was going to find his own similarly appetizing, he determined to test the waters.

The next time they were drying off together alone in the locker room, and Dodge's cock got fully hard after he dried his back, Harp turned around and asked Dodge to dry him off for once. As Dodge toweled him, far more slowly than necessary (lovingly would be a better description), Harp stroked his cock so that when he turned around it was standing straight out in its extremely impressive glory. His erection actually bumped against Dodge's when he turned around, and they both laughed nervously.

Dodge stared at Harp's huge cock. "Damn, Harp, you sure are hard!"

Harp reached over and enclosed Dodge's lesser, but still impressive, shaft in his hand. "I don't think I'd call this a soft-on, Dodge!"

Dodge's hand almost jumped to seize Harp's cock. He stroked it with his fist, "Jesus, yours is so fuckin' big and hard! Man, I wish I had a dick like that!"

Harp was confident enough of his grasp of the situation that he swallowed hard, looked at Dodge directly, and took the plunge. "Well, you can have this one for a while if you want." His fist began to travel the length of Dodge's cock. "If I can have yours for a while!"

Dodge looked stunned, but he kept on stroking. "You mean ... you mean you wanna...?"

A sly grin lit up Harp's face as he cupped Dodge's balls with his other hand. "C'mon Dodge, you've been wanting to do this for a long time now."

"I don't know what...." He lengthened his strokes and his other hand sought Harp's balls. "Yeah, Harp. I want it, okay?"

"I hope you know what to do with it once you've got it."

Dodge released Harp's cock, stepped backward, and looked around to be sure they were alone. He returned to Harp, sank to his knees and engulfed about half of his cock in one plunge. He sucked wildly for a few seconds, then stopped, looked up at Harp and grinned. "You have something like that in mind?"

Harp smiled back. "That's amazing, Dodge, that's exactly what I had in mind!" Dodge held Harp's cock up and out of the way as he began to lick his balls and caress his ass with the other hand. Harp took him by the shoulders and raised him to his feet. "This isn't the right time, and it sure as shit isn't the right place! Where can we go?"

"Come to my house tonight. We can study chemistry together, and you can sleep over." Both were in the same class, with a fairly important test imminent, so the excuse made sense. Although he had spent the entire night there only occasionally, Harp had often visited Dodge's house, where his bedroom was isolated in the attic. Dodge grinned and added, "We may not get much sleep, though."

Harp knelt in front of Dodge and with one quick movement deep-throated his entire cock, and he used his tongue inside his mouth to lick its underside. It was a bit bigger than Doug's, but he didn't gag; Doug had taught him well. He sucked eagerly for only ten or fifteen seconds, then stood and kissed the stunned Dodge on the lips and whispered, "We may not get any sleep at all!"

Dodge was stunned. "Jesus, Harp, I don't know what to say! Christ, when can you come over?"

"I'll be there around eight. We really should study for a while, you know."

Dodge grinned and again grasped Harp's huge, still fiercely hard shaft. "Yeah, right!"

They quickly dressed and separated, sharing a brief, furtive kiss before they piled into their separate cars and went to their homes.

They didn't study any chemistry that night, but they devoted quite a lot of time to the study of anatomy! They did find time to talk a while, following a brief session of hugging, groping and kissing. A certain amount of pretense for Dodge's parents was required as prelude to turning out the lights (not much—they were somewhere between extremely liberal and totally spaced out), but after a fairly brief verbal exchange, they closed the door to Dodge's bedroom and resumed their foreplay of that afternoon.

Dodge admitted he had been more and more attracted to Harp lately. "I know that makes me a queer, but, damn, when I see your ass walkin' down the hall, or see that big ol' dick of yours in the shower, I know I want to go to bed with you. And I was so glad when you started to suck my dick this afternoon, because ... well, I mean I was really glad you did, but I also knew if you'd do that, you weren't gonna tell anybody about this—about me being a queer?"

"Shit, Dodge, doesn't this make me a queer too? I think you're hot, and I know you've been paying an awful lot of attention to me since we got back to school this fall, and I wanted you to, you know? And I wanted to show you I was interested too, but until just a little over a week ago, I was afraid to do anything about it."

"What happened?"

"This is strictly between us, okay?" Dodge nodded assent. "I've been seeing this older guy. I can't tell you who he is, so don't ask. Well, a couple of weeks ago we went to bed and shot our loads all over each other, and then last week he sucked me off three times one night, and I sucked him off twice, and it was the hottest thing that ever happened to me."

"I guess you probably won't believe me," Dodge said, "but I've never had a cock in my mouth until this afternoon in the locker room. But I've wanted to suck yours for a long time, now, and almost every time I see your ass, 'specially when you're naked. I get so fuckin' horny I have to go and jack off somewhere."

"Funny, the guy I was with last week told me my ass was

the hottest thing he'd ever seen, and I know he wants to fuck it!"

"Jesus! Are you gonna let him? Do you do that?"

Harp snickered, "Shit, Dodge, except for screwin' Maria Jenks and a couple other girls, I'd never done anything before, certainly not with a guy. But I don't know, we watched some movies at his house of these really hot guys sucking each other off and fucking each other's asses, and it was fantastic. I'm sure he wants me to fuck him, and I want to. Yeah, I think it's gonna happen next time we get together."

"Wow! But ... does that mean you're gonna let him fuck you?"

"I'm gonna let him try, I know that. It sounds hot to me, and I hope I like it. I've thought about it a lot lately. Have you ever thought about it?"

"Harp, I can tell you this, now that you've told me what you did ... well, I've thought a lot about sucking a cock and getting mine sucked, and fucking a guy, And even takin' a dick up my ass. Except for playin' around a little in Scout camp, and stuff like that, you know, watchin' each other jack off 'n' all, I've never done anything. I know when I see your ass I want to kiss it and I want to stick my dick in there, at least between your cheeks, almost as much as I want to suck your cock."

At that point, Harp walked over and quietly locked the bedroom door. Standing next to it, he watched Dodge eyeing him as he slowly took off all his clothes and stood naked before him. Then he walked up to him, kissed him, turned around, and bending over slightly to offer his stunning ass to view, smiled back at him over his shoulder. "Look good?"

Dodge knelt and began to kiss and lick as his hands ran slowly over Harp's legs and his beautiful buttocks. He continued for some time, before he whispered in awe, "Jesus, you're beautiful Harp!" and his hands went around Harp's waist and he sank his face deep into the heaven that lay between those perfect buttocks. He licked and kissed the opening for several minutes, and then Harp thrilled to the invasion of his hot tongue, which flitted in and out, and danced around inside him, providing him a sensation as euphoric as anything he had ever experienced. While Dodge continued his worship, Harp used his hands to pull his face into him as tightly as he could.

Turning abruptly, Harp said, "I don't want you to stop, but if you keep that up I'm gonna come!" He raised Dodge to embrace him, and just before he drove his tongue into his mouth, he whispered, "And I want to come the first time in your throat, okay?" It was more than agreeable with Dodge of course, who again sank to his knees and resumed his worship of the stupendous shaft he had been wanting for so long.

Initially, Dodge only took about half of Harp's monster cock in his mouth as he sucked, and while it felt wonderful to Harp, it offered nothing like the rapture he had felt when he had been buried deep in the hot recesses of Doug's throat.

After a few tips from Harp, Dodge was soon able to take almost all the of the adored object deep inside him without gagging. Harp rewarded his admirer's efforts with an extraordinary flow of cum, which Dodge kept in his mouth and for a long time used to bathe the organ that had delivered it, while he continued to suck in rapt adoration. When every drop had been drained, and when the ecstasy of Dodge's absolutely virtuosic maiden effort at cocksucking had lessened somewhat, Harp raised him to his feet and kissed him deeply, only to find the mouth his tongue invaded was still full of his own cum. Harp had often masturbated while lying on his back alone, directing his orgasm into his own mouth, so the taste of what he was sharing with Dodge was familiar—and exciting. They passed the mouthful back and forth repeatedly, and finally Harp retained about half of it and swallowed. He grinned at Dodge, "The rest is for you!" Dodge swallowed, and returned the grin before he stripped off his clothes and the two fell into bed, lights still on, still 'studying.'

Harp came in Dodge's throat two more times that night, and once again the next morning before they got out of bed. Invariably, when they were engaged in 69-ing, since he knew that Dodge hadn't been screwing around, he eagerly brought his lover to climax in his mouth each time. Dodge's emissions didn't explode like his own did, but they were voluminous, and Harp adored both the sensation and the unique taste. Moreover, Dodge's cock was not as big as his own, and he was able to take every last bit of it deep inside him.

Before having to forsake their love-making and leave for

school, Harp positioned his body over a supine Dodge's face and did amorous push-ups into his still hungry mouth while he fucked it, and climaxed a fifth time into it in a space of some twelve hours! Euphoric, grinning, satisfied beyond words, Dodge provided the same liquid salute to Harp's throat—his fourth in that same time period.

There was no time to sit down and have the bacon and eggs Mrs. Venturi offered them that morning, but still the two extremely happy youths walked into Oconee High together after having shared two helpings of the most delicious breakfast imaginable.

That night of sex with Dodge, which would ultimately prove to be only the first of a long series of such encounters, was astonishingly rewarding to both of them. Harp was glad he had told Dodge about Doug, because he was eager to explore his sexuality further with the older man.

While he had greatly enjoyed the experience with Dodge and wanted it again, he also wanted to be with Doug again even more keenly. He asked himself if he was going to be able to get fucked. He wanted to be sure Dodge understood that was going to happen.

As exciting as Dodge's adoration of his cock and his ass had been, he really looked forward to the greater control he felt Doug exerted over him. He realized that he enjoyed himself more when he could sense someone else directing the action. This surprised him, but he knew it was true, nonetheless.

The next time he had sex with Doug, they first shared a passionate and wonderful mutual blowjob before—as planned—taking up where they had left off, with each having a finger up the butt of the other. Doug guided his young lover to a delirious mastery of the rapture of buttfucking. Harp proved to be a quick study, and before the evening was over, had spent at least an hour-and-a-half of actual time with his cock buried as deep inside Doug's ass as it could go, and that was very deep indeed, to Doug's utter delight! Harp screwed him as he knelt on all fours, as he lay on his back, as he rode him every way imaginable. In fact, Harp was unable to decide which position was most pleasurable, and his research led him to try all positions a number of times, and defer judgment until he would be able to conduct considerably more research.

The sensation was almost nothing like screwing a girl. Well, it was like it, but the intensity of the feeling was so much greater inside Doug than it had been with any of the girls he had fucked that it was of a totally different order. Holding Doug's waist while he drove into him, and studying the face and body of the handsome man, Harp was in heaven, and it was obvious from Doug's almost continuous, delirious, panting commentary that he was enjoying it equally. Doug had not experienced the unique thrill of feeling the orgasm from a bare, unsheathed cock explode deep inside him in a long time, and when Harp first erupted there while he lay on his back with his legs on Harp's shoulders, he was so moved he began to kiss the young stud with such passion that the magnificent shaft impaling him never lost its incomparable rigidity and the fuck continued unabated for another quarter-hour until Harp had produced another explosion.

As a pupil of passive fucking, Harp did not prove to be quite the quick study he had shown himself to be in the active role. The thrilling multiple orgasm he had just delivered to Doug had drained his passion to a considerable extent, of course, but he was still anxious to take Doug inside him. Doug's reaction to his fuck had clearly shown him what rapture lay in store for him as the "bottom" in such an experience. Kevin Williams taking Mike Henson, and Mike Henson taking Jeff Stryker the same way on video had been very convincing, but observing the total ecstasy Doug experienced when he drove himself in, he could see in person what a delirious experience awaited him. He was eager to find out, but although Doug's finger felt absolutely wonderful when it plunged eagerly in and out of him, he found he was too tense to relax his sphincter as Doug urged, and the pain of admitting the much greater bulk of a cock was more than he could stand. Doug managed to get the head of his cock inside, but Harp insisted they would have to wait for another time, so Doug had to settle for masturbating on the peerless ass he so eagerly sought to penetrate.

Later, Harp delivered another orgasm into Doug as the latter rode his cock, at almost the same instant Doug directed his own orgasm on the chest and face of the beautiful boy on whom he was impaled. With Harp still inside him, Doug kissed him and whispered, "You are the most wonderful fucker! I love you!"

After a long, sweet kiss, Harp smiled and whispered back, "I love you too."

Doug had felt a number of considerably larger cocks than even Harp's prodigious monster inside him, and as recently as a month or so earlier had told a Farrar student who was burying one of those titanic organs inside him, probably a thrilling inch-and-a-half longer than even Harp's, that he was the best fucker he had ever known. In spite of the splendor of Harp's achievement, that record still stood. Still, it was a nice thing to say to a sweet, exciting young man who had just serviced him so very, very well.

Both Harp and Doug, in saying "I love you" really meant to convey feelings that might more accurately have been expressed by saying "I like you a lot, and sex with you is terrific!" or words to that effect, which would have accurately said what they actually meant: they had extremely terrific sex together.

Harp promised he would continue to try to give his ass to Doug, as he was quite honestly eager to do. He practiced opening his ass with all sorts of vaguely penis-shaped substitutes: animal (his fingers), vegetable (carrots, cucumbers), and mineral (candles), and was finding it more and more easy to do, and more exciting. Yet, although he was preparing himself to welcome Doug inside, it turned out that it was someone else who finally took the precious gift of his anal virginity.

The student body at Oconee High comprised a fairly representative sampling of rural Southern boys, which meant there had to be at least one who was fairly effeminate, and who suffered because of it. There were actually several at Oconee, however, and they had to endure the usual condescending sneers and innuendoes high school boys are inclined to direct against such subnormal masculinity. When Harp had heard his epicene schoolmates derided for their lack of manliness, he never took part in what their tormentors thought of as fun. Although he was completely masculine himself, he had sensed for a long time that he probably shared their appetites for sex. He now knew that when he heard one of them referred to as a 'cocksucker', the reference could apply equally to himself. Furthermore, the adjective would be accurate in his case, whereas that proclivity was only alleged in the instance of the other boys.

Oconee High was small enough that everyone knew everyone, but, of the effeminate boys there, Harp had more than the barest nodding acquaintance with only one of them: Jeremy Lee.

Jeremy was of average height, perhaps an inch or two taller than Harp, slim, very blond, and with delicate features. He was, in the opinion of many, simply too pretty to be a boy. His manner was more fussy than effeminate, but there could be no mistaking that he was considerably less masculine than his classmates. His interest in classical music, his apparent lack of interest in things athletic, and his considerable talent as an artist set him apart further. Still, although he was something of a pariah, he maintained a friendly and cheerful attitude toward all but the most virulent "fag-baiters."

Harp had shared classes with Jeremy, even though he was one year ahead of him in school, and in study hall the younger boy had often helped him with academic problems. Jeremy did not "suck up to" Harp as most did; he obviously liked him, but was not at all impressed with his athletic achievements. Harp found that refreshing, if just the tiniest bit annoying. Still, although they were not close, the two were more than just acquaintances, and while Harp had not actively defended Jeremy, or any of his other less-than-masculine schoolmates, when he had heard him referred to as 'queer', or 'fag', or 'cocksucker', he had certainly never taken part in such slander.

After discovering that he very much liked sucking cock, he immediately began chiding those who used those terms. Given his popularity and his obvious masculinity, Harp was able to quell a considerable amount of subtle fag-baiting in the student body. He thoroughly dressed down one of his classmates who was slandering Jeremy and making cruel remarks about his presumed gayness, surprising himself almost as much as he did the slanderer.

Jeremy got word of Harp's defense of him, and as he was getting into his car in the parking lot after school one afternoon, he spotted him heading for his own automobile. Standing next to his car he called out to him, "Harp, can I talk to you for a minute?"

Harp came over. "Sure, Jeremy, what's up?"

"I hear tell you've been defendin' me."

"Defending you?"

"Yeah. I got the word that Rod Buell was bad-mouthin' me as usual, and you told him to shut up. Or something like that."

"Look, Jeremy, Rod was being an asshole. There's nothing strange about that. Rod usually acts like an asshole. He said some shit about you and I told him to shut up, that's all."

"Harp, I know the kind of shit Rod and a lot of those guys say about me, and it doesn't much bother me. None of 'em know shit, but they gotta run their mouths about somethin', and since I'm different from them, they figure I'm some kinda freak. Let 'em. I don't give a shit."

"Yeah, but Jeremy, you ought to give a shit. He was saying you ... well, he said some pretty nasty stuff."

"I'm a faggot, right? That what he said?"

"Yeah, that's right. And I told him he didn't know you at all, and didn't know what the hell he was talking about. And I told him to quit calling you names, and I also told him calling anybody a 'faggot' was about as proper as calling somebody a 'nigger'."

Jeremy snickered. How'd he take it?"

"Well, better than I expected him to, actually. He shut up and didn't say anything more."

"He'd better not. I could tell you ... oh, never mind. I just wanted to thank you, that's all."

"Hey, that's okay, Jeremy. Look, even if you were gay, it wouldn't make any difference to me. I figure it's none of my business one way or the other what someone else likes to do."

"Even if it's someone who ... likes to do things different from the way you do?"

"Like what?"

"Oh come on, Harp, you know what I'm talkin' about. If you found out I was gay, what would you do about it? I'm not sayin' I am, just askin', okay?"

"Look, let's go for a ride for a few minutes and talk."

Jeremy was taken by surprise, but he recovered himself and said, "Sure, we can go in mine." They got in the car and as Jeremy drove, they talked further.

At first their talk was general, and after a few minutes, as they neared a state park along the road to their school, Harp told Jeremy to pull into the park and stop. Jeremy parked in a remote section, switched off the ignition, and turned to face Harp. "So, what do you wanna talk about?"

"Well, you asked me what I'd do if I found out you were gay. What I think you really asked me was would I tell anybody if I found out you were. Am I right?"

"Yeah, well, something like that, I guess. Well, would you? Tell anyone else?"

"Jesus, Jeremy, you know I wouldn't. Hell, would you tell anyone if you found out I was gay? No, you wouldn't. I know you wouldn't."

"Of course I wouldn't. But that's not about to happen."

"Look, Jeremy, this is none of my business, and just tell me so if I sticking my nose in where it doesn't belong. And remember, we're talking privately here."

"Harp, you're the nicest guy I know in school. You can ask me any damn thing you want to."

"Okay. Are you gay?"

Jeremy looked levelly at Harp for a long time before he replied. "Yes, Harp. I'm gay. Okay? Curiosity satisfied?"

"No, it's not just curiosity, Jeremy, I ... look, I'm kind of glad to find out you're gay, because ... oh hell. Jeremy, you're not any gayer than I am."

"You? You're gay?" Harp nodded. "I can't believe it, Harp, you just don't seem the type."

"Come on, Jeremy, you're talking like Rod in a way. Do you have to be a *type* to be gay? Because I play football and you like operas, does that mean we can't both like to ... well, to ... Oh shit, you tell anyone this and I'll kill you!"

A stunned Jeremy nodded as Harp added, "Yeah, I like to suck cock, okay? Do you?"

Jeremy smiled. "Yeah, Harp, I love to suck cock. And I like doin' more than just that, and I do it with a few guys you know—guys who you'd never suspect would wanna do it with me."

"Who?"

"Harp, I'd never tell you, or anybody else. Any more than I'd tell anyone that you like to suck cock. Jesus, I can't believe you even told me that."

"Well, I did. So there you are. And it may surprise you to know that I like to do more than just suck cock."

"No!" Jeremy feigned shock. He was a good actor.

"Yes. Why, just a little while ago I found out how much I like to fuck butt."

"No!" Jeremy had all he could do to keep from giggling.

"Yes, and ... and ... well, hell, I've said this much, I might as well say it all. I want to get fucked in the butt myself. I've tried, and it hasn't worked yet, but I'm gonna keep at it, because I know I'm going to love it."

Jeremy grinned. "Yes, you will. You will love it, Harp. Believe me, there's nothin' like it."

"You ... you like getting fucked, Jeremy?"

"I love takin' a big ol' dick up my ass, the bigger the better. And I've had quite a few of them! But you know, I think I do more fuckin' than I do gettin' fucked. Look, I won't say who they are, but there are four guys on the football team who I fuck regularly, and one on the basketball team—no, actually two on the basketball team, but one of 'em is one of the football players. They all love gettin' fucked."

"No!" Now it was Harp's turn to act surprised.

"Yes, and for about every two times one of them fucks me, I fuck him three times! And there are other guys, too."

"Jesus, Jeremy! How many guys do you go to bed with?"

"Actually, I don't go to bed with any of them more than just once in a while. They don't wanna be seen with me, or have me over at their houses, 'cause they're afraid someone will think they're queer, so we go off to someplace deserted and throw a blanket down on the ground or something, and we suck each other off and fuck each other, and then nobody can get any ideas. Hell, I don't really care, but it's usually only when I can actually go to bed with one of them that we kiss and hug, and it's like makin' love instead of just fuckin'." He snorted. "And that hardly ever happens."

"And that's what you really want?"

"Hell, Harp, don't you?"

"Oh, sure. I like the kissing and hugging almost as well as I do the other. I really want to make love with a guy, not just have sex."

"Harp ... do you ... I mean...?"

Harp finally broke the long silence that ensued. "Ask me, Jeremy. We're friends, aren't we? I mean we've always kinda been friends, but after today, I think we really are friends. Whatever it is, it's okay. Just ask."

"Okay. Do you want to make love with me, Harp?"

Neither boy spoke or moved for a seemingly long time. Finally Harp leaned over, put one hand behind Jeremy's neck and drew him to him. His other hand stroked Jeremy's cheek as he kissed his lips very gently and sweetly. Jeremy's arms went around Harp's body and held him tightly as he kissed back, still sweetly, but with the tip of his tongue licking Harp's lips as Harp did the same. Finally they broke, and Harp whispered, "Yes, I want to make love with you, Jeremy, if you want it."

Jeremy whispered, "I want you more than any boy I've ever seen. I've wanted you for three years now. I wish I'd never made love with anyone else, so you could be the first."

Harp sat back and smiled at him. "I can't be the first, Jeremy, any more than you can be the first for me." He kissed him again. "But I can be the next if you want."

"Oh God, yes! Make love to me, Harp!" Their arms went around each other, and they embraced and kissed passionately.

"I think I know where we might go. Right now, if you want."

"Anywhere, Harp. Now! I want to feel you inside of me! We can go out in the country. I know lotsa places we can go. I've got all the stuff we need."

"If we have to, Jeremy ... but I'm gonna try to find a way we can go to bed and make love—at least today, okay?"

"You're some kinda guy, Harp! Jesus, I can't believe this is happenin' to me."

"It's not happening to you, Jeremy. It's happening to us!" Harp sat back on his side of the car and rested his hand on Jeremy's leg. "Drive into town so I can make a call."

Jeremy drove to town, and Harp called Doug at his office at the University. He explained that he needed a really big favor, no questions asked. Doug was curious, but agreed to help if he could. "I want to use your bed for a couple of hours."

Doug paused for a second. "You don't want to use it by yourself, I guess."

"No I don't, Doug. Please? As a special favor?"

The next pause was even longer, then, "Okay. Sure, Harp. We don't own each other, but I hope this doesn't mean you don't want to see me any more."

"God, no. No. I want to see you very soon. I don't want to stop at all. I love being with you, and it's important to me. I hope this doesn't make you want to see me less. It's just, well, I want to do this too, okay?"

"You're very important to me too, Harp. Look, use the guest room, okay? I might get home before ... well, before you're through. That will be okay, I can get out of the way when you're ready to leave. The door on the lake-side porch is unlocked, just go in there, and make yourself at home. Do you ... well, if you need anything, you know where things are in my bedroom."

"You're great, Doug. I'm gonna fuck you extra hard next time! And I'm practicing so you can do me, too ... soon, I hope."

Doug laughed, "I hope so too. Have a good time!"

At Harp's direction, Jeremy drove out toward Doug's lake house, and Harp slouched down in the car as they passed his own house. When they began to make the last turn, Jeremy laughed. "We're goin' to Doug Truax's house, aren't we?"

"Yeah. How do you know Doug?"

"And I'll bet I know him the same way you do!"

"Yeah, but wow! This is weird. Have you known him a long time?"

"Doug picked me up one night when I was a freshman, about two years ago. He didn't live out here then; he lived in a house on the Farrar campus."

"You were having sex when you were a freshman?"

Jeremy barked a laugh. "Harp, I was fuckin' my best friend when I was thirteen, and we'd started suckin' each other off when we were twelve! When Doug picked me up, I knew what I was doin', and he knew what I wanted to do, too."

"What did you want to do, Jeremy?"

By this time they had arrived at Doug's house. Jeremy pulled into the parking area and switched off the engine. He turned and look at Harp. "What I wanted to do was get my cock sucked, and probably suck his, and fuck his ass, and probably get him to fuck mine. That's pretty much what I want to do with you Harp, except there aren't any 'probablies,' okay? I know I want to suck your cock, and I know I want you to fuck me. How's all that with you?"

Harp leaned over and kissed Jeremy. "It all sounds good to me. Why don't we get to it?" Jeremy grinned, and they both got out of the car. Harp stopped. "Oh shit!"

"What?"

"Won't Doug recognize your car, Jeremy?"

"No, it's okay, he wouldn't recognize it. He's always picked me up. You've got a key?"

Harp explained about the unlocked porch door.

They went in, and spent a long time standing and kissing, exploring each other's bodies with their hands.

By this time, both were fiercely erect, and as Jeremy's hand began to massage Harp's enormous bulk, he shouted, "Oh my god, your cock is really big!"

"I want it inside you!"

"Oh Jesus, me too. I've wanted it inside me ever since I got to know you. I just didn't have any idea it'd be so big!"

"If it's too big, we can...."

Jeremy dropped to his knees and began to unbutton Harp's Levi's. "Oh, no, it's gonna be just perfect, I know. I can't imagine anything *more* perfect!"

At that point he dragged Harp's pants and shorts below his cock, which sprang up to meet the younger boy's gaze. "My God, Harp! Oh my god!" He opened his mouth wide, and took the entire impressive length of Harp's cock inside him.

Jeremy was young, but it was perfectly clear that he was exceptionally accomplished at what he was at that moment doing. He had not only practiced the art for several years, he had practiced it assiduously. But he also brought to his present ministrations a prodigious natural talent. Add to this the fact that he had been dreaming of doing exactly this with the handsome, sexy Harp Harper for over two years, and the upshot is that young Jeremy was giving Harp a masterful blowjob! Harp cooperated fully, and his deep thrusts into the hot, moist, intense vacuum were rewarded with thrilled murmurs and a ring of lips traveling tightly the entire length of his shaft. Harp's hands eagerly fondled Jeremy's head, and the sensation of Jeremy's hands feverishly exploring the contours of his ass added to the thrill, and neither was anxious to break the moment.

Eventually, Jeremy had to 'come up for air," and as he did so, Harp fell to his knees, took him in his arms, and kissed him passionately. "I want to suck you too, Jeremy. Let's get undressed and go into the bedroom." They both stood, Harp pulled his pants up, and he took Jeremy's hand to lead him into Doug's bedroom. Jeremy began to undress, but Harp told him to wait, took lubricant and towels out of the night stand, and then looked at Jeremy. "We're gonna go in the guest room. Do we need rubbers?"

"It's the only safe way. Don't you use 'em?"

"Well, I've only screwed around with two other guys, Jeremy, and neither of them has fucked me yet. Doug's the only one I've ever fucked, and Dod ... er, the other guy I've messed around with, has never done anything with anybody else, so I guess I'm safe with the HIV thing."

"Jesus, you can come in my mouth, then? And in my ass?"

Harp grinned and kissed him lightly. "You better bet I'll come in your mouth—and in your ass, too. Doug told me when I shoot a load, I *really* shoot a load. He likes it a lot."

"Oh my God, Harp, I can't wait. I wish I could tell you I want to shoot a load in you, but...."

"I've never been fucked, Jeremy."

"I know that, but I mean ... well, you know, I mean to shoot my load in your mouth, but I can't do that to you Harp. I'm sure I'm okay, but I've been with an awful lot of guys, and everybody says you gotta use protection. So don't let me come in your mouth, or ... well, you know."

With his lips a scant inch from Jeremy's, Harp completed his sentence, "Or fuck me without a rubber? Okay. You gotta use a rubber when you fuck me, or anyway when you try to fuck me, okay?"

"You want me to try, Harp?"

"Oh yeah!" He kissed him and took a package of condoms from the night stand. "Let's go in the other bedroom." They entered the guest room, and closed and locked the door.

They watched each other undress. The sight of Jeremy's body produced no particular surprises for Harp: he was fairly thin, hairless, and nicely built, though anything but muscular. He had a cute little ass, Harp thought, which he looked forward to penetrating, and his dick was longer than Harp expected it to be—not as long as his own, but not missing that dimension a great deal, although it was considerably more slender. Jeremy, on the other hand, feasted on the sight of Harp's body, and declared his ass the most beautiful one he had ever seen—an opinion that seemed to be shared by everyone whom he had experienced sex with, Harp thought.

Their first 69 was not mutually consummated. Lying under Harp, Jeremy took every drop of his explosive orgasm deep in his throat, and gloried in it before swallowing, but as he himself neared ejaculation, he made Harp stop. "I want to try to fuck your ass, okay?"

Harp was agreeable, and continued to kneel over Jeremy as the younger man worshipped his ass with his hands, and eventually began to use his tongue to penetrate the sought-after prize, much to Harp's considerable enjoyment. After Jeremy had brought Harp to a state of great excitement with his tongue, he continued his exploration with one finger, gently inserted, then two, aided by lubricant. As Harp's obvious enjoyment of the sensation increased, Jeremy began a rather determined assault with his two fingers, until he heard Harp pant, "Fuck me, Jeremy!"

Jeremy withdrew his fingers from Harp, and his body from beneath him. He directed Harp to lie on his side, in a fetal position, and he applied considerably more lubricant both to Harp and to his cock, now sheathed by a condom.

As he gradually began to insinuate himself inside, Harp complained of pain, but Jeremy worked very slowly and gently, and the exclamations of pain gradually became sighs of appreciation. In a few minutes, Jeremy was buried inside Harp, and began a slow and very sensuous series of deep, but gentle thrusts that elicited cries of delight from their recipient. "Oh Jesus, Jeremy, your cock feels so good! Fuck me, Jeremy! Do it easy, but fuck me with your big cock!" And Jeremy's cock did indeed feel big to Harp, but as he gradually began to relax and truly enjoy the sensation, he started to work with Jeremy, and soon the two were locked in a passionate, frenzied fuck.

Harp felt unbelievably warm and filled, and complete, and

discovered a new depth of sexual relationship and connection with another that overwhelmed his senses. Put quite simply, and in far less elegant terms, Harp adored getting fucked, even much more so than fucking. He came to this latter conclusion later, on reflecting on the experience, and it surprised him somewhat.

Careful to keep the plunging delight of Jeremy's cock still inside him, Harp maneuvered so that he was now on all fours, with Jeremy kneeling behind him. In this new position, Harp began to buck savagely, and Jeremy began to plow deep and hard and fast, and although it lasted quite a wonderful, timeless while, it was all too soon at an end, and Jeremy unceremoniously pulled himself out of Harp, and stripped the condom from his cock just as he spewed a huge, hot orgasm all over his partner's beautiful body and matchless ass. They fell flat on the bed, gasping in passion, and Jeremy kissed Harp's neck and shoulders as they slowly calmed down and cooed appreciation to each other for the sublime thrill each had experienced—Jeremy in the wonder of finally capturing the prize he had so long dreamed of, and Harp the discovery of a level of rapture he had never known.

Harp turned over, and they lay together in gentle, sweet embrace for some time, until the growing bulk of Harp's cock against Jeremy's belly signaled a resumption in activity. Knowing he did not have to ask, Harp rolled Jeremy on his stomach, and applied lubricant to him. As he began to penetrate him, Jeremy asked, "Do you have a rubber on, Harp?"

"No, I don't need one. I told you, I know I'm safe."

"Put one on, Harp, and promise me you always will. I'm sure you're safe, but ... just never screw a guy without a rubber, and never let anyone screw you without one. Okay?"

Harp was grinning as he peeled a condom from the package with his teeth, and as he rolled it on his massive shaft he said, "Yes, mother!"

Jeremy proved to be an even better partner than Doug, and his appreciation of both the gigantic size of his organ and his skill at employing it inspired a performance on Harp's part that they were careful to prolong and savor, and which ended with Jeremy on his back and his legs on Harp's shoulder. The assault on Jeremy's wildly appreciative bottom lasted over twenty minutes, and concluded with a copious orgasm deep inside it. Removing the condom from Harp a few minutes later, Jeremy emptied the contents on his stomach, and was astonished at the quantity of the offering, and deeply appreciative of the beauty and the expertise of the stud who had delivered it into him.

They lay together another hour, kissing, sucking, probing, and enjoying each other. Jeremy was in absolute ecstasy, and could not sufficiently express his admiration for Harp, for his dick, for his technique, for the perfection of his ass and body. Harp finally simply told him, "Hush. You can't imagine how much I'm enjoying this either!" Jeremy tried to fuck Harp again, but he was too tender, although he promised to give him what he wanted again and soon.

Jeremy was not tender, however, and delighted in kneeling to submit to another assault, which he called a halt to before orgasm, so that he could turn over and enjoy another explosion of Harp's love in his mouth. Harp also enjoyed the explosion Jeremy then produced, although it was more in the nature of a shower, rather than a drink. Once they had calmed down again, Jeremy said, "That was the last time you should come in somebody else's mouth, okay?" Harp sadly agreed that he was right.

It was getting quite late, and each phoned home to say he would be late for supper. As both were drying off from a most enjoyable, but rather inefficient mutual shower, they heard Doug come into the house. Harp told Jeremy, "I'll get him to hide when you're ready to go, so he won't see who I was with."

Jeremy giggled and got into the bed, lay naked on his back and said. "He won't care. I'll cover my face; get him to come in here and see if he recognizes me."

Harp called Doug in, saying "Someone here I want you to meet."

Doug kissed the still naked Harp and fondled his ass as he came in the door. Looking at Jeremy's body he laughed, leaned over and just before he took Jeremy's cock in his mouth, he said, "This looks good enough to eat, Jeremy!"

Jeremy threw the pillow off his face and laughed. "I wondered if you'd recognize me!"

Doug tried to persuade the two youngsters to stay and initiate a threesome, but they each had to get home. Harp promised to call Doug later that night, and on the way back to pick up his car, Jeremy agreed that they might think about a threesome with Doug. "Could be fun."

Harp asked, "Have you ever done that before? With two other guys, I mean?"

Laughing, Jeremy replied, "I did it once with Doug and ... someone else you know, actually. And once I did it with three other guys. But it's not near as much fun as being alone with someone you really like. I'd a lot rather be with just you, Harp!"

They agreed they would at least consider a threesome with Doug, and also determined to get together for a return engagement very, very soon. They parted as two very happy young men, both having realized prized ambitions that afternoon.

It happened that Doug was not at all offended that Jeremy had taken the prize of Harp's virginity. "I want to make love with you. I don't have to be the first to do anything, okay?"

And although Doug was not the first to screw Harp's ass, he was the second one, and his achievement followed Jeremy's by only a day or two. Within a week, Harp had been screwed three more times by Jeremy (on two occasions), and four times by Doug (also on two occasions). Although he never failed to provide ample, and delightful return services, Harp realized that he was a more natural "bottom" than he was a "top".

The next time Harp went to bed with Dodge he introduced him to his new exercise, and Dodge enjoyed it so very, very much that he strove diligently to determine for himself why it seemed to be so much fun. Eventually, with Harp's monster dick driving deep inside him, he came to realize that while it may be more blessed to give than to receive, it's often more enjoyable to receive than to give.

With Doug and Dodge and Jeremy, Harp achieved an ideal symbiotic sexual relationship. He and Doug were equals in love-making, with neither seeming to be the dominant partner, giving and taking, topping and bottoming with equal gusto. Dodge was completely besotted with Harp, and while he was an eager and effective aggressive sex partner, he was obviously more happy when he was servicing Harp's magnificent endowment by providing hungry and seemingly insatiable orifices to shelter it and receive its thrusts. Strangely enough, since he was the only one of the three who was somewhat effeminate, it was Jeremy who really dominated Harp. Although he loved playing passive partner to the beautiful stud, he tended to command their sex play most of the time, and Harp preferred it.

Jeremy and Doug and Harp did occasionally meet for a 3-way, which proved relatively satisfactory, and it was the youngest and least overtly masculine of the trio who dominated and directed the proceedings.

Neither Doug nor Jeremy really wanted to share the glorious Harp with another, so although Harp greatly enjoyed having two guys on hand to screw him, he was usually with only one of them at a time. Only Harp knew of Dodge's interest in gay play, so Jeremy never suspected that Dodge was one of the "others" he thought Harp was playing around with, and no possibility of a 3-way with him was ever a consideration.

In fact, although there were three other guys Harp had sex with during his senior year, no lasting relationships developed. One of these was with a man who picked him up one night as he was doing some work in the university library—and did nothing but take him out in the country to give him a blowjob. Harp neither learned, nor cared to get, his name, and found the furtiveness of the experience distasteful. The second was one of the football coaches who was married, with children, and yielded to his total fascination with Harp's luscious ass and impressive dick only after the greatest soul-searching and inner struggle. And although it was fully realized and mutually rewarding, the coach felt so guilty that he never even contemplated repeating the ecstasy he experienced on the one occasion when he managed to meet Harp alone in the training room and share the wonder of this boy's now quite sophisticated sexual precocity. Harp, on the other hand, would have been happy to repeat the experience endlessly: the coach was handsome, had a big dick, and fucked like a stallion.

Jeremy had mentioned that he had been having sex with a boy who was on both the football and basketball teams, but would never reveal the names of any of his other sex partners. [Jeremy had replied, "You wouldn't want me to tell them I'm having sex with you, would you?" Harp said "no," but he wasn't sure if he was being completely honest!] There were only two guys who fit that description, and since one of them was so totally unappealing, it seemed clear to Harp that Eddie Williams had to be the one. Eddie was pretty cute, and was a nice guy, and the body and endowment he showed in the shower was quite interesting. By now, Harp was regularly checking everybody out.

Seducing Eddie was simple. Harp first buddied up to him for a week or so, and invited him to spend the night at his house. Long before going to bed, Harp stripped naked, and sat around that way as they talked. Before turning out the lights, he stretched and treated Eddie to a great show of his body, especially his ass, which recent adulation had brought him to conclude was the best among his many very fine assets. He was pleased to note that as Eddie stripped off his shorts and slipped under the bedclothes, the endowment he had been considering in the shower room lately was much more worthy of consideration now, and apparently ready for action.

Within five minutes after getting in bed, Eddie's hand was on his ass, and, five minutes later, Eddie's lips were around his dick.

Before the night was over his considerable endowment had delivered itself of four, or maybe even five, doses of the medicine Harp had hoped to have administered when his cute house guest had crawled into his bed. Between getting into bed and going to the breakfast table, Harp screwed Eddie three times, each time producing copious liquid evidence of Eddie's appreciation at the same time that Harp was producing the same product inside the latex sheath buried deeper inside Eddie's willing recesses than any other shaft had yet plumbed.

On the other hand, Eddie screwed Harp only once, which was disappointing in terms of frequency, and while enjoyable in terms of quality, was somewhat below the ecstatic level of Harp's own performance. Their kissing during the course of the memorable night had been so passionate, and they had both sucked cock so eagerly, and at such length, that their lips were sore. They dissolved in a fit of giggles when they found that neither of them was able to produce a whistle the next morning.

Although Eddie repeatedly made it clear he was anxious to pursue sexual adventures with him on a regular basis, Harp only repeated the experience with him twice before graduation, as it turned out that it just wasn't as much fun as it was with either Jeremy or Doug or Dodge. Analyzing it, he knew it was because while Eddie was an insatiable and appreciative bottom, he was, at best, a lackluster top. It was now clearly the bottom role which also appealed more to Harp. Harp felt no guilt whatever about later denying Eddie's overtures, since he was fairly positive that Jeremy was fucking Eddie's brains out with great regularity. Knowing the excellence of Jeremy's services along those lines, he was sure Eddie's desires (or perhaps needs, given the strength of his demonstrated appetite) would be satisfied expertly.

By the time his last semester in high school began, Harp was balancing three full-blown sexual relationships, so he really didn't have time for much extra-relational sex play anyway.

He spent the night at Dodge's house at least once a week. Dodge's parents were rather "spaced out," and gave no consideration to the frequency or the details of their 'sleeping' arrangements together. Dodge staying at his house was more of a problem, as they had to exercise much greater caution; as a result he seldom 'slept over' with Harp. Doug could not, of course, spend the night at Harp's house, but at least once a week, Harp spent the night at his, and Dodge 'covered' for him if his parents asked questions. Strangely, Dodge didn't ask questions himself. He was so deliriously happy that Harp was screwing him regularly, that he would have done anything to please him. Sensible lad.

Jeremy lived with his mother, and she regarded Harp as one of Jeremy's "little friends," so she was amenable to Harp spending every night with Jeremy if he wanted. Still, considerable caution was necessitated at Jeremy's house, so Jeremy slept over with Harp about as frequently as the other way around.

The upshot of his complicated sex life was that Harp was spending at least three nights away from home every week, and Jeremy was spending one or two nights each week with him.

His parents did not seem concerned, as long as his grades held up. And they did. Harp was not an unusually good student, but he was passably capable and interested. And, sad to say, that alone seemed enough to carry him well above the average level of scholastic achievement. In addition, he was an extremely handsome, polite, star athlete. Good grades seem to come naturally to those who meet those qualifications.

Although he had no clear idea what he wanted to do for the rest of his life, Harp planned on entering college. Screwing seemed to be the only clear passion of his life. It was obviously something for which he had an enormous aptitude. But, on the assumption that he would sooner or later settle on something practical, he applied to, and was accepted by, Farrar University.

Graduation came and went. Relationships with his three partners continued, although Doug was not teaching for the summer and was gone frequently. Doug gave Harp a key to his house, and encouraged him to consider it his home if he wanted. There were no restrictions, as long as he acted responsibly. Harp did not abuse the trust Doug bestowed on him.

But, since his parents knew nothing of his relationship with Doug, he couldn't make much use of his house for anything except swimming and skiing, and an occasional "overnight" with Jeremy or Dodge or, if he was home, Doug, if a cover story could be produced to allay his parents' suspicions. That situation changed significantly and swiftly one evening in early July.

Harp had asked Jeremy to spend the night with him at his house, and Jeremy had accepted eagerly. His parents had gone to a church meeting and were not expected home until fairly late. With his bedroom window thrown open to the warm summer night, Harp took advantage of his time alone in the house with Jeremy to pursue the passionate love-making they so enjoyed, without the caution they normally had to exercise when they were there.

After having shared mutual oral love-making for some time, Jeremy eagerly knelt on all fours to receive Harp's frenzied assault. Following the climax of Harp's vigorous efforts, Jeremy lay on his back while his idol mounted him. Impaling himself on Jeremy's familiar, but still thrilling shaft, Harp spent a rapturous ten or fifteen minutes riding the adoring younger man. After Jeremy registered an intense orgasm inside him, Harp took over the eager exercise Jeremy's fist had been engaged in, and with his head thrown back and his eyes squeezed shut, he brought himself to another explosive and massive ejaculation.

After prolonging his efforts until he had deposited every drop of his emission on his partner, Harp's chin fell to his chest and he let out a great sigh of satisfaction, "God, that was great, Jeremy!"

"You fuckin' covered me with your load!"

Harp smiled and opened his eyes to look down at the evidence of his orgasm on Jeremy's body. Illuminated by the spill of light from the bathroom, he could see his milky offering puddled on Jeremy's stomach, spattered all over his chest, and a gob on his chin just below his broadly smiling mouth. Even his hair showed traces of Harp's copious orgasm. Harp leaned over to kiss Jeremy and lick the semen from his chin, straightened up, and looked out of the window, directly into the eyes of his watching father.

With a loud "Jesus Christ!" Harp leaped up and watched his father turn and walk away from the open window.

"Whatsa matter?" asked Jeremy.

"Shit, Jeremy, my father was watching us!"

"God!" They stared at each other. "What'll we do?"

"Get dressed and get out of here! I don't know what to do!"

In a near panic, Jeremy dressed and left the house by the bedroom window; Harp heard his car starting and leaving as he threw on a T-shirt and some pants. With his hand on the bedroom doorknob, Harp tried to think. What could he do? What could he say? Deciding he had no idea what the answers to those questions were, he nonetheless took a deep breath and entered the living room to face the music. His father stood there alone, Harp uttered only one word, "Dad ... " and ran out of things to say.

Mr. Harper looked at him in stony silence for some time. Finally he said quietly and evenly, "Go to bed, David. I will talk to you in the morning. You will not leave the house until I do, is that clear?" Harp nodded and began to try to say something, but his father held up his hand to forestall him, and turned and went to his bedroom, where, Harp assumed, his mother had already retired.

Sick at heart, Harp stumbled back to his room, closed the door quietly and flopped across the bed, still dressed. His father's use of his middle name, something his parents employed only when angry at him, and the tone he had employed in using it suggested he was furious. But there had been more. While his parents were not unduly strict, nor unduly moralistic, the look he had seen in his father's eyes as he held up his hand to him had suggested both disgust and condemnation. Loathing? Yes, loathing, too.

Harp dozed a few minutes at a time during the night. He was still lying there, staring at the ceiling when his father knocked firmly on his door the next morning. "I will meet you in the front yard in five minutes, David." He heard the footsteps leave his door, and a moment later the sound of the front screen door opening and closing.

He splashed some water on his face and slipped into his shoes. Gathering his strength, he left the bedroom, and as he passed through the living room he saw his mother sitting on the couch, staring at the floor, tears streaming down her face. He stopped, knowing she could see him peripherally, but she neither looked up at him or offered to say anything. Since he could think of nothing whatever to say to her, he turned and went into the front yard. His father was standing there, looking away from the house. He approached and stood behind him. He said nothing, but Harp knew his presence was acknowledged. In a minute his father began to speak quietly, without turning to look at him.

"I do not have a child who could do what I saw last night. I have made your mother understand she doesn't either. I don't have any idea how long you've been doing ... that, but as long as that's what you do ... well, what you are, I guess I should say ... you are not my son. I will not talk about this now, and your mother has promised me she will not either. You're of age now, and can do what you want, but if what you want to do is ... is what I saw you doing, we want nothing to do with you."

"Dad, I...."

"No, David. I'm leaving now, and your mother is coming with me. We'll be back by noon, and I want you gone. If there are things you need, but can't take with you, stack them in the barn and get them some time when I'm not here. If you wish to leave some things here, that's okay. They will still be here if you should come to your senses and change your ways." He turned toward him, and his face was stony, "And if you sincerely do, I will listen to you. But that can't happen for a while. I am too disgusted and ashamed right now."

Harp had absolutely nothing he could say. He was sobbing, anyway, and probably would not have made himself understood if he had been able to formulate a reply.

"I don't know where you will go right now, and I don't want to know. You are not part of this family, at least for a while. Your mother may tell you to keep in touch with her. Do not do that. If you really change your ways sometime, you may call me when you do. I want you off the place by noon."

Sobbing, thunderstruck, totally bereft, Harp stood in the field and watched his father return to the house, where his mother joined him on the porch. Both avoided looking at him as they drove away.

Harp went numbly through the motions of gathering his clothes and possessions together, and putting them in his car. It was clear that there was nowhere to go initially other than Doug's, so it was there he unloaded his meager possessions, making three trips rather than stockpiling anything in the barn. He knew that although Doug was *in absentia* at the moment, he would not mind his moving into *his* house at least temporarily.

For the next day or so, he simply sat around, wondering what to do. He called a very worried Jeremy, who had heard nothing whatever said about the discovery of their sexual relationship and told him he would call him soon. He was safe at Doug's house, he told him, and he would contact him again when he felt he could talk about plans. Even before that, he had called Doug and explained what had happened.

"Are you all right, Harp?"

"I don't know what I am. I'm just here."

Doug changed his immediate plans, amorphous at best, anyway, and returned home the next day. He offered Harp permanent sanctuary in his home—with no obligations, and without sexual favors as payment—for as long as he needed it. For three nights he cradled Harp in his arms, and never once initiated sexual contact with the distraught young man. He encouraged Harp to continue with his plans to attend Farrar that fall. His tuition and fees were already paid for the first semester, and Doug even volunteered to help Harp find a way to pay those fees himself if his parents sought a refund.

By their fourth night together, Harp sought the comfort of sexual liaison with his host, and both were pleased to note that he seemed to bring no baggage of guilt to their reunion. Jeremy and Dodge, neither of whom had heard any talk about his exile from home yet, were soon offered complete updates and welcomed into his new bed in the guest room at Doug's house.

It was his grandfather who proved the greatest immediate comfort, however, when he drove up one morning about a week later, hugged Harp without saying a word, and said simply, "We have to talk, son."

Harp had always found his paternal grandfather a valuable source of friendship, comfort, and extra spending money. Since Harp's grandmother had died a few years earlier, the elder Harper visited the farm far less than he had before. Harp had only marginally concerned himself with any possible reason for this, but since he had always known it was his exuberant grandmother who engineered and directed visits, he thought that mourning the loss of his wife accounted for the increased insularity of his grandfather. Nonetheless, he himself had continued his regular visits to the old man at the house he and his grandmother had shared in Oconee for almost the entire duration of their marriage. Harp was very close to his grandfather, although he sensed his father was not. It was not something he had stopped to think about, and the few tentative questions about it that he posed to his father had been deftly, but rather abruptly turned aside.

Grandfather's sudden appearance at Doug's house was cause for great joy on Harp's part. He had wanted to call him, but had no idea how he would react if he learned of his activities from his father, and he could not know whether or not the silence his parents had apparently been keeping extended even to Gramp.

Following his opening remark, Gramp continued to hold the boy tightly in his arms for a long time, still saying nothing, and patting his back as Harp cried quietly and hugged back fiercely. He took Harp's hand and led him to a bench next to the driveway. "Sit here and let's talk." Harp mopped up, using Gramp's handkerchief, and they sat.

"Gramp, how did you...?"

"Never mind, son. It doesn't matter how I found you. I found you, that's all." Harp never did learn how Gramp had found him, in fact; it didn't matter—he was here for him. "Now tell me what in holy hell this is all about."

"Did Dad tell you what he ... did he say I was ... Gramp! I don't know how to tell you ... I don't know if I can tell you."

"Harp, nobody else'll tell me anything about what happened, or didn't happen. Looks like *if* I'm gonna learn anything, you're the one who's gotta tell me, and I don't know how you're gonna do that, or even if you're gonna do that, but you can tell me, that's for sure, whatever it is. We've always been friends, haven't we?"

Gramp's sympathetic ear had been a source of great comfort to Harp many times over the years, and he had never needed it more than he did then. He decided he could tell Gramp the truth, as long as he kept the details general enough.

"Gramp, Dad caught me ... well, I was doing something with a friend of mine, and Dad caught me, and he threw me out of the house, and Mom wouldn't even talk to me."

"You want to tell me what you were doing with your friend? You don't have to. I can't think of anything you coulda been doing that would shock me, or cause me to love you one tiny bit less than I always have. But you don't need to tell me if you don't feel like you can."

"I don't know how to tell you, Gramp."

"Just tell me if you want, Harp. Of if you don't want, we'll skip that part and just figure out what we're gonna do about this mess."

"I need to tell you, I think; it's just that ... that...."

"Let me maybe make it easier for you. And if I'm completely off here, don't get mad, okay?" Harp nodded his agreement. "Look at me." Harp complied. "Was your friend another boy?" Harp looked away again as he nodded. There was a long pause, and Harp could almost feel his grandfather's steady gaze. "Are you gay, son?"

Completely taken off guard, Harp swerved his head to look into the old man's eyes for a long time before mumbling, "Yes, Gramp, I am ... but ... how did you...."

Gramp put his arm around him. "Never mind, son. Oh, I didn't suspect anything, but the way your father reacted, I ... Look, I'm gonna tell you a long story, and ... oh, Harp, son, if you happen to be gay, that's it, that's all there is to it—you just happen to be gay! I'm not gonna feel any differently toward you than I always have, and I just want you to give me the same respect when I tell you what I think it's time you heard, okay?" Harp nodded, but only by way of saying "go ahead." He didn't understand anything yet.

"I was twenty years old when the Japs bombed Pearl Harbor in 1941, and I joined the Navy right away. The draft was already going on, and I knew if I didn't join up, I'd wind up in the Army, and I always thought the Navy was exciting, or ... glamorous, I guess." He laughed heartily. "Boy, was I wrong! Well, anyway, after boot camp and a little detached training duty, I spent the whole war on a cruiser in the North Atlantic—the old *Amarillo*. I won't go into all my war stories. Hell, you've heard a lot of 'em anyway. But there's just one I've gotta share with you.

"I had a shipmate on the *Amarillo*; he was two years younger than I was. His name was Mark Gordon."

"Mark Gordon! That's dad's name!"

"That's right, Harp. Your dad is Mark Gordon Harper. He was named after my shipmate Mark Gordon."

"How come I've never heard of him then?"

"Let me tell the story, Harp. This isn't easy."

"Sorry, Gramp."

"Well anyway, Mark and I got to be closer than I ever thought I could be with anybody. He was handsome, he was fun to be around, he was a good, good friend. But mostly, I guess, I sorta fell in love with Mark."

"You mean ... fell in love with like ... like really fell in love with?"

"Yeah, Harp, that's what I mean. Now just listen. I loved Mark Gordon more than I ever loved anything in the whole world. We were always together, we did everything together. We got scared shitless together when we thought there was a German U-boat around, or we were under attack by a plane, and we cheered together when we knocked out a German plane or sank a German ship. And we sank three of 'em! But the times that came to mean the most to us both was when we were together with our arms around each other, and kissing each other, and ... well, I guess you know what I'm gonna say now: when we were making love to each other.

"It was hard to find a place on our ship where we could make love, but we managed. And we had some help from other shipmates who were like us, or who understood what we were feeling. Anyway, we found time on ship, and any time we were in port, we went to the nearest hotel and spent the whole time in bed together. This shocking you, Harp?"

"No, Gramp ...no! It's just that...."

"I'm too old a guy to be having sex? And especially to be gay? Well, remember, I was twenty-four and Mark was twenty-two when the war ended. Sex was mighty important to us. As far as being gay is concerned, well, we didn't call it that back then. In fact, we didn't talk about it at all, we just lived it.

"Well, anyway, after the war was over, both Mark and I wanted families. He lived in Kentucky, by the way, Corbin, Kentucky, and we knew that we couldn't very well have it both ways, have kids and be respectable in our home towns, and still be *queer* or be *fairies*. That's what we woulda been called. Be out, I guess you say these days. So we decided we'd only be able to see each other once in a while, but we'd always love each other and ... express that kind of love only when we could be together. We swore we wouldn't share that kind of love with any other man. So I guess you could say we swore to be true to each other, but we'd have wives and families to be true to along with it. You following me?" Harp, stunned, nodded his head in wonder.

"So once or twice a year I'd go visiting to Kentucky, and Mark would come down here to visit about as frequently. Our wives knew we were best friends. Hell, your grandma adored Mark, and was happy to name your dad after him! But they thought we got together to fish and tell war stories and bullshit, and they always gave us plenty of slack. We probably spent only ten or twelve days a year together, Harp, but when we were together, we loved each other, and it was a very special, regular part of our lives.

"We were as careful about getting together as we could be, and there was only one time we were caught making love with each other. Can you guess who caught us, Harp". He looked into his grandson's eyes for a long time.

Harp began to see where this was leading. "Dad! Dad caught you, didn't he?"

"That's right, son, he did. Your dad was about your age. No, I guess he was a year or two younger. But anyway, Mark and I thought we had the house to ourselves all afternoon, 'cause your grandma and your dad had left to go shopping over in Greenville. It turned out your dad didn't go at the last minute, and I didn't know about it, and he walked into the guest room where Mark was staying, and he found us together in bed."

"Jesus! What happened, Gramp?"

"That's just it. Nothing happened. He took it all in, turned around, and walked out and left the house. I got dressed right away, and tried to find him to see if there was some way I could ... I don't know, I couldn't have made him understand, of course, but I thought maybe I could ... well, anyway, I couldn't find him. And when he showed up for supper that night, he never said anything. He was kinda cool, but he didn't really act rude, or say anything at all about what he'd seen. For a long time I tried somehow to talk to him about it, and try to explain, but he always acted as if it hadn't happened, as if he hadn't seen anything. But I saw his face that afternoon in the bedroom. I know he saw everything. He didn't seem to be mad at Mark, he didn't start to want to be called a different name, he didn't get all strange when I'd go to visit Mark in Kentucky, or when Mark came back here. It was as if it hadn't happened. But it did happen, Harp, and I don't know what you and your friend were doing when your dad caught you...."

"Gramp, I just can't tell you!"

"I don't wanna know, Harp. But you were making love, weren't you? You weren't hurting each other, or you weren't making each other do something he didn't want to, were you"

"No we weren't, Gramp. I know Dad didn't see it that way, but Jeremy and I were, well, making love."

"Jeremy? Is he a nice boy?"

"He's a real nice guy, Gramp, but ... well, we were just enjoying ourselves."

"Fair enough. Anyway, whatever you and Jeremy were doing together, I think when your dad saw you, he just ... what's the word you use these days?"

"He freaked, Gramp."

The older man chuckled. "Right, he freaked. He over-reacted, probably. But son, I guess he had reason to, and I guess what I'm saying is that's it's maybe my fault. After all these years, you're paying for my indiscretion over twenty years ago."

"Gramp, it's not your fault at all. It's my fault!"

"Harp, it's nobody's fault. It happened, and I'm sorrier than I can say. I don't know if your dad will come around or not, but whether he does or whether he doesn't, I want you to bear a couple of things in mind. First off, it's nobody's fault. You've just gotta deal with the situation, whatever it is, and move on, and put it behind you. You're smart, you're independent, you're tough, I think; you can do it. Second, I want you to know that I'm here for you all the way, and that I 'm gonna do for you whatever I can. I kinda suspected something like this had happened. Oh, I didn't have any reason to suspect you were gay, son, but ... hell, I know what gay is. I've been gay all my life, and ... well, let's just say it didn't surprise me, but it could've come as a helluva shock to anyone who wasn't gay himself. You follow me?" Harp nodded.

"Anyway, I knew that if I was right, I had to tell you my story. I've never told anyone else, but I hoped it might make things a little easier for you."

Harp grinned and hugged his grandfather. "It does, Gramp. Thanks! So, did you and Grandma ever ... well, talk about you and ... Mark Gordon?"

"No, we never did. Mark died before he was sixty, back in '82, almost the same time as his wife. I loved him, Harp, but I loved your grandmother too," he chuckled, "and except for having a life-long love affair with a man, I was faithful to her all those years. She died knowin' I loved her all that time, but I think she knew I was in love with Mark all those years, too. But she knew it didn't take away from my love for her and your dad, or from my duties as a husband and a father. Your grandmother was a wonderful woman."

"She sure was, Gramp, and you know what? She married a wonderful man!"

Too moved to speak for a while, they sat there until Gramp was able to finish what he had to say. "So, son, I don't know if your Dad will come around or not. He may not, remembering how he dealt with finding me and Mark. And your mother's gonna do what he says, we both know that. But if he doesn't, just try to understand. He loves you, but ... well, I think that's an area he just can't deal with. But you and I have to deal with it. So, here's the scoop: I want you to stay in college, and I'm gonna take care of the bills until you can take care of yourself. And I'm not even gonna consider taking 'no' for an answer. If you want to live in a dorm or an apartment ... what do you want to do about that? This Dr. Truax who owns this house ... are you ... or is he ... "

"He's gay, Gramp, and we mess around, but we're not serious about anything. He's a really nice guy. He wants me to stay here in the guest room as long as I want. He even says I can live here if I want— no strings attached."

"You reckon he means it? I dunno. If I was his age, and I wasn't your grandpa ... "

"Gramp. Please!" They both laughed. "Doug's fine. I'll be fine, and I know you wouldn't offer to see me through if you didn't want to, so okay, I'll take you up on it. I'll stay here with Doug for the time being, and classes will be starting soon, and I've got the car you gave me. I'll be fine. Thanks Gramp, you are the very best! But Gramp, promise me one thing?"

"Sure, son, anything."

"If you have problems with boyfriends, you won't share them with me!"

Gramp laughed and tousled Harp's hair. "Not very likely at this point! But if you have boyfriend problems, I'll be there if you want to talk. I know I'm an old fart, and all that, but I hope after this you'll realize I just might understand. I might not have any answers, but I can listen, and I'm sure you know I love you. And that's the most important thing of all!"

It looked as though Harp's parents never would come

around. Although he repeatedly took tentative steps to effect a reconciliation, they remained adamant, but with his grandfather's unflagging support and understanding, he got on with his life. So close-mouthed were his parents, in fact, that few people realized there had been a rift.

He decided to accept Doug's offer of residency at the lake house, and they quickly became confidants and friends, roommates who shared household duties, and regularly shared each other's beds. On many occasions, given the proper mood and mutually desirable prospects, they also exchanged and shared bed partners.

Jeremy was a constant visitor, often joining Harp in his bedroom for love-making, often visiting Doug's room for the same purpose. More often than not, however, when it was only Harp, Doug, and Jeremy in the house, they wound up in Doug's big bed as a very compatible and extremely passionate threesome. Harp probably enjoyed this three-way arrangement more than the others, because both Doug and Jeremy were so completely captivated, thrilled, enamored (what you will) by the utter perfection of his matchless ass, and so constantly stimulated by it, that they unrelentingly provided the kind of attention, service, worship to it that he more and more enjoyed. Any time the three of them were together, Harp knew he was going to be screwed in sequence by both Doug and Jeremy at least once apiece (more often than not at least twice). He found that especially satisfying. Harp was still a very powerful and dedicated top, but he was becoming an absolutely consummate bottom, and given his dedication and expertise in the bottom role, along with the physical magnificence of the receptacle he provided anyone who topped him, everyone whom Harp admitted to his bed was privileged, delighted, thrilled (again, what you will) to fuck the handsome, appreciative young stud.

Both Dodge and Eddie Williams were due to go off to school in the fall: Dodge to Florida State, and Eddie to Clemson. Before leaving they both visited the lake house often. While Dodge enjoyed several lengthy and rewarding private sessions with Harp, sessions with Eddie were anything but private. Harp had told Jeremy of his seduction of Eddie after he had deduced that Jeremy and he had had been screwing around. Jeremy was not afraid, therefore, to suggest to Eddie one evening that he come with him out to the lake house for a threesome with Harp. Eddie was eager, Harp was agreeable, and Doug was on hand as an unplanned, but very active participant in the first of several extremely active foursomes which left Eddie's seemingly insatiable thirst for the bottom role almost slaked. Harp managed to get himself slaked a lot as well. Fortunately, Doug proved as potent and indefatigable in those sessions as the young, unbelievably masterful Jeremy; both rose to the occasion as often as any of the participants could have wanted.

3.

Once classes began in the fall, the sexual activity around the lake house slackened, but only marginally. Both Doug and Harp were busy, but Jeremy still visited frequently, and the three of them continued their sex play together. Almost any night that neither Doug nor Harp had a 'trick' in his bed, they slept together and made love as though they were dedicated lovers. But there was an ample supply of others: some Harp met or picked up, some Doug found or were revisiting his bed; some they shared, some were either reticent about being part of a three-way or (as was the case on a number of occasions) who were so stricken with Harp's beauty and his matchless ass that they didn't want to leave his arms; some were not interesting enough to schedule another visit with, but a few were either so well built, so good in bed, so handsome, or (best of all) so hung that repeat encounters were sought and frequently arranged.

Through it all, Harp enjoyed himself enormously, but didn't come close to falling in love with any of his sex partners, although any number of them were clearly ready to admit they loved him. He did love Doug, he did love Jeremy; he was not in love with either of them however. He felt sure that Jeremy was in love with him, but he quietly discouraged any declaration to that effect, as he had to do with a more obviously smitten Dodge almost every time he joined him in bed during week-end or holiday visits.

Harp did not prove to be a particularly good college student. Perhaps he lacked motive or direction, perhaps he was too taken up with his unusually active, but quite satisfying, love life, but most likely he simply was not of the intellectual bent that leads to clear success in higher education. He had a good mind, but he was not a scholar. He had, for all practical purposes, coasted through high school on his good looks and athletic accomplishments. At the end of his freshman year at Farrar his grades were sub-standard, and although Gramp offered to continue paying his expenses, he felt guilty about taking the money, and decided he should at least take a break from school and go to work to support himself in the interim. He began working full time as a waiter at The Steak House, a local restaurant that attracted a clientele from all over the Upstate South Carolina region.

Although his pay as a waiter was not very impressive, his income from tips was quite good. Not only was he a hard worker, but he was also both friendly and handsome, factors that added considerably to his ability to inspire generous tips. The 'uniform' for The Steak House was white shirt with khaki pants and a short apron. His muscular body and the rotundity of his perfect 'bubble butt' filled out his tight shirt and khaki pants nicely, and added greatly to his appeal for prospective tippers who admired the masculine form.

Doug would accept no money from Harp for rent or household expenses. Since he normally ate his big meal of the day at the restaurant, he had almost no expenses. Dating cost him nothing whatever. Between his regular love-making with Doug and Jeremy, he enjoyed the occasional tryst with a 'one-night-stand'; Eddie was only a few miles down the road at Clemson, so he frequently visited to bed down with Doug and Harp, and, when possible, Jeremy as well. Even Dodge got home from Tallahassee occasionally, and invariably spent most of his time back in town satisfying his craving for love-making with Harp. Jeremy was going off to Richmond, Virginia in the fall to study Art, but his forthcoming absence seemed unlikely to necessitate Harp's seeking partners to take his place, although both he and Doug would miss his dominant mastery in their sex play. If anything, the slim and faintly effeminate Jeremy had grown from the unexpectedly aggressive young man who took Harp's anal cherry to an even more commanding and fairly fierce top. Some lucky guys in Richmond had a real treat in store for them.

So, aside from incidentals and automobile expenses, Harp spent almost no money, and found he was soon building up a rather impressive figure in his savings account. He began to supplement this legitimate income in a way he had never envisioned, and on a scope he would not have dreamed possible.

One night after he had been working at The Steak House for a couple of months, he became aware that a man sitting alone at one of his tables was very clearly 'checking out' his ass and flirting with him, often calling him by name (Harp had, of course, introduced himself as "your waiter tonight"). The man was probably in his forties, obviously educated and affluent, and even rather attractive. Harp flirted back, to a certain extent, well aware of the effect it might have on his tip.

As the customer prepared to leave, and Harp brought his change back to the table, he handed over a twenty-dollar bill as a tip. "I really enjoyed my meal, but I especially enjoyed your service."

"I enjoyed serving you sir, and this really is a generous tip. Thanks!"

"I hope you're not going to get upset about my asking this, Harp, but I'm going to ask anyway. What time do you get off work?"

"I'm usually through a little before ten ... why do you ask?"

"Well ... and again, I hope you aren't offended ... I was just wondering if you'd have a drink with me."

"Well gosh, that's nice of you, but I don't...."

"Just a drink or two in my room. I'm staying here at The Inn, [the attached hotel was generically named like The Steak House] and I sure would like some company for an hour or so."

"I don't know, I...."

The man looked Harp in the eye. "I'd be very generous. Look, you won't be off for an hour or more, think about it. I'm in room 211, and if you decide you'd like to visit, I'll be there. And as I said, I'll be generous, and if you decide you'd be willing to stay for a while longer and share a lot more than just a drink with me, I'll be even more generous. I hope that doesn't offend you, but I think you're a very attractive boy. Do you understand what I'm saying?" He continued to gaze levelly at Harp.

Harp finally found his voice. "I understand, sure. I know what you're saying, but ... I don't know, I ... look, I'll think about it, and I may come down and have a drink with you, okay?"

The man smiled. "Great! And if it's only for a drink, that's fine, and I know I'll enjoy it. But think about the other, too, okay?"

"Yes sir, I will, I promise." The man smiled and left.

During the time before he finished his duties, Harp

determined he would at least share a drink with his customer. He wasn't sure about the other. Even though he did think the man was reasonably attractive, did he want to get into that? Still ... well, he'd see what the man wanted to do, and how it went.

Shortly before ten he knocked on the door of 211, and was eagerly welcomed by the man, whose name turned out to be Joe LaValle. During the course of his first drink, Joe moved ever closer to Harp, resting his hand frequently on his leg. No sooner had he accepted the second drink than the hand moved slyly up to his crotch, where it brushed against a now-erect organ of such unexpectedly pleasing dimension that Joe abandoned all attempts at subtlety. He began to stroke Harp's cock. Harp sat back, spread his legs, and allowed the manual admiration to continue.

Within a few minutes, Joe had convinced Harp to strip, and it was hard to decide which thrilled and excited him more: the splendor of Harp's huge rock-hard cock, or his perfectly glorious ass. He decided to be fair and he paid as much attention to one as to the other.

Harp was pleased to note when Joe stripped that he had a good body, and was very well-endowed himself. He might not have been someone Harp actively sought out as a possible sex partner, but he certainly did not turn him off! Still, Harp was not required, apparently was not expected, to return the passionate attentions Joe turned to him.

Joe feasted on Harp's cock. Harp found him to be a very talented, even virtuosic cocksucker. Joe also enjoyed fondling Harp's balls and kissing his ass. He was sufficiently artful that Harp's erection never flagged, and he shot one enormous load all over Joe's face a split second after he withdrew from his worshipping mouth, and another on his own stomach while he lay on his back, legs resting on a crouching Joe's shoulders as the older man masturbated him and plumbed the depths of his ass with a very talented tongue! Returning Harp's still very hard, dripping cock to his mouth, Joe re-commenced his sucking while he brought himself to an explosive discharge of his own.

When Harp left Joe's room, he had one hundred dollars more than he had when he entered it, and had agreed to engage in another encounter with Joe next time he was in town. Harp was surprised to find that he had actually enjoyed the occasion, and thought he would probably bring a greater degree of personal interest to a return engagement.

Within a week, Joe was back; he worshipped Harp in the same way. He was back a week or so later, and things escalated. Within three months, Harp was seeing Joe at least weekly, and they were engaged in fully reciprocal, extremely satisfying sex. The first time Harp had both screwed Joe and returned the oral favors Joe so splendidly bestowed, his 'fee' was voluntarily raised twenty dollars, and every time after Joe finally began screwing Harp, there was a guaranteed $150 to be had, usually accompanied by a generous tip. Joe was a masterful lover, and it was an extremely pleasant way to make money.

By Christmas, and with Harp's consent, Joe had passed the word to a number of his friends, mostly from the Atlanta area, where Joe lived, about the unbelievable talent that was waiting tables at The Steak House. They began making regular pilgrimages to sample it. As far as Harp could tell, going to bed with him seemed to be the principal reason for visiting. Joe was very fond of Harp, and only told friends whom he knew Harp would find reasonably attractive, so that even when Harp began accepting frequent trysts with others at The Inn, it was still fun. So satisfactory were his services that almost all his clients tipped him well. They were by now clients, no longer just customers he waited on at The Steak House. He arranged meetings completely apart from his work as well, and was soon 'servicing' four, and sometimes five, clients every week.

Harp found that many men were perfectly content to merely fondle him and watch him masturbate. A few simply wanted him to strip for them and tease them with his body. Most wanted to suck him off, and practically all devoted a considerable amount of time to worshipping his peerless ass. For those who wanted to be fucked or sucked, Harp obliged, as he did for those who wanted to fuck him; he did not charge extra for such services. Satisfaction was what he sought to provide his clients. Most were reasonably well built, young, and good-looking, and Harp enjoyed making love with them for the act itself. A few ranged from less attractive to unattractive; these he closed his eyes for, and pretended he was having sex with Doug, or Dodge, or Jeremy. A few of his clients were quite attractive, and four or five had endowments of sufficient size, and they employed them with enough skill, that Harp not only enjoyed them without having to resort to fantasy, but looked forward to repeat sessions with them. For the most part, sex with his clients was strictly business, but often business mixed with considerable fun and gratification.

Only one strange incident marked Harp's first season as an escort. He had accepted a telephone appointment to meet a prospective client at a hotel one evening, and when he appeared the client introduced himself as Rudy. Rudy was probably in his early forties, reasonably handsome and trim; Harp's initial reaction was positive. The door to the adjoining room was standing open.

Rudy explained that what he wanted was for Harp to make love to his son in the adjoining room, while he sat and watched without actually participating. Harp expressed uneasiness at the proposed arrangement, but Rudy promised to add a very generous tip to Harp's fee. He added that if Harp found his son unattractive, or his own observation of their sex acts unnerving, he would still pay Harp's fee without requiring consummation of the arrangements. Harp agreed that it seemed reasonable, and they went into the adjoining room together.

A young blond boy sat on the edge of the bed. He was rather thin, but very attractive facially—almost pretty. The boy stood, and Rudy introduced him to Harp as Don Williamson, adding, "He's eighteen. It's okay."

While he shook hands with the boy and exchanged the usual pleasantries, Harp observed a high degree of effeminacy in him that he normally would have found disconcerting. But given Don's good looks, and the extremely seductive way he looked Harp over while fondling a well-filled and promising crotch, Harp thought the sex could prove to be very rewarding on more than just the monetary level. After all, Jeremy was somewhat effeminate also, but he was still one of the hottest and most satisfying buttfuckers Harp had ever encountered.

During the many threesomes Harp had with Doug, he had

often fucked someone else while Doug watched, and vice-versa. He felt sure Rudy's presence as an audience-of-one would not be a problem. He grinned at Rudy and said, "Looks like fun!" He gave Don a quick kiss and began to undo his belt. As he knelt and dragged Don's pants and shorts down he said, "Let's see what you've got for me here."

Don's cock sprang up as soon as it was released—thin, but lengthy, and throbbing in full erection. Harp looked up at Don and smiled, "This looks decidedly good enough to eat!" Don seized Harp's head and drove his cock deep into the welcoming hot mouth. Effeminate he might be, but this was a boy who knew what he wanted, and was not shy about going after it! Harp reached behind Don to fondle his soft and undulating ass while it drove his cock with a ferocity totally at odds with his apparently feminine nature.

Harp heard Don say "Thank you, Dad" just before he raised him to his feet and urged him to remove his clothing.

Harp stripped naked, and Don followed suit. Rudy had placed a chair near the bed, and sat there watching the two boys while they admired each other. By now both were completely naked, and both had raging hard-ons.

Don moaned, "My God, you're beautiful!" as he enfolded Harp in his arms and began to kiss and fondle him. After a very thorough manual inspection, Don began to lick and kiss Harp's neck, shoulders, and chest before sinking to his knees to kiss his stomach. He held Harp's cock and balls reverently in his hands while he expressed his admiration, and proceeded to lick and suck them with equal devotion. His reverence soon turned to fierce hunger as he deep-throated every bit of Harp's cock and drove his lips all the way up and down its shaft. It was clear to Harp that the youngster kneeling before him was an accomplished cocksucker.

Looking down at Don feasting on his prick, Harp was surprised to see him hold out his hand toward Rudy. Rudy leaned forward and held it in his own while his son continued to nurse eagerly. It seemed to Harp as if Don was somehow *sharing* the experience with his father. Without Harp having observed it, Rudy had also stripped off his clothes, and now sat there naked, stroking his erect cock.

Using his hands to turn Harp's body around, Don expressed

awe at the wonder of Harp's ass, which he kissed and licked, and then invaded with his busy tongue. Eventually, Don stood and led Harp to the bed, where they fell together in "69." Harp knelt over Don, sucking his cock, and Don alternated sucking Harp's cock and eating his ass with equal enthusiasm.

Rudy had moved his chair until he now sat right next to the bed. Don frequently held out his hand for his father to take. It seemed to be a gesture to offer him vicarious participation in the sex play.

After an extended period of rolling on the bed as they double-sucked, Don reversed his body and held Harp in his arms while they kissed with as much eagerness as they had brought to their sucking.

Don whispered in Harp's ear, "Please fuck me!" Harp began to get up to get the lubricant and packet of condoms he carried in the beach bag he took with him to assignations. He had only put one foot on the floor when Rudy held out a condom and a lubricant dispenser to him. *Service with a leer!*

Harp stood next to the bed and rolled the condom onto his cock, while Don moved to the side of the bed and knelt on all fours, with his toes hanging off the side. Harp applied lubricant to his own cock, then squirted it generously on Don's asshole; he worked it in, using his finger to 'test the waters.' Don groaned and urged him, "Give me that big prick! Fuck me hard!"

As Harp stood next to the bed and poised his cock for tentative penetration, Don drove his body backward and impaled himself with one violent thrust and a near-scream, "Give it to me, Harp!"

Harp fucked with all the rapacity the boy's delirious hunger invited. The head of his cock almost emerged from its sanctuary each time he drew back, while at the same time Don's ass gripped his entire prick tightly and pulled on it as he propelled his body forward. Harp's balls slapped audibly against Don's ass each time he drove himself in to meet the fierce backward shoves that greeted his thrusts—all accompanied by gasps of appreciation and hoarse exhortations to fuck harder and faster. It seemed only polite to accede to his partner's wishes, so Harp held Don's waist tightly and fucked as hard and as deep as he could. At the same time, Don often reached out to communicate and share his excitement with his father, who continued to stroke his own cock excitedly.

Nearing orgasm, Harp paused for a moment to ask Don if he was ready for him to blow his load. "No, please! Not unless you can keep fucking me after you do," Don answered. Harp considered that although he would probably have no trouble in continuing to fuck after a climax, he was in ho hurry to bring this encounter to a close—this kid was a great fuck! So they disengaged and rested for a moment, with Don on his back and Harp lying on top of him sharing kisses.

They kissed tenderly at first, but gradually they began to grind their cocks together, and their asses began to undulate. Both boys heard Rudy emit a gasp, and they looked over to see him leaning back in the chair, with his eyes squeezed shut and his head thrown back; he clutched his cock as it discharged the evidence of his excitement on his chest and stomach. Apparently Rudy thought their kissing was as exciting as their fucking. The truth was, however, that a more important factor in bringing Rudy to climax was the sight of the undulation and humping of the most sublimely perfect ass he had ever seen. Rudy had good taste.

Soon both Harp and Don were once more fully aroused, and Harp whispered, "I want to fuck you again!" Don spread his legs and lifted them, locking them around Harp's waist as he raised his ass to welcome him back inside. With one quick movement, Harp's prick was again buried in the appreciative boy, and they resumed their interrupted fuck with even greater enthusiasm. Again, their fucking grew in intensity until Harp was pounding Don's ass savagely, burying his prick all the way inside with each plunge, and the fiercely hungry ass was slamming backward to increase the ferocity of their love-making. At the same time, their mouths were locked together, and their tongues intertwined while their kisses paralleled the growing passion of cock and ass.

Although Harp did not yet appear ready to climax, Don cried out, "Get on your back, Harp—let me ride your cock while you get your load!"

Harp quickly withdrew and lay on his back, holding his cock straight up as a target. With no hesitation, Don positioned his ass over that throbbing target and sat down heavily while Harp began humping upward. After bouncing up and down as far as he could, uttering moans of ecstasy all the while, Don moved his feet forward, and leaned his body backward. With his feet and hands, planted solidly on the bed, the boy used them for leverage while he continued his frantic ride. As he did so, his entire body rode up and down the considerable length of Harp's thrilling shaft, and his long cock bobbed and swayed in a wide arc. In only a minute or two, and without touching his cock, Don's copious orgasm began. His cum was flung widely as it erupted from his wildly bobbing prick in eight or ten generous spurts. He continued his eager ride long after his load had been expended. He re-positioned himself so he could kiss Harp and lick his own semen from his face, without abandoning the thrill of the large cock which continued its rapacious invasion of his ass.

Harp began humping wildly as he panted, "I'm about to come, Don!"

Don quickly dismounted and flopped on his back as he said, "Shoot your load on my face!"

Harp seized his cock and began to masturbate furiously as he knelt over Don's chest. In just a moment, he began his orgasm, which he directed at Don's face generally. Don opened his mouth wide and managed to take most of the hot white fluid inside, and before Harp's cock had spent itself, he raised his head to take the erupting shaft inside, and suck the last drops from it.

Harp fell heavily over Don's face. Don continued to nurse on the beautiful prick which had fed him so amply, and at the same time his hands reverently fondled the succulent globes of Harp's ass.

When Don finally had to come up for air, he and Harp lay next to each other while they kissed and embraced tenderly. Don turned to face Rudy, and held out a hand to him. As Rudy took the offered hand, Don said, "God, Dad, that was incredible!"

Rudy's eager masturbation had resumed, and he panted a fervent reply to his son, just as he reached another orgasm, "He's the hottest ever, Don!" With his hand still clutching Don's, and his cock discharging its load, he managed to gasp "God, Harp, what a gorgeous ass, and what an incredible fuck!

You boys are absolutely perfect together!"

All three calmed down, and Harp excused himself to go pee. When he returned, Rudy had put his pants back on, and he motioned for Harp to follow him into the adjoining bedroom.

"You're a beautiful boy, Harp, and I've never seen anything quite as marvelous as your ass while you were fucking Don. How I wish I could fuck you!"

"Rudy, I'd be glad for you to . . . "

Rudy put his hand over Harp's mouth as he replied. "No, you're my special treat for Don tonight. Maybe another time." He took out his wallet. "You quoted $150, here's twice your fee. Stay with Don for a while if you will. I know he'd like for you to fuck him again, if you can, and I'm pretty sure he'd be anxious to fuck you if that's agreeable." Harp began to speak. "No, that's up to you—just stay with him a while longer and do whatever you both want to. You were about to offer to let me fuck you, so I guess you'd be willing to let Don fuck you. Believe me, he's very, very good at it!" He kissed Harp lightly. "Go to him."

"Okay, Rudy, but I don't understand what . . . "

"Maybe Don will explain things to you, maybe he won't; that's his decision. Don't just fuck with him, though, Harp, *make love* with him. Okay?"

Harp smiled. "You got it, Rudy. Another time, maybe?"

"Sure, Harp," Rudy said, and he closed the door behind Harp as he returned to the other bedroom.

Don was sitting on the bed, still naked, propped up against the headboard. "Hi!"

Harp climbed on the bed and lay down on it, opening his arms to welcome Don back in his embrace. He kissed the end of Don's nose, and returned his greeting, leading to an extended period of mutual caressing and kissing of the most tender and affectionate variety. At one point he looked down and observed that the sweet blond boy was quietly crying.

"What's the matter?"

Don laughed nervously, and swiped the back of his hand over his eyes. "It's nothin'. It's just that you're so beautiful and so wonderful, and so . . . so sweet! I'm really happy, Harp."

"I'm glad you're happy, Don. I'm happy too, you know. I really enjoyed making love to you. You're . . . I don't know, so

. . . "

"Such a good fuck?" Don giggled.

"I was gonna say you're so sweet too, but yeah, I'd also have to say you're a great fuck! Any guy would be lucky to fuck you—or to get fucked by you," Harp replied.

"You wanna try your luck again?" Don asked as he smiled.

"Oh yeah!" Harp grinned, and reached down to hold Don's cock in his hands. "I'd love to feel this big long dick of yours all the way up my butt—almost as much as I want to feel your hot butt squeezing mine tight again."

The kiss that Don gave Harp was passionate. "Thank you! God, that's what I was hopin' you were gonna say. Dad's always so . . . he's such a wonderful man, I just wish he'd let me show him how great I think he is."

Voicing a suspicion which had been growing steadily in his mind, Harp said, "Don, you don't need to tell me anything—I mean, I know it's none of my business, but . . . Rudy's not really your father, is he?"

Don smiled and answered, "No he's not, but he's so much better to me than my real father was. It's a long story, but if you want, I'd be glad to tell you why he was sittin' there watchin' you fuck me while he beat off."

Harp sat up, propped his back against the headboard while he cradled the boy in his arms, and said, "I'd like to know, really."

"Okay, it'll take a while, but hell, we can both be restin' up so we can work up another big load to give each other." He grinned up at Harp. "Okay?"

Harp kissed him. "Sounds perfect! Tell me about it. But be sure you're working on building up that load at the same time."

Don began his story.

"My real dad was a mean, drunk, redneck sonofabitch, and I hated him as far back as I can remember. He was always gettin' drunk and beatin' up on my two brothers; Tim is two years older'n me, and Andy's one year older. The three of us slept in the same bedroom, and I always had to watch while be slapped 'em around. He never hit me, 'cause he always said I was like a little girl, and he didn't hit girls.

"And it was true—I did act like a girl. I dunno why, I've

always been like that. Anyway, he didn't hit me, and he never hit Mom either, but he was mean as hell to her. He took his real meanness out on Andy and Tim.

"Mom died two years ago, by the way, when I was fifteen, so I'm only seventeen, not eighteen like Dad told you. When I say 'Dad' I mean Rudy, of course—he's a real dad to me. We always called my real father 'the old man,' except to his face; he made us call him 'Daddy' then.

"Anyway, after my Mom died, the old man got even meaner, and was drunk even more, too. One night he came home quiet for once, so we didn't hear him, and he came into our bedroom and found me kneelin' on my bed with Tim fuckin' me up the ass while I was suckin' Andy's cock. He went ballistic, and really beat up on 'em, and told me I was a little faggot whore. Then he stumbled into his bedroom and passed out.

"Tim and Andy and I had been suckin' each other off as long as I could remember. Hell, we didn't have much else to play with! I started swallowin' their loads long before I shot my wad the first time. In fact, Andy and I were actually suckin' each other's cocks right at the very moment I got my first load; Andy got so excited he blew his load down my throat while he was drinkin' mine. I musta started eatin' their loads before I was twelve! But we didn't fuck each other, even though we tried a lot, until Tim fucked one of his buddies at school. I was about fourteen by then, and Tim found he liked fuckin' butt so much, he kept after Andy and me until finally I took him up my ass, and I just flat-out loved it once I got over the pain. Tim wouldn't even let us try to fuck him; he probably drank about five gallons of mine and Andy's come, but I still think he's straight. Andy never did let Tim fuck him, though. Tim's got a really huge cock, and Andy couldn't take it—but it felt great to me. Every once in a while, when Tim wasn't around, Andy'd let me fuck him. And I really loved screwin' him, too, but I knew I liked him screwin' me even more. Tim's big ol' prick was the best, though. So anyway, when the old man walked in on us with both of their cocks inside me, it wasn't anything new—just the first time we got caught.

"The very next night the old man came in drunk, and ran Tim and Andy out of our room. We woulda locked the door, but he never let us have a lock on it! He took his clothes off and started callin' me a 'faggot whore' again, and stuff like that, and then he threw me down on the bed and said he was gonna show me what it felt like to get fucked by a real man, not a couple o' kids. He made me show him where we kept the Vaseline, and he greased me up and fucked the hell out of me. Tim's cock is a lot bigger, but the old man's hurt a lot more—he was so fuckin' drunk and so fuckin' rough, I could hardly stand it. He shot his load in me and staggered out.

"When Tim and Andy came back and found out what happened, they were ready to go kill him, but we cooked up a plan instead. We figured the old man'd be back to fuck me again some night soon, so Tim borrowed a flash camera and hid it in the living room. A couple o' nights later, the old man staggered in wearin' just his socks, and wavin' his dick and shoutin' for Andy and Tim to get out. They left, and he started fuckin' me again, and just about the time he was ready to come, Tim threw the door open and took a picture with the flash camera, and started runnin' like hell.

"The old man jumped up, and started runnin' after Tim, naked. Well, he still had his socks on, but that made him look even more naked. As soon as they were gone, Andy came in and I got dressed right away, and we ran off together. The old man was too drunk to catch Tim, and besides he was naked, and drunk as he was he knew he couldn't go runnin' down the street that way. So Tim got to the police station, and we met him there like we'd planned. Tim told the Police Chief, who knew my old man was a piece o' crap, that he'd just taken a picture of our dad fuckin' me, and we wanted protection. The chief took the camera and had one of his people take it over for the picture to be developed that night, while he went out lookin' for the old man.

"They found him in a field, naked and passed out, and arrested him. They charged him with all kinds o' shit, and he went to prison for fifteen years. The judge was real nice to us. She put Tim and Andy with different families, and she sent me to live with Rudy. It seemed kinda strange that Tim and Andy got put with regular families and I went with a man who lived by himself alone, but it turned out that the judge was Rudy's sister, and she and Rudy'd been scared of their old man when they were kids, and he'd done pretty much the same thing to Rudy that my old man did to me. She told me that Rudy knew what I'd been through, and she knew he could never do anything like that to me. And she even said that I'd be good for Rudy!

"I don't know if I've been good for Rudy or not, but he tells me I am. And he's the nicest man I've ever known. He's what a real father oughta be like. After I found out how great he was, I asked if I could call him 'Dad,' and he broke down and cried while he hugged me an' told me there wasn't anything that'd make him feel more honored.

"I knew he was gay—and so did the Judge, for that matter. Hell, he didn't even bother to hide the porn or the gay magazines from me. He said that after all I'd been through, there wasn't much reason I couldn't see 'em too if I wanted, but not to tell anybody about it.

"I got horny as shit seein' all those hot guys in the movies and the magazines, and I was really wantin' to fuck, and suck cock again. I knew it was kinda crazy, but I loved Dad so much, and I was so grateful to him for what he was doin' for me that I finally came right out and asked him to have sex with me, to let me show him how much I loved him. Hell, my real dad fucked me and I hated him. Now I had another dad that wasn't really related to me, and who was gay, and who I loved—why couldn't he fuck me? And I mean fuck me because he loved me, not outa hate like the old man did. I really wanted him to, and . . . hell, you've seen him, he's a hot guy for his age.

"It totally blew his mind; he said he couldn't do that, but I convinced him to try. I could tell watchin' him look at videos that he was really hurtin' for sex with a guy. I asked him why not me? Wasn't I good-lookin' enough? Didn't he know I wanted him to make love with me?

"It took a long time before he came around to my way of thinkin', but one night we tried, and we watched videos together and he got horny as hell, but every time I started to suck his cock, or get him to try and fuck me, he lost his hard-on right away. He told me, 'If you were that guy in the video I'd wanna fuck you, and I'd wanna spend hour after hour suckin' your cock, but you're my son, Don. I can't do that with you.' Then he told me he loved me all the more for havin' tried to give him the most precious thing that anybody'd ever offered. That was his word, 'precious.'

"Then he said that if I wasn't his son, he'd be so hot for me he'd do anything to get me in bed. He said that any guy'd be lucky if he got a chance to make love with me. When I told him I really needed to have sex with somebody pretty soon, he offered to find someone for me.

"About a week later we drove to Atlanta and went to this guy's house. He called himself a model in the magazine, but what he meant was that he was sellin' his ass, and Dad was buyin' it for me. The guy was big, and really cute, and built like a brick shithouse, and he seemed nice, and Dad was gonna leave me there with him for a while, but I convinced him to stay there with us. He sat in the living room while I went into the bedroom with the guy, who pulled off his clothes and showed me where he was really big; hell, his meat hung halfway down to his knees! I'd never had a cock like that up my ass, even though Tim's was mighty big. But it wasn't any problem. He stuck that thing all the way up my butt, and fucked like there was no tomorrow!

"We were havin' a great time when I thought about how miserable Dad must be, sittin' in the next room, and I asked the guy if he minded my askin' Dad to watch us have sex. He said it was fine with him, and I went in and made Dad come in and sit next to us and watch. I told him to pretend the guy makin' love with me was really him, and I'd pretend the same thing. The guy didn't mind, hell he was gonna get paid either way.

"It mighta been a crazy idea, but it worked. Dad enjoyed it as much as I did. He was beatin' off like crazy, and a little while later, right after the guy we were visitin' shot this huge load all over me, Dad blew his own wad all over himself. The guy wanted me to fuck him back, which sounded great to me, but as soon as I rammed my cock up his butt and started fuckin' it, I looked over at Dad, and he'd lost his hard-on. He never wants to watch if I'm fuckin' someone. He's doin' like I said, he's pretending he's the guy I'm screwin' with, and he said he couldn't take a guy up his butt—he had hated gettin' fucked by his father so much that he would never do that again if he could help it. But he knows I like fuckin' butt, and the reason he left us here alone was so I could fuck you, if you want.

"Dad's taken me to see quite a few different guys, whenever one of his friends tells him about one who's really hot, but who's nice as well. A buddy of Dad's from Gainesville told him he'd been over here to see you, and he said you were the best. I gotta admit it, he's right!"

"That's really a wild story, Don," Harp said, "thanks for telling me. It sure explains a lot. And, if I'm not mistaken, I seem to remember you saying just before you started telling it to me that you'd fuck me if I wanted you to."

Don kissed Harp fiercely and said, "Jesus, do I ever want! Your ass is the prettiest thing I've ever seen. Yeah, please let me fuck you!"

Harp smiled and quickly was on his back, his legs spread to welcome Don's invasion. He soon found that the boy was as talented a top as he had been a bottom. His recent orgasm lent a staying power to the fuck Don administered to Harp's ass which was deliriously satisfying. By the time Don blew his load inside the sheath buried deep in Harp's body, he had been fucking steadily, and with a savagery that astonished Harp and completely belied the boy's effeminacy, for over a full half-hour! He continued to fuck with almost undiminished zeal, and without even losing his erection, for another five or ten minutes. Harp was enjoying it enormously, and considered lying there while Don worked up another load to give him, but he could not hold off his own orgasm much longer.

Harp's legs had been locked around Don's waist the entire time he had been thrilling to the boy's precocious mastery. Now he spread them, planted his feet on the bed, and arched his back—and with Don's still-hard cock continuing its work, he began to masturbate. Don took over for him, saying "When you're ready to get your load, let me know."

It took little time before Harp's orgasm loomed. He cried out, "I'm about to come, Don!"

Don immediately pulled out and leaned down to completely engulf Harp's wildly driving cock in his mouth. After only a minute or so of ecstatic sucking, the hot, delicious nectar he craved began to erupt in his throat. Both boys moaned and gasped in excitement while Harp fucked Don's mouth savagely, and delivered a load as copious as his first.

They lay and kissed for some time more, but the hour was by then quite late, and Harp took his leave. Before going he lectured Don about the dangers of ingesting come, and both expressed the hope that circumstances would find them together again soon.

Unfortunately, it was the only time Harp ever saw Don Williamson, but he did get a report on him a few years later, when he was working in Atlanta. Rudy recognized Harp at the Lenox Square shopping mall, and accosted him. He told him that Don was now a student at Georgia Tech, and was doing well. He said he and Don continued to have sex with each other vicariously, but the stand-in for Rudy was now Don's regular boyfriend, a fellow student at Tech who was not only extremely nice, but who was as devoted to Don as even Rudy could desire. He laughed when he told Harp that Don's relationship was monogamous, but that they welcomed his audience while they practiced their monogamy.

By spring, Harp had long since stopped putting money into a savings account. There was far too much of it to be explained to the Internal Revenue Service, so he was depositing it in a safe-deposit box. He especially wanted to avoid accounting. He didn't mind getting fucked by his clients, but getting fucked by the IRS was another matter indeed.

Gramp had made it clear to Harp that he would continue to help him out financially even though he was no longer in school, but Harp, with genuine love and gratitude, had gently refused his help. As the first anniversary of his beginning work at The Steak House came around, Harp was amazed to learn that aside from legitimate money he could justify earning in an audit, he had put more than $21,000 in cash into his safe deposit box.

In spite of the frequency of sex with his clients, Harp continued his activity with Doug, alone or with his 'tricks'. His own 'dates' fell off slightly in number, but he still went to bed with quite a few guys he found attractive. The only marked change following his new 'career' was his limiting masturbation to once or twice a day. Still, Doug began to suspect something was up, and Harp confessed that he had, for all practical purposes, become a prostitute. Doug was not horrified, in fact he was not even judgmental, but he did make Harp promise to exercise great care in practicing safer sex with his clients, and he acquainted him with the term *escort*.

"You're escorting clients. If you were a prostitute, you'd be fucking tricks!"

Harp laughed, "Well, we couldn't have that, could we?"

In the fall of '93, two years into Harp's new lucrative career Doug came home following the first day of classes. He was raving about a student enrolled in one of his sections of Junior-level Spanish. According to Doug, this student, Steven H. Rommel, was probably the most attractive man he had ever encountered in any of his classes: blond, tall, very muscular, friendly, charming, and handsome.

Once before, only a year or so earlier, Doug had raved about the beauty of one of his students. In fact, the description of Rommel at first blush seemed almost to fit the one Doug had tendered a year ago. Doug had been so excited about the earlier blond hunk, Til Mayer, that he found an excuse to get him out to the lake house for Harp to meet. Doug avoided sexual relations with any students currently enrolled in his classes, but he wanted Harp to 'scout out' this one for possible action as soon as final grades went in.

Til was very attractive, but it had been Harp's initial impression that he was straight. Nonetheless, Doug had purposely left the house, allegedly on an errand, leaving Harp and Til alone. After he excused himself to go to the bathroom, Til returned, stark naked, and with his cock erect.

"I figured this might look good to you guys."

In fact, it looked extremely good to Harp. The fat seven-plus inches of smooth, nicely circumcised meat standing straight out from Til's muscular body looked very good indeed, but Harp played his cards fairly close to his chest. "Well, you've got a great body and a nice big cock, but why do you think that either Doug or I would be interested?"

Til leered as he approached the seated Harp, stroking the shaft of his delicious cock, "C'mon, I'm not stupid. Two guys livin' alone like this, both really good-lookin' guys, askin' me out here. I know what you want!" He stepped in front of Harp, the mushroom head of his throbbing cock only inches from his mouth. "This looks good to you, don't it? C'mon, check it out!"

And it did look good to Harp, and as Til took the back of his head in his hand and pulled it inward, he opened his mouth and accepted the offering. As Harp fondled Til's balls and savored the delicious mouthful, Til drove himself deep into his throat with savage thrusts for some time, but then unceremoniously pulled out and led Harp to the bedroom, where he flopped on his back and smirked, "Make love to this big cock!" As Harp stripped off his clothes, knelt over the supine Til, and again began to suck and lick the exciting shaft, Til purred, "Yeah, suck me off!" and moaned encouragement to Harp in ever-increasing passion as his thrusts grew faster and deeper. Holding Harp's hair tightly in both hands and forcing his head up and down the lengthy shaft, Til was fucking his mouth with real ferocity and obviously nearing orgasm. Harp barely managed to pull his head away before Til's massive emission spattered them both with his violent discharge.

Even as he panted in the throes of ejaculation, Til almost shouted to Harp, "Tell your roommate how good this is. He's gonna want it too!" Harp was deeply offended by Til, but nonetheless the extreme passion of the moment was exciting, and with his face dripping with Til's come, he masturbated and deposited his own on the latter's chest.

Til grinned up at him. "Man, that's hot! I'll bet your roommate's gonna fuckin' love eatin' my dick!" He began to caress Harp's ass. "You like to get fucked? Why don't you siddown on my big cock and ride it, and let me show you what else I can do for your roommate!" He scooped Harp's emission from his chest and used it to lubricate his own, still magnificently erect cock. "C'mon, ride this baby!"

Til's cock looked tempting, and Harp was almost aching to mount it, but horny or not, he was by now thoroughly turned off by Til's attitude, and managed to escape his further attentions, saying after he came he was no good for sex for the rest of the day. Still lying below him, Til began to masturbate violently. "Just watch this!" Soon another series of spurts shot upward as Til groaned, "Oh, yeah! Tell your roommate I can give him a lot more than just one load!"

As they were dressing, Til dropped to his knees and took Harp's cock in his hand and almost kissed it. He grinned lewdly up at Harp, "Tell him for a really good grade, I can get real cooperative." He stroked the firmness of Harp's cock and watched it grow. "Too bad you're not the one givin' out grades. I could do somethin' with this baby!" Til shrugged, released Harp's cock and stood to dress.

When Til prepared to leave, after Doug had returned, he winked at Doug as he went out the door, saying. "See you in class, professor, but Harp here can tell you I do my best work outside of class!"

Doug turned to Harp after Til drove away. "Well?"

"Doug, if you have that asshole out here again, just be sure I'm not here, and don't tell me about it, okay?"

Til kept coming on to Doug for several weeks without result, but dropped the class before mid-term, with a test average far below that of the second-worst student in his class! He was not heard from again.

There had, actually, been another 'prospect' Doug had wanted him to check out—not blond, but handsome as the very devil. This one had completely resisted Harp's blandishments; if he was gay, or even agreeable to gay sex, he was impervious to Harp's charm. Given both Harp's physical magnificence and his considerable charm, only the most devoutly heterosexual could have resisted. Harp's report on that one had been "Forget it!"

Now, Doug told Harp he had asked his new muscular blond Adonis, Steve Rommel out to the house for a beer, and again wanted Harp to scout the territory for possible invasion. Harp earnestly hoped he was not going to prove to be another Til.

Steve Rommel turned out to be anything but another Til Mayer, in spite of certain surface physical resemblances. Like Til, Steve was tall and blond, but he was even taller, a towering six-three, and his blond hair was a golden crown of matchless beauty. He had a winning smile, brilliant white teeth, penetrating green eyes, high cheekbones, and a strong jaw; he was, in short, a stunning man. Harp was soon to learn he had an extremely well-developed, gym-built body, was well tanned (with an extremely sexy tan line, much like his own), and his cock was not only as fat and beautiful as Til's, it was a wonderful inch or more longer.

Til had been physically beautiful, but Steve was even more attractive, and he turned out to be a sweet, thoughtful man as well, no comparison at all to Til in that sense.

The first night, as Harp and Doug visited with Steve, they learned a lot about him, but not yet what they most wanted to know. They learned he was twenty-six, three years older than Harp, and rather old to be a college student. He had spent four years in the Marine Corps as soon as he finished high school, and then enrolled in a junior college in low country South Carolina. After two years he was now transferring to Farrar as a Junior, majoring in Business Administration, but with no clear-cut professional ambitions. They learned he wasn't dating any girl seriously, but further questions about his romantic life were sidestepped.

When Doug left for a time, again on a spurious errand, Steve did not reveal any more of his private life to Harp. They sat next to each other on the couch, and their legs brushed together frequently. In conversation, Harp frequently let his hand casually come to rest on Steve's leg, and was never rebuffed. However, when he began to move his hand up Steve's leg toward his beautifully bulging crotch, Steve moved from the couch and sat on a chair.

Harp thought there was going to be no pay-off with Steve, but when Steve prepared to leave, and bid Doug good night, he asked Harp to walk with him to his car. At the car, Steve asked Harp, "Can I see you again?"

Harp was standing quite close to Steve, but moved in even closer and said quietly, "Do you want to see me again?"

Steve put a hand on Harp's cheek. "God yes! I want to see you again soon!" Harp pressed his body against the tall beauty and looked up at him, without saying a word. Steve bent his head down and kissed Harp very sweetly. "I hope I can see all of you next time."

Harp's hands now held Steve's head. "Can I see all of you?" Their bodies were now pressed tightly together, and Harp could clearly feel that Steve was as fully aroused as he.

Steve reached up and took one of Harp's hands in his own, then guided it to the bulge of his erection. "You can see every inch of me!"

Harp fondled the extremely hard, extremely impressive bulge. "This feels like a lot of inches."

By now Steve's hand had sought Harp's cock. "Jesus, Harp, so does this! Do I get to do more than just see this?"

"You can do anything with it you want."

They spent several minutes kissing and fondling each other passionately before Steve prepared to leave, after exacting a promise from Harp that he would visit him in his dorm room the next afternoon. "I don't think I can wait until night."

"Will your roommate...?"

"No roommate. We'll be alone."

"I can't wait, Steve, why don't you come in now, and we could...."

"No, I'd feel funny, with Doug and all. I'll see you tomorrow."

Deciding neither really wanted to wait even until the next afternoon, they agreed to meet at eleven the next morning, as soon as Steve finished with his classes.

Harp watched Steve drive off, then went into the house. Doug looked at him? "Well?"

"Jesus Christ! I think you found a treasure this time!"

Not since his first experiences with Doug and Dodge, and the night Jeremy had become the first to fuck him had an experience been more exciting and meaningful to Harp than his first sex with Steve the next day in his dorm room. He arrived there promptly at eleven to find it empty, with the door standing open. He went in and sat down. A minute or so later, Steve appeared, fresh from the shower, wearing only a towel around his narrow waist. As appealing as his body had looked the night before in tight polo shirt and shorts, it was even more stunning now. A huge grin broke over his face as he saw Harp sitting there. He closed the door and held out his arms to Harp, who went to him and the two embraced and kissed hungrily.

Coming up for air, Steve whispered in Harp's ear. "I wanted you so bad last night I could hardly sleep. Would you believe I had to jack off twice before I could get you off my mind?"

Harp smiled. "I guess I'm just losing my sex drive, I only jacked off once thinking about you, but I made it last, and I saw your face and body every stroke, and I wanted to be giving that load to you so bad! I was so horny this morning I wanted to jack off again, but I saved it for you instead!"

Steve began to unbutton Harp's shirt. "I hope you've got more than one load for me! I know I've got a lot of 'em for you!"

Harp was soon undressed, and as he dropped his shorts, Steve gasped, "My God! Your cock's huge! And you are so fuckin' beautiful. Jesus, Harp, I'm sorry, but there's no other word. You're beautiful!"

Harp stepped forward, dropped to his knees in front of the blond Adonis and dragged the towel from his waist. The rigid prick that had been tenting the towel sprang up to accept Harp's kiss. It looked enormous even to Harp's practiced eye, and was as beautiful as the man it adorned! "I don't think I've ever seen anyone as beautiful as you!" He looked up at Steve. "Look at you, you're perfect!" He stood and again enfolded him in his arms, "Really, Steve, you're the most beautiful man I've ever seen!"

And it was true. Harp and Doug had frequently marveled over the incomparable beauty and sexiness of the movie star Brad Pitt, and compared the relative merits of exceptionally beautiful porn stars like Ryan Idol, Rex Chandler, Tom Steele, Erik Houston, and the totally incomparable Steve Fox, but here in his arms was a manwhom Harp found every bit as sexy and stunning as any of them.

For some time as they fondled each other and kissed hungrily, they hoarsely exchanged compliments, each claiming the other was the most beautiful in the world. And, based on the perceived dimensions of the two fiercely hard cocks they were grinding into each other, each also claiming the other was better hung.

Which of the two was more beautiful was an insoluble matter, of course. But each was certainly stunningly handsome. Which had the larger cock was easily determined later. As it turned out, they were, for all practical purposes, the same size: nearly eight inches of fat shaft. Almost every one of the hundreds and hundreds of men who were later to watch the two make love to each other thought Harp's cock was a good inch or so longer than even Steve's generous endowment. The discrepancy was easily explained: Steve was approximately seven inches taller than Harp, whose 10% shorter frame made his eight-inch prick look 10% longer in relation to his body height. Both were beautiful, both had big cocks, and they fully appreciated the fact that fortune had smiled on them in bringing them together that day.

If Harp had wondered about Steve's level of sexual experience, any question was put to rest when the latter dropped to his knees, opened his mouth and completely engulfed Harp's big cock in one dive, burying his nose and upper lip in the generous thatch of pubic hair, with his lower lip pressing against the equally generous ball sack. Harp fucked eagerly, and the suction and tongue action Steve supplied made it perfectly clear that this was the mouth of an extremely talented and accomplished cocksucker.

Judging by their grunts and moans of excitement, each was enjoying himself as much as the other, but Harp longed to nurse on Steve's magnificent tool as well, so he withdrew and led him to the bed. They lay together on their sides in 69, and as Harp returned to the sanctuary of Steve's mouth, his own accepted his partner's fat shaft down to its very roots, and their moans of passion increased as they noisily sucked, slurped, and feasted voraciously on each other. They paced themselves carefully, prolonging the rapture as much as they could, but they were so completely hungry for each other that eventually neither could hold off any longer. A split second before ejaculation, Harp pulled from Steve's mouth and exploded a copious load on his adoring partner's face. Only a few seconds later, Steve barely cleared the tight rim of worshipping lips before his own huge orgasm showered Harp.

They lay speechless in utter bliss for several minutes before Steve reversed his body and smiled into Harp's face. He rolled Harp on his back, knelt to straddle him, and with great ceremony scooped the generous deposit of semen from his own face. Still smiling, he reached behind himself and made it clear he was lubricating his ass with Harp's ejaculate. Then he scooped his own semen from Harp's face and reached down to lubricate Harp's still fiercely hard cock. Then he closed his eyes, and with a look of utter bliss, settled down and took Harp inside him.

He rode slowly, dreamily, raising himself to the point where Harp almost slipped out, and settled gently back down as far as he could go. His head was thrown back and Harp thrilled not only at the sensation of this tight, unbelievably hot asshole gripping his prick as Steve fucked himself on it, but at the sight of the matchless beauty of his passenger.

Steve rode for a long time, gradually speeding up as Harp began to thrust upward into him. "God, Harp, I've probably had a thousand different pricks in my hand and in my mouth, and hundreds of them up my butt, but yours is the hardest one I've ever felt!"

Feeling another orgasm impending, Harp said, "Roll on your back and give me a rubber!" Steve dismounted and handed a condom to Harp from the stand next to his bed. He lay on his back and raised and spread his legs. Harp quickly rolled the condom on and drove himself back into the delicious moist grip as Steve's legs rested on his shoulders and he recommenced his deep penetration. The break had delayed his orgasm sufficiently that he was able to fuck savagely for another five minutes, each thrust countered by the exciting backward drive of Steve's undulating ass. With a cry he plunged himself in as far as he could, and erupted inside the condom, as he felt Steve's ass gripping and contracting around him to squeeze out every drop.

He stayed inside Steve as he fell on top of him and they kissed and embraced for a very long time. He raised his head and grinned at the blond, who grinned back, "God damn, I like to get fucked, and you are the best!"

Harp grinned back. "Guess what? I love to get fucked too, and I suspect you're gonna be even better at fucking than I am. You ready to show me?"

Steve took Harp's head in his hands and their lips were next to each other as he said, "Oh yeah, I'm ready to show you. I want to sink into that beautiful ass of your and never come out again!" He kissed him. "Roll on your stomach."

The perfection of the two velvet globes that Harp offered when he did as he was bid took Steve's breath away. He fondled them and his hands played gently and lovingly all over the rounded perfection before he began to worship similarly with his lips and tongue. "I've never seen anything so beautiful in my entire life!" Harp raised his ass as Steve's tongue began to slip into him, and soon he was humping and writhing in ecstasy. Steve's oral virtuosity was obviously not limited to cocksucking! Steve rolled him on his back and raised his legs so that he could bury his entire face in the paradise Harp offered him. The agility of his driving tongue raised Harp to rapture, and when Steve rolled a condom onto himself and prepared to replace his tongue with his cock, Harp was almost sorry to get fucked by his cock, since it meant the end of the most perfect tongue fuck he had ever experienced.

Once Steve's massive cock was in him, and it entered in one endless, inexorable, thrilling thrust, any qualms about cessation of tongue-fucking were lost in the delirious thrill of Steve's equally virtuosic ability as a buttfucker. Countering the deep, brutal thrusts excitedly, Harp enjoyed watching the perfect face wreathed in passion almost as much as he gloried in the rapture of being impaled on the huge cock driven so expertly by this stallion.

Steve paced himself carefully so that he could share the ecstasy of the fuck with Harp for a maximum time. Long before he neared orgasm, be had Harp turn over and kneel on all fours. "I want to look at your fabulous ass while I fuck you!" He continued to plunge deeply and ever more fiercely as Harp began to drive his ass violently backward to meet each thrust. With a fierce cry, Steve wrapped his arms tightly around Harp's waist and his thrusts grew extremely fast and short as he expended himself inside the hot receptacle.

Harp and Steve spent a long time getting acquainted, but never stopped caressing and kissing or enjoying each other's beauty as they talked well into the afternoon.

When Harp asked Steve if he had been exaggerating about the number of cocks he had known ("a thousand different pricks in my hand and in my mouth, and hundreds of them up my butt"), he was astonished to find that it had probably been an accurate assessment, rather than hyperbole.

"Hell, during the four years I was in the Marines, I think I spent more time on my knees than in any other position! If some jarhead didn't have his cock down my throat or up my ass, I probably had mine buried inside his. I don't think a day went by when I was in the Corps that I didn't fuck at least one jarhead or swabbie ass, and have a dick or two up my own, and getting out of the shower without getting or giving a blowjob (or both) was practically unheard of. I can remember times at sea when we'd be lined up to fuck and suck each other! My D.I. got so turned on fuckin' me he liked watching other guys screw me after he loaded me up. One night he made me lie down on a table while he watched nine other boots line up and drill my ass, and he wouldn't let any of 'em stop until they'd come inside of me. And then he finished up by fuckin' me again!"

"Jesus, that must have been terrible!"

Steve smiled, "Well, it was a little scary, but it was fun, too! Except I sure was sore a few times. I'd only been fucked by six or eight different guys before I went in the Corps, but after four years in there I got to where I almost had to have it. After I got out of the Corps and started going to college in Charleston, I used to go down to the Battery at night and let guys pick me up. Usually there wasn't anybody there I really wanted to fuck around with, but I wanted to fuck around with somebody, and there were always guys there willing to give me plenty of money to fuck 'em or suck 'em, or let them fuck or suck me. Shit, I paid my way through school and even saved up a lot of money that way. So, anyway ... yeah, I wasn't exaggerating about the number of cocks I've had in my hand or my mouth or my ass, but I also wasn't exaggerating about yours. I've never felt one as completely hard as yours, and I've had some so big you wouldn't believe it, but never one that felt better inside me than yours. And you are the handsomest guy I know, and your ass really is the most perfect thing I've ever seen. No exaggeration. No bullshit. You know the worst about me. And I don't know why I'm telling you all this. I've never told it all to anyone before, and I sure as hell don't want to scare you away. This has gotta be just the first day for us!"

Harp kissed him. "Only the first out of many, okay?" He laughed. "And all that sure makes it easier for me to tell you what I've been doing the last couple of years."

In fact, the story of his gradual move into escorting might have been embarrassing for Harp to tell had it not been for Steve's admission to selling his own ass as well. Steve was especially interested, since he had hoped to somehow continue making money with sex, but had seen no way it was going to happen in Oconee. In fact, he had found little sexual outlet at all in the few weeks he had been here. Aside from one cute guy who had cruised him in the college library and wound up planted deep up his butt an hour later, and another attractive stud who lived down the hall, and had followed him from the bathroom to his room and had already proved to be an avid top and bottom on three separate occasions, Steve's fist had been getting a lot of exercise.

"When Doug asked me out to his house, I felt sure he was coming on to me, and I was looking forward to it. He's a damned good-looking guy. Are you two ... well, I guess you are, huh?"

Harp laughed. "Oh yeah, Doug and I share a lot of good times. He's really hot for you, too, but he won't do anything as long as you're in his class."

"Shit! That means we can't do anything ... well, I was hoping the three of us might get together."

"I'll work at getting Doug to make an exception. I'll talk to him."

Before Harp left to go to work, he and Steve spent a lot of time cuddling and kissing, talking, and, in spite of the fact that they had just really met, planning. Harp sensed that something fairly involved was going to develop between them; he knew he wanted it to. They also spent a lot of time having sex, but Harp had to limit himself to one more orgasm, as he had a client to see that night after work, but since Steve had no such obligations, he treated Harp to several more generous liquid offerings.

Harp stopped back by Steve's room after his client, and even though it was near midnight, they made love again, and agreed to meet the next afternoon, after Steve's two o'clock chemistry lab.

Their next afternoon together was again ecstatic, and since he had no client that night, Harp picked Steve up right after work and took him out to the lake house. Having been coached by Harp, Doug assured Steve that anything that happened out at the lake house had nothing whatsoever to do with his work or his grade in his Spanish class. By the end of the week, Steve was sleeping with Harp almost every night. By the end of the second week Harp had convinced Doug that Steve could separate his sex life from his school work, and Doug began to join the two lovers in bed from time to time. Shortly after that, Steve moved out of the dormitory and into Harp's bedroom.

Harp knew he could fall in love with Steve easily, and he sensed that Steve could easily fall in love with him as well. Given his work as an escort, he knew that would present difficulties, but he wanted sex and friendship with Steve, close friendship, and lots of sex. He was pleased that Steve took so readily to admitting Doug to their sex play. It seemed to indicate he was not interested in getting serious with Harp.

Another indication that Steve was not interested in getting serious about their relationship was the fact that he asked Harp to help him line up an escorting clientele for himself. Harp felt sure he could get Steve on as a waiter at The Steak House, and he also felt sure he could suggest to several of his regular clients that they might wish to employ Steve's more personal services as well.

By this time, many of Harp's 'dates' had nothing to do with the restaurant at all. He had his own escort telephone line, and most of his regulars called him and arranged trysts that way. He had even begun making trips to Atlanta and other cities in the area to visit clients in their homes. Gramp's old car was still purring along fine, and although he could easily have afforded to drive anything he wanted, he saw no reason to replace his first car just because it was old. He was probably seeing two or three regular clients a week in Oconee, maybe had three or four new clients contact him at the Steak House each month, and was traveling out of town for sex three or four times a month as well. On average, he was probably having sex for money fifteen to twenty times a month, and since he was living off his salary and tips as a waiter, he was putting around four thousand dollars or more into his savings deposit box every month. There was obviously plenty of latitude to work Steve into his escort business. As it turned out, Steve worked into the operation quickly and easily, and in no way distracted from Harp's income.

Steve was readily hired as a waiter at The Steak House, and he was a good worker as well as an absolutely gorgeous addition to the staff. The first time Harp suggested to one of his clients that he might wish to consider Steve instead, the client looked at Steve and suggested Steve *and* Harp join him in his room. That particular client was one who had mostly sucked Harp's cock and had him tease him and pose for him while he masturbated. With Steve added to the mix, the client was satisfied to watch Steve and Harp make love to each other, and basically all they did was let him watch while they did what they normally did together every night when they got home. It was, in fact, the first time anyone paid to watch Harp and Steve have sex together. The client was so thrilled with the exhibition that he promised to return for more of the same, and asked if it were all right if he suggested to some of his friends they might wish to hire the two together also. Harp and Steve were more than happy to agree, of course.

Both Harp and Steve serviced clients individually through the restaurant and, after Steve was established, word of mouth quickly brought them all sorts of dual engagements, in town and out of town. Often they would service a gay couple, fucking each other and swapping partners as well, but the first time they were asked to make love together for a group of gay men to watch they were, understandably, hesitant.

The party in question was in Atlanta, and they would have turned down the offer to "put on a show" for the guests had it not been for the fact that the host was one of Harp's well-established clients, who assured them the entire affair would be low-key and controlled. So they accepted, and a week or so later they spent a memorable hour fucking each other on a makeshift platform in a lavish Atlanta living room in the presence of a dozen or so naked, masturbating men. They were not only extremely well paid for their appearance, they were almost immediately booked for another appearance later that month in Atlanta.

The host for their second party appearance provided a bedroom for them following their show, and it was there that several of the guests visited them following their hour-long fuck show and sampled the matchless talent for themselves. That night Harp and Steve team-fucked several different guests, lay or knelt side-by-side and watched each other get fucked repeatedly, and slept soundly on either side of a contented host who ended the night by sucking both of them off.

An apparent network of well-heeled gay men seeking novelty was activated, and soon Harp and Steve were doing their act two or three times a month, often flying all over the country to do so, usually spending a couple of days in each city they visited to allow time for individual sessions with guests they met at the parties.

The pattern for their appearances became fairly well established after the great financial success of a party they performed for in St. Louis. They would spend an hour embracing, kissing, fucking, and sucking each other, ending with each ejaculating on the other's body or face. They always used condoms when fucking, and might have preferred to come inside each other, but the guests always wanted to see the come fly.

Following their performance, they stayed together in plain view of the party guests and allowed a number of them to fuck either or both of them, usually as many as wanted to, with them personally monitoring the safe-sex status of the participants, and with the host providing additional compensation for each guest who wanted to fuck them. Any guest was free to masturbate and discharge on any of the performers as they fucked or got fucked. Harp or Steve (or both) occasionally fucked a guest or two in the presence of the others, but normally that was reserved for private encounters arranged for in advance. It was not uncommon for each of them to get fucked by six or eight different men at a party, and spend the night and part of another day servicing clients individually or, more frequently, as a duo.

Each party was exhausting physically and sexually, but they rarely returned home with less than three thousand dollars apiece for the effort! Steve seemed to glory in the parties. The more times he got fucked, the happier he was, no doubt fondly remembering his D.I. lining up Marines to gang-fuck him. At first Harp had enjoyed the feverish ecstasy and the unbridled passion of the orgies, but it began to strike him more and more as totally impersonal. The anomaly of considering a series of hard cocks up your ass as impersonal was not wasted on him.

Their frequent absences necessitated a number of changes. Steve had to drop out of school, both had to quit their jobs at The Steak House, and Doug was becoming very unhappy about the living arrangements.

When they weren't servicing clients or fucking each other for an audience, Harp and Steve had become more and more like lovers. Neither sought other sexual partners, although they welcomed Doug into their bed frequently and had sex with Dodge or Eddie or Jeremy when they visited. They especially enjoyed Jeremy's visits: the slim young art student had become more of an accomplished fuckmaster while living in Richmond. Doug still thrilled to sex with both Steve and Harp, of course. How could he not thrill, after all? Two matchlessly handsome, well- built, well-hung sexual virtuosos—what's not to thrill to? But he began to resent Steve's presence in their lives as the catalyst for the deterioration of the closeness to Harp he had known. He actually loved Harp, if truth be told.

Inevitably, the relationship between the three of them dissolved. Each agreed they should seek other arrangements while they were still friends, so they agreed to separate. Since so many of their clients lived in or near Atlanta, and given the vastly simpler travel arrangements which could be made from that city, Harp and Steve rented an apartment in a new complex in the Virginia-Highlands area of Atlanta.

4.

Before the move to Atlanta in the summer of '95, Harp's only real tie to Oconee was broken. Gramp, who had been in good health at seventy-four years of age, and whom Harp had lunch with weekly, was found to have died quietly in his sleep. He had already made his own funeral arrangements, and paid for them. Under the terms of those arrangements, his body was cremated and his ashes divided between two containers—one to be buried in Oconee next to his wife's body, and the other entrusted to Harp to deliver to a funeral plot he had purchased in Kentucky.

There, in a cemetery in Corbin, half of Gramp's ashes were to be interred, adjacent to the resting place of his life-long friend Mark Gordon, identified as such in the funeral documents. The fact that Mark had also been his life-long lover was known only to Harp, but probably suspected by his father as well. The will directed that Harp empty Gramp's house and dispose of all his personal effects in any way he saw fit.

The house itself, once emptied, was willed to Harp's father, but the balance of his surprisingly large estate went to his beloved grandson, along with a quotation from *Hamlet*:

This above all: to thine own self be true,
And it must follow, as the night the day,
Thou canst not then be false to any man.
Farewell: my blessing season this in thee!

While Polonius' advice to Laertes seemed generally appropriate for an older man to tender to his grandson, Harp alone understood the special significance of this message from his grandfather. It probably had considerable impact on his later decision to abandon the increasingly unbridled lust of his relationship with Steve.

Harp understood Gramp's instructions for him to conduct a sort of triage among his effects when, in the process of sorting through them, he encountered a large package of letters from Mark Gordon, addressed to the senior Harper. A note was on top: "Harp: I couldn't bring myself to destroy these, but I ask you to do so by burning them, and adding the ashes that remain to my own before you deliver them to Kentucky. I hope you will be interested enough to read them, and will understand that the deep love for me that Mark shows in these letters was matched by my own for him, which I tried to express in those I wrote him. I pray you will find a love as lasting and real, but that you will be freer to express it than I was ever able to. I doubt your father will ever forgive you for being too much like his own father. Nonetheless, forgive him and get on with your life, which I pray will be a very happy one. I love you, son. Gramp"

There were hundreds of letters. Yet, considering the fact that they spanned fifty years, that was a surprisingly low number. While Harp did not read every word of every letter, he spent almost an entire day, frequently crying, reading enough that he knew the depth of love that his grandfather and the man after whom his father was named had shared for so long. As he burned the letters in the fireplace he knew he wasn't destroying them, but simply preparing them so they could stay with his beloved grandfather forever.

Now driving his newer car, the second his grandfather had given him, Harp completed Gramp's funereal assignment, and on his return from Kentucky loaded up his few possessions and put South Carolina behind him. While his peerless fuck-partner accompanied him, he left behind a considerable balance in his legitimate savings account as well as an astonishing amount of cash in a safe-deposit box.

Harp and Steve settled into their new apartment, signed up with a gym to keep themselves fit, and quickly made new friends in their mostly gay apartment complex. They put separate, individual classified ads in the "Models/Escorts" section of the gay Atlanta weekly *Hotlanta 2-night*, and got separate beeper numbers for clients to use. Their new apartment had two bedrooms, and they used the 'guest room' to service clients on "in calls," but actually preferred the impersonality and efficiency of "out calls," especially to hotels.

As new escorts in town, fresh meat, they took a huge number of calls in their first months, often having to use both their own bedroom and the guest room for simultaneous appointments. Each had stated in his classified ad "second stud available," and they occasionally serviced a client or a gay couple together. Needing *noms de guerre*, they laughingly hit on "Louis" for Harp and "Clark" for Steve, but it was only when they serviced a client together that the "Louis and Clark" joke became apparent (and since those professional names were almost never actually written, it is doubtful that anyone knew they were misspelling Meriwether Lewis' surname) . After a few months, the frequency of their calls decreased, but they still stayed busy and developed a considerable following of 'regulars.'

Their dual specialty act remained popular, but almost always out of town. They continued to use their real names for those appearances. Although they traveled to cities all over the country, and had repeat calls in Chicago, Houston, Miami, Seattle, and especially Minneapolis and San Francisco, more and more they found they were going to the Los Angeles area to fuck each other at parties and for private sessions following. Their services for this were never advertised in print, but word-of-mouth engendered as many such engagements as they wanted, quite a few more than Harp now wanted, although Steve seemed to thrive on the orgy scene. He was never happier, it seemed, than when he had a line of horny men waiting to fuck him.

For almost a year they stayed together, but by the next spring it seemed to Harp like the only time they connected was when one of them had his dick inside the other one. Steve had begun to immerse himself in the Atlanta gay-bar scene, which held little interest for Harp, and more and more he had begun staying all night with clients on out-calls, or having in-call clients sleep over. Harp didn't know what Steve did on his out-calls, but judging by what he heard coming from the guest room during his in-calls he could tell he pretty well fucked non-stop for hours. He was probably giving a lot more than he was getting paid for, in Harp's estimation. In orgy situations at parties, Steve almost seemed out of control with lust at times. While Harp also took cock after cock up his ass or down his throat, he never lost sight of the fact that it was business, no matter how much he might be enjoying it at the moment. Harp did still enjoy it, incidentally, or he would not have been doing it (he didn't really need the money any longer). Although he much preferred one-on-one sex, it was still exciting to be surrounded by a gaggle of hot hard cocks wanting in, and fun to satisfy himself by satisfying the demands of those hot cocks.

Neither Harp nor Steve had ever been much for alcohol, but Steve was now drinking more than before, and he wasn't much fun to be around when he was drunk, or even tipsy (who is, for the sober person?). Although Harp suspected Steve might be involved to some degree with drugs, he never found evidence of it; of course he didn't look for evidence. Steve was his fuck buddy and his partner in sex shows, not his spouse or his moral responsibility. He did not really consider 'poppers' to be drugs, and he was accustomed to the sight of Steve sniffing on a bottle of inhalant and shouting in the suddenly-heightened passion it engendered while he was nearing orgasm or, more usually, taking a particularly satisfying prick up his ass.

At several West Coast parties men who claimed to be movie or television directors or producers had tried to interest Harp and Steve in working with them, especially in pornography. Both had learned enough about the L.A. scene to know that at least 99% of the business propositions made at parties is seduction by bullshit, so they never seriously considered any of it. Only a handful of men they knew to be major names in the industry had ever been with them at any of the parties where they had entertained, and none of those had ever offered them anything but a dick or a butt or a mouth to deal with, or money for services rendered.

Harp was of two minds when Steve told him following a party in West Hollywood in May, 1996, that he had been offered a chance to break into film and television, and was going to re-locate to Los Angeles.

In the first place he was surprised that Steve had believed the impressive, but too-slick agent who had made the offer. The same man had made an offer to Harp also, but had hinted that work in the porn industry might precede 'breaking into' legitimate film work. Harp suspected the same terms had been involved when he spoke with Steve, but he guessed that Steve was probably interested in the porn work also. He himself was probably not interested in making porn movies. He knew it did not pay particularly well, and served mostly to popularize the star as an escort. There apparently are no porn actors—just porn stars. A star could justify higher fees for his clients.

Harp already had as much escorting work as he wanted, and from what he had observed and learned from a few minor porn stars whose 'charms' he had shared at West Coast parties, he didn't think he wanted to be part of the porn scene. He tried to convince Steve to reconsider, and think the plan through more carefully, but Steve had made up his mind.

In the second place, he had to admit to himself that he felt a bit relieved. Steve was incomparably beautiful, he had a fantastic body and a wonderful big cock, he was a passionate and ultimately satisfying sex partner, and he liked him a great deal, but in recent months they had simply grown apart. He no longer felt they had much in common except sex, and he welcomed a separation so that he might look for someone to love, a different place to live, a different life style, a ... he didn't really know what. Steve was making it easy for him to re-focus his life without having to hurt his good friend—his treasured fuck partner—by suggesting a break-up.

Steve wanted to keep their dual act viable. They could, after all, meet wherever they were needed, and God knows they needed no further rehearsal. But Harp said it was a good time to bring the whole thing to an end. He knew he was not really going to miss it, but at the same time he knew that Steve's expression of regret was completely sincere.

Just about the time the Olympics came to Atlanta, Steve left for Los Angeles.

Harp—and, from what he could gather, practically all the escorts in Atlanta—were unusually busy servicing Olympic visitors during the entire long, hot summer of '96, but when it was all over he took stock of his situation, and as he was shaving one morning he simply concluded that since Steve had gone to L.A. he had almost nothing tying him to Atlanta.

The only close friends he had made in the city were his neighbors, Brent and Tad. He had met Brent at the apartment complex gym, and they discovered they shared more than just mutual South Carolina birth. Brent and his partner Tad had both been students at Clemson University while he had been working at the Steak House in Oconee, just a few miles down the road from Clemson, so all three shared familiar backgrounds. He would miss them, but it wasn't enough to keep him in Atlanta. And he really hated the traffic. So he decided to leave.

The question of just where he would go offered no great dilemma. From the first time he saw San Francisco he knew that he had found his favorite city in the world. True, he hadn't seen too many of the world's cities, but he couldn't imagine one more beautiful or more friendly than Baghdad by the Bay. He had also been very impressed with those same qualities in Minneapolis, but he had once visited there during the winter—which effectively ruled it out. He and Steve had first flown to San Francisco for a party appearance in '94, and both had fallen in love with it—and each time he had returned he felt as though he were coming home. There was no question in his mind where he would go after Steve had departed for California and he had finished his duty as a good American by providing much-needed services to the many in town for the Olympic Games.

Although he felt reasonably sure he would see them again, and probably often, he embarked on a trip to say goodbye to those people who had meant most to him. He drove up to Cincinnati, where Jeremy was now living, apparently in a fairly serious relationship with an older man. He spent two days of almost non-stop sex with the boy who had first fucked him, and who had grown to manhood as a much more exciting lover than ever. Nick, his older companion, was charming, and apparently did not resent Harp's dalliance with Jeremy. He was, in fact, eager to see in person what Jeremy had described to him as "the hardest cock and the most perfect ass in the history of the human race."

Nick laughed as he explained how he had informed Jeremy nothing could be most perfect—it was either perfect or it was not—but after joining Jeremy in worship of Harp's special assets he had to agree. Certainly he had never made love to a harder cock, and there was no question that the ass he watched driving that incredible shaft into his lover had to be regarded as well past just 'perfect.'

From Cincinnati, Harp headed south to Oconee, to see both

Doug and Dodge. The latter was now back home, or very close to it—he was teaching in a small town just over the Georgia line. Doug was happy to hear the sounds of Dodge and Harp in riotous sexual reunion in what he still thought of as Harp's room, since he occasionally joined them there. Before driving back to Atlanta, Harp spent two full days alone with Doug in the bittersweet joy of leave-taking lust.

As he drove up the road from Doug's house, he took the side of the loop going to it which passed his father's farm (since being ejected from that farm six years earlier he had always taken the other side in going to the lake house), and saw his father working in a field. He pulled to the side of the road and stopped briefly, wishing things were different, and especially wishing he could say goodbye to his mother, but the callus he had forced himself to grow over his feelings toward his parents enabled him to drive on, although his eyes were blurred for several miles.

Knowing that initially he would not want a car in San Francisco, he sold his and on a sunny October morning boarded a United Airlines flight for the next step of his destiny.

His familiarity with his new home town was rather slight—he and Steve had managed to explore a bit on their previous visits—so he decided to stay in a motel or hotel for a couple of weeks and combine sightseeing with apartment hunting. He directed the cabbie at the airport to take him to a hotel near the Castro Street area. The cabbie agreed to drive him, but offered little hope he would find a hotel room in the Castro at that particular time, since the "Castro Street Fair" was in progress. He smiled as he noted he and his lover would be enjoying the fair later that day themselves!

Surprisingly, the second motel they stopped at—a Travelodge only a few blocks from Castro Street itself—had just had a cancellation, and Harp rented a room there. He was not especially horny, and had even decided he would take a vacation from sex for a week or two while he looked around. But this was his first night in his new home town, and it was the gay capital of America—he was going to initiate his new residency with a good fuck if at all possible. In San Francisco during the Castro Street Fair, a gorgeous, well-built young man with a huge basket in his tight jeans and a universally-admired ass was probably not going to have any difficulty arranging for sex.

After a nap and a shower, he walked up Market Street, passed the famous Safeway store, observed any number of gay couples walking hand-in-hand in the warm weather, and was astonished at the press and variety of the celebrants at the fair. He was 'cruised' constantly, and he cruised right back. It seemed fairly plain he would have no trouble picking someone up to share his bed.

Dining in a restaurant on Market Street, he was served by a tall, extremely muscular blond in very faded blue jeans and white tank-top shirt so tight they might have been painted on his glorious body, and who was dazzlingly beautiful in addition. Harp felt sure this one was 'spoken for,' but he struck up a conversation with him anyway, and learned that (a) he did have a lover (Shit!), (b) said lover was out of town (Oh, really?), and (c) the aforementioned lover need never know if he had a drink with Harp after he got off work (Yes!). It was only halfway through their first drink that the blond, who actually reminded Harp of a young Steve Rommel, agreed enthusiastically to (d) do a lot more than just share a drink with the hot guy with the adorable ass and the bulging basket sitting across from him (Thank you, Jesus!).

This table-waiting beauty was named Steve Adams (Harp thought, "Steve Fox, Steve Rommel, Steve Adams—my god, are all tall, muscular, gorgeous blonds named Steve?") He had no way of knowing, of course, but he was soon to meet a couple of other gorgeous blonds who would affect his life considerably, and who were not Steves.

In Harp's motel room shortly thereafter, the stunning blond unreeled a very significant piece of meat from his own bulging basket and proved very eager to stuff it repeatedly deep inside the adorable ass he admired so! When Steve excitedly yanked Harp's Levi's down, the cock he discovered inside the bulging basket he had admired so much in the restaurant excited him enough that once he had satisfied his immediate desire to fuck this magnificent ass, he wanted to waste no time in getting his own needy ass fucked by it. Harp proved to be quite as capable of satisfying Steve's deep-seated needs as the blond surely had been in plumbing his depths.

Butts sore, mouths stretched, covered with come, totally exhausted, and as sexually satisfied and happy as humanly possible, Harp and Steve drifted off to sleep finally only after the next day had dawned.

Welcome to San Francisco! Have a nice life.

. . .

For a week Harp "did" San Francisco as a typical tourist: Fisherman's Wharf, Golden Gate Park, cable cars, Sausalito ferry, Chinatown, etc., etc. As his second week began, he decided he needed to find a place to live. Dropping in on the restaurant where he had met the incredible blond hunk who had made his first night in 'The City' so memorable, he managed to snag a table where he would again be served by the unforgettable beauty. He learned that Steve's lover was back in town, so he didn't ask him to share his stunning cock and stupendous body again (although he was taking a vacation from sex, Harp would have been glad to make an exception in this case), and settled instead for asking him if he had any leads on apartments in the area.

Steve referred Harp to a gay real estate firm in the Castro, and after looking at several available apartments in the area, he settled on a small two-bedroom apartment on one floor of a newly remodeled Victorian on Page Street, within easy walking distance of Castro Street itself. It was fairly expensive, but the recent remodeling and like-new appliances and furniture made it well worth the cost—which Harp could easily afford, anyway. Once his sexual vacation was over, he planned to put his fabulous ass back on the market, and judging by the classified ad pictures of his potential competitors shown in *The Golden Gate Nation*, he thought he could develop a ready clientele without too much trouble.

Several of the pictures in the "Models/Escorts" section looked to promise keen competition, however, and once Harp was settled in and ready to go back to work, he decided to engage the services of one of the better-looking escorts (assuming the pictures in *The Nation* were genuine) to get advice about starting his own escort work. He didn't plan to pay for sex with him, but figured he might be willing to share a few tips in exchange for his fee.

He was ready to go back to work for something to do, but he was also completely rested from his sexual vacation, and was actually getting unbelievably horny. It was either start escorting again, or start acting on some of the very clear invitations to sex he had been receiving both obliquely and blatantly ever since he had come to the city. His unaccustomed disinterest in sexual congress over the previous week or so had not left him with a massive load needing release, however,. He had actually purchased the latest 'signature' dildo to hit the market, and had employed it regularly and enthusiastically on himself to ease the itch. Harp had to admit he wished during the critical moments on those occasions that it was the real Tom Chase's monster cock buried inside him rather than just the latex alternative which bore his name and dimensions. The "Tom Chase" model seemed to be about as challenging as Harp thought he could personally accommodate. He thought he would have needed a garage to be able to find a place to park the "Ken Ryker" model.

Halloween morning, the new issue of *The Golden Gate Nation* hit the street and Harp scanned it as he drank his morning coffee, and determined to call the escort whose picture was especially appealing to him: dark, with an extremely sexy trim muscular build, apparently quite handsome (the area around his eyes was obscured by a black band), and with something of a brooding look.

He called in the late morning, and agreed to meet with "Angel" at his apartment near the Embarcadero at two o'clock in the afternoon. Angel had a wonderfully sexy voice, and agreed to talk with Harp about setting up his own escorting practice. When he suggested, "Yeah, we can fool around and then later we'll talk," Harp had instinctively felt he *was* going to want to 'fool around' before talking. His intuition was fortuitous, as it turned out.

Angel's apartment was, incidentally, only a bit more than a hundred yards from the very spot where Harp would experience a significant turning point in his life a few months hence.

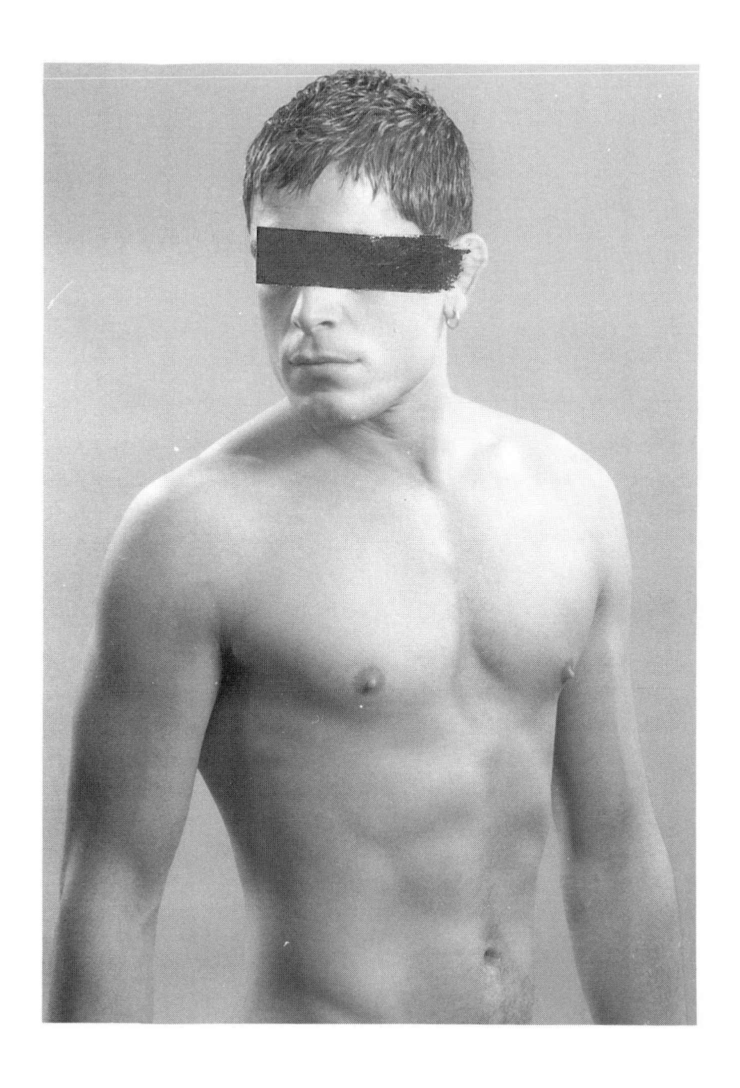

...The dark young man who met him at the door, Angel, was anything but brooding. A New Yorker of Puerto Rican extraction, he was pleasant and quite friendly, well built and extremely handsome—and very sexy.

The dark young man who met him at the door, Angel, was anything but brooding. A New Yorker of Puerto Rican extraction, he was pleasant and quite friendly, well built and extremely handsome—and very sexy. They chatted a few minutes and Angel told Harp to take his clothes off, which Harp eagerly did as Angel dropped his shorts to reveal a huge, fat shaft of tempting meat hanging between his legs. Kneeling in front of this massive beauty, it took Harp only a few licks and kisses to bring it to throbbing, superb rigidity and very impressive dimension. Harp's own cock was almost painfully erect at the prospect of enjoying this beautiful offering.

Angel smiled down at him, "You like my cock?" By this time Harp could only answer "MmmmmHmmmnn!" as his mouth was full, really full, of hard dick. "Oh, you do like my cock, huh? Gonna fuck that mouth of yours."

Angel proceeded to drive his thrilling shaft deep into Harp's hungry throat for some time before the two naked studs fell to the mattress spread on the floor and embraced and kissed passionately for some time. Angel played with Harp's cock and ass as lovingly as Harp rendered that same tribute to him, and each expressed admiration for the beauty of the other's body, ass, and dick. Grasping Harp's head tightly, Angel pushed it downward to take him inside again. Harp eagerly sucked and drove his lips up and down the long, fat shaft as Angel murmured his enjoyment and humped upward unto the source of his pleasure. ("Man, you can really suck cock!")

He rolled over, pinning Harp's face under him, and delivered a mouth-fuck as exciting as any Harp had ever experienced. Angel's balls pressed against Harp's chin, and his entire titanic organ was buried as deep in the hot, hungry throat as it could go. Still he humped, and Harp's eager hands caressed his ass and invaded and fucked his asshole with an apparently much-appreciated finger. He was encouraged by Angel's exhortation, "Yeah, play with my ass!"

Angel's arms locked around Harp's head and he continued to fuck fiercely, gradually moving Harp's entire body up against a wall. Harp could barely breathe, but he succeeded. Not wanting to relinquish this stupendous shaft plumbing the depths of his mouth, all his senses were drugged by the taste, the smell, the lip-stretching bulk, the impassioned thrusts of this throbbing, steely-hard wonder.

He had no idea how long he reveled in the joy of this invading presence in his throat, but it seemed far too short when it was withdrawn and Angel declared he had to rest a minute or he would be unable to avoid coming.

As they nestled together and Angel's hands played appreciatively over his body, Harp whispered, "Fuck me!"

Angel grinned. "Yeah? You want me to fuck you up the ass?"

Matching the engaging grin, Harp said, "If you fuck my ass like you fucked my mouth, you're gonna have a really happy camper on your hands!"

Angel stepped into his bathroom and returned with lubricant and a condom, which he peeled as he told Harp, "Lay on your stomach and show me that pretty ass." Harp rolled over and Angel knelt straddling him as he began to caress and fondle the rounded twin velvet globes offered to his appreciative gaze. "My God you've got a beautiful ass. I'm really gonna enjoying fuckin' this!"

And Angel obviously did enjoy fucking Harp's ass, but not one bit more than Harp did. Of the untold number of cocks Harp had taken up his ass, there had been a significant number of large ones—and several of those even larger than this one. But none had probably thrilled him quite as much as Angel's. It was not just the size—enormous and enormously satisfying as that was—it was the complete passion and dedication to fucking that Angel brought to his ravenous assault. Harp felt completely filled by this magnificent shaft, and Angel drove it into him so savagely and unrelentingly that he all but screamed his appreciation. Angel pinned him flat to the mattress and lay heavily down on his back as he drove himself ferociously into Harp's hungry hole. Normally, Harp was accustomed to getting fucked as he knelt on all fours, or as he lay on his back with his legs spread, and often as he settled down for a wild ride on a cock below him, but at that moment any way this plunging, throbbing, huge and thrilling piston of steely hard flesh wanted his hungry ass was exactly the way he also wanted it taken.

He eagerly raised his hips from the floor to drive his ass back in perfect synchronization to meet the forward thrusts of this plunging, ravaging monster until his ass-ring was buried in the nest of pubic hair at its base with each inward thrust, then tightly grasped the shaft with it as maximum withdrawal without actual loss of contact was effected each time Angel drew back to ready himself for another plunge. The relentless, irresistible shaft buried deep inside drove all reason from him. His mind was awash in a searing hot glow of complete animal lust.

Angel again fucked him so hard that he gradually drove his body up against the wall, where Harp lay pinned while Angel's hands held his shoulders and his hot ass drove the thrilling shaft rapidly and inexorably until Harp was alternating between screaming for more ("Fuck me! Fuck me harder with that beautiful big cock!") and begging for mercy! ("Oh god! Stop! Oh shit, that hurts!"). Mercy was apparently not in Angel's repertoire at that moment, although more seemed to be—he drove harder and, seemingly, deeper and faster, with an almost continuous hoarse litany: "Gonna fuck you! Yeah, Fuck you up the ass! Yeah, you like this cock? Take it up your ass!"

After what seemed like both an eternity and yet a cruelly short period of time also, Angel finally pulled out of a gasping, ecstatic Harp, quickly tore the rubber from his cock, and began to shoot a generous load of scalding hot come all over his body.

Harp had been very close to orgasm himself for a long time, and just as Angel pulled out, he rolled on his back, seized his cock, and without a stroke it began to spew a veritable fountain of white cream a foot or two into the air, covering his hand and his belly, and splashing off Angel's chest—which was still heaving with passion while he continued to explode his own prodigious emission.

After a minute or two of gasping, Angel fell on top of Harp, and the two beautiful men kissed and embraced while their joint emissions mingled and caused their bodies to slide sensually against each other. Later, thinking about the encounter, Harp realized that although it was one of the most thrilling and satisfying sexual experiences of his life, two things that he would have assumed would probably have negated its impact set it apart from any he had known before: he had paid for sex, and it had been basically one-sided. But whatever the cost, whatever the extent of mutual gratification, it had been probably the most enjoyable hour of his life.

From that memorable day seven years earlier when young Jeremy had first penetrated him, until this month, he had never gone more than three or four days without getting fucked. Except for the only partially satisfying application of the mammoth latex Tom Chase stand-in, this was the first time he had been fucked in two weeks, and it had been worth the wait! Still, Harp knew it was not just hunger which had made this particular fuck so outstanding. Angel was an unparalleled fuckmaster; he could not help but think, *My God, if he fucks like this for money, what must he do for love?*

Harp was so thrilled and happy that he almost forgot to pursue the subject that had really brought him to Angel's apartment—but the huge driving Latino prick had only temporarily driven it from his mind.

Angel gave him a few pointers about the San Francisco escorting scene, told him who to see at the *Nation*'s classified ad desk, and gave him the name of the photographer who had taken the sultry photo of himself that had so appealed to Harp. The subject of a name to use for escorting arose. Angel confessed that his real name was "Louis."

Louis had remarked when they first began to embrace, that since he was an Angel, he was going to show him how well he could play a Harp.

After they had finished, Harp affirmed that this Angel was able to play this Harp as well as anyone he had ever been with.

Harp had laughed about a further coincidences of names. He had called himself "Louis" when he was escorting in Atlanta, should he continue to do so here? Louis said, "You were Louis before, let Louis become an Angel in San Francisco like I did."

"You think I should call myself Angel too?"

"There are millions of angels in heaven so I think there's room for two in San Francisco. Besides, I don't use the name in my advertising anyway." So Harp decided to become another Angel in the heavenly host of San Francisco escorts.

Harp took Louis to dinner, and got acquainted with this astonishingly attractive person, who proved to be as enjoyable socially as he was sexually. He was a thoughtful, sweet, and extremely pleasant man with a ready and totally captivating laugh, but one who could also be a voracious, insatiable, and virtuoso fuck machine.

. . .

The classified ads in the mid-November issue of the *Nation* contained a new photograph of Harp's muscular, ultimately desirable body—nude, but cut off at the top line of his pubic hair, with his face partially obscured by a black bar, as Louis' was in his ad, and the caption: "ANGEL! 25, five-eight, 160 lbs,, guaranteed eight inches of fat, iron-hard meat, to-die-for ass, handsome, hot, and versatile. This angel may not have wings, but I'll sure spread 'em for you anyway. Or, would you rather spread 'em for me? Let Angel usher you into heaven. Out calls only." His pager number followed, and within hours of the time the paper hit the streets his pager began to ring.

Three days after the ad appeared, during which time Harp had already serviced seven or eight grateful, happy clients, Louis called to compliment him on it and wish him luck. Harp had decided it was time to put the business of providing pleasure for others ahead of his own immediate personal gratification, but was still anxious to seek another sexual tryst with Louis some time fairly soon. The first man he fucked after Louis called had no idea that as Harp pounded his ass unmercifully with his driving cock, he was pretending it was really the sweet and beautiful Latino fuckmaster who was underneath him, receiving a fuck as epic as the one he had given Harp.

Thanksgiving was surprisingly busy, which was fortunate, since it allowed Harp no time to dwell on the fact that he was all alone for the feast day. While his friends back east were probably with their families stuffing themselves at the traditional Thanksgiving table, he was stuffing his dick into the mouths and asses of strangers—but they did pay well for the service, and while several of them returned the favor, at least one of them did so with equipment of such satisfying dimensions that Harp felt it had been an exceedingly good weekend.

The phone didn't ring on Monday after Thanksgiving until about nine at night. The caller identified himself as Brad. The voice was hoarse and sexy, but Harp had long ago learned that prospective clients usually assumed unnaturally sexy voices when they first talked with him. He couldn't quite say why, but he also realized he did the same when he returned a pager call to a number he did not recognize. He was, after all, in the business of sex—might as well sound sexy to an inquiring client.

Phony voice or not, Brad seemed nice, and Harp agreed to meet him shortly at his apartment near the Embarcadero. Although he wished he was in that part of town for another encounter with the exciting Louis, who lived very nearby, Harp was pleased to see that the tall blond man who opened the door to him was extremely handsome. He was clad only in a fairly skimpy towel tied around his waist, which clearly revealed the fact that he also had a terrific body—a good start!

"Hi! Angel? I'm Brad. Come on in."

Entr'acte: BRAD AND HARP

The current that passed between the tall, blond, forty-six year old Bradley David Thornton and the short, dark, twenty-four year old Mark David Harper when they first looked into each other's eyes on the Monday evening following Thanksgiving of '96 stimulated a subliminal perception in both of them that a significant moment had just arrived. It was not love at first sight, although there may have been an element of that in it, but if we were to call it full blown, galloping, rampant, undeniable lust at first sight it is doubtful we would be far off the mark.

Brad's initial reaction was that Harp looked like Paul Stavros. Harp thought that Brad looked like Steve Rommel. In both cases that 'snap' comparison was extremely flattering to the subject that occasioned it, but there was more to it than just the appeal of physical beauty. Electricity, instinct, prescience, ESP, call it what you will, Brad and Harp *connected*.

Harp took Brad's hand as it was offered to him in greeting, and the two men forgot to shake hands, but looked into each other's eyes for probably a full half-minute before they realized what they were doing—or, rather, what they weren't doing. With a nervous laugh, Harp finally shook Brad's hand and muttered the expected, "Hi, Brad, I'm Angel. It's nice to meet you," and entered.

Brad closed the door behind Harp and turned to face him again. Harp stepped in and began to trace Brad's shoulders, arms, chest and stomach with his hands. He returned his attention to the large bronze nipples adorning the impressive twin swells of Brad's chest and fondled them as he grinned, "This looks like it's gonna be a lotta fun." He dropped his hands to the towel, pulled it away to let it drop to the floor, and sank to his knees. With one hand he cupped Brad's balls, and with the other he held the shaft of his cock, which immediately began to grow and harden.

Harp looked up and grinned again, "Oh yeah, I'm looking forward to this!" He returned his gaze to the head of the massive and now throbbing cock trembling only an inch from his lips, and murmured, "Shit, this is beautiful!" just before he opened his mouth wide and took every impressive inch deep inside him.

Harp's nose was buried in Brad's pubic hair, and he could feel the large ball-sack resting against his chin. While Harp exerted maximum suction to this impressive mouthful of cock and teased its underside with his busy tongue, Brad very gently held his head and plunged his dick deep into the worshipping throat. Harp's hands found the writhing buttocks driving the thrilling shaft into him, and fondled them as both men murmured and cooed their delight.

The tight ring of Harp's lips began to travel the entire length of Brad's cock as the rounded buttocks ceased to writhe and began to drive it fiercely in and out. Harp sat back, and allowed the cock to slip from his mouth as he used his hands to rotate Brad's body. "Jesus, your ass is as beautiful as your cock!" And with that, Harp began to kiss and lick the velvety surface of Brad's muscular ass while his hands explored his stomach and chest from behind. Brad bent over, and he used his hands to spread his buttocks, allowing the worshipping mouth and tongue easier access to what had obviously become their goal. Brad gasped with pleasure as Harp's tongue entered him and the busy dance of the darting muscle inside him filled him with ecstasy. His hands pulled Harp's face tightly into him and he rotated his hips for maximum effect.

Finally, Harp stood abruptly, gasping for breath, and began kissing Brad's neck passionately while the unmistakable bulge in his Levi's ground against his bare ass. Brad turned around in his arms, and they embraced fiercely while their tongues intertwined and their mouths tried to devour each other. When they broke, they grinned happily for a moment before either could say a word.

Finally, Brad pulled Harp to him again for a quick kiss before he exploded, "Wow! That was fuckin' incredible!" and began pulling Harp's tight T-shirt from his Levi's.

Harp began to kick off his shoes and unbutton his pants. "I think you're gonna like what I've got for you, too!" Since he was wearing no shorts, his fully erect cock sprang up as soon as he dragged his pants below it. "Think you're gonna be able to do anything with this?"

Brad threw Harp's T-shirt to the floor and knelt before the

monstrous shaft of unbelievably hard flesh quivering magnificently before him. Taking it tenderly in both hands, he whispered in awe, "Jesus, Angel, it's huge!" He gently kissed the swollen, plum-colored cock-head and the tip of his tongue teased the opening for a moment before it began a general worship of the throbbing organ.

After several complete traversals of the long, fat shaft, Brad took the impressive balls into his mouth and sucked greedily while one hand stroked the cock and the other caressed and explored Harp's ass.

Harp groaned, "That feel so fuckin' good! Yeah, suck my dick!" and held Brad's head absolutely immobile while he drove himself violently into his willing mouth. While Harp fucked fiercely, Brad reveled in the frenzied attack, only occasionally gagging as the huge cock penetrated the deepest recesses of his throat. After several minutes of rapture, Harp pulled out and turned around, presenting his ass to the kneeling worshipper. "You like this too?"

Brad sat back on his heels and looked in amazement. His hands began to play reverently over the velvety perfection, and he could only utter an awe-struck "Jesus!"

Harp looked back over his shoulder and asked, "Whaddaya think?"

Brad looked up at him in adoration, "You *are* an angel! No human should be allowed to have an ass this ... *perfect*. That's the only word to describe it: perfect!"

Harp laughed, then turned and knelt in front of Brad, taking him in his arms. He laughed, "Hey, I'll bet you say that to all the guys...."

"Hardly."

They kissed very tenderly, and at great length before Harp whispered into Brad's ear, "I want you to fuck this perfect ass with that perfect big cock of yours!"

"I couldn't possibly fuck that ass! I can ... no, I *will* make love to it! Yes, I'll worship it with my prick, okay?"

Harp smiled at him. "Fair enough! I hope you'll let me make love to yours, too!"

"No one leaves this room until I've had an Angel up my ass!"

It was quite a while before either one had the other up his

ass, however, since each was so completely lost in oral adoration. They lay together kissing and embracing for a long time, but not nearly as long as they lay together end-to-end, mutually feasting on the cocks they had buried deep in each other's throats. Harp lay on his stomach while Brad spent a heavenly eternity adoring his perfect ass with hands and mouth, stroking himself until orgasm was imminent. "I'm about to come!"

Harp looked back at him and smiled. "Shoot your load on my ass! Oh, that'd really be hot!"

"But I want to fuck you!"

"Shoot on my ass now! I promise you, you can fuck it later!"

With that, spurts of scalding hot emission began to cover Harps' back and ass as Brad panted in wordless passion. He straddled him for some time, shaking every drop from his still rigid cock, finally falling on Harp's back and kissing his neck. "God, you're beautiful!"

"That felt so good, so hot! Get a towel and clean me off so I can do the same to you!"

Brad raised his body somewhat. "I've got a better way to clean you up!" He began to lick the ejaculate from Harp's neck and shoulder, working his way down until he was licking the rounded buttocks clean, and eventually finding lingering traces of his own semen in the heaven that lay between them. Harp moaned and squirmed as the busy tongue apparently looked for further manna deep inside!

By the time Harp had made good on his word, covering Brad with his own emission, and following Brad's example for cleaning up afterward, they again lay together kissing and caressing for some time, sharing personal information. Brad learned, for instance, that he was actually in the arms of Harp, not "Angel," and Harp learned Brad's age, and was astonished.

"My God, you're the same age as my father! I can't believe it! You're so hot and so ... God, beautiful is the word ... you just don't seem any older than I am."

Brad laughed. "I have to admit I don't feel the least bit fatherly toward you! I've got a son, and believe me, what I want to do to you is not something fathers do to their sons!"

Harp kissed him. "You still want to fuck my perfect ass,

huh?"

"More than anything I can think of! But Jesus, Harp, look at the time! You said you'd give me an hour and we've been at this close to three hours!"

"Forget the time. Forget the money, I ... "

"No, I agreed to pay you. You're not doing this for love, after all!"

"Brad, I promised you an hour for $150. We used that up a long time ago. Since then I may not have been doing this for love, but I sure as hell love what we're doing! So we're not doing it for money now, okay?" Brad smiled and nodded. Harp laughed, "Good! Now how about that fuck?"

"Comin' right up! Do I get one too?"

Harp laughed. "Oh yeah! I'm gonna bury this cock so deep inside your ass you're gonna think I moved in!"

If Brad's cock wasn't quite as big as Louis' was, and if the pounding he gave Harp's ass wasn't quite as savage and ravenous as the one Louis had subjected it to, neither missed by much!

When it came time for Harp to return the favor, he couldn't resist emulating Louis' style and ferocity at first, but soon he was just Harp making love to the beautiful blond Brad beneath him, whose murmurs of satisfaction gradually grew into hoarse cries, and finally muffled screams as he thrilled to the ever wilder invasion by the colossal, unbelievably hard dick. Even though Brad had discharged an enormous second orgasm as his condom-sheathed cock plumbed the hungry depths of Harp's ass, he involuntarily discharged another one when Harp drove deeply inside him and his passionate groans signaled his own explosion. Brad was on his back, with his legs wrapped around Harp's waist, so his orgasm splashed off Harp's chest before coating their bellies and gluing them together, and they continued to kiss and embrace while the condom buried deep inside him filled with Harp's emission.

Brad made drinks, and the two sat and talked for a long time. Neither dressed, each agreeing that he wanted to continue enjoying the beauty of the other's body and dick. It was warm enough in the apartment that neither needed clothing, and even warm enough outside, surprisingly so for the second day of December, that they left the window partially open.

This apartment was dedicated to sexual play, so Brad had made no efforts to conceal its furnishings. He had even eschewed the services of a cleaning person so that he might feel free to leave anything in plain sight. Anyone who visited here was going to be here for purposes of fucking and sucking. His Tom Fox and Jeff Styryker dildos were lined up on a bookshelf filled with porn videos, and on either side of the bed a lubricant dispenser sat next to a saucer filled with condoms. Harp complimented Brad on the apartment, laughing about the two huge dildos and admitting he had recently added the Tom Chase model to his own apartment.

The only picture in evidence was a framed 11 x 14 inch print of an often-seen photograph of Race Rivera, standing and grinning at the camera, with his hard cock stretching out for miles past the fist that grasped it at the base, and with a thick strand of come dripping from the end of it. Harp noticed it was autographed, and picked it up to examine it, saying "Yeah, Race Rivera! This is a hot man!" He read the inscription inked on it: "For Brad: I'm sure glad my load landed where it did that day at the theatre! I've enjoyed every load I've given you since—almost as much as I have those you gave me! Love, Gundo ("Race Rivera")."

Stroking his cock, which was in the state of erection this famous photograph regularly provoked, Harp said. "Jesus, you fuck with Race Rivera?"

Brad told the story of his first encounter with Gundo at the Top 'n Bottom, and their subsequent friendship and meetings. Hearing of Tom Hunt's appearance in the story as second father to 'Race Rivera' (along with his identical-twin stud-lovers) interested Harp especially; he picked up the Tom Fox dildo and examined it. "Wow! You got this from the model for it, huh?"

"Yeah, what a souvenir, huh? I wish I could say the same thing for my Jeff Stryker model!"

"I feel the same way about my Tom Chase model," Harp laughed, "Makes me hungry all over again!" He went to Brad and kissed him. "I'd love to get that big dick of yours up my butt again, but I've got to be going. Will I see you again?"

"You'll see me again just as soon as you'll let me see you, okay?" Brad slipped on his shorts while Harp dressed quickly, and he slipped two hundred-dollar bills into his shirt pocket.

Harp took Brad in his arms and they embraced and kissed tenderly. "Brad, I've had such a good time, I ... this was so much more to me than a client call. I don't feel right about taking your money."

"It was the best money I ever spent. I don't feel right about your having spent ... Jesus! ... four hours with me! You only agreed to an hour!"

"The first hour was for money, okay? The rest was because I wanted to make love with you. Next time, if you want me, there's not gonna be any money involved."

"If I want you? C'mon, you know I do. But this is the way you make your living."

"I'm not gonna stop takin' money to screw and be screwed, and who knows, next time I see you I may have already been with a couple of clients that day ... and you're right, it's my business, so okay, I'll keep taking your money, if that's the way you want it. But I'll turn my pager off when we're together and give you everything I've got left. Okay?"

"Jesus, Harp, you're as sweet as you are hot!"

"That's me baby, the whore with a heart of gold. Do I wait for you to call me, or will you give me your phone number? I already have the one you gave me for here, but ... is it okay to call you where you live?"

Brad gave Harp his home phone number and explained that his son might be there, but he would not ask questions. "Call me as soon as you're willing to see me again! I don't need to call, I'll want to see you again the second you walk out the door tonight!"

"In case you do want to call," Harp said, "here's my telephone number, and you have my pager number. I don't know when I can see you again. Let's see, today's December 2nd; is ... oh, let's say December 3rd too soon?"

"If we really have to wait that long, I guess we can!"

"I know I'll have to see a client or two tomorrow, but I'll be here tomorrow night, okay?"

"I'll be here, just let me know when. Or don't even bother to call, just come!"

"Believe me, I'll come!" He kissed Brad before he left. "I'm looking forward to tomorrow night already!"

"If you're with a couple of clients earlier in the day will you still be able to ... well ... "

Harp laughed. "Brad, I had two clients today before I came here tonight! Didn't I do all right?"

"Jesus, Harp, if you'd have done any better I wouldn't be able to walk!"

They kissed and embraced one final time, and Brad was left alone with the memory of one the most enjoyable sexual experiences he had ever known, shared with one of the sexiest, most handsome men he had ever seen. He couldn't wait for tomorrow night!

Lust at first sight followed by ... what? Something much more, perhaps?

Brad had almost no experience with escorts, so he only suspected his encounter with Harp had been very special. Harp, with considerable experience in the field, knew it had been very special indeed, and he wasn't at all sure why. Brad was extremely handsome, of course, and well built and well hung, and Harp actually preferred older men, but that usually meant men five or ten years older than he, not men the same age as his father, for God's sake!

Harp had three clients to service before he met Brad again the next evening, but they were not demanding. Even given his fairly extensive experience as an escort, he was still surprised at how many of his clients were content to bring themselves to orgasm while they sucked his dick, or watched him strip or masturbate. At any rate, he showed up at Brad's apartment on Tuesday night, and their sex was as satisfying as it had been at their first encounter.

A week later, after several more meetings with Brad, Harp began to get concerned; he was enjoying it too much. If Brad wasn't the savage, demanding fucker that Louis was, and if his cock wasn't quite as stupendous, he was still an extremely intense and satisfying top with a very impressive dick! Almost as important to Harp was the fact that Brad was also a talented and appreciative bottom, who took every inch of his own shaft all the way inside him with a joy and a hunger that inspired him to efforts as a top that probably equaled Louis'. All that was fine, but Harp began to wonder if he might not be in danger of falling in love with Brad.

As much as he had loved Steve and Doug and Jeremy, as close as he had been to Dodge, Harp had never been in love with them. He had come close to falling in love with Steve in the early stages of their relationship (he was the most beautiful man he had ever seen), and even closer with Jeremy. Jeremy would always be very special to him of course, and it wasn't just that he was the first guy to fuck him, although almost every gay man probably falls in love to some degree with the first guy who takes him that way, unless there is a component of rape or degradation. He didn't object to falling in love, but he was selling his ass for a living, how could he reconcile that career with a love affair? Considering how much he enjoyed Brad's company and his love-making, he had obliquely sounded him out on what his attitude might be if they did become lovers and he continued to escort. If Brad knew what Harp was actually trying to learn, he didn't let on, but he did make it clear that he would probably have a considerable problem with a lover who was available as something of a temporary sex partner for rent to others.

Harp decided he needed to cool his growing passion for Brad—but only cool it, not quench it.

On the other hand, Brad realized after their first few meetings that what he felt for Harp was rapidly turning into something emotionally meaningful to him. Here was a young man about as beautiful as any he had ever seen (including Paul Stavros, something of a high-water mark in setting standards of male beauty), with a dick as relentlessly hard as any he had ever had inside him, and one that approached the Whopper Toole/Gundo Lopez/Tom Hunt standard of enormity! In addition, he had the most spectacularly perfect and adorable ass he had ever laid his eyes on, much less penetrated, and was a passive fuck-partner as talented and appreciative as any man could want, and yet a thrilling, demanding top as well. Add to this the sweetness and intelligence that became more apparent with each meeting, and it would have been strange if Brad did not fall in love with Harp.

It became clear to Brad that Harp wanted to slow the momentum of their relationship, and it alarmed him. Following magnificent, exhaustive sex one night, Harp broached the subject.

"Brad, I think this is starting to get serious, and I'm not sure that's bad, but I do know it's happening too fast. I know I like you as much as anyone I know, and I enjoy making love with you ... well, you can tell how much I enjoy that! But look, I'm having sex with other guys at least ten or twelve times a week, and that's the way I make my money. I can't get serious about anybody."

"I know that, Baby (a pet name for Harp that Brad had begun to use some time earlier, without objection from the 'baby' himself), and I have to admit I hate sharing you with anyone. I wish you would consider letting me...."

"I know what you're gonna say, Brad, and I appreciate it, but I'm not ready to settle down just yet. I don't do it with other guys because I enjoy it, I ... no, that's not true. I do enjoy it with other guys, well, most of them anyway! But I'm doin' it for the money, okay? And look, I'm still taking money from you every time we get together, right?"

"Well, yeah, but you're not taking any more than you would if I were a regular client, and we spend hours making love. And correct me if I'm in error, but I think we're making love, not just screwing each other—or am I reading you wrong?"

Harp kissed him tenderly. "No, you're not wrong. I know it's special when we get together, but I'm just not ready to get serious right now, okay? Brad, just don't push it, okay? Look, let's keep on making love, and you can keep on paying me, and if I tell you someday that I won't take any money from you anymore, that's the day I tell you I'm ready to be your lover."

"Okay, Harp, I'll wait for the day."

"Now understand I'm not saying that day's really gonna come, right? Let's just stay good friends and we'll fuck, and we'll see what happens. Look, you're gonna see Race Rivera again, aren't you? And what about, whatsisname, the Greek guy you say I remind you of?"

"Paul."

"Yeah, Paul. If he comes out here again, aren't you gonna want to see him? And make love with him too? And make love with Race Rivera too. Shit, why would anybody not want to make love with him if he got the chance?"

"Would you?"

"Just try me if he comes up here and sees you again, just see if I'd say yes to a threesome with Race Rivera!"

Brad laughed. "Okay, you made your point. I love you, baby, I think I may be in love with you, but we'll just chill, like Josh says, and see what happens. And it's about time Gundo was back up to dance at the Top 'n Bottom, so we'll try for a threesome if you want!"

"Fantastic! Oh yeah ... deal! So, anyway, I gotta go."

"So do I, I'm late already. Josh is going to be there tonight, and he'll be wondering where the hell I am."

"Is he cute? You've never showed me a picture of him, you know. How about seein' if he'd like 'a date with an angel!' "

"You know, I don't know if he'd like it or not. He's pretty private about his personal life. That's fine, he'll talk to me if he wants to, he knows he can. And no, I've never showed you a picture of him—he's so goddamned cute I think you'd forget me in a minute!"

"Okay, you fix you and me both up with Race Rivera when he comes to town and I'll forget Josh, how about that?" Harp laughed. "And give me my goddam money before I leave. We ain't lovers yet!"

"I like the sound of that 'yet' in there!"

Harp got serious. "I like it too, but let's just wait and see. Oh, and in the meantime, whatever it means, I do love you."

"I love you too, Baby."

Harp had not brought the subject up in his discussion with Brad, but he wanted to consider the possibility of dating others, beyond escorting, of course, before 'settling down' with one man, if in fact, that was what the future held for him. A couple of his clients, and he was already developing some dedicated 'regulars', had made it rather clear they hoped for something like a relationship with him. As he had not done with Brad, he made it clear to them that such was not a possibility.

He had never serviced a client at his apartment, although he had invited Brad there for a drink once when they had gone out to dinner. This is not to say he had never had sex in his apartment, however. He felt the interaction with his Tom Chase dildo did not count as sex. On several occasions he had met someone who took his fancy, and was obviously interested in taking something more from him than just that! It was common for men to approach him in bars and other public places and 'hit on him.' If he were not 'working,' and the guy looked and sounded interesting, he was happy to have a drink or chat. He had accompanied a half-dozen of them to their apartments for sex, and he had invited three or four to his own apartment to share his body and his bed.

Only one of these 'non-business' encounters had led to anything other than a meaningless, however enjoyable, one-time sexual encounter.

He had met Jay in a bar on Castro Street one night in mid-January. Although there had been few customers at that early hour, the tall young blond had moved stools to sit right next to Harp a few minutes after he entered. Harp had been as taken with the blond's rather breathtaking good looks as the blond had apparently been taken with his.

They had talked only a few minutes when Jay rested his hand on Harp's arm and said, "I'd like to ask you to my place for a drink or something, but I live a long way from here. Would you consider going anyway?"

Harp put his hand over Jay's. "I live close; we can go to my apartment and have a drink there if you want, but it's the or something that sounds interesting to me! Let's go!"

Together they strolled to Harp's apartment, and shared a very satisfying two hours in bed. Jay was young, barely legal, but mature for his years. Once in bed, it became obvious he was a veteran of a multitude of sexual skirmishes. Their oral lovemaking was extremely passionate and satisfying, and Jay obviously enjoyed getting screwed, but he seemed happiest when Harp's ass was impaled on his generous cock. This arrangement suited Harp fine.

Jay said he was a college student, and was a San Francisco native, but he did not want to provide any particulars. "My family lives here, and I've got to be very careful. They have no idea I'm gay."

"Would they be horrified, or something?

"No ... they're pretty liberal, actually. But I don't see any need for them to know just yet. I know that someday I'll have to come out to both of them."

"Both of them? They wouldn't find out together?"

Jay frowned. "No ... they're divorced. I live with my dad."

Harp kissed Jay and held him close. "Look, Jay, you don't need to tell me anything about yourself until, or if you want to. There is one thing you can do before you go, though ... no, two things."

Jay laughed and kissed him. "Name it, you've got both of them if it's even remotely possible."

Harp smiled at the beautiful young blond for a long time before replying. "First, promise you'll see me again, soon."

"That one's easy—you've got it! In fact I was going to make you promise me the same thing. What's the other?"

"Just fuck me once more before you go!"

Jay laughed aloud. "Funny, that's another thing I was going to ask you for too!"

All their wishes were granted!

Within a month, Jay was visiting Harp's bed regularly, and in addition to enjoying sex with him almost as much as he did with Brad, Harp began to feel he was perhaps falling in love with the young stud. The trouble was, he was also more and more realizing he was falling in love with Brad. Both of them were making it clear by their actions that they were not falling in love with him—they were already there!

Inevitably, Harp had to tell Jay what he did for a living, and it was painful to watch how it hurt the youngster. Although he accepted the fact intellectually that Harp was having meaningless sex with quite a number of different men every week, it was very difficult for him to accept it emotionally. Harp knew that Jay was soon going to begin lobbying him to stop escorting, and he didn't know how he was going to react. Hell, he was seeing Brad at least two or three nights a week, and he hadn't even told Jay about that.

One night in late April, in Brad's apartment, Harp took the next step. He was lying on his back with Brad's cock inside him and his legs on the older man's shoulders. They had been kissing wildly while Brad fucked and Harp masturbated himself. As he filled the condom he wore deep inside Harp's appreciative chamber, Brad panted, "God, Harp, I love you so much!"

Harp's orgasm splashed over their two chests a moment later, and following the long and passionate kiss that ensued, he answered, "I love you too, Brad. I really think I love you!"

"Do you mean ...? Harp, I ... God, Baby, I'd be happy to be with only you for the rest of my life!" He raised his head and looked into Harp's eyes. "I don't want anyone else in the world if I can have you."

With two fingers Brad scooped up a generous portion of Harp's orgasm and studied it before he opened his mouth and moved to lick it from his fingers. Harp grasped his wrist and stopped him; he shook his head 'no' at Brad and smiled before he pulled the fingers into his own mouth, where he licked them clean. He smiled at Brad. "I think we need to talk. Make us a drink."

Brad did the honors at the bar, and sat on the bed waiting for Harp to return from some cleaning up in the bathroom. Harp returned, kissed Brad, and sat in a chair near the bed.

"When I say I love you, Brad, I guess what I mean is I think I'm falling in love with you." Brad began to speak. "No ... just let me finish.

"I've loved you, of course, for a long time now—meaning just that, that you're a lovable guy, and I more than just like you. I love my friends back home, I love Steve Rommel." Brad knew the story of Steve, since Harp had told him his entire life's story in installments—and Harp had heard Brad's in return. "So, yes, I love you, too. But lately I've been feeling more than that, and as strange as it seems, I don't think I've ever been *in love* before. I told you about Jeremy, the first guy who fucked me in high school, and I think I came close to being in love with him. And I think I came real close with Steve the first year or so we were together. But with you ... I dunno, it's just that lately I feel like I want to be with you all the time, and I keep thinking of you and me together years from now, and ... I just can't explain it. I know it makes me feel good all over when I even think of you, and about half the time when a client is fucking me, I fantasize about it being you doing it. A couple of times lately I've slipped and said your name while I was coming with a client. One of them thought it was funny; another one wasn't amused at all.

"I enjoy sex, you know, and actually I enjoy my work most of the time. But lately I've been getting this feeling that I don't want to have sex with anybody but you, and ... "

Brad leaped from the bed, kissed him, and took his shoulders in his hands. "Harp ... don't have sex with anybody but me any more! I love you; I'll do anything to satisfy you!"

"Please Brad, let me go on, okay? I know you love me, and I am saying that from now on, I do not want you to give me any money. We both know I said that when I stopped taking money from you, I'd be saying I was ready to be your lover." Brad, kneeling in front of him, with his hands still holding his shoulders, again began to speak; Harp put his hand over his mouth. "Wait!"

"I'm going back on my word. I'm not ready to be your lover, but I can't keep taking money from you for sex. I love you, I love sex with you, but I want to have sex with you because I love you, and only for that reason. I know the money doesn't mean anything to you, and you know it doesn't mean a helluva lot to me. But you are not a client any more, not in any way." He kissed Brad and held his head as he looked into his eyes. "Okay?"

Brad smiled wistfully. "I hope you're saying you're closer to agreeing to become my lover. What I really hope is you're saying you're closer to becoming my partner as well as my lover!"

"I am closer, Brad. But, I have to make a living, and ... "

"We'll get you a job. You can be working for my travel agency tomorrow, or we can get you in school, or...."

"Okay. We'll talk about that. I like the sex, but I'm probably willing to give up selling my ass. I don't know for sure if I'm willing to stop fucking with anyone else when it's not just money involved. I've never been in a situation where I wasn't involved with a couple of guys at the same time. Even if I fall completely in love with you, I don't know if I can be happy sexually without seeing someone else too once in a while."

"Is there someone else now?"

"I have to admit there's someone who I know is falling in love with me, and who I like a lot. I'm sorry if this hurts you."

"I'd rather know than be surprised. I've always assumed ... I don't know why I should have assumed you might not be interested in someone else. You're so fucking attractive, and I'll bet half of your clients fall in love with you. Is it just one guy? Is he young? Is he a client?"

"There's just one guy, Jay. He is young, he's very young, but he's not a client. Hell, he's a college student! He can't afford me!"

Brad stood and walked back to the bed. This was sobering news, but he was going to try to face it calmly. "And you think you're in love with him? I'll bet he's gorgeous!"

Harp came to him, lay on the bed and drew Brad in to him. "He is gorgeous! In fact he even reminds me of you. That's how fuckin' gorgeous he is! But I'm not in love with him. I do love him, like I love you, and I'm pretty sure he's in love with me. I don't think I can see myself falling in love with him, but right now I don't see myself not seeing him any more, either. Does that make sense? If you and I become lovers—or, better yet, partners—I won't be selling my ass any more. I might give it away, like to Jay, but it'll really belong to you. And you'd better keep telling me it's the prettiest ass you've ever seen, too!"

"Jesus, Baby, it is the prettiest ass I've ever seen, and you're the only one I've wanted to fuck for a long time now."

"Not even the fabulous Paul? How about Race Rivera? Gundo, right? If Gundo walked in here right now, you wouldn't want to fuck him?"

"Well, Race Rivera...."

Harp laughed. "Right! If Race Rivera walked in right now, I'd be damned sure he didn't walk out until he had fucked my ass at least once! And if both Paul and I were kneeling on the edge of this bed, showing you our butts, you'd only fuck mine?"

Brad grinned at him. "You do like to make it hard, don't you?"

Harp moved his body downward and said, "I love to make it hard!" just as he took Brad's cock in his mouth and began to suck it. Brad moved so that he could take Harp in his mouth, and they occupied themselves in a playful "69" for several minutes. They were not serious about it, however, and were soon simply holding each other, fondling each other's asses lovingly, and planting sweet kisses on each other's stomachs and cocks.

"Brad?"

"Yes, Baby."

"Quite seriously, how do you feel about threesomes? I know you told me about your trip to L.A., and Tom Hunt and the twins along with Gundo, but that's the only one time you've ever mentioned where you had sex with more than one guy. And that was ... what, a fivesome?"

"Well, I also told you about the gang-bang that led to Chris Drake and me becoming lovers, but that was strictly one-on-one, even if poor Chris did get eight or ten loads up his ass."

"Poor Chris? I've had eight or ten cocks up my ass in one night several times—hell, a lot of times, actually—and loved the hell out of it! And I seem to remember you told me you put more than one load up Chris' ass that night yourself!"

"Okay, but it was strictly one-on-one as soon as I started with him, but ... hell, let's don't talk about Chris. Let's talk about you and me. Aside from that trip to L.A., I've never had sex with more than one guy at a time. You want to know how I would feel about a threesome with you?"

"Yeah, what if Paul or Gundo were here? would you want to watch me fuck Paul, or watch Gundo fuck me, or watch me sucking Paul's cock while you fucked him, or ... "

"I get the idea! And the answer is a very clear, and very definite I don't know! I honestly feel I could deal with it, and even enjoy the hell out of it if it was just for fun ... if we were in love, and were just having fun without any kind of meaning or ... shit, I don't know, Baby. Do you want to try a threesome?"

"Brad, I think if there's any chance for us to become partners, threesomes are going to be involved. I think if we were partners I'd be happy to have sex with you alone most of the time, and even when there was someone else involved, I'd like you to be there too. So yeah, I want to try a threesome. And there's something else we need to talk about."

"Okay, what?"

"Being partners isn't just about sex. You realize I've never met any of your friends? I've never even seen where you live, and aside from walking or going out to eat, every time we've been together we've either been having sex or talking together before or after sex. We need to start finding out if we work out together around other people, and outside of bed!"

"You're right, and it isn't as if I haven't thought about that. Hell, I want you to meet my friends, and become a part of my regular life. I want you to meet my son, so that you can be over at my house, and he'll accept you as a part of my life. Maybe someday he's going to accept you as my lover, I don't know. I hope so, though. He's really a good kid, and he's very broad-minded, I think. You're gonna flip, he's so handsome. How could my son, or my friends, or anybody I know not like you, though?"

"It doesn't have to happen overnight, Brad. We'll work into it gradually. I've got to see where this thing with Jay goes—if anywhere. He's a sweet guy, and I do love him, and I definitely don't want to hurt him. Hell, maybe we'll wind up having a threesome with Jay."

"Now that could be interesting. Anyway, a threesome it is. Who do we get to join us?"

"I know just the guy. You remember Louis, who helped me get started escorting? He lives only about a block from here, and he's gorgeous, and hot as hell, and hung like you wouldn't believe. I don't know if he'd go for a threeseome, but we can try."

"Sounds great. Do you know his number?"

"Do you have a copy of *The Nation* around? His ad's in there." Brad had picked up a new issue of the paper only a few days earlier, and they found Louis's ad.

During the time he had been escorting in San Francisco, Harp had spoken with Louis several times, and even had lunch with him on two occasions. Remembering the spectacular quality of his love-making, he had been anxious to lie under the Latino stud again, but each had been busy with his own clientele when they had spoken or met. The last time they had lunched, however, Louis had told Harp, "I sure want to fuck you again soon! Boy, that's some pretty ass!"

Harp grinned at him. "That is some pretty cock you've got, and I'm ready to take it up my pretty ass again!"

"Pretty, huh? Big too, right?" Brad returned the grin, in silent agreement. Louis continued. "Well, you know, we should get together for a professional courtesy exchange soon. And I think I might like to have you fuck me up the ass, too. I haven't been fucked in quite a while. I hardly ever let a client do that, but I remember what a big, nice cock you've got, and anyway, you wouldn't be a client, right? Yeah, let's get together soon and fuck each other!"

Harp had wished he hadn't already promised his time that day to clients, and could go to Louis' bed right at that very minute. He was anxious to re-experience the savage fucking Louis provided, and he also looked forward to giving the dark fuckmaster a taste of his own medicine!

Louis answered his phone right away, and after Harp had explained the situation, he agreed to a threesome at Brad's apartment, saying he'd fuck Harp for fun and fuck Brad for $150.00! "After I fuck him, he can watch while I fuck you and you fuck me!"

Both Brad and Harp had already shot two loads apiece together that night, and Harp had even serviced three clients earlier in the day, so it was no time to start a fuck-fest with Louis. They settled on the next afternoon for their threesome. Louis laughed just before he hung up. "A client sucked me off this afternoon, but that's the only time I got off all day." His voice lowered, and became very sexy. "I'll save up for tomorrow afternoon. I want to give each of you a nice big load!"

Harp spent the night with Brad, and the two slept in each others arms, often waking to kiss and fondle. Both were stunningly horny the next morning, but they sublimated their natural inclinations to breakfast and a morning of shopping, each wanted his own 'nice big load' to give Louis in return for his! Before returning to the apartment, they dropped in at the branch of Brad's travel agency located in the financial district, where Brad introduced Harp to his employees, as a friend, with no explanations offered. As they left the office and began to stroll back to get ready for their tryst with Louis, Harp grinned at Brad. "Thanks, I'm beginning to feel like a part of your life outside of bed!"

That afternoon Louis called and said, "I'm going out the door, be there in five minutes. Get out of your clothes and get those dicks hard, I wanna fuck some ass!" Five minutes later both Harp and Brad opened the door to him, completely naked, and with their very impressive cocks standing straight out!

Before even closing the door, Louis took Harp's cock in his

hand and leaned in to kiss him. Brad closed the door behind the two as their arms went around each other and they kissed passionately, Louis still fondling Harp's impressive erection, and Brad admiring the very comely Louis. Then they broke, and Louis turned to Brad. "Damn! You're hot too," and he took Brad's cock in one hand while he stepped in and fondled his ass with the other. "Yeah, two hot men to fuck!"

Brad embraced Louis and his hands explored his body as he smiled at him. "Talk about a hot man! This is gonna be fun!" And they kissed passionately as Harp came up behind Brad, his hard cock pressed against his ass, and he embraced the two eager men together.

Their threesome was lengthy, lusty, and completely joyous. Louis' fucking was every bit as tireless and fierce and satisfying as Harp remembered!

Brad watched in awe as the huge Latin cock plunged relentlessly in and out of Harp's perfect ass, and Louis' own wildly-writhing and driving ass was also a joy to behold. As Louis neared orgasm, he told Brad to play with his ass, and with two of Brad's fingers tightly clenched deep within him, Louis delivered his load in six or eight spurts, deep inside the passionately appreciative Harp. He continued to fuck for quite a while after his orgasm, and turned his head to murmur to Brad, "Your fingers feel great in there, but I'm looking forward to that big hard cock inside me, get a rubber and fuck me up the ass while I'm still inside Harp."

A quick application of lubricant and a condom, and Brad was poised at Louis' twitching sphincter. "Give it to me—hard!" With a fierce lunge, Brad's cock was completely inside, and if he thought Louis' ass writhed and drove wildly when he was fucking Harp, it was nothing compared to how it grasped and pulled on his cock to counter the deep penetration he was obviously thrilling to. "Oh God, yes! Fuck my ass hard!"

Harp raised his ass so that Louis' cock—which stayed huge and hard throughout Brad's fuck—would not slip out. In effect, Brad was fucking both lucky young men at the same time, since the force of his body pounding his cock deep inside Louis, drove Louis' own cock deep inside Harp. All three were panting and gasping in passion as Brad's relentless fuck continued for ten or fifteen minutes of mindless lust, ending only as Brad drove himself as deep as he could, and froze there while he filled the rubber inside Louis with a huge emission.

Louis continued to writhe. "I'm ready to shoot another load!" The pace of his humping picked up, and with Brad's cock still buried in him, he added another load to the one already in the rubber inside Harp's ass, which so stimulated Brad that he began humping wildly and added another load to the condom he was wearing inside Louis!

As Louis and Brad began to calm down, Harp said, "That's it, I've gotta fuck some ass myself!" He pulled himself out from under Louis, and lost little time in lubricating and sheathing himself. Louis and Brad separated, and rolled on their backs, side by side, grinning up at him, both their cocks still enclosed in filled condoms. Harp stood over them, his prick throbbing in anticipation. "Who gets this?"

Brad raised his legs and spread them. "Fuck me, babe, while Louis watches!" Harp knelt between Brad's legs, which came to rest on his shoulders. He pulled the condom from Brad's cock, and drizzled its considerable contents over the asshole presented to him, and as Louis whispered, "Fuck him up the ass!" Harp slowly, but inexorably sank into Brad's willing body, while Louis pulled the condom from his cock and coated Brad's chest with his double emission, which he played with as Harp fucked.

Harp fucked long and relentlessly, often kissing Brad as he buried himself deep inside. "Did you like watching Louis fuck me?" he asked. Almost delirious with the force of the frenzied thrusts of Harp's cock, Brad could barely pant, "Oh God, yes! He's so fuckin' hot!" Harp continued to pound as he asked, "And d'you want him to fuck you too? Want him to fill up your hot ass with that hard monster dick of his?"

Brad turned his face to Louis and panted "I want that big fuckin' prick of yours inside me too!" Louis leaned over and kissed the ecstatic Brad, whispering, "Gonna fuck you up that hot ass until you scream!"

Finally, with a wild cry, Harp pulled himself out, tore the condom off, and spurted a massive load of hot, white come on Brad's chest and face, and on the side of Louis' head as he was kissing Brad's ear.

A break for drinks brought a time for relaxation and laughing about the wonders of the incredible sex they had just enjoyed. Harp promised to fuck Louis, and Louis promised to fuck Brad as planned. It was possible that Louis enjoyed the fierce and inspired plunging of Harp's huge cock up his ass as much as Brad enjoyed the savage fuck Louis' monster administered, but Brad himself couldn't imagine anything much more enjoyable or exciting than the feel of the Latino stud's immense uncut prick driving into him endlessly and brutally, culminating in a splash of hot come on his ass! A new demigod was added to the Pantheon of Supercocks I Have Known in Brad's mind, Whopper, Gundo, Tom Hunt, and now Louis!

Brad agreed with Harp that Louis was a perfect fuckmaster, and Louis admitted he had never serviced two hotter or more attractive men than the two whose asses were raw from the breathtaking fucks he had just given them—and grinned as he admitted his own ass was satisfyingly sore from the two beautiful cocks that had fucked it! When the three went their separate ways, they were all exhausted, but completely, rapturously satisfied—and happy.

Louis and Harp both had to meet with clients that evening, but where they were going to find the strength to service them after the ecstasy of their afternoon threesome was anybody's guess. Josh was due home for the evening, so Brad was going to meet him. As he kissed Harp goodbye, he agreed that the threesome was a complete success, and while he still wanted to make love privately with Harp most of the time, he also looked forward to other sessions with Louis, and maybe with others.

Harp grinned. "Race Rivera?"

Brad grinned even wider. "Maybe ... want me to call him?"

"I lined up Louis for your sake, so how about lining up Race Rivera for mine?"

"I'll call him tonight if I can. You up for a trip to L.A. to get fucked by a porn star?

"Call the airline as soon as you line up Gundo, I'll be packing my bags!"

As it happened, Gundo was both delighted to hear from Brad, and eager to meet Harp. The prospect of a threesome was something he expressed great enthusiasm for, and they set a date slightly more than two weeks hence, when Gundo would be home from appearances at strip theatres in Washington and Chicago. He asked if Brad and Harp would like to get together with Tom Hunt and the twins also while they were visiting. He said those three had especially enjoyed Brad's visit the fall before, and had instructed him to line up a return engagement when he could.

Brad happily acceded, adding "I feel sure Harp will be even more excited once he examines my Tom Fox Dildo. And I know both you and Tom and the twins are going to be excited once you get a look at Harp's ass. It's simply the most beautiful thing I've ever seen!"

Gundo laughed, "Hey, we'll all keep it busy! You want me to put another Tom Fox Dildo in the mail to you, so you guys can practice together?"

"Nah, it'll be fun using mine on each other and pretending we're Tom when we do!"

For the next two weeks, Brad had sex only with Harp. Harp continued to service Jay and his usual clients, but he was excited about meeting Race Rivera, and getting to have sex with the legendary Tom Fox and the twins as well, it looked like a helluva visit! They planned to spend four days in L.A., taking in some of the sights while they were there in addition to feasting on Gundo, and his mentor and his twin playmates as well! Harp could hardly believe that Tom Hunt's cock was going to be the same size as his Tom Fox signature dildo, but Brad assured him he was in for a very special treat. "And I'm looking forward to watching the twins double-fuck you, it's really something, believe me!"

Jay was very unhappy about Harp being gone for four days, but Harp thought how much unhappier he would be if he knew why he was going, so he told him it was strictly a visit to be with a client in Los Angeles. Besides, the prospect of becoming a full-fledged, loving partner with Brad seemed ever more likely. Jay would just have to get over it, Harp really didn't want to hurt him, and he really didn't want to think about giving up sex with him completely, either. Hell, he was young. Maybe he'd accept the fact that Harp was taken, and might even be willing to join him and Brad for threesomes. That would be fun—two gorgeous, tall, big-dicked blonds to fuck and, much more to the point, to get fucked by!

There was little time to see the sights once they got to Los Angeles. They were so busy with sex that when they weren't engaged in that, they were too tired to do much but nap and hang out by the pool. The planned meetings with Gundo, Tom Hunt, and the twins were supplemented by another encounter they never would have anticipated.

Gundo met them at the airport, and drove them directly to his apartment, where he could hardly wait to see if Harp's ass was as magnificent as Brad had promised, and as it looked in his tight Levi's! The way he buried his face in that magnificent feature, and the time he spent exploring it with his tongue indicated he was more than satisfied. The way he fucked it subsequently—and fucked it, fucked it, and fucked it, repeatedly—indicated a great reverence and appreciation for its merits!

For two days the three men fucked each other and sucked each other endlessly, in every imaginable way, with huge orgasms coating happy bodies and cocks. Harp was thrilled at Gundo's sexual expertise and his gargantuan prick, and took it every way he could, repeatedly. He rode Gundo's monster cock as he lay on his back, and barely dismounted in time for Gundo to tear the condom off and display his famous "Vesuvius" shot, which splashed over Harp's smiling face—and with that orgasm dripping from him, a laughing Harp used his fist to elicit an equally large load which he directed all over a grinning Gundo's face! Gundo and Harp managed to save enough of their energy to service Brad's ass as well, and both Brad and Harp spent a considerable amount of time with their own cocks buried deep inside an appreciative Gundo! Sucking, double-sucking, rimming, kissing, fondling—all found time for plenty of these as prelude and accompaniment to the fucking.

The afternoon and evening they spent at Tom's house was as wild as Brad had promised it would be. The great beauty of the identical blond twins was almost as impressive to Harp as the unbelievable size of Tom's always steely-hard cock. The latter proved to be as satisfying as any cock Harp said he had experienced, and just as thrilling as Brad remembered it. Tom fucked Gundo as well, and indeed seemed to be completely indefatigable. He did not fuck the twins while Harp and Brad were there (he did that almost every night, after all), saving himself for his appreciative guests—all of whom returned the favor at least once, and all of whom offered their asses to the long, slim cocks of the beautiful twins.

One of Tom's cameramen was on hand the whole time with a video camera, filming everything, but with Harp and Brad's approval, since he assured them there would be no copies made; the resulting tapes would be a souvenir, which they were free to destroy if they wanted.

The twins ate and fucked Harp's ass with particular delight, declaring it (as, it seems everyone always did) as beautiful as any they had ever seen. Harp was anxious to experience the twins' infamous double fuck, and he was not disappointed. As one of the twins (each was completely indistinguishable from the other to Harp) lay on his back, Harp knelt over his long, hard cock, and gradually settled down on it. With that cock completely inside him, he leaned forward, and the other twin knelt behind him and began to put his own cock next to his brother's inside Harp's chamber. The two cocks moved in and out together, and Harp felt like he was being fucked by a single prick that was as fat as any might possibly be! Then, apparently at some kind of signal (the twins had done this literally thousands of times) they shifted, and one cock drove in as far as it could, while the other pulled back almost to the point of withdrawal, and they fucked this way for some time; Harp later told Brad the sensation was as thrilling as anything he had ever known. Brad understood his enthusiasm, remembering it well from his first visit with the twins, and experiencing it again the same night Harp discovered it. Then, at another signal, they shifted back to the original paired penetrations, and fucked that way for a while before shifting back to the simultaneous in-and-out. Harp shot a huge load on the bottom twin's chest as they were doing this, but insisted they continue.

The twins had unbelievable stamina, and performed their specialty on Brad's eager ass, and on Gundo's as well before they finally declared themselves near orgasm. They stood close together and masturbated for only a few strokes before they shot their loads on each other, almost simultaneously. Then each licked his own emission from his brother, and they embraced passionately and invited Harp and Brad to fuck them as they stood there kissing. Gundo and Tom knelt behind Harp and Brad and tongue-fucked them as they serviced the twins, who continued to kiss and embrace each other and play with each other's cocks.

Tom was so impressed with Harp that he expressed a very keen interest in having him test to see how he looked and performed formally in front of a camera. He thought he could have a great career as a porn star. Harp was flattered, but not interested, even though Gundo offered to be his on-screen partner for the test, and do absolutely anything with Harp that he wanted.

Before they left, Tom asked Gundo to try and get together the next night with television star Richie Hassler and fuck with him to see how he thought Richie might do as a porn actor; if Gundo thought him promising, they would set up a test shoot. Richie had been so impressed with Gundo's work in video, that he especially asked to get together with him to "practice."

Tom explained that Brad and Harp would still be with him, but his two guests agreed to go out and do something else while the session between Gundo and Richie went on, but they both expressed the hope they could at least meet Richie before they left, if he was willing.

Richie Hassler was the star of a TV sitcom called *Hall Pass* that beginning in '90 had been, despite the mediocre acting and the inanity of plot and dialogue, rather popular with teen-agers, and a surprising number of gay men, for three seasons. The teen-agers were attracted by the high-school setting of the show, and the teeny-boppers and gay men were attracted by the clean-cut and sexy young male actors. The second lead on the show, the dark and obviously Latin Monte Alvarez, was as sexy and attractive in his own way as Richie. In addition to the beauty of the two leads, the gay men loved watching Monte, whose young muscular body was normally clad in tight Levi's or gym shorts that revealed a huge, bulging crotch. Richie's body was slight, but lightly muscled, and he had an adorable little bubble butt, which showed up nicely in the frequent beach and gym scenes. His crotch promised nothing of the massiveness that Monte's suggested, however, but the face and the butt more than made up for this failing.

After the show ceased production and went into syndication, Richie and Monte were seldom seen. They made a feature movie based on the show, which bombed. Thereafter Richie more-or-less disappeared from public view, and Monte only appeared in the occasional 'made-for-TV' movie aimed at youngsters. A year before Brad and Harp's visit, Monte had married, and Richie had been best man at his wedding. Just a few months before their present meeting, however, Richie, now twenty-six, had been arrested in a police raid in Griffith Park in Los Angeles, where, according to newspaper and TV accounts, word of mouth, and reports in the tabloids, he had the cock of one naked man down his throat, the cock of another naked man up his ass, and four more naked men waiting their turns! There had been no denying the much-reported event, so after Richie's lawyer got the case quietly set aside, Richie came out to the press and admitted he was gay, and that his encounter in the park had been very indiscreet.

Monte Alvarez was interviewed on the subject of Richie's troubles, and stated that he had been taken by surprise, that he had never suspected his friend was gay, but that he was still his friend and he wished him all the best. Since Richie knew his movie and TV career was at an end, he decided he would do what he had secretly aspired to for years: he contacted Tom Hunt and told him he wanted to talk about doing a porn movie, bottoming for Racc Rivera.

"I asked the kid if he thought he could take you," Tom said to Gundo. "He laughed his ass off and asked me if I was familiar with the Jeff Stryker, Ken Ryker, Brad Stone, Kris Lord, and Tom Chase dildos as well as my own. I told him I was, of course, and he said he not only used all of them regularly, but he'd even had the original models for two of them inside him several times! He offered to take the original of mine any time I wanted to give it to him, but he really wants to work with you, says he thinks you're the hottest guy in porn. I told him I'd have you call him if you were willing to audition him, and report back to me. He mentioned tomorrow night as being good, but I get the feeling almost any night would be okay."

Gundo laughed. "Shit yes, I'll try him out. I just wish it was the other guy, Monte Alvarez. God, I used to drool over him all the time, but I gotta admit I also dreamed about fuckin' Richie a lot when I watched the show. So you think he's serious, or does he just want to fuck with Race Rivera?"

"I think he's serious, and it doesn't look like he has an awful lot to lose. I know the video could sell twenty or thirty thousand units easily. If he never does another one, we could all do pretty well on it, and if he's good, well ... who knows? He says he's pretty much strictly a bottom, but so were Kevin Williams and Joey Stefano, and now Kevin Kramer, but he'd be starting out with a famous name and a million guys around the country who've dreamed of fucking him for a long time even before the first video was released! I think it could be sensational." Tom gave Richie's private telephone number to Gundo.

As they were leaving to return to Gundo's apartment, Tom presented Brad and Harp with the videocassettes that had been shot that night, and told them he hoped they'd send him a dub of some of the sections with Harp's ass on display. Harp stepped up to Tom and kissed him. "You want to take a few minutes right now to make another special tape just for you to watch?" Tom agreed that he would like that very much, and with Brad, Gundo, and the twins looking on, and with Gundo more or less directing the cameraman, they filmed a session of Harp displaying his ass for Tom to caress and tongue-fuck, taking Tom's monster cock inside it, and undulating that beautiful object seductively while he returned the favor and fucked his host. Each achieved an orgasm while riding the other's cock and masturbating, and each concluded by licking his own emission from his partner. Tom promised to get a copy made for Harp. Other than that, to keep the tape strictly private, and he promised to beat off to it often—a plan which Harp said he would follow himself. Had the cameraman turned around, he could have filmed the twins on their knees sucking Gundo and Brad off while they watched. An,d as Harp and Tom were licking their own loads off each other's stomachs, Gundo and Brad were licking theirs off the twins' faces.

It had been as sexually frenzied an occasion as Brad had experienced since he rescued Chris from the gang bang over twenty years ago, or the fivesome he had had with these same people (less Harp) the previous fall. It was the wildest thing Harp had experienced since he and Steve Rommel had folded their act. Tom, the twins, and Gundo were no strangers to scenes like this, but they all agreed it had been one of the best!

Gundo called Richie Hassler late the next morning, and the two set a meeting for late that afternoon at Gundo's apartment. He gave Richie instructions to find it, and then asked if he would mind if Harp and Brad stayed around until he arrived, so they could meet him. Richie said he would be happy to meet them, and when Gundo informed him they were both cute, built, hot, and hung, Richie said he might like for them to stick around and watch—or maybe even participate in his informal audition!

Richie proved to be every bit as cute in person as he had been on *Hall Pass*. Although the show had been off the air for about four years, he didn't look a day older—he was twenty-six, and looked about sixteen. He was wearing a tight T-shirt and even tighter Levi's, which showed he had apparently been doing some gym work to build up his body, and that his butt was as cute as ever! The only difference between this real Richie Hassler and his character on *Hall Pass* was a slight, but unmistakable effeminacy and an unrelenting air of seductiveness. This was obviously a guy who was looking for cock!

Shaking hands with Gundo, Richie was almost drooling. "I have absolutely loved your videos! You've gotta be the hottest man in porn!"

Gundo pulled Richie in to him, and fondled his ass. "I hope I'm gonna prove it isn't just an illusion."

Richie returned the embrace, then fondled Gundo's crotch and said "I can feel this is no illusion—this is major meat! Jesus, I've been wanting to sit on Race Rivera's fabulous cock for a long time!" By the time the two began kissing passionately and grinding their pelvises together, it was clear each had a throbbing erection!

Gundo grinned into Richie's face. "This is gonna be fun, I can tell. And I want you to meet Brad Thornton and Harp Harper. I think you'd have fun with them, too!"

There was no question that Richie was impressed with both Harp and Brad, as he shook their hands he was obviously sizing them up. When they began to talk about *Hall Pass*, he cut them short. "Look, we'll visit later, and we'll talk as much about that as you want, but right now I'm horny as hell, and I want to get fucked! I can't wait to get Race ... Gundo up my butt and down my throat, and if you guys look half as good naked as you do with your clothes on, I know we can find some room for you, too—if you're interested."

Harp laughed and embraced Richie. "I've been interested in your butt ever since I first saw you on TV, and from what Brad has said, I know he feels the same way." The last part of this was a total lie, Brad hardly ever watched *Hall Pass*. "I guarantee you we can both fill you up with about as much cock as you can handle, maybe not quite as much as Gundo's got, but damned near!"

"Ooooh! I think I may be in love," Richie said as he began to fondle Harp's crotch and then with his other hand provide similar attention to Brad. He soon had both cocks straining the bounds of their pants as he kissed one, and then the other, and then grinned at Gundo. "Why don't we find your bedroom, unless you guys are ready to fuck my happy ass right here."

Gundo caressed Richie's tempting butt and said, "Let's start in the bedroom, anyway!" Gundo led the way, and the other three followed. Once inside, Richie kicked off his shoes and began peeling off his skin-tight Levi's and tee-shirt. He had an adorable body—slight, but with quite nicely developed musculature—and a perfectly rounded, perfectly magnificent, perfectly edible and fuckable ass! His cock, which was standing straight out from his body and throbbing in erection—about average size—but perfectly formed, and promised to be a tasty treat indeed.

All three had been so fascinated watching Richie strip, that they were still fully clothed when he threw himself on Gundo's king-size bed. He rolled on his stomach and leered at them, humping the bed and running his hands sensuously over his undulating ass. "I want to see some big cocks!"

Gundo, Brad, and Harp all stripped seductively for Richie, who expressed eager approval and spent a considerable period of time kneeling before each of them to demonstrate a cocksucking talent which was nothing short of astonishing—able to take even Gundo's stupendous prick completely down his throat, with his nose disappearing in the thatch of pubic hair over it and the Latin stud's enormous balls pressed against his chin.

Although both Brad's and Harp's dicks were also impressive, they presented no problem whatever for the apparently bottomless throat of the adorable little blond. And it wasn't simply that he could accommodate those huge cocks—he provided equally impressive vacuum and oral stimulation as he did so.

And if Richie's throat seemed bottomless, it was nothing compared to the hungry depths of his surprisingly tight butt. He not only rode each of them, he actually bounced savagely up and down as his body gripped their cocks in a vise-like hold that guaranteed each would not stop until orgasm had been achieved. When he knelt before each to receive their thrusts, his body drove wildly backward to meet them, and intuitively provided perfect synchronization for maximum penetration and withdrawal. Combined with the ever-tight hold he seemed to always maintain on an invading cock, he again was guaranteed the fuck would continue to orgasm.

He lay on his back for each to receive equally enthusiastic "missionary position" fucks from them—with his legs wrapped around their waists, his hands feverishly exploring the body of the fucker-of-the-moment, his mouth eagerly performing a feverish dual tongue-fuck, and his ass slamming in to meet the thrusts of his fucker. Any time he was kissing or sucking, he was murmuring impassioned groans of lust, and when his mouth was not filled with tongue or prick, he was loudly urging whoever was inside him to fuck harder and faster and deeper. He frequently sniffed the bottle of poppers he clutched in his hand, and each time it drove him for a few moments to almost insane heights of passionate talk and delirious driving on the prick he was receiving.

If Richie's dick was not unduly long, his tongue seemed to make up for it. As he rimmed the three men, it became obvious he loved eating ass as much as he did sucking cock. It was equally obvious, however, that he loved nothing quite so much as getting fucked. He managed to suck cock and eat ass much of the time while he was getting fucked, and he was at all times so clearly appreciative of what he was receiving, that all three of his welcome assailants concentrated their efforts on servicing him. Uncharacteristically, they hardly played with each other at all, devoting their efforts to pleasing the guest of honor.

Richie was an indefatigable "bottom" of matchless talent. After almost three hours of relentless sex play, the four collapsed on the bed in total, deliriously happy exhaustion. Richie was virtually covered in come—he had inspired Gundo and Harp and Brad to impressive heights of semen production, but a good bit of the slimy and sticky discharge coating the hot blond's cute body and face was his own.

After a short respite, Gundo and Brad and Harp agreed they wanted to get serviced by Richie too, so their guest joyously fucked their mouths and offered his cute ass to their tongues before plowing each of them in missionary position, and each agreed the famous face looked adorable with their legs framing it while he went about his work. Although his cock was only of average size, he was a very capable fucker who satisfied each man he screwed—and concluded each fuck with a few generous spurts proving his satisfaction.

Gundo assured Richie that he was positive a video starring the two of them would be as sensationally successful as it would be unbelievably enjoyable to make, and that he would so recommend to Tom. He kissed him and laughed, "But I think we'll need to get together and practice a lot before we start. And I know Tom will want to audition you himself as well—and he's got the biggest cock I've ever seen!"

Richie was especially pleased with the latter comment, noting he often fucked himself with the Tom Fox Dildo, and was eager to enjoy the original inside his eager ass.

A wonderfully enjoyable four-way shower ensued, and all settled down for a drink and a visit. Richie freely admitted that he had been acting pretty stupid lately, that what the police who caught him in Griffith Park didn't know was that two of the naked guys standing there had already fucked him! "I had to promise my dad I'd stop that kind of thing, and I know I've got to. I'd been getting pretty out of control."

"Did your dad knows about you being gay before that?" Gundo asked.

With a big grin, Richie replied, "My dad knew I was gay before anyone else did. Who do you think sucked me off the first time?"

"Your own father?"

"Well, he wasn't my real father. I'm not sure my mother even knew who that was, but the man I always knew as my dad married her, and formally adopted me—and she disappeared a few years later. He couldn't have been nicer to me if he'd been my real dad, and if he wanted to suck my dick, it was his! Anyway, he obviously enjoyed it—he started doing it when I was about twelve, and it wasn't long before he convinced me I should be doing the same thing for him! I didn't screw around with anyone else until Dad started taking me to auditions. He all but promised directors, and producers sex with me in exchange for a break in movie or television work, and I had to come through on quite a few of those promises, but I didn't have to do too many dirty old men before I was on that show and by that time Dad had lined up a young lover who seemed to keep him satisfied."

"God. What about your mother?

"Who the hell knows? Who the hell cares even? I don't even remember her. After the show started, we thought we'd hear from her, but we never did. I promised Dad, and I had to promise Monte too that I'd be a lot more careful in the future."

Gundo, Brad, and Harp had all been especially hot for the hunky Monte, and asked if there had been any off screen hanky-panky between the two.

Richie laughed. "Ha! Hanky-panky? Listen, the first day we got together and read through the script for the pilot, Monte knelt between my legs and sucked a huge load out of my cock, and almost before he had swallowed, he was shooting an even bigger one down my throat! I was nineteen, and I'd sucked a lot of cock along the way, but nothing to compare to his.

"Monte has one of the biggest, most gorgeous pricks I've ever seen. They tried to hide it for the show, but his box was still so big you could hardly take your eyes off it. We're talking something like ten or eleven inches here! I could only take about half of it in my mouth the first time I sucked it, but he was patient with me, and worked with me so that in a couple of weeks he had every inch of that gorgeous monster all the way down my throat—and I sucked at least two loads out of that cock every day from the first reading of the pilot script until the night before his wedding.

"And it sure as hell wasn't one-sided. He loved nothing more than sucking a couple loads out of me every day. Well, I say he loved nothing more than that—that's wrong. What he loved more than that was exploding one of those huge loads all the way up my butt! I'd never been fucked by anything near as big as his dick before that. Again, I could hardly take him when he first tried to fuck me, but it wasn't long before I was loving every fabulous fat inch he could shove inside me, and, honey, that cock of his was fat, too, and hard as a rock.

"God, he was a fabulous fucker—correction, unless something has happened in the last few days, he *is* a fabulous fucker. Anyway, I loved nothing better than feeling that huge load of his blasting inside me—almost made me come every time he did."

The three listeners were fascinated. Brad asked, "Did Monte let you fuck him?"

Richie laughed. "Let me fuck him? Ha! He would have made me fuck him if I hadn't wanted to, but you can bet your sweet ass I wanted to! Surprisingly enough, considering how many guys had fucked my eager ass before that, Monte was actually the first guy that I fucked—and that was the same day we first had sex! He always wanted to get it while he was lying flat on his stomach—and that was great as far as I was concerned. I can't think how many times I gave it to him that way—and gave him some mighty big dildos up his ass the same way—*and* fucked him while he had one of those huge things already in him.

"We blew our loads inside each other for a long time, until we both decided we'd better start practicing safe sex, but the rubbers didn't make it one bit less enjoyable."

"And you fucked each other the night before he got married?" Gundo asked.

Richie leaned forward and kissed Gundo. "And he blew three big loads in me; I don't know how much come he had left for Alicia on their honeymoon, but he damn near drowned me with it the night after they got back!"

"And you were best man at his wedding?"

"No, no, honey, Monte was the best man at the wedding! If you'd ever been fucked by that big thing of his, you'd know that! I was just the luckiest man at the wedding!"

"And didn't he tell some reporter he was surprised to hear you were gay?"

"Yeah, and ain't that a kick in the ass? He'd just finished screwing me when he told me had said that!"

Harp asked, "Did he screw other guys too?"

"Well, he sure as hell screwed a lot of other guys before he started fucking me," Richie said. "But aside from some unbelievable threesomes we had with several very famous guys I'd better not mention, I think he regarded us as lovers from the first time we got together until the show folded, and he took that seriously, I think?"

"Did you?"

"Well ... pretty much so, but I have to admit I sucked a few cocks and got fucked by a few other guys along the way. Actually, most of the guys on the show were gay, or could certainly be had, but Monte and I kept it to ourselves. I think all the other guys thought we were screwing each other, but they never found out for sure, except for Hill Earthman. You remember him? Tall, dark-haired, gorgeous hunk who played the lifeguard on the show? He caught us one time, and promised to keep quiet about it if he could fuck both of us, and he did. And we both fucked him, too, and we got together with him every now and then so that he could renew his vows the same way.

"After the show broke up, I started branching out regularly, and Monte didn't seem to mind. I guess doing the show was part of our love affair. When it was over, they were both over. Obviously, we still see each other and enjoy screwing. Even though he's married, I know he's been having an affair with ... well, I'd better not say, but you'd be very surprised."

Gundo tried very hard to get Richie to set up a meeting with him and Monte, but Richie said he couldn't promise anything, that since his marriage, Monte was keeping a pretty low profile, still seeing Richie and having sex with his famous lover when he could, but not taking any chances past that. "After all, he's still got some kind of career in movies," Richie said.

"The two of you could have an incredible career in fuck movies," Gundo said.

Richie kissed him and said, "I promise you Monte's not gonna ever be seen in a fuck movie. But I sure hope he enjoys watching me in a lot of them!"

Gundo kissed him back, "And your first one is gonna have Race Rivera's cock so far up your ass you're gonna be screaming!"

"I think we all had better practice a little more," Richie said as he dove into Gundo's lap and started getting Race Rivera's cock ready. The other two cocks were soon ready also, and before the evening was over, Richie had been double-fucked by both Harp and Brad while Gundo was plumbing the depths of his appreciative, and seemingly bottomless throat.

Later, as Gundo was standing, holding Richie's body in his arms while he was impaled on the giant prick, Brad came up to them, and squeezed his own big cock inside Richie's ass along with Gundo's, to deliver another, even more stunning double fuck to the slim blond! Richie wanted to double-fuck someone along with Gundo, so Harp obliged him by riding Gundo as he admitted Richie's smaller, but still quite satisfying prick alongside Gundo's monster.

When Richie left a few hours later, all said they looked forward to a repeat soon.

That particular group never managed to meet again, although Race Rivera and Richie Hassler were subsequently paired in several very successful videos. Richie proved to be an extremely popular porn star, and many of his videos matched him up with Latinos like Gundo, obviously wanting to capitalize on the memory of his television work with Monte Alvarez. Within two years he was the pre-eminent bottom in the business, the most accommodating and exciting since Joey Stefano, and every major porn star, except those who were under exclusive contract, and couldn't appear in films by Tom's company, Fox Hunt Productions, was filmed fucking Richie.

Richie seldom fucked in his films, but for special contrasting effect, Tom occasionally had him top some of the biggest, most gym-built muscular men in porn—several of whom were regarded as strictly tops. One of the few things more stimulating than watching Richie's cute little bubble butt getting fucked by a big cock was watching that same adorable ass driving and writhing while he buried his own cock into the generous, muscular ass of a super-macho porn stud. As voracious as Richie was, he never got fist-fucked (at least on camera); fisting was regarded as both dangerous and anti-sexual by Tom Hunt.

Tom, using Gundo to convince him, did manage to talk Harp into acting in a porn video, which proved so successful that he actually appeared in an entire series of them, but his face was never seen—which had been the agreement reached before the first was filmed. He appeared in the videos as "Cal LaPidgin," a pun on an obscure word that Tom knew, for some equally obscure reason, "callipygian," which means 'having well-proportioned buttocks.' In simpler words, one who is callipygian has a cute ass—and Harp certainly qualified if anyone ever did.

Even though his face was never shown, Harp was for a time one of the most popular performers in male pornography, often capturing first place in various polls and awards ceremonies, though he never accepted an invitation to appear at any of the latter. His ass proved to be as glorious on camera as it was in the oh-so-beautiful flesh. The camera loved it, as did anyone who ever touched it, kissed it, rimmed it, or fucked it. Not only Richie and Race, but some of the biggest and most celebrated cocks in porn were shown penetrating the depths of Harp's perfect fundament. This included a brief return of Tom Hunt to video, in his persona as Tom Fox, where he was shown stroking his gargantuan cock while he explained that he could not resist making a one-time comeback in order to fuck what had to be the most beautiful ass he'd ever seen. Harp's voice is heard as he says he's never seen a cock he wants inside him more than this one, and he uses his hand to guide Tom's cock to his hole, after which one of the most splendid and exciting fucks ever filmed ensues.

It was a one-time comeback for Fox, but it was anything but a one-shot appearance. He generated no fewer than four loads for Harp's (and the camera's) gratification in their unforgettable shoot. Harp gave Tom three in return, including one in a condom buried deep inside the legendary ass. It would have been seen as a less impressive performance if viewers knew it had been shot over a period of three days.

The beauty of Harp's ass in Richie's video with "Cal

LaPidgin" so impressed his fuck-buddy and former co-star Monte Alvarez that Monte asked him if he would try to set up a secret threesome with them and "Cal." Harp was thrilled to comply, and one of the most pleasant afternoons of fucking he ever enjoyed was the result. Not only was Monte as breathtakingly handsome and well-built in person as he appeared on TV, but his cock was as long, as fat, as hard, and as thrilling as Richie had promised it would be—and he was as delighted to take Harp's own impressive prick deep in his mouth and his ass as he had been to bury his in the legendary "Cal LaPidgin." Indeed, the Latino stud exploded his most impressive load of the afternoon all over Harp's face while he rode his cock, with Richie buried inside him as well, double-fucking him! It is a great shame that particular threesome was not filmed.

In every film he appeared in, Harp's perfect ass is shown as it drives his generous and equally photogenic cock savagely into whomever has just been filling it! In all his videos, every guy who screws Harp then proceeds to suck his cock and eat his perfect ass, before submitting to the enthusiastic and obviously satisfying long, ecstatic fuck he receives from "Cal" in return. The series became the vehicle for the first on-screen kissing, cocksucking, rimming, and bottoming of several porn stars who had claimed they were completely straight, and never sucked or got fucked!

In one of those appearances, the model for the all-time best-selling 'signature dildo' pounds Harp's perfect ass and barely gets his mammoth prick out and stripped of its condom before he literally coats that perfect object with come. Then his hands are seen massaging that come into a now-standing Harp's ass while he kneels before him, apparently sucking cock. The camera pans around Harp's body, and it can be seen that the stud definitely is administering a very impassioned and impressive blowjob. He removes his mouth from Harp's cock momentarily, grins at the camera, and explains, "I don't suck cock or take it up the ass, but fucking Cal's ass was so hot I've just gotta have this pretty dick of his as far inside me as he can get it, and it looks like when I get it warmed up right, he's gonna slip me a whole helluva lotta fat, hard prick!"

He then deep throats every inch of the aforementioned

'pretty dick' for several more minutes before kneeling in front of Harp to receive another of the porn world's all-time classic ass-poundings! In the course of that historic coupling he enjoys Harp's ferocious, seemingly endless fuck so much that as soon as Harp blasts a huge load on his back, the former exclusive top settles his ass down over a supine Harp's still throbbing cock and rides it while he jacks off and shoots an even more copious load than his first.

The final scene shows him licking his own come from Harp's chest and face, although the camera angle makes it impossible to distinguish the features of Harp's face. The super-top's first on-screen kiss ensues, and as Harp rolls on top of the stud, they begin to grind their pelvises together, kissing rapturously, and before the scene fades for the final credits, the viewer has the feeling that another exchange of fucks is going to follow! In fact, Harp and the superstud who'd lost his ass-cherry to Harp on camera, but who loved getting his ass screwed in real life, and who enjoyed nothing in the world more than being fucked by the massive dildo molded from his own cock, exchanged fuck after fuck after fuck for three straight days after making the video—but, regrettably for porn fans, they were not captured on film.

The sex they had the next day in Gundo's apartment was great, but anticlimactic. All were so exhausted from their session with Richie Hassler the day before that they just hung out by the pool, and although there was a lot of kissing and cuddling, and everyone got a blowjob or two, no one got fucked that day! The next morning, before Harp and Brad had to leave for the airport was quite another story, and all were left with the indelible memory of spectacular "going-away" fucks.

Back in San Francisco, Harp felt he had to 'mend fences' with Jay after his absence, and so he left Brad to fend for himself for the next several days, which stretched to a week when Harp rented a car and took Jay up to the Russian River for a long weekend. After three days, Brad was so horny he scanned the pages of the "Models/Escorts" section in the latest issue of the *Nation*, seeking a playmate to hire for an hour or two of true love. One new ad caught his attention right away.

It was indicative of the growing seriousness about his feelings for Harp that Brad had not even looked at the escort section of the newspaper for several weeks, and so he had no idea how long this particular ad had been running. He felt sure it had not been running the last time he scanned the ads, because he could not have missed it! The editor of the *Nation* was no doubt aware of how eye-catching this particular ad was, since he had placed it in virtual dead-center of the penultimate page, which almost entirely comprised photo-ads for escorts.

It showed the torso of a nude man from about his shoulders to mid-thigh. It was a very attractive body, but what caught the eye, and made the heart beat a lot faster, was the fact that the only thing covering this man's sizable cock was a dish towel. The thatch of pubic hair above the cock was quite visible, and the balls were just barely concealed, and the cloth draped over, and clung to the no-doubt luscious organ in such a way that it was even quite evident that he was circumcised.

It was, hands down, the most blatantly sexy photograph Brad had ever seen in this newspaper. The caption read: "Like the looks of this bat? You ought to see the balls! Let's play! I like to pitch, I like to catch! Andrew: nineteen years old, drop-dead gorgeous, versatile, and horny as hell. This is a current picture, and it's exactly what $150 will get you. Out calls only." There was no question in Brad's mind who he wanted to spend some time with that evening.

He called Andrew's number, but got only an answering machine. In a very sexy, hoarse voice, Andrew said, "Hi! This is Andrew. I'm afraid I can't see you today, but I hope you'll call me another time. If you can, just save it up for me. If you can't wait, think of me when you're giving it to someone else, and then call me to see how I compare. I just know I won't disappoint you." Just the voice and the message added to Brad's horniness. So he called another escort, Steve, whose photo-montage also looked very promising.

Steve was available, so Brad went to his apartment. It was very near where Harp lived, actually, and he spent two eminently enjoyable hours. Steve was a tall, long-haired blond with super-long legs and a luscious ass, and he delighted in wrapping the former around Brad's waist as Brad plumbed the latter at great length—and, according to Steve, at very satisfying depth also. He was also a very eager and commanding top, with a relatively long, extremely fat "beer-can" dick, and Brad enjoyed bottoming for him as much as he had enjoyed topping him. The two had prefaced their fucking with passionate kissing and embracing, and lengthy and enthusiastic mutual oral worship. Eventually, Steve gave Brad two loads, but Brad returned three! It was an experience Brad expressed eagerness to repeat, and after he had described Harp, Steve agreed that it would be fun for Brad to bring him along with him next time. Steve added that his own lover/roommate was "in the business," and showed Brad his picture ad in the *Nation*. They both agreed that a foursome might be even more fun. Steve's lover had a great body, and, according to Steve, an even bigger and fatter cock and an unusual talent for multiple orgasms.

Brad told Harp about his encounter with Steve the next time they met, and Harp detailed his love-making with Jay on their Russian River trip, with the predictable result that they got so horny they spent the night re-enacting those activities with each other.

For the next month they dedicated themselves to each other. Harp did continue to see Jay, but they had no threesomes, although Harp did think a session with Steve and his lover sounded promising.

It was becoming clear to Harp that he was going to have to decide soon if he could continue dating both Brad and Jay. Both were after him to stop escorting, but Jay could offer no compensation except his love, while Brad could offer either a position with his company, education for another profession, or even just supporting Harp if that was the way he might want it.

They decided to celebrate the first day of summer with a threesome—with the exciting Louis. When they called him in the late afternoon, Louis regretted that he had to decline their offer. He had just serviced a client, and had another one scheduled for early evening. He laughed, "And Harp, the guy I was just with was from South Carolina, like you. Older guy, but nice, a retired professor. I oughta tell him about you, you South Carolina guys could hook up.

"But he's coming back to see me later this week. I promised

him a big load, he said he wants this big cock of mine up his ass again soon."

Coincidentally, Harp later learned that Louis's South Carolina client had retired from teaching at Farrar University, the very same school Harp had attended for a year, and where Doug Truax taught.

They decided to call Steve to try and set up a threesome (or perhaps even a foursome, with his lover), but he was already engaged as well.

Harp had agreed with Brad that the ad for 'Andrew' was as sexy as any he had seen. "If you and Jay didn't keep me so busy, I'd be tempted to call him myself, and see if he wanted to exchange a courtesy fuck. But, hell, I wouldn't mind paying for what's under that towel!" So, they hoped Andrew would be amenable to a threesome with two appreciative fans.

The same sexy, hoarse voice that had been on Andrew's answering machine responded in person to Brad's call. Brad put on his usual, sexy, husky voice to talk with the youngster.

"Andrew, this is Brad. My friend and I are wondering if you'd be interested in a little 'party'."

After Brad described himself and Harp, Andrew said it sounded exciting as hell, and promised to be a lot of fun. Brad said, "We're both anxious to see what's holding that towel up in your ad. Is it as big as it looks?"

Andrew laughed, "Oh yeah! If I was short, it might not be as big as it looks in the picture, but I'm tall, and I know you're not gonna be disappointed. Do you think it looks good enough to eat? I sure hope so!"

"Absolutely, we're both looking forward to a big meal. You up to a two-course dinner yourself?"

This time Andrew's laugh was more a low, sultry snicker. "I can't wait. Only thing I like better than a cock down my throat is one up my ass. I guess tonight I can get both at once, can't I? And I think when I turn around, you're gonna be almost as happy as you will be when you see what the washcloth is hiding! You guys like to receive as well as get? I like to give, too, I really like to give, and I'm damned good at it!"

It was Brad's turn to laugh. "I'll bet you are! I've always heard it was better to give than to receive, but that sure as hell doesn't mean I don't like to be on the receiving end—and my friend likes receiving especially. And I don't think you've ever seen a prettier ass than my friend is gonna show you."

"Well, I've got a lover, and if your friend's ass is half as beautiful as his, I'm gonna love plugging it! Does, say, $250 for it sound okay?"

Brad declared the fee acceptable.

"Tell me when and where, then," Andrew said.

Brad gave him the address, and Andrew said he would be there in an hour. "I have to get a quick shower, and I live clear across town from the Embarcadero, but don't start without me, okay?" And they both expressed eagerness about the little 'party'.

The hour passed slowly, and both Harp and Brad were anxious for Andrew to appear. Slightly more than an hour later, the telephone rang. Brad picked it up, "Yes?"

The sexy voice: "Brad? Andrew. Buzz me in and get ready!"

Brad pressed the buzzer to open the front door downstairs, and Harp headed for the bathroom. "I'm gonna take a pee and get ready." Brad kicked off his shoes and slipped his shirt over his head. A minute or two later, there was a knock on the door. Peering through the peep-hole, Brad saw the back of Andrew's head as he looked back down the hallway, a beautiful crown of golden hair.

Brad opened the door, saying, "Andrew, come in, I'm...." And he froze as "Andrew" turned his head to greet him.

It was Josh—his son!

Neither could speak for a moment. Finally, Brad gasped, "Josh, what in hell is this? My God ... you're Andrew?"

"Dad? You're the Brad I'm here to meet?"

"Yes, I ... no! Oh shit, get in here! You've got a lot of explaining to do!

"I think maybe you've got a few things to explain to me, too, Dad!"

"Jesus Christ, I can't believe this! Come in here and...." He took a deep breath. "Yes, you're right, Josh, I guess I owe you an explanation too. Come on in and let me get the door closed."

Josh came in to the room, looking around. "What is this place, Dad? What are you...?" He stopped short as Harp emerged from the bathroom.

Harp was totally naked, and he was holding his erect cock in his hand and grinning. "You guys ready for some of this?" He stopped, and his jaw dropped as surely as if he had been doing a vaudeville take. "Jay!"

It was Josh's turn to do the take. "Harp!"

The stunned silence which ensued was probably as *fraught* as a silence can be.

JOSH

1.

The argument concerning Nature vs. Nurture, or Heredity vs. Environment, is a relatively new one in the instance of homosexual orientation. Until fairly recently, everyone apparently assumed that if a man or boy was queer, it was because he had either: (a) been subjected to a sexual encounter with an opportunistic faggot which infected him in some way, transforming the hitherto normally oriented poor soul into some sort of raging, flaming (albeit perhaps secretive) queen who referred to everyone as "Miss Thing"; (b) been pampered by an over-protective mother, or lived in an overly-feminine household, which led him, of course, to adopt the feminine lifestyle and apparent thirst for cock which females are known to harbor—an absent or abusive father was a helpful accoutrement in laying the blame; (c) decided to humiliate his family or wreak revenge for no doubt imagined wrongs done him, by embarrassing all his relatives; or (d) been possessed of the devil.

Over-exposure to Broadway show-tunes or the ballet were also suspected root causes of adoptive homosexuality. A lack of enthusiasm for sports was a strong symptom of the deviant orientation. Parenthetically, it was assumed that all effeminate men were homosexual, and effeminate boys obviously apprentices, and that all homosexual men or boys were effeminate.

Of late, however, there has been conjecture, perhaps even admission, in a number of ever more influential quarters that some guys might just be born with a taste for cock. The things we do not learn, we are, apparently, born with as a result of genetics. The question naturally arises: how, then, could a predisposition to a nature that tends to provide no offspring be passed on? Would it not die out? A good point. One possible explanation might be that there are married men or women, fathers and mothers, who are homosexuals. But, on the other hand, this could not explain the dilemma, since married people couldn't be queer. They're married, for godssake!

Most homosexuals will freely admit, although mostly only to one another, or to their confessors, whether clergy, counselors, or shocked family members, that they have known they were gay all their lives, that they knew they were attracted to members of their own sex long before their first sexual experiences. Demonstrative of heredity/nature over environment/nurture? No. Far too simplistic. The jury is still out.

To conclude the parenthetical proposition stated above, regarding effeminacy, it is becoming more and more understood that while the vast majority of effeminate men or boys are probably homosexual (or would be, if they exercised their choice), the vast majority of homosexual men and boys are not effeminate! How then to spot a queer? Alas, it ain't easy, and it's sometimes difficult for the fag basher to spot his prey!

Certainly Joshua Andrews Thornton was aware from his earliest sexual stirrings that his life story was never going to be the boy-meets-girl one if he had anything to say about it. He came from a happy home with both parents present and apparently compatible. His mother was anything but domineering at home. She was loving and attentive when she was there, but admittedly her work consumed more and more of her time, especially after she assumed editorship of *Bitch* when Josh was nine years old, and she was the only feminine element in his home. He had no early traumatic sexual experiences with homosexual men. He was to have plenty of anything-but-traumatic ones when he reached sexual maturity, but he either welcomed or initiated most of the earliest ones. He loved both his parents, so there were no perceived wrongs for him to avenge by turning queer. And it seems highly unlikely that he was possessed.

He had not been exposed to much Broadway show music at home, and everyone in his immediate family despised ballet. And he enjoyed sports, both as an avid spectator and as a naturally athletic, reasonably gifted participant.

So, how to explain that Josh turned out gay? True, his father was gay, but had he passed that along to his son in his genes? Who knows? And if he had simply learned to keep it in his jeans ... well, that's pointless speculation as well as a rather forced pun!

The neighborhood around the house on 36th Avenue in San Francisco, where Josh grew up, was an ideal place to raise a child, and equally appealing to the child, also. His elementary school was less than a block away, his high school was within four blocks. Golden Gate Park was a few blocks south, and Lincoln Park as easily reached to the north, both magnificent recreational areas, and the seemingly endless ocean-front beach was less than a mile away. It was a quiet, upper-upper middle class neighborhood, with few traffic problems, little crime, and no homeless vagrants. If it were foggy more than one would have desired, and if the months of summer vacation were often among the coolest of the year, well, it wasn't perfect.

Josh himself wasn't perfect either. He occasionally was cranky or petulant. He didn't always remember to do chores assigned him commensurate with his age, nor did he always perform those chores or specially-assigned duties with the greatest willingness or enthusiasm. He rarely was insubordinate or disrespectful of his elders, but those traits weren't entirely unheard-of, either. He enjoyed goofing off as much as anyone, and as a result was occasionally prone to procrastination. He was seldom guilty of more serious infractions. However, the one time he appropriated some money from his father's wallet without permission (i.e., although it's not nice to say it, he *stole* it), he was apprehended, punished, and learned an excellent lesson about honesty and property rights.

But if he wasn't perfect, he was a damned good kid. He had a sunny disposition, a generous and affectionate nature, love and respect for his parents and relatives and friends, a considerable intellect (and the intellectual curiosity to put it to use), and industriousness.

Physically, he may not have been perfect, but it's hard to think where any imperfection lay. He was always tall for his age, finally topping out at over six feet. He had a magnificent head of golden hair, perfectly balanced features, wonderful skin which seemed to glow with health, a naturally muscular body which he kept toned unconsciously through play and exercise, and the facial features of an Adonis. Those who were privileged to see him naked after he reached sexual maturity, which he did at an extremely early age, were treated to the sight of beautifully rounded buttocks and a perfectly shaped, quite lengthy penis.

He not only resembled his handsome father physically, he was his father's son in other ways as well, especially in the matter of sexual precocity. His father had experienced his first full-blown sexual encounter when he was only fourteen, in the arms and mouth of his first prep-school roommate. His son beat him by a year, as a thirteen-year-old, with his best friend in a pup tent on his backyard lawn.

Josh's first erections not induced by bladder pressure, friction, or some other such involuntary or inadvertent cause, arose when he saw pictures of handsome men or older boys, or admired a tight pair of pants or shorts displaying a well-filled crotch or a tantalizingly bulging posterior. Mercifully, the sight of nude boys his own age failed to stimulate him, unless they were perhaps as developed as he, and he was usually spared locker-room embarrassment. At first it confused him. It actually took him some time to make the connection between his erections and the visual stimuli which evoked them. Before he reached his teenage years, he began to realize he was attracted sexually to members of his own sex.

It did not devastate him to realize he was probably gay. He lived in a city that was as welcoming of gay people as could be reasonably desired, and at a time when positive gay characters began to appear on television, and even gay characters in movies were not necessarily sissy, screaming-queen stereotypes. He came from liberal parents who would no more tolerate references to 'faggots' than they would to 'niggers'.

A good many of Josh's schoolmates used the term *fag* rather indiscriminately, and anti-homosexual comments and jokes were not at all unusual. Still, on balance, the dawning realization of his own homosexuality did not trouble Josh.

He began doing something about it the way almost all boys begin doing something about their sexuality, whether hetero-, homo-, bi-, omni-, or whatever: he discovered that masturbation, which he had not yet even learned a word for, seemed like a natural thing to do when stimulated, and felt absolutely wonderful in the bargain.

At the age of twelve, with pubic hair at last clearly evident on his pubes, his masturbatory exercise led him one night to an unusually good feeling—a *spectacularly* good feeling—and he experienced his first orgasm. Not knowing what had just happened, it frightened him, at first, but he instinctively knew that anything that felt that good couldn't be bad. He managed to synthesize the various unorganized bits of sexual information floating around in his brain, and had to come to terms with a concept which had hitherto been unclear to him, but which he had been too embarrassed to ask about. Guarded and oblique inquiries of his friends made him conclude that they were not yet experiencing orgasms.

Josh found that his fist was suddenly his very favorite playmate. When Damon Matthews became his friend, he found another, equally enjoyable playmate.

Josh had enjoyed playing soccer in school, and frequently he joined in on impromptu games in Golden Gate Park. The age range of players in these 'pick-up' games tended to be from fourteen to eighteen, high school age, but a few more mature younger players took part. Josh qualified, and enjoyed playing with the older boys. He was immediately attracted to the handsome Damon, and not just physically. There was no doubt Damon was physically attractive: a handsome fifteen-year old boy with an unruly shock of dirty blond hair, a compact muscular body (broad shoulders and a narrow waist), and an infectious, almost omnipresent grin. The grin accurately suggested his personality as well, friendly and happy-go-lucky, with an appetite for fun and a keen sense of humor. At times his insouciance almost suggested a kind of loopiness or goofiness, but it was just evidence of his innate good nature and optimism. Everyone liked Damon; it was unavoidable.

The first time Josh noticed Damon was when they were teamed together in a soccer game in the park, and Damon looked like God to the younger boy. He was handsome as the devil, and he was built, and his sweaty tee-shirt and shorts showed off an ass and a large bulge at the crotch that Josh ached to see naked. Several times when they made contact, Josh, then barely thirteen but already in the full throes of puberty, had to work hard to conceal a recurring erection. Their team won the game, and Josh was thrilled when the ebullient, grinning Damon threw a sweaty arm around his shoulder and asked him if he wanted to go get a Coke.

During the next two hours Josh virtually fell in love with Damon, realizing his physical beauty was matched by a charm and enthusiasm that he found irresistible. They were both quite late for supper at their respective houses that evening, since they had lost track of time while they were getting acquainted. Although he was two years older than Josh, Damon treated the younger boy like an absolute equal. Josh would not enter high school for another year, but Damon was already a sophomore—and yet there was never a suggestion between them that one was a lowly junior-high student. In view of what was soon to happen, it is likely that Damon was as physically attracted to Josh as the latter was to him.

Within a short period, they were together much of the time outside of school. Josh's two closest friends of long standing, Kyle McFarlane and Eric Neely, remained his closest associates in school (they were all in the same grade), and Josh did not ignore them. Damon just became his closest close friend, not his only one.

Late in the fall of Josh's eighth-grade year, he and Damon decided to camp out in Josh's back yard. The close contact of the tent precipitated a sexual encounter that had been brewing for several months.

Both boys had 'slept over' at each other's houses any number of times, but each had twin beds in his bedroom, and although they tussled and lolled around with each other on one or the other bed, they slept apart. This is not to say, however, that they were not becoming keenly aware of each other sexually.

The first time the boys had been together naked, each freely admired the other's body and cock, and traded expressions that said, in effect, "You've got a great body," and "You've got a big cock" —both positions were clearly founded in fact, incidentally! After a few exchanged visits, and an increasing frequency of exposure to each other's naked bodies, they began to stop their practice of hiding their erections from each other, and let their obvious stimulation lead to talk about sex.

The first really overt move between them came one evening at Damon's house. They had been playfully wrestling, dressed only in their underwear, when Damon, who was straddling a supine Josh, put his hands on Josh's shoulders and grinned down on him. "Jesus, Josh, look what you made me do!" He looked down at his crotch, and his very hard cock was protruding from the fly of his boxer shorts.

Josh grinned back. "If you'll get off me, I'll show you what you did to me!" Damon dismounted and knelt next to Josh on the bed, as the latter pulled down the waist band of his briefs, to expose an equally hard and equally imposing erection, which Josh took in his hand and began to stroke gently. "I think I'm gonna have to jack off."

Damon stood on the bed and peeled off his shorts. His cock stood straight out from his body, and Josh was thrilled as he looked up at his handsome, exciting idol. Damon began to stroke his own cock. "I know I'm gonna jack off!"

As Josh peeled off his own underwear, Damon lay down next to him, and each watched the other stroke his cock, in long, slow movements. "Oh man, this feels so good! I love it," Damon said as his strokes increased in speed and intensity. Josh accelerated his own efforts, and soon both boys were panting as they masturbated furiously. Damon gasped, "You want to see me shoot my wad?"

Josh stopped stroking and propped himself up on one arm to watch his friend's ever-more-frantic stroking. "Yeah, let me see you come!" In a few minutes, Damon stiffened his legs, and arched his back several inches off the bed, and as he continued to masturbate savagely, his hot discharge erupted into the air, splashed on his chest, and coated his hand. His body fell flat to the bed, but he continued to stroke himself feverishly with one hand, and massage his orgasm into his chest with the other. "Oh God, Josh, that felt so good!" Josh watched, fascinated, as transfixed by Damon's beauty as he was thrilled with his friend's cock and orgasm.

Finally calming down, Damon's hands fell to his sides. His dick flopped against his belly as he turned his face toward Josh and grinned hugely. "That was fun!"

Josh's hand sought out Damon's chest, and he moved the palm of his hand around tentatively on the slippery, come-covered surface. "Man, Damon, you've got a big dick. And you really can shoot!"

Damon took hold of Josh's hand with his own, and guided

it around his slick chest. His grin softened into a smile, then after a minute, his look became serious. He stopped moving Josh's hand and simply held it to his chest. "You've got a really nice, big dick too, Josh. Can you get your load yet?"

It was Josh's turn to grin. "You wanna see me do it?" He fell on his back and began stroking himself as Damon propped himself up to watch, fascinated. It took only a few minutes before the frantic beating Josh was administering to his throbbing cock began to achieve results. He had been very near orgasm a few minutes earlier when he stopped to watch Damon's climax. "I'm gonna come, man! I'm gonna get my load!" With an unfocused look of complete ecstasy he smiled sexily at Damon.

Damon was seized by the same rapture as he put his hand on Josh's stomach, at the base of his cock, and said, "Let me help you!"

In a total fever of lust, Josh released his cock, dropped his hands to his side and panted, "Yeah, jack me off, Damon!"

Damon eagerly seized Josh's cock, and after only a few savage strokes the younger boy's emission was spurting out. One of Josh's hands seized Damon's arm as he continued to use it on the exploding cock, and his other hand cupped the back of Damon's neck. His head whipped from side to side in passion as he ejaculated, and pulled Damon's head down until their faces were only inches apart; he whispered, "Oh God, you make me come, Damon, you make me shoot my load!"

Damon's hand continued to stroke Josh until his orgasm was completely through. Then with his hand he began to spread the copious, still hot ejaculate on his friend's belly as he looked very seriously into Josh's eyes. He murmured, "You made me come too, Josh, you made me shoot my load! I didn't know if you were able to come yet, but I was hoping you could. I wanted you to ... and you came a lot for me!"

They looked at each other very seriously for a long time, and their lips were moving together almost imperceptibly. Before a kiss became inevitable, Damon ginned and broke the mood. "We're a fuckin' mess! Let's get cleaned up!"

They showered together, and surprisingly without any kind of embarrassment at what they had just shared. Inevitably, they both got erections again, and Damon took hold of Josh's for a moment. "Big dick, man!" He guided one of Josh's hands to his own erection. Josh eagerly seized it, trembling with excitement as Damon added "Two big dicks!" and bestowed his irresistible grin on his friend.

They continued to play with each other for a few minutes, and very soon they were at the point of no stopping. Each continued to masturbate the other until he shot another load. It took quite a while, and the hot water was all gone long before that, but they simply turned off the shower and thrilled to the exercise. They climaxed at almost exactly the same time, while they grinned at each other without saying a word.

After their mutual orgasm, Damon pulled Josh's body in toward him, and the two ground their pelvises into each other. "Man, I want to do this with you again, okay?"

Josh, completely stupefied with happiness, said, "Yeah, and I want to do it again soon, too!"

Josh would have been happiest if it had happened again that very night. Before he could get to sleep, he had to beat off yet again, with a vision of Damon vividly consuming his mind with every stroke.

Between that night, and the night a few weeks later when they pitched the pup tent in Josh's back yard, they enjoyed mutual masturbation twice again, once when Damon was staying over at Josh's house, and another very exciting time on a sunny afternoon in the bushes in Lincoln Park, where, when they had both shot their loads, they discovered a man watching them and masturbating himself. He begged them to let him give them both blowjobs, but they pulled their pants up very hurriedly, and fled, giggling.

The night they pitched the tent in the yard succeeded a day that had been so warm they decided it would be fun to sleep outdoors. In addition, they both knew they would also have an excuse to be sleeping together side by side, and they looked forward to playing around with each other again. Josh especially looked forward to lying in Damon's arms and caressing his fine body most of the night. He had no way of knowing it, but Damon was equally interested in extending the affectionate part of their growing relationship.

The kiss-that-didn't-quite-happen when they had ended their first shared orgasms had not again seemed imminent, although

Josh had "played it" again and again in his mind. He longed desperately to kiss his older friend—almost as much as wanted to hold his dick in his hand again—but knew that if it was going to happen, Damon would have to initiate it. They actually almost never talked about their sexual experience. They had both made casual reference to "having fun," and while actually masturbating with each other they expressed their passion and pleasure freely—they just didn't much talk about it when they weren't doing it.

They watched TV in Josh's room until about nine that night, and then went in the backyard, where they lay on a blanket outside the tent for a long time, talking, and very tentatively touching each other. Finally, Damon's hand boldly and suddenly cupped the crotch of Josh's Levi's, and he whispered, "Why don't we go inside and get undressed?" In his groping, which was enthusiastically returned, Damon was delighted to find that Josh was obviously as horny as he was.

They stripped to their underwear outside the tent, but as soon as they got inside, Damon slipped out of his shorts and guided Josh's hand to his throbbing erection as he said "You want this?" He began to tug at the waistband of Josh's briefs as he said it.

Josh squeezed the solid and sizable organ he wanted so badly and said, "I want it more than anything I know!"

By this time Damon's hand had worked inside Josh's shorts and found something equally firm and impressive to squeeze. "And I want this just as much!"

Josh had brought a battery-operated lantern out to the tent, and he switched it on as soon as he had taken his shorts off. Both boys looked admiringly at each other's cocks as they began to fondle them. Lying on their backs side by side, they stroked each other for some time before rolling on their sides to face each other as they continued their mutual manual stimulation. Their faces and lips were only inches apart again (as they so often were in Josh's dreams), and they looked seriously into each other's eyes as they stroked.

One of Damon's hands began to explore Josh's body, and he eventually began to caress his ass. "Mmmmm—that feels good, Josh! Roll on your stomach and let me play with your ass!"

Without a word, Josh smiled at Damon, and assumed the

requested position. Damon knelt, straddling Josh's legs, and soon both his hands were caressing the smooth, rounded globes of the younger boy's matchless ass. Josh murmured his contentment as he undulated his buttocks in rhythm with Damon's caresses. The loving hands moved upward on Josh's body, and as they caressed his back and shoulders, Josh could feel Damon's very hard cock pressing into the crevice between his buttocks. Instinctively, he began to raise his ass, opening the crevice to admit Damon better.

"Fuck! You feel so good, Josh!" Damon said, and he lowered his body , inserting his cock between Josh's legs and beginning to fuck slowly and deeply. His chest was pressed against Josh's back and his mouth was at Josh's ear as he whispered hotly, "It feels so wonderful to fuck you like this. Do you like it?"

"It feels really exciting—I love the feeling! You've got such a big prick, Damon!"

"Your prick is just as big, and you're two years younger than I am. Think how big it's gonna be when you're my age!" He pulled them onto their sides, continuing to hump into Josh's legs as his hand went around and played with Josh's cock. Josh's hand went behind them, and pulled Damon's ass in toward him while he fondled it. "Damn, that feels good, Josh. Turn around and face me!"

Josh turned to face Damon, and he separated his legs for a moment to re-admit the driving prick between them. Their arms went around each other, and Josh's painfully hard cock pressed against Damon's stomach as he humped in rhythm while Damon continued to fuck his legs, below his balls. Each caressed and explored the other's ass at the same time they pulled their bodies in together. Their faces were so close their lips were almost touching.

Damon was barely audible as he said, "You feel so good, Josh, I...." He moved even closer and whispered only one word before their lips met: "Josh!" And as they kissed, their hands ceased moving feverishly, and they held each other in a tender, innocent transport of love.

Their kiss was not passionate, it was not hurried, nor did either make a sound—it was chaste, it was sweet, it was for each his first romantic kiss. They lay holding each other and kissing gently, very gradually opening their mouths to each other's tongues. They frequently stopped kissing, separated a bit, and shared a smile before resuming their innocent love-making—innocent even though their two fierce erections continued to hump! Finally, Damon whispered, "I want to watch your cock while I jack you off—and I want you to jack me off while I do it. Okay?"

Josh smiled at him and kissed him. "I want to see you shoot your load up close!" He reversed his body, so that they still lay on their sides, but each boy now had his face near the groin of the other so he could clearly see the cock he then began to stroke. As they stroked, each used his free hand to caress the ass of his partner, and where they had been kissing each other's lips a few minutes earlier, they were now planting kisses on their respective stomachs and legs.

Damon stopped kissing, and held Josh's cock while he slowly kissed its tip; Josh followed suit, and they were soon kissing up and down each other's shafts. Only a few minutes later, Josh felt the warmth of Damon's mouth as it opened and took his cock inside. He stopped kissing long enough to murmur, "Oh God, that feels so good!" Then he too opened his mouth, and soon each had his cock buried deep in the moist recesses of his best friend!

They began to move the ring of their tightly-held lips up and down each other's shafts, and their murmuring became feverish. Neither boy had ever felt anything as stimulating as the feel of his friend's mouth and tongue servicing him, or the taste and sensation of the other's hard cock driving into his own mouth. As the tempo of their sucking and the degree of suction they exerted increased, they began to plunge fiercely into each other. Within minutes Josh and Damon were engaged in a magnificent mutual mouth-fuck! With their cocks deep inside each other's mouths, their hands were freed, so each could use both to cup and fondle the buttocks of the other while he pulled them in tightly with each inward thrust.

It took little time before a gasping Josh spoke around the driving cock filling his mouth, "I'm gonna come—you better stop!" But Damon only sucked harder, and gripped his ass tighter. Josh drove his cock fiercely, and in a moment, he buried himself as far inside as he could, and his emission shot forth deep inside Damon's throat. Damon was so stimulated, that only a few seconds later—without warning the younger boy—his own discharge flooded Josh's throat. Neither stopped sucking or murmuring. Instinctively they kept each other's loads in their mouths and used their tongues to roll it around and bathe the cock with it. Nothing in their lives so far had ever come even close to exciting them as much as this!

Eventually, Damon swallowed the mouthful of hot ejaculate, and gasped, "Jesus, Josh ... Oh God! That was wonderful!" He pulled away and reversed his body while Josh swallowed and savored the miraculous nectar his best friend had given him. Damon threw his arms around Josh and pulled him close. He kissed him hard, and forced his tongue deep inside the willing younger boy's mouth. Soon their tongues were doing a frantic ballet, their bodies ground together in ecstasy, and their hands explored one another's bodies while they murmured passionate appreciation.

It took them a long time to calm down, but eventually the feverish kissing and caressing became sweet and tender, and the cocks meeting between their nestled bodies lost their rigidity. Damon whispered in Josh's ear, "I can't believe we swallowed each other's loads, but I never wanted anything in the world more when we were doing it. You tasted wonderful, Josh!"

"I couldn't have tasted as good as you did! I've never been as excited as I was when you were coming in my mouth, and I've never felt better than I do this very minute. I love being with you, Damon! Have you ... ever done this with anyone else?"

"No, Josh—and I don't want to do it with anyone else. You're my best friend, I ... you're more than my best friend. I always want to do this just with you!" He was silent a moment as they kissed, then he pulled away suddenly. "Have you ever done this with anybody else?"

Josh laughed. "God, Damon, I'm thirteen years old! No, I've never done this with anyone else." He kissed Damon and hugged him tightly. "And you're the only one I want to do it with too! Gosh, Damon, I ... I like being with you more than anything in he world!"

"Me too!" It was as close as either one could come at that point in their lives to saying I Love You, but that was the sentiment their words actually expressed.

They switched off the lantern and lay in each other's arms, talking quietly until they fell asleep. Josh's dad woke them the next morning by banging on the tent pole. Had he put his head inside the tent, he would have found his thirteen-year-old son in the arms of the older boy who had become, for all practical purposes, his lover!

Strangely, they did not suddenly seek constant repetition of their first fully shared adult sexual experience. It was another week before they repeated the kind of love they had shared in the tent—and since they were in Damon's bedroom when they did, they had to be fairly restrained. From that point on, however, they did look for other opportunities, but without discussing it. They only spoke of their great appreciation for each other's sexual attention after they had begun to have sex, and in the delicious afterglow following shared orgasms. But each knew he wanted the other, and they tacitly seemed to find means to express their passion and affection in the way that had become almost a holy ritual to them. Any time one slept over with the other, they feasted on each other's cocks and bodies, and kissed so long and so passionately their lips would become sore. They even managed to sleep with each other all night, since each had a lock on his bedroom door, as well as parents who respected their privacy. They invariably took great delight in messing up the guest bed, so that it looked like a boy had spent the night in it. From their very first session of love-making they had discovered they did not have to stop at one orgasm apiece, and messing up the guest bed often involved an enthusiastic mutual blowjob shared on it.

They discovered many new positions to adopt while they shared "69," and all sorts of other ways to approach satisfying their raging sexual needs. They played with each other's asses frequently, and they often fucked each other's legs, but neither apparently thought anal sex was yet something to consider, if they even considered it desirable or even possible. Damon and Josh were lovers for well over a year before the next major change in the level of their homosexual love-play.

Both boys were popular with their classmates at school, and

each had his own group of friends. While they neglected their other friends to a certain extent, in order to share their companionship and their love-making, they attended different schools, and so they moved in different circles much of the time. In their impromptu games in the park, Damon came to know Kyle McFarlane and Eric Neely, Josh's classmates and best friends, and Josh became familiar with several of Damon's friends. Kyle and Eric were both awed and envious seeing Josh so close to an older boy, and especially one so charismatic as Damon, and Josh was sufficiently mature that Damon's friends seemed to forget he was still a junior high school student. Both boys had a large number of friends, of course, but Kyle and Eric are especially singled out for mention here because of what later transpired with them. It should not be inferred that all of Josh's friends turned out to be gay and he wound up having sex with them, as delightful as that might have been.

By that fall, when Josh entered the same high school where Damon was starting his junior year, they were confirmed lovers, but they still practiced their love, rather than talked about it. In their own respective circles of friends they continued the kind of sexual talk and speculation about girls that was expected of them. Alone together, they did not engage in the hypocrisy of talking about girls as desirable sex objects. If their private talk turned to sex, they usually got naked and began to make love to each other.

If either Eric or Kyle suspected Josh was having sex with Damon, they said nothing about it. They did, however, talk about their growing interest in sexual matters with their friend—and at great length. The three were often together, and each was a frequent "sleep over" guest at Josh's house. Eric had a good, solid, two-parent home only a few blocks from where Josh lived, and the extra bed in his room was actually a bunk bed, so both Josh and Kyle spent the night there regularly, too. Kyle's home life was apparently not pleasant—he almost never talked about it. Josh thought his mother probably was an alcoholic, his father was long gone. They almost never even visited Kyle at home.

When the three were together, their sex talk was typically more boastful than when only two were present—when it was more likely they would share actual confidences and discuss questions that had begun to arise in their minds. Neither Kyle nor Eric suspected that their best friend was a practicing cocksucker of ever-growing excellence, or that his older friend returned the favors he received by slaking his own thirst while he nursed in the same way!

Josh had a VCR in his room to record his favorite programs, and he often watched them with his friends. Two of his three favorite shows were remarkably similar. One was the teen-age sitcom *Saved by the Bell,* starring the adorable blond Mark-Paul Gosselaar as Zack, and the very well-built, handsome, and unbelievably sexy young Mario Lopez as his best friend A.C. Slater. The second, *Hall Pass,* was unquestionably a copy of the first, with Richie Hassler as "Richie," and Monte Alvarez as "Monte" (his Latino best friend). If privacy permitted,he massaged his cock while he watched these programs.

His other favorite show was *Baywatch,* with plenty of cute, older guys to watch, running around in their revealing bathing suits. After David Charvet joined the cast in Josh's sophomore year, he never missed an episode.

All of Josh's friends regularly watched tapes of his favorite television shows when they visited, and there was sufficient presence of cute girls in all of them to justify their enthusiasm for doing so, but when it was just Eric or Kyle watching with him, it seemed to Josh they were as attentive as he to the heavenly male talent.

Comments about how good-looking Mark-Paul, Mario, Richie, and Monte were became increasingly common among Josh and Eric and Kyle. Watching an episode of *Hall Pass* one afternoon, showing Richie and Monte at the beach, wearing very skimpy and well-filled Speedos, Kyle spoke out and became the first to open up a subject that was apparently on all their minds. "Monte Alvarez must have the biggest dick in the world!"

Eric was obviously attuned to the suggestion, since his immediate reply was, "Yeah, or else he's got the biggest set of balls in the world."

Josh, his eyes glued to the image of the sexy Latino with the big basket, murmured, "Maybe both!" All three were quiet for several minutes, digesting that possibility and admiring the beauty whichoccasioned the thought.

Another time Josh broke them all up as he paraphrased an old Mae West line the three had heard somewhere, and which had amused them so much they often quoted it to each other: "Is that a pickle in your pocket, or are ya just glad ta see me?" They were watching an episode of *Hall Pass* where Richie and Monte were dressed in light slacks, going to pick up their girls. The bulge that so magnificently adorned Monte's groin in tight jeans, now seemed to be swinging freely. Josh said, "Look at Monte—is he just glad to see Richie, or is he smuggling a salami in his pants?"

The three dissolved in giggles, and wrestled on the bed, pawing each other's crotches and quoting the line Josh had formulated. Their horseplay became the indirect stepping-stone that eventually led them to sex as more than just a topic of conversation. As Kyle had his hand on Josh's crotch, joking about the possibility of his concealing a salami inside, it became obvious that something was indeed growing very large in his hand, and was becoming extremely hard—and Josh noticed that Kyle's pants began to bulge significantly while his hand lingered just a moment too long for a casual, playful grope to that growing salami. Josh filed this information away for future reference.

Kyle was perhaps not as mature or sexy as Damon, but he was a good-looking guy—sandy hair, fairly thin, a cute butt (not quite of Richie Hassler caliber, but it was getting there, Josh thought), a Roman nose, and relatively prominent ears. These last two features, instead of detracting from Kyle's appearance, added character to it, and actually made him more attractive. One of Kyle's most fascinating features, as far as Josh was concerned, was an unusual penis. Josh had only seen Kyle's cock a few times. It had always been flaccid—or nearly so—and it was unusually thin, but it promised to be unusually long as well. Since Josh had only been given time for very short appraisals, he had never really been able to drink in its features. He looked forward to an opportunity to quench his growing thirst with Kyle as well as with Damon, and after having watched Kyle's erection fill his pants while he groped Josh during their horseplay, he felt it was probably just a question of time! In fact, he had only a fairly short wait.

Thanksgiving is a family time, of course, and while the Thornton family planned its usual at-home turkey dinner, the even smaller McFarlane family was apparently going to be unable to observe any special holiday meal. Kyle's mother was going to have to go to Los Angeles for the holiday weekend, for some unspecified reason if she could farm Kyle out to friends' families. Brad and Gwen Thornton were quick to offer Josh's spare bed for as long as Kyle wanted to use it. Both boys were delighted.

Kyle seldom talked about his home life, but over the course of their friendship, Josh had gathered that his mother was pretty much "on the make," with a succession of boyfriends sharing her bed sporadically.

As they were talking before bed on Thanksgiving Eve, Kyle admitted his mother was going to L.A. to meet a boyfriend who had spent a few days, and noisy nights, with her in San Francisco recently. "This one wasn't too bad. I like her friends fine, but I hate most of the guys she ... dates, though. This one was at least nice to me, and acted like he knew I existed."

"Doesn't your mom want to date anyone regularly?" Josh asked.

Kyle frowned. "Most of her close friends are gay. They're mostly men, but she's got a few gay woman friends, too, and that seems to give her all the companionship she wants, except once in a while. Then she gets all excited about some guy, and he comes around for a while, and ... spends some time with her, and then we never see him again."

"Do her gay friends ever look funny at you? The guys, I mean. Do they say anything, or act like they want to ... well, you know, do anything to you?"

Kyle seemed surprised at the question. "No! They're nice guys, really. You'd never know some of 'em are gay, either, but a couple act more like girls than guys. They're really nice to me, and only one of them ever acted like he thought he might want to ... well, you know."

"What did he do?"

With a nervous laugh, Kyle replied, "He didn't really do anything. He just looked real close at me for a long time once when Mom had gone to the bathroom, and he came up and put his hands on my shoulders, and said 'You're gonna be a real heartbreaker, you know that?' Then he put one hand on my cheek and grinned at me and said, 'I remember how hard it is to be fourteen. Hurry and grow up, Kyle. You can break my heart any day!' Then my mom came back, and nothing else was said. And he never said anything again."

"Wow! You know what?"

"What?"

"I think ... *Kyle's got a boyfriend!*" Josh sang this several times, to the traditional tune, until Kyle playfully wrestled him to the floor, and the two dissolved in giggles.

With a guest on site, Thanksgiving Day was especially festive in the Thornton household, and Josh's parents treated Kyle as though he were a part of the family. Early that evening, after the huge holiday meal had begun to settle, Damon came over to visit, and Josh called Eric to join them. The four played cards and watched TV for some time before Damon and Eric returned home.

Josh asked Kyle if he wanted to watch anything special on TV before turning in. Kyle asked him to re-play the episode of *Hall Pass* they had recently watched, the one where Monte appeared to have a salami in his pants. Kyle did not specify why he wanted to see that particular episode again, but remembering what had followed it earlier, Josh had a pretty good idea that he was going to see considerable growth in the bulge that had appeared in Kyle's pants when he had groped him before. Without Eric around to watch, it could be a promising situation.

The promise was fully realized.

This time as they watched Monte's cock swinging in his pants, they talked about it without joking, as they had when their other friends were present. Kyle murmured, "God, that Monte Alvarez must have a huge dick!"

"Yeah, he's a sexy guy, isn't he?" Josh said, and began to gently caress his growing erection. He noticed that Kyle saw him doing it—and he could see that his erection wasn't the only one in the room.

How completely astonished both boys would have been if they had known that six years down the road Josh's father would be fucking the adorable blond Richie Hassler in the very place that Monte Alvarez' dick regularly found thrilling and welcomed refuge.

On the screen, Monte stepped over Richie's legs stretched out on a footstool, and the outline of Monte's magnificent monster was momentarily visible if one was really looking for it; both Kyle and Josh were looking closely for it. Kyle mumbled, "Jesus what a dick!"

Josh rewound the tape to re-play the scene, and then hit the "pause" button to freeze the scene. Monte's cock was clearly the cause of the exciting, long, fat bulge in his trousers. Josh said "Wow, look at that!" as he stretched the fabric of his own trousers tightly over his now-complete erection, outlining it clearly. "But look at this: mine's pretty big too!"

Kyle studied Josh's crotch for a moment, saying nothing, and then looked up at him before saying, very tentatively, "Will you let me see it?"

Josh stood and grinned down at him; his hard cock now tenting his pants, which he began to unzip. "Sure you can see it!" He let his pants slide to his feet, and then pulled his shorts below his cock, which stood straight out from his body, throbbing and bobbing. He gently moved his hips so that his cock swayed from side to side. "Whaddaya think?"

Probably without realizing he was doing it, Kyle began to massage his own erection while he stared at Josh's impressive endowment—almost as if he were hypnotized. He sat forward in his chair—with the throbbing cock only a foot or so from his face. "Jesus, Josh, you've really got a big one! And it's a *really* nice one! I mean it, really nice."

Josh wiggled his eyebrows and did a fairly recognizable Groucho Marx imitation as he said, "The better to fuck you with, my dear!" Kyle looked up quickly in alarm, almost as though he had been slapped. Josh laughed, "Jesus Kyle, it's Little Red Riding Hood; I'm only kidding!"

Laughing nervously, Kyle said, "Oh, yeah."

Josh knelt in front of Kyle and put his hand on his knee. "You gonna let me see yours?" He moved his hands up to the bulge. "It looks like you're pretty big, too!"

"What if your parents come in?"

"My folks haven't come in my room without knocking and asking if it's okay for years. But if you want, I'll lock the door, too."

Pressing Josh's hand down on his dick, Kyle said. "Lock the door."

After doing as Kyle had asked, Josh returned to stand in front of him and look at him steadily while he removed his shirt and pulled his tee-shirt over his head. He kicked his shoes off, pulled his shorts down, and stepped out of pants and shorts to stand before Kyle fully nude—and fully erect! Aside from a brief and obviously thrilled glance at Josh's prominent cock, Kyle never lost eye contact as he stood and shed his clothes. The last article of clothing for Kyle to remove was his shorts—and it was clear that his state of arousal was fully as advanced as Josh's. As he pulled his shorts down, his cock sprang out—pointing to the ceiling and throbbing in anticipation!

Kyle's cock was not as big as Josh's, but it certainly wasn't small. It was clear, though, that Kyle was afraid Josh would find him lacking; he looked at him anxiously. "Okay?"

Josh nodded and grinned. "Okay? A lot more than okay! It looks great!" Josh stepped forward to take Kyle's cock in his hand, and stroke it lovingly. "Feels great, too."

Kyle's hand encircled Josh's cock and he exhaled the huge breath he had been holding in. He was actually trembling as he held the treasure Josh extended to him. "God, Josh, your cock feels wonderful. And it's so big and ... I'm so glad you're letting me feel it. I've really wanted to. You know?"

Putting a hand behind Kyle's head, Josh pulled him in and gave him a quick kiss. "Let's get on the bed." He went over to the bed and lay flat on his back. Holding his dick in his hand he smiled at Kyle. "Come and get it!"

Looking as though he had just been awarded the prize in a major contest, Kyle advanced and stood next to the bed, drinking in the sight of Josh's beauty and stroking his cock. He whispered, "I've wanted this for a long time, Josh!"

Josh stroked himself slowly and grinned at his friend. "Lie down on top of me, Kyle—and let me kiss you right!" Kyle climbed on the bed, and stretched his body over Josh's. Their arms went around each other, their painfully hard cocks rubbed together as they undulated their asses, and their lips met in a long kiss. Although their kiss began as a chaste, sweet demonstration of affection, their mouths opened, their tongues probed and danced, and it gradually turned into a hungry expression of lust. They sucked each other's tongues and groaned in passion while their hands explored territory each was bent on conquering.

It was obvious Kyle was new to this, but Josh's love-making with Damon gave him the kind of experience that allowed him to lead Kyle quickly past the initial mutual masturbation he and Damon had practiced as prelude to more complete love-making, and within minutes Kyle and Josh were locked together in "69," with their cocks buried deep in each other's throats. They fucked each other's mouths savagely until Kyle panted around the big cock lodged in his mouth, "If you don't stop, Josh, I'm gonna come in your mouth!"

Josh's hands pulled Kyle's undulating ass in toward him as he also spoke around an invading dick, "Give it to me, Kyle!" He began to suck even harder, moving his lips up and down the entire length of Kyle's cock. Just as Kyle began to cry out in orgasm, Josh drove his lips down into the pubic hair at the base of his cock, and he delighted in the thrill of a massive orgasm shooting into the back of his throat in copious, spurts—eight or ten discharges that filled his mouth and spilled out around his lips as he kept sucking.

Kyle whimpered, "Give me yours, Josh!" And in a moment Josh drove himself as deep into Kyle as he could. Kyle gagged, but managed to keep sucking and to accept the huge flood of hot semen that rewarded his efforts!

The two boys embraced as they savored the wonderful liquid each had given the other. Kyle finally swallowed, and switched his body so he could kiss Josh. As he began to penetrate Josh's mouth with his tongue, and Josh opened to admit it, Kyle found his mouth suddenly filled with his own come, which Josh had saved to share with him. With a thrilled "Mmmmmm!" Kyle shared this treasure with his friend, passing it back and forth until each finally swallowed his half.

They kissed and snuggled for a long time, hands very gently and sweetly now exploring each other, now-flaccid cocks pressed together tightly, tongues and lips engaged in tender love-play. Finally Kyle whispered, "That was the most wonderful thing that's ever happened to me, Josh. I've wanted to do this with you for a long time."

Josh's smile was almost audible in his voice as he kissed Kyle's ear and whispered, "Why didn't you tell me? I've wanted you, too."

"I was afraid you'd get mad, or make fun of me, or call me a fag and never want to see me again," Kyle said.

"And now what do you think?"

"I think you're the most wonderful guy in the world. And I want to be with you like this all the time."

Josh laughed. "I think being like this all the time would cause us some problems. But we can be like this a lot, if you want."

"Oh yes, Josh ... please! Hold me and kiss me!"

For the sake of appearances, they mussed the guest bed, but Kyle lay in Josh's arms all night, and they woke early to salute the next day with another mutual blowjob. And this time Kyle retained Josh's orgasm in his mouth to share with its donor when they kissed afterward.

By the time his mother had returned home and he had to leave Josh's house, Kyle knew several things he had not known before Thanksgiving, but which he had begun to suspect: he was gay, he loved to suck cock, and he loved Josh Thornton!

Circumstances did not permit love-making between Josh and Kyle more than once a week or so—and even then it had to be practiced in the afternoon and during stolen moments ... and between those treasured times Josh and Damon were burying their cock in each other's throats.

More and more it struck Josh that his other close friend, Eric, might welcome sex with him, and he began to think that could be considerable fun indeed. He was having wonderful, passionate, fulfilling sex with both Damon and Kyle regularly, but he still thought it would be even better to number Eric among his blow-job buddies as well! Although he made any number of suggestive remarks, and provided rather broad opportunities for negotiations to begin, Eric did not seem to rise to the bait.

Josh was determined that the passionate and wonderful sex he had been sharing with his older lover, Damon, would not diminish—and it didn't! In fact, only a couple of weeks after first trading blowjobs with Kyle, he and Damon advanced a major step in their relationship.

One night in early December when Damon was sleeping over, the two boys lay on Josh's bed, naked, sucking each other off. After a very long period of foreplay, Josh lay on his back while Damon knelt over him in the "69" position, with his ass presenting a very attractive prospect to treat Josh's eyes, and his cock hanging down into Josh's eager mouth to treat him in other ways, which had become their favorite way to make love. Josh was caressing Damon's ass, and the tip of his forefinger was teasing his hole; as he did this, Damon's finger began to explore Josh's hole, and actually began a shallow penetration.

"That feels good, Damon, but it kind of hurts too!" Instead of answering, Damon reached back and gripped the finger Josh was tentatively pressing against his own hole. He pushed it tightly, until the tip penetrated a bit. Damon then seized Josh's entire hand and pulled on it to force most of Josh's finger inside him.

Still gripping Josh's hand, Damon began to drive the finger in and out. After only a few moments, Josh's finger was buried completely inside on the "in" strokes, and Damon began to murmur, "Oh God, that feels so good!" Damon's ass gripped Josh's finger tightly as it began to undulate, and at the same time he drove his cock into the depths of Josh's worshipping throat. He returned Josh's cock to his own mouth and began to suck wildly, gripping tightly with his lips and driving his mouth as far up and down the shaft as he could. Josh enthusiastically fucked him with his finger and Damon moaned around the shaft of the dick filling his mouth, "Yeah, fuck me, Josh. Stick it in me!"

Josh eagerly and enthusiastically complied, and the gentle probing of Damon's fingertip into his own asshole hurt considerably less now as he finger-fucked his friend. Damon was now wildly driving his ass backward to meet the thrusts of Josh's finger while he continued to moan ("Fuck me, Josh! Fuck me hard!") until he reached behind and again grasped Josh's hand, pressing it hard into him as a veritable flood of his hot come began to spurt down into Josh's eager mouth. Josh fucked Damon's mouth as hard as he could, his hips driving upward with savage jabs, while he sucked all the harder and used his finger to fuck all the harder. In a few minutes, his own powerful explosion shot upward into his friend's mouth, and both boys were murmuring their thrill around huge mouthfuls of hot semen! They bathed each other's cocks for several minutes as they calmed down, eventually swallowing, and switched their body position so they could cuddle and kiss for a long, wonderful time.

Finally, Josh said, "That was so exciting, Damon. God, I was fucking you with my finger. Did you really like that?"

Damon's grin was huge. "I thought you could tell I did, wasn't my load big enough?"

"Yeah, oh yeah! Big fuckin' load ... I loved it!" He smiled and kissed Damon deeply and the boys savored the taste of their come mingling in their mouths. "But ... we've never done that before. Why did you decide you wanted me to do that?" Josh asked.

After a brief hesitation, Damon said, "You know Dan Bliss? Tall, cute, dark-haired guy? He's a senior."

Josh looked puzzled. "Yeah. Well, no ... I don't know him, but I know who he is. What about it?"

"He helps the coach in my swim class. He's on the swim team, you know. You think he's good-looking?"

"Yeah ... sure, he looks good. He looks fine," Josh answered.

"Well, I see him in the shower almost every day, and you oughta see him naked—he really looks good then!"

"Looks good *how*? He doesn't look like's he got a great body. I mean it's okay, but he can't be a bodybuilder or anything." He grinned. "Looks BIG DICK kinda good, ya mean?"

Damon almost leered. "Dan Bliss has got the biggest prick I've ever seen in my life! It must hang down halfway to his knees when it's soft—and it's fat as hell, too. I saw him with about half a hard-on one time in the shower, and almost fainted—it was unbelievable! I mean, when you see him in his swim trunks, you can tell he's hung, but you'd be amazed if you could see how MUCH is hiding in those Speedos!"

If Josh's expression wasn't quite a leer when he replied, it didn't miss it by a lot! "Sounds interesting." In fact, it sounded much more interesting to Josh than he was prepared to admit to Damon at the moment. "So ... what's this got to do with my fucking you with my finger?"

Damon proceeded to relate his recent experience with Dan: The swimming class that Damon was enrolled in met during the last period of the day, so there was never any real urgency to finish showering and leave. On the Monday after Thanksgiving, Dan offered to work for a minute or two after class with Damon on his 'butterfly stroke.' By the time they had finished, and got to the locker room, the coach put his head in and said, "Lock up, will you, Bliss? I've got to go to a meeting."

Dan said, "Sure coach." He looked at Damon as he began to peel off his trunks. "Come on, let's get a shower."

Damon didn't always shower after swim class. After all, he was clean, even chlorinated, at the end of a session, but the prospect of showering with the massive meat that fell out of Dan's trunks as he slipped them off was too good to pass up! Dan reached in his locker and took out his gym bag, which he placed on the bench just outside the shower room as Damon followed him in. Damon had watched Dan walking in front of him, and thought that his ass looked almost as tempting as his cock.

By the time Dan started the shower and turned to invite Damon to "Get in," Damon's cock was well on the way to erection—not yet standing straight out as it did when he was registering full sexual excitement, but well engorged and quite large—and beginning to rise to the hoped-for occasion. Damon noted with excitement that although there was a whole row of shower heads on the wall, Dan had turned only one of them on as he invited Damon to join him. It seemed obvious he wanted to be close, and eyeing the monstrous cock hanging down in front of Dan, Damon was hoping to get very close indeed.

Dan handed a cake of soap to Damon and turned away. "Do my back, okay?" Damon proceeded to soap every inch of his back very slowly, and with great attention to detail, savoring each minute of caressing this hot body. He gradually began to soap around Dan's body from behind, extending his loving ministrations even to his chest and stomach. "Boy, that really feels good," Dan murmured. Damon began to soap a bit lower—almost reaching the pubes, then moved his busy hands back to the tempting dorsal side of the tall stud's body, and

Dan's head was rolling as he almost purred his satisfaction with Damon's ever-more sensuous ministrations.

Soon the purr turned to a moan of satisfaction as Damon began running his excited palms over the slick surface of Dan's ass, and Dan accompanied his fondling with subtle rolling and humping of his buttocks.

Dan turned his head and grinned back at Damon. "Now that! Mmmmm, that really feels good!" He turned to face Damon, whose heart leapt to this throat: Dan's cock was standing out parallel to the floor, obviously in full erection (Dan had been secretly masturbating while Damon soaped his back). The shaft was not only the biggest prick Damon had ever seen, it was unquestionably the most exciting thing that he had ever so much as thought about. He couldn't conceal his awe—almost staring at the glorious cock that Dan was apparently offering to share with him.

"Jesus Christ!"

"Sorry, I got a hard-on. But wow!" He grinned slyly. "It looks like you did too!" And there was no question that Dan was right. As Damon had soaped the older boy's body, his cock had grown fully erect, and it now throbbed and ached for attention as much as Dan's apparently did. If Damon's cock wasn't as enormous as the one the incredibly endowed boy presented to his delighted gaze, it was still very impressive, but if Dan was impressed, he didn't immediately show it. He took the soap from Damon's hand and said "Turn around, I'll do your back."

The feel of Dan's hands exploring his body as he soaped was exciting Damon enormously. He turned his head, and spoke over his shoulder. "Can I ask you a personal question, Dan?"

"Sure ... ask anything you want." His hands were now reaching around Damon's body and were caressing his stomach, and subtly dipping down into the thatch of pubic hair above a cock beginning to need some serious attention. The fact that Damon could feel the head of Dan's magnificent monster cock pressing against his ass did not in any way lessen his growing excitement!

"Just how big is your cock anyhow? I've never seen anything like it."

"I guess I've got a full nine inches, and when I get really

excited, it's even a little more than that." He pressed his body against Damon, and his gargantuan prick slipped between Damon's soap-slick legs. "Right now I think it's gotta be a lot more than nine inches, 'cause I'm really excited!" His hands slipped down and one circled Damon's cock while the other cupped his balls. He put his mouth almost into Damon's ear and whispered, "And I can feel how excited you are, too!" He nibbled the ear, and kissed it. "Do you want it, Damon? I really want yours."

Damon reached down with one hand and caressed the enormous tip of Dan's cock as it extended below his ball sack, while with the other he reached behind to pull Dan's ass in toward him. "Yeah, I want it Dan. But what if somebody walks in?"

Dan's hands were now caressing his chest, and the fabulous prick was driving in and out between his legs. "I already locked the door. It's just you and me, and we can do whatever you want." The shower was still playing hot water over their bodies. Dan reached over and turned it off, then knelt behind Damon and began to kiss his buttocks and caress his hips. Damon's hand reached back to hold Dan's head as he kissed. Soon Dan's kissing was deep into the crevice between Damon's buttocks, and he muttered, "Bend over!"

Damon bent over, and Dan's lips sought the tight muscular ring of his sphincter. Murmuring in ecstasy, Damon bent over farther and used his hands to spread his ass-cheeks wide so that he could admit the driving, hungry tongue which invaded him; ecstasy turned to rapture as the busy, naked muscle worshipped his asshole. Damon had often teased his asshole with his finger while he masturbated. It had been a delightful sensation, but it had only begun to hint at the thrill of this hot boy fucking it with his busy tongue. God! Dan's tongue felt as big as his cock—and how he loved it.

After several minutes of this divine play, Dan stood. "Stay right there." He went over to the door and retrieved a tube of lubricant from his gym bag. He was squeezing some on his hand as he returned to Damon. Damon watched Dan's unbelievable cock bob and sway as he returned, and he could not help but masturbate as he thrilled to the sight. Dan was grinning. "You don't need to beat off. I'll take care of that for you."

Dan swiped his lubricated hand over his asshole, and backed up to where Damon stood. "Jack me off from behind—I want to feel your big hard cock up against my ass while you do."

The warmth and smoothness of Dan's ass felt wonderful as it pressed back against Damon's cock. Damon played with Dan's nipples with his left hand as his right hand busily stroked the vast bulk and length of the hard prick Dan was driving fiercely into his fist. One of Dan's hands reached behind, and took hold of Damon's cock. The hand was heavily coated with lubricant, and as it stroked his cock Damon thought he was in heaven. But heaven *really* opened for him a moment later when Dan used his hand to guide Damon's achingly hard cock-head up and down between the cheeks of his ass, then positioned the cock-head at his anal sphincter. He cried out "Shove, Damon!" and violently drove his ass backward so that every inch of Damon's cock sank deep inside his body. Damon gasped in surprise and thrill, and instinctively began to fuck as the incredibly tight chamber completely grasped his cock and pulled forward until it almost slipped out, and then slammed back on it to start the process again and again.

In a delirium of lust, Dan moaned "Fuck my ass! Oh God, I love your cock! Please, fuck it!"

Damon screwed with more abandon than he had ever been able to display before, he could not drive his cock into Josh's mouth this deeply or this hard. It was unbelievably exciting! His hands held Dan's waist tightly. Dan bent over and he reached back to pull Damon's humping body in toward his ass in sync with each savage thrust it was receiving. Dan's ass 'worked' Damon's cock as expertly and thrillingly as Josh's mouth ever had. Damon was so completely caught up in fucking this incredible boy that he even forgot to play with the biggest, most exciting cock he had ever seen, even though it was only inches away from his hands.

With a loud cry, Damon bent over Dan, hugged his waist with his arms, buried his cock as deep inside as he could possibly go, and froze in that position while an enormous, violent orgasm exploded all the way up inside Dan's hot body. Dan cried almost as loudly, "Oh Jesus, I can feel it shooting! Fill me up with your come, Damon! Keep fucking me! Give me your big load!"

The moment when Josh had first sucked a load from his cock, when each boy had given, and received his first blowjob, had been by all odds the most exciting moment of Damon's life to that point. But this—this was more gloriously exciting by several magnitudes. He had just shot what had to be the biggest load of come he had ever produced deep inside the most exciting boy he had ever seen—in his mind at that moment, the boy with the hottest ass and the biggest prick in the world. He dreamed of sucking an equally gigantic load out of that stupendous cock while he continued to press Dan's body to him, and Dan kept driving his tight, hungry ass back on his cock. Damon stayed hard and plunged in and out in the welcoming, hot pool of his own discharge, deep in the moist, welcoming recesses of Dan.

Damon continued to fuck as long as he could, but after shooting every drop of the most thrilling orgasm he had ever experienced, he was so drained of energy for a few moments that his erection eventually wilted inside Dan, even though Dan's ass continued to grip it and work it expertly. His cock may have momentarily lost its erection, but Dan's ass still felt better to Damon than anything he had ever encountered—beautiful, welcoming, exciting. ["Filled to overflowing with my hot come!"]. In his mind he feverishly anticipated taking Dan's prick deep in his throat and sucking the load of come such a magnificent tool must have in store for him.

Finally, Dan stood, letting Damon's cock slip out. Dan turned around, and enfolded Damon in his arms. Their lips met passionately, and they fondled and caressed each other endlessly as they kissed. Dan lubricated one hand by swiping it across his ass, and, coated as it then was with the residual lubricant and the come Damon had deposited there, he used it to caress Damon's ass feverishly, and gently insinuate a finger into his sphincter. Damon gasped again as Dan's finger gradually went all the way up his chamber and began to fuck. "Does that hurt?" Dan asked.

Although he had delivered a massive orgasm only minutes before, Damon was still completely caught up in the ecstasy of this unbelievable experience (his cock had returned to full erection as Dan probed his ass). The probing finger did hurt a bit, but it felt wonderful, also. He moaned in Dan's ear, "It hurts a little, but keep fucking me with it! I want it inside me!" His hands feverishly grasped Dan's writhing ass as he added, "I want you inside me!" By now, Damon was hungrily accepting Dan's finger, and he drove his ass back on it eagerly to meet its thrusts.

Dan whirled Damon around, put his enormous cock inside the crevice between the cheeks of his ass, and bit his neck in near delirium. "Let me fuck you, Damon; let me inside this hot ass!"

"I want you to! I'll try, but your prick is so huge!" He undulated his ass against the vast bulk of Dan's shaft. "Fuck me with your finger again for a while. It felt so good in there—almost as good as your tongue did. Just fuck me with it again for a few minutes." He couldn't see the grin that split Dan's handsome face as the older boy slowly sank two fingers all the way into the beautiful ass presented to him when Damon bent forward and arched his back to offer it. Damon writhed and moaned in ecstasy as the fingers fucked eagerly, and his cries of pleasure increased when Dan's other hand came around and grasped his cock—and as the eager fist grasped him tightly and stroked up and down his entire length, he turned his head, and with eyes glazed over with passion said, "I want to fuck your ass again, Dan!"

Dan continued to stroke Damon's cock and to fuck his ass with two fingers as he bent forward to kiss him. "You will! I'm not letting you out of here until you fuck me again, believe me! But first, let me give you a load up this hot ass!"

Damon turned around, took Dan's face in both hands and looked deep into his eyes. "I'll try, but you're gonna have to help me. Take it slow, and be gentle. I've never had anything but your tongue and your finger in my ass."

Dan grinned and kissed Damon lightly. "You just had two fingers inside you!"

Returning the grin, Damon said, "Even better—two fingers, but that's a long way from that monster dick. But I want to give you what you gave me if I can. If I can't take it, promise me you'll keep trying, and let me suck you off this afternoon. I know I can do that. I may not be able to take all your cock down my throat, but I'll take as much as I can, and I'll suck that beautiful, fuckin' giant cock of yours dry, okay?"

"Sounds great! Also sounds like you've been sucking some cock, huh?" Damon smiled and nodded. Dan went on. "I love sucking cock almost as well as I love getting fucked! I'm gonna suck you off too. I can't think of anything I'd like better than taking a hot load from Damon Matthews in both ends!"

"I've got a buddy, and we ... well, our favorite thing is sucking each other off at the same time. We'll do that, if you want, and I promise I'll suck two loads out of you if I can't take you up the ass, how's that?"

"You got a deal, Damon. As long as I can put a couple of loads inside you, and you put at least one more load inside me, I'll be happy as hell. For this afternoon, anyway!" They kissed for a long time, passionately, while their bodies ground together and their hands explored feverishly.

Dan spread a pallet of towels on the locker room floor, and had Damon lie on his back on it. Kneeling next to him, Dan used his fingers to massage a considerable amount of lubricant into the younger boy. He leaned over Damon's face, and they kissed as Damon raised his legs high, and spread them as wide as he could, allowing access to first two, and then three of Dan's exploring fingers. "That feel so fuckin' good, Dan! Try to fuck me!"

Having learned it initially from the first man to fuck his ass, and having of necessity taught the lesson many times himself (very few guys he fucked had ever taken anything as big as his gigantic nine inches before), Dan knew how it was easiest to accept a cock the first time—or the first time for one like his! He had Damon lie on his side in a fetal position; Dan lay on his side behind him, and told him to raise his leg and spread his cheeks as far as he could. Dan 'warmed him up' with three fingers for several minutes, then generously lubricated his huge cock and positioned the tip at Damon's eager hole. In spite of his eagerness to fill the chamber he sought, he very slowly and gently began to press against the opening. "Work with me, Damon!"

Damon revolved his ass and humped on the enormous cock head, pressing backwards as he undulated—and very tentatively, he was able to accept the very tip of Dan's prick.

"Oh, Jesus, that hurts like hell!"

"But you'll love it once it's in. Try to take a little more."

Dan continued to press, and Damon continued to move to meet him, until soon the entire head was inside. Dan began a very shallow fuck, with his cock penetrating only about two inches. "Let me keep fucking you deeper as long as you can take it. Your ass feels incredible—so hot and tight!"

Damon worked with Dan, and he was thrilled with the feeling of this massive cock inside him, but also in considerable pain. He stifled his pain as long as he could, and, finally,with about three or four inches of hard, fat meat fucking him ever more enthusiastically, he made Dan stop. "I just can't take it all! It hurts too much. But I want you to fuck me like I fucked you! I just can't take it yet! I'm sorry."

"We'll get there. I'm nearly half-way in, and I just want to ram my cock all the way inside and fuck you like I've never fucked before!" Damon turned his head to accept Dan's kiss, and Dan very gently continued to move his cock inside him.

"I'll practice. I promise. Next time I'll try to take more. Maybe pretty soon I can take all of you. I really want to!"

"I know we can get there. Practice with the guy you suck cock with. How big is his cock?"

A dreamy smile suffused Damon's face. "Oh it's big! Nothing like yours, but still plenty big. I'm gonna try to get him to fuck me next time."

"You sure as hell don't need to practice fucking ass, though," Dan said, "not the way you fucked mine!" He broke into a huge grin. "You are one good buttfucker! But maybe he'll let you fuck him too—show him what he's missing!"

Damon laughed, "Yeah, and when I've got him broken in, you're gonna want to fuck him, right?"

Looking quite serious, Dan asked, "How would you feel about that?"

"Can I be there too?"

"Maybe we can have a three-way fuckfest, how's that sound?"

Damon became serious also. "I don't really know how he'd feel about that, but I think I might be able to talk him into it. It sounds fantastic to me! Ouch!" Dan had begun to fuck a bit deeper. "Please take it out of me! I just can't take it all!"

"I've got to get my load, Damon. Will you suck me off?"

"Sure I will. I'm dying to get your load!"

Dan carefully withdrew from Damon's ass and cleaned up. Damon lay on his back and Dan straddled his chest, his cock seeming to stretch out for feet over the admiring boy. Damon took it reverently in his hand and kissed the tip. "Nine inches! Jesus, what a fantastic dick!"

With Dan smiling down at him, Damon licked the bottom of his shaft, and sucked on his balls. After kissing every one of the nine long and fat inches of this glorious wonder, Damon began to suck the tip, and gradually opened wider to admit the demanding fat shaft.

He was unable to take all of Dan's cock, but he managed to get most of it into his throat, and Dan's exclamations and cries of delight indicated he was doing a good job of servicing this incomparable teenaged stud.

Dan's hands gripped Damon's hair and pulled his head in toward him as he fucked the worshipping throat as hard and as deeply as he could. "God, you're a great cocksucker, Damon! Eat my big fuckin dick!"

After a long time, Damon had to stop for a minute to rest his mouth. Dan said he was glad for the respite, since he was very near coming, and didn't want this expert blowjob to end too soon. Damon fondled and kissed the gigantic shaft towering over him. "This is the most amazing prick I've ever seen!"

"You believe it's nine inches?"

"I believe it's at least nine inches! To tell you the truth, I've never seen anything like it!"

"Some guys don't believe ... wait, stay right there." Dan stood, leaving Damon lying there, and went over to his gym bag. He came back with a ruler and knelt next to Damon. "I quit trying to convince anyone. Look." He laid the foot-long ruler along the top of his cock, with the end touching his pubes, buried in the luxuriant thatch of pubic hair. He could easily have made his cock appear to measure an inch longer had he pressed the tip of the ruler into his stomach, but he simply rested it there—this was an accurate, and astonishing measurement! The tip of the fat, beautiful prick extended over a quarter-inch past the nine-inch marking on the ruler! "See? And it's six inches around, but you'll have to take my word for that right now."

Damon grinned at him. "The way my mouth feels, I think it's a lot more than that! Like I said—what a fantastic dick!"

"It's even more fantastic with you," Dan said. "It's usually exactly nine inches—you inspire me! Let's check that big thing of yours!" He laid the ruler over Damon's prick. "Wow—seven and a half inches! No wonder you felt so good in me! That's a lot more than most guys have. Even my ... the guy I fuck with most often doesn't have that!"

He again knelt over Damon's head. "Suck a load out of this hot nine inches!"

Damon smiled as he kissed and licked the huge cock-head. "Nine and a quarter hot inches!"

"That nine-and-a-quarter inches is all yours—suck every drop of come out of it!" Dan leaned forward, and Damon grasped his hips tightly and opened his mouth wide to admit the magnificent monster again. Dan stretched his legs back and began doing push-ups over Damon's mouth. Damon sucked hungrily, and Dan drove his cock as deep as the eager throat could accept.

It was a shame no one was there to observe the sight: Dan's ass was perfection as it writhed and plunged the unbelievable shaft downward. His magnificent busy ass rose almost a full nine inches with each stroke—the cock-head was partially revealed at Damon's lips when it rose to its height—and then began its inexorable drive downward into the boy. One of Damon's hands was now excitedly caressing Dan's chest, and his other was stroking his own sizable cock, between Dan's lower legs. Dan was murmuring, "Eat my cock! Take my load!" and the like, and Damon's mouth was so full of dick that he could only murmur a delirious "Mmmmmmm!" as he sucked and slurped.

Had this beautiful scene been witnessed by an observer, he would no doubt have his own cock out stroking it while he watched—only the most unimaginative, the heterosexual, or those of the feminine gender would have been able to abstain.

With growing rapture, Dan's fucking grew more rapid, and almost all of his fat shaft was sinking into Damon's throat. Then, with a loud cry of "Take it!" his orgasm began.

Damon did his best to accommodate Dan's emission, but it

was so copious, and so violently discharged, he gagged somewhat, and some of the hot white ejaculate spurted out around his lips. Dan gripped his head in both hands and continued to fuck wildly. They rolled on their sides, where the massive cock continued to fuck, and Damon continued to suck every possible magic drop from it, while his hands caressed the still-humping ass which had earlier received his own monstrous discharge.

Dan licked his come off Damon's face and lips, and the two boys lay embracing and kissing for a long time, murmuring thanks for the magnificent way each had gratified the other. At one point, Dan said, "I've wanted to have sex with you since I first saw you in the shower at the beginning of the semester."

"I'm so glad it happened, Dan. I've been thinking about your cock ever since I first saw you in the shower! I've hardly been able to take my eyes off it when I've been there with you."

Dan grinned at him. "I noticed, believe me. I knew you were interested, and one of the reasons it looked so big to you was that it was always a little bit hard when I saw you naked! Did you like my ass?"

Damon kissed him and returned his grin while he caressed the subject of his question. "Nice ass!"

"Well, you saw a lot of it because I had to turn away from you so I could lose the hard-on you were giving me!"

Before they finally left the school it was dark, and each had experienced two more orgasms. They had climaxed almost simultaneously as they sucked each other, locked in a heated 69. Later, Dan had knelt on all fours to accept another exciting fuck from Damon, and just before they showered again, Damon had knelt in front of Dan while he masturbated, and thrilled while the older boy splashed a huge load all over his face and into his open mouth.

As they parted, Damon promised to practice so he might be able to take all, or at least more, of Dan's cock up his ass the next time, and Dan again urged him to see if "his friend" would be interested in joining them.

One thing they both knew without question: there would be a next time very soon.

Damon finished his narrative of the encounter with Dan, and

concluded by kissing Josh and saying, "I hope you're not mad at me."

"Of course I'm not mad. I'm a little jealous of you maybe! Well, what I mean is I'm jealous that it wasn't me who got to fuck him and suck him, and, well, you know, his prick sounds incredible! Do you think he was serious about the three of us getting together? I want to see that cock!"

"I believe he's dead serious—and damn the three of us could have a hot time together! I know he'll want you to fuck his ass, too—and you're gonna love fuckin' it, and I'm gonna love watchin' you do it, too! You know, I'm glad of it, but I wonder why Dan picked me out to fuck with."

Josh laughed. "I know why he picked you out!"

"Why, smart ass?"

"Because you're the best-looking guy in school!"

Damon looked soberly at Josh for a few moments before responding. His reply, when it came, was quiet: "Thanks, Josh." They shared a long, very sweet kiss before he continued. "I can't be the best-looking guy in school though, because there's one guy who's a lot more handsome than me or anybody else!" He put a finger over Josh's mouth before he could ask the obvious question. Then he bent his head so that his lips were only an inch from Josh's as he added, "And he's my best friend, and I've got about a gallon of his come in my stomach right now!"

"And are we gonna work on getting another gallon in your ass, so you're ready for Dan?"

"You read my mind," Damon said as he kissed his friend's lips with something much more than just friendship. "And maybe we can work at getting your ass ready for that super cock too! Jesus, I'd love to fuck you, Josh!" Josh grinned at him, and Damon thought, "My God he's cute!" He had thought Josh was unbelievably cute the first time he saw him, but he had never looked cuter than at that very moment.

"Judging by the way you say Dan reacted," Josh said, "and the way you acted with my finger up your butt, I think that might be a lot of fun! I'm sure willing to try!"

Both boys were fairly exhausted from the huge loads they had exchanged only shortly before, so they decided to watch television for a while, and postpone exploring the possibilities of fucking each other until morning. After watching part of a "movie of the week," they abandoned it to watch a tape of some *Saved by the Bell* episodes, lying next to each other on the bed, naked and on their stomachs

"God, I'd love to fuck Mark-Paul Gosselaar like I did Dan Bliss," Damon said. "Even without practice, I'd let him screw me. What a really cute guy!" His hand was caressing the velvet roundness of Josh's ass.

Josh laughed. "I'd a lot rather screw Mario. He's just as cute, but he's twenty times as sexy. I'd love to get screwed by him, and I wouldn't be surprised if his cock isn't as big as Dan's! If it hurt too much, I'd chew a pillow or something while he stuck it in!" He reached over and began to explore Damon's ass, first caressing it, moving his hand up and down in the crevice, and then beginning to tease the hole with his finger. "I'm horny as hell again ... you want to pretend I'm Mark-Paul? What's the difference if it's one blond or another trying to fuck your ass?"

Damon rolled on his side and enclosed Josh in his arms. They kissed, sweetly at first, but with gathering passion, until their tongues were frantically intertwined and their bodies grinding together, their cocks obviously in full erection.

Breaking their kiss to smile at Josh, Damon whispered, "The blond I want to fuck my ass...!" His smile turned into a huge grin, then he wenton: "Well, the first blond I want to fuck my ass is Josh Thornton. Mark-Paul is gonna have to wait his turn. You got anything to grease us up?"

The only thing Josh could find was a jar of Vaseline, but it was as good as anything. No doubt there have been tens of millions of men who first got fucked by a prick coated with that time-honored product.

Damon lay on his back with his legs spread, grinning lazily as Josh liberally applied the ointment to his asshole. He started penetrating with one finger, which, judging by the smile and the pleased murmur, felt fine to Damon. Two fingers driving in and out produced the same result. As he began to insert three fingers into his friend, the pleased murmur became a gasp. "Ooooh! Take it easy!"

"Does it hurt?" Josh asked.

"Just a little ... go slow, I think it's gonna feel great once you get 'em all the way in." Josh worked slowly, and soon had his three fingers as far inside Damon as they could go, his entire hand pressed firmly against the now undulating ass. Damon closed his eyes and sighed, "Oh yeah! That feels wonderful!"

Josh leaned over to kiss Damon as he finger-fucked him. Damon held Josh's head and they feverishly sucked on each other's tongues and fucked each other's mouth's with them. Finally Damon panted, "Try your dick. I really want your dick inside me, Josh!"

"How do we do this?" Josh asked.

Damon rolled on his right side and raised his left leg. "Lie down behind me, and go slow!"

Josh applied more lube to Damon's asshole, and liberally coated his cock as well. Then he positioned the tip and began to press. He panted into Damon's ear, "Let me in your beautiful ass, Damon! I love it! I wanna fuck it!"

"Oh yes, fuck me, Josh! Give me your big dick—but take it easy until it's all the way in!"

Josh's fingers had prepared the way adequately and, proceeding slowly, the considerable length of his prick slid easily all the way into his friend's writhing ass with almost no difficulty. As Josh drove in the last inch of his cock, burying himself deep inside, Damon's legs straightened out, his head rolled back, and he moaned in ecstasy, "Oh Jesus, Josh. I love it! Fuck me with your big dick!"

It would have been impossible to say which boy was more ecstatic.

Damon was completely suffused with a thrilling heat as the bulk of Josh's dick slid in and out, and he was stimulated as he had never been. The sensation was thrilling. Even the pinnacle of lust and ecstasy he had achieved when he discharged his load into the hot, tight recesses of the magnificent Dan's ass was now surpassed. He knew now why Dan had thrilled so to his own fuck, as Josh's huge, adorable, treasured cock plunged into him, thrust deep inside him, impaled him with commanding piston strokes of joy.

While Damon was experiencing his first taste of this ultimate thrill, Josh was taking the next step toward it.

To Josh, the grip of Damon's undulating ass was incredible—every square inch of his driving cock was held tightly by the moving muscles inside, and those muscles pulled on every square inch as he backed out, before plunging again and again into the hot, tight chamber.

Both boys were in a complete delirium of lust. The tentative beginning of the fuck accelerated and intensified, but they instinctively interspersed their frenzied love-making with short periods of rest, so they could delay their orgasms and prolong the rapture. Eventually, Josh's frenzy could not be stopped, and he brutally rolled their bodies so that Damon lay flat on his stomach with Josh on top of him. Josh continued to fuck with ever-growing savagery, while Damon's ass bucked upward to accept the brutal thrusts—and as Josh emitted a loud cry Damon could feel the eruption inside him in a series of eight or ten spurts.

Damon continued to grind his ass around Josh's cock as the latter slowly stopped fucking. Both boys agreed it had been the most thrilling moment they had ever experienced. Josh whispered, "I can't wait for you to fuck me. I want to give you the thrill you gave me."

"You have no idea what a thrill you gave me," Damon said. "Now, look, I've fucked butt, and I've been fucked, and now I think getting fucked may be even better than fucking, if that's possible!"

You could almost hear a dreamy smile in Josh's voice, "I wanna find out! Stick your cock in me, Damon. Fuck ... my ... ass ... with your ... beautiful ... big ... prick!" Josh kissed Damon's neck between the words.

"I think we're gonna have to wait until morning."

"Why?"

Damon snickered. "Put your hand on my belly." Josh reached beneath Damon, who still lay face down on the bed. His hand encountered a a puddle of cum. "I shot my load while you were coming in me. I couldn't help it."

Josh giggled and rolled Damon on his back. He began to lick the come from Damon's belly and even sucked a bit out of the end of his now-flaccid dick as well. He kissed Damon with his come-covered lips. "God, the bed's a mess."

"What will your folks think?" Damon asked.

"Well, my mom sends the laundry out, and so far it's no questions asked. I guess she'll assume I just had one helluva wet dream!"

They agreed that Josh would put off giving his cherry to Damon until morning, and moved over to the guest bed and fell asleep in each other's arms.

The next morning, as planned, Damon's love-making brought Josh to the pinnacle of joy he had experienced himself the night before. They woke very early. It was just beginning to get light, but Damon's cock was pressed against Josh's ass, demanding entrance. After brushing their teeth, knowing that "morning breath' would diminish the pleasure of their kissing, they kissed and nuzzled and sucked each other, and with Damon's tongue busily fucking the orifice he hoped to plant this cock in very soon, Josh panted, "Fuck me. God, I want you now!"

Even granting that Damon prepared Josh for his cock with a great deal of manual exercise and liberal amounts of lubricant, the actual penetration was much more easily achieved than either could have imagined.

Damon finished his preparation with Josh lying face down, and as he started to roll the younger boy's body on his side, Josh raised himself on all fours and lay his head down on the bed, raising his ass and presenting it to his friend. The three fingers Damon had been fucking him with in that position had felt so wonderful, Josh hoped he would be able to take all the seven-or-more exciting inches he was now craving in the same way.

Damon was gentle, but insistent. Josh worked hard at spreading his cheeks, wriggling his ass, and pressing backwards to meet the forward drive of the ever-more delightful thrill of Damon's cock entering him. With almost no apparent pain from the boy he was entering, Damon found his pubic hair was pressed tightly against his young lover's ass, and his throbbing erection was buried to the hilt. Dan's ass had been beautiful and hot. This was perfection. This was his very best friend—the first guy who ever fucked him, and he was fucking his beautiful ass now. Josh's reaction was exactly what Damon's had been the night before, he discovered the total bliss of a rock-hard cock fucking his ass.

The gentle, increasing-to-insistent, and insistent-to-ferocious thrusts of Damon's prick ("How big it is," Josh thought, "I never realized his cock was so huge!"), the heat which the bulk of that busy and thrilling cock generated, the pressure of this treasured friend's body pressing against him excitedly, these all combined to bring Josh to orgasm even before Damon's wildly plunging cock erupted deep within him. Damon was fucking him with ever-greater excitement and moans of rapture when Josh raised himself to his knees, arched his body backwards, threw his head back and closed his eyes, and uttered a delirious cry, "I'm gonna come! Keep fucking it!"

Damon continued to fuck like a savage as his hands left Josh's waist and his arms encircled his body. One hand feverishly played with Josh's chest while the other seized Josh's cock and masturbated furiously. Josh's two hands went behind their bodies to pull Damon's wildly driving ass in to him.

Damon's hand could feel the come coursing through Josh's cock while he masturbated it and listened to the hoarse moans of passion as Josh's orgasm shot forth, propelled four feet to splatter against the headboard of his bed in large white gobs! As Josh began his climax, he increased the frenzy of his backward drives on Damon's cock, and he was almost instantly rewarded with the thrill of the older boy's come exploding deep inside him, spurt after spurt of that same precious hot liquid he himself continued to spurt on the bed.

By that time Damon's fuck had become totally unrestrained, and he was driving every inch of his cock in and out, as wildly, as rapidly, as deeply as he could. Long after his thrilling eruption, Damon continued to fuck his friend, who had again fallen to all fours, and Josh continued for some time to drive his ass backwards to receive the masterful thrusts of his friend's continuing invasion.

Later, they lay in each other's arms, kissing and embracing in the sweet. affectionate love into which their lust had gradually subsided. Neither could find words to compliment the other sufficiently on his performance as both fucker and fuck-ee, so their kisses and busy hands and murmurings ("God you were wonderful!") had to tell the story.

They finally got in the shower, and between finishing that and getting dressed, they had fallen to the bed again, locked in "69" while each had sucked yet another massive load from the other.

Just before unlocking his door and going outside to face the day with his lover-friend, Josh held him and kissed him as he said what both felt. "I wouldn't have believed I'd love anything more than sucking you off, but fucking you is so good. I can't decide if fucking you or getting fucked is better."

Damon ginned. "I won't make you decide, if you promise not to make me decide!"

On the way to school, Josh told Damon it was all right to tell Dan about their experience of the night before, and he assured him he would not be upset to hear that he had succeeded in taking Dan's alleged stupendous cock up his ass ("Just be sure to tell me all the details!"). Damon agreed to keep Josh's name out of it for the moment. But, if things went as he expected them to, he would suggest to Dan that all three get together for sex. Josh was eager to see Dan's cock and, given how relatively easy it had been to accept Damon's own very generous cock inside him, he thought perhaps he might be able to experience an even greater thrill with the Dan Bliss supercock buried to the hilt inside him.

2.

Dan was excited to learn that Damon had bottomed. "You think you're ready for mine yet?" he leered.

Laughing, Damon said he thought he might need more practice.

The next day Dan caught up with Damon in the locker room at the end of swim class. Damon grinned, "We gonna drill for oil when Coach leaves?"

"I wish we could," Dan said, "but Coach is gonna be here for a while, and I've gotta get home and meet my dad. He's not home a lot, and I need to be there when he is."

"How come your dad's gone so much?" Damon knew Dan lived alone with his father. "Are you all alone when he is?"

"Look, after dad goes away again, I'll get you to come over to my house. I'll tell you all about my home life. I can't tell many people about it, but I think I can tell you now, and I think you're gonna be really surprised! And if we haven't made it all the way by then, we can keep practicing there. Shit, if we have managed to go all the way by then, we can do it some more. And we don't have to worry about the coach, or anyone else catching us. And maybe we can get your mysterious friend to join us?"

Damon laughed. "I know I'd like that. I think my friend would too."

Checking to be sure no one was around, Dan pulled a gym bag out of his locker. "Look, I'm gonna give you something to practice with. I'm pretty sure that if you can take the biggest one of these, you're not gonna have any trouble taking me. You got your gym bag here?" Damon found his own bag and Dan transferred three latex dildos to it, in graduated sizes, with the smallest probably six inches in length, and the largest looking absolutely enormous to Damon. "The biggest one is almost exactly the same size as my cock." He grinned, "And it really feels good when I use on me!"

"Jesus!" Damon exclaimed, "where'd you get these?"

"They belong to my dad. He hardly ever uses 'em. He won't know if they're gone for a while. But listen, this is strictly between us, okay?"

"Well sure, Dan, but ... I mean these belong to your father?"

Dan looked at the floor for a few seconds before he looked up and replied soberly. "Look, I'll tell you all about it when you come over to my house. I said you'd be surprised. Hell you might eventually meet dad, and ... well, he's a great guy, and I know you'd like to meet him ... at least."

"At least?"

This time Dan's expression was anything but sober. "A surprise, remember? And don't say anything about where I got these dildos if you and your friend practice together with 'em. In fact, be sure he does practice, okay? I wanna meet this guy, and slip some meat to him too!"

"I'll try to get us both ready! And I'll bet you'll enjoy the meat he's got to slip to you!"

"You did, right?"

"Oh yeah," Damon grinned. "And between these things here, and his meat and my meat, we'll both be ready for you soon, I hope."

"Sounds fantastic! And maybe we'll still be able to get together here at the pool before the both of you are ready. But it'll be even better at my house. We can watch some porn videos to get warmed up."

"You've got fuck movies?"

"They're my dad's too, but we both watch 'em. He's got lots—Jeff Stryker, Ryan Idol, Tom Steele—all the big ones. Well, the big guys with the *big* ones, I should say!"

"Your dad ... "

"I'll tell you all about it soon. This isn't the time or the place."

"Your dad is beginning to sound more interesting all the time."

Dan grinned. "Hey, your friend is beginning to sound more interesting all the time! Just practice with these, and when you and your friend are fucking each other with the big one, just pretend it's me, and pretty soon I'll be shoving the real thing in you both!"

In spite of his promise to Dan, Damon told Josh where the dildos had come from. He could see no harm in doing so. The two boys speculated endlessly about Dan's father as they assiduously applied themselves to the delightful task of learning to accept the biggest of the three dildos (which, had they known it, was modeled from Jeff Stryker's actual cock, and which was a toy Josh's own father would own and employ in a few short years).

By the time the second semester began, Damon and Josh were almost able to accept the Jeff Stryker dildo fully. Damon, in addition to the pleasant 'stretching exercises' he had been enjoying with Josh, had shared his love with Dan twice more, once in the locker room at the pool, and once in the bushes in Lincoln Park (since school had closed for the Christmas vacation and Dan's father was home for the entire holiday period).

Damon's work with the dildo was beginning to pay off for them; on both occasions he had experienced the thrill of Dan's copious load shooting into his ass, but the magnificent tool that delivered it had to be confined to a very shallow depth (oxymoronic perhaps, but better than nothing).

Both boys eagerly looked forward to the time when all nine-plus inches of Dan's prick could be buried deep inside Damon to unburden itself. The skill that Damon brought to sucking that colossal tool, and the eagerness with which he accepted its length and bulk that way—to say nothing of its thrilling eruption—went a long way toward easing Dan's disappointment in not yet fucking his friend's ever-more tantalizing ass.

Josh did not let his excitement over his affair with Damon, cool his lovemaking with Kyle. Quite to the contrary. Shortly after he had mastered the ability to take Damon's cock up his ass, he had successfully instructed Kyle in that valuable and satisfying skill one night in his bedroom, only the first such encounter in what would prove to be a very, very long series.

Good deeds are often rewarded in kind: within the next six years, Josh would kneel behind no fewer than four hot young men eager to accept his cock up their asses, and who had mastered the ability to do so from Kyle's ever-more-skillful instruction in the technique. As capable as Kyle became in practice, however, this was an instance where the pupil never surpassed the master.

There is no question that Josh and his friends were

considerably more active in bed (and on the floor, and in the shower, and in the locker room, and in the bushes, and so on) than others of their respective ages. Perhaps for some of them at least, their sexual precocity was genetically derived: Josh's father had begun sucking and fucking at the beginning of his freshman year in high school. Kyle, of course, had no idea what his father was like, sexually or otherwise, but at that point in his life, unknown to his son, the father was tending bar in Los Angeles.

The elder McFarlane's experience with Kyle's mother had soured him sufficiently on women that he cheerfully accepted the invitations to sex and the accompanying money that male patrons offered him. His good looks and the carefully arranged outline of his long cock in his always-tight trousers ensured that those invitations would be forthcoming regularly.

Damon's parents had produced a precocious, voracious sex machine without any apparent genetic contribution to his hypersexuality. As for Dan's father ... well, that story was to be revealed on a very dramatic night in the very near future.

Eric was, to the best of their knowledge, not even sexually active yet, although they regularly watched for signs that he would be willing to join them in their sex-play. Like Dan's, his story was also to be revealed somewhat later, and like Damon there was nothing in his family history to suggest a genetic predisposition toward homosexuality.

Josh found he was able to accept every bit of the Jeff Stryker dildo with only a little work, after which he gloried in the feel of it when Damon plunged it in an out of him. Damon did not have to 'warm up' to that monster device by using the small or the middle-sized dildo. The boys discovered that Josh's cock was, for all practical purposes, the same size as the middle one, perhaps even a bit larger. Naturally, the real thing which Josh employed was much more satisfying for both of them than the latex alternative. Soon they discovered that Josh could very gradually introduce most of the small dildo into Damon's ass while he already had his own cock buried inside. From there it was a simple step to Damon's ability to master 'the Jeff Stryker Challenge'—and not just tolerate it, but savor it as Josh was doing.

For Damon, meeting with Dan at the pool was no longer as easily arranged as it had been, since he was no longer enrolled in the swimming class. Still they found a few occasions after the new semester began.

One afternoon in early February, Dan was in the locker room, crouching over Damon, impaled on his cock and busily licking his own cum from his forehead, where he had shot it while thrilling to his mutually satisfying ride. It was in this position that Damon asked, "Do you know who Josh Thornton is?"

Dan admitted he did not.

"He's only a freshman, but he's blond and tall, and unbelievably good-looking, and he's got a great body, and ... " Damon smiled suggestively, "he wants to meet you."

Realization dawned as Dan grinned. "And you two have been fucking each other, and you're ready to take my cock up your asses! I sure as hell hope that's what you're planning to tell me."

Damon pulled Dan's face to his, and the two kissed deeply for a minute before Damon said, "And we're both ready for you. We've been wearing your dad's biggest dildo out thinking about it."

Dan's father was away again, so they scheduled a night late that week to meet as a threesome at his house. Dan, still embracing his younger friend, suggested that he and Damon didn't necessarily have to wait. Damon agreed, and they spread a pallet of towels on the floor. Damon at last felt the thrill of the astonishing Dan Bliss cock fucking his ass, so long and so hard, and driven in so deep that he felt as though he were in heaven, and when he felt the explosive discharge of a huge load erupting significantly deeper inside him than Josh had been able to accomplish, he knew heaven had arrived!

Their parting words that afternoon were excited plans for Friday night at Dan's house. "Be sure to tell Josh what he's got coming," Dan said. "And after you both get it, I expect the two of you to fuck me silly!"

The next day, Dan stopped Damon for a minute between classes. "I just found out who Josh Thornton is, and I'm twice as excited as I was. I've seen him around school before, and he's damned near as sexy as you are. I introduced myself, and my dick kept getting harder and harder while we talked, and so did his, and I think we spent most of the time watching each other's cocks grow. God, I can't wait until Friday!"

The threesome that met at Dan Bliss' house that February Friday had high expectations for sexual thrills. They were in no way disappointed.

Dan lived in a well-appointed, remodeled Victorian two-story house in the Seacliff section of the city, not far from Baker Beach. Responding to Josh and Damon's enthusiastic comments about the house, Dan gave them a brief tour, including the three bedrooms on the second floor, his own, his father's, and one which was obviously devoted to some special purpose.

The special bedroom contained nothing but a king-sized bed, really only box springs and mattress, in the center of the room, with end tables next to its head. There were large mirrors on all four walls , as well as one on the ceiling, centered over the bed. Bright, but not harsh lighting came from a large number of track lights mounted on the ceiling around the room, and all aimed at the bed. A stack of towels sat on the floor next to the bed.

Since Dan had said nothing when he admitted them to the special room, Damon asked. "What in hell is this for? Who sleeps here?"

Dan laughed. "Nobody gets much sleep in this room! I guess you can figure out this room is made for sex, so we're gonna stay here for a while, okay?" All agreed that sounded like an ideal plan. "For right now, just get out of your clothes and get on the bed. I'll explain it all later." He began pulling off his clothes, and in a minute all three boys were naked, and judging by their erections, ready for action.

This was the first time Dan and Josh had seen each other's bodies, and each was impressed for different reasons—Dan for the beauty of Josh's body and cock (he already knew how handsome he was), and Josh for the gargantuan throbbing prick that stood out from Dan's body, begging to be serviced. Dan was relatively handsome, and had a good body also. But Josh was so thrilled by the sight of the matchless cock he could think of nothing else for the moment, and sank to his knees to kiss and fondle the object of his admiration.

Within minutes, the three were on the bed, doing much more to each other than just kissing and fondling, although those two activities occupied a generous percentage of their time.

Dan produced ample lubricant from an end table, along with a bottle of poppers. The stimulating poppers were totally unnecessary, each of the three was both hungry for sex and fully attracted to his partners. Still, the occasional sniffing added a delirious fever to their actions, and the next couple of hours were the most erotic and thrilling Josh and Damon had ever known. As they learned soon, Dan had experienced many other such sublimely impassioned encounters on this very bed, but even for him this occasion was special. He had never before fucked with boys his own age here, with friends, and it made the occasion very special for him.

At Dan's suggestion, the boys had arranged to spend the entire night together, so there was no need to hurry their love-making. And, in spite of Josh's eagerness to get fucked by the most exciting prick he had ever seen and Dan's eagerness to fuck this golden-haired Adonis, the three spent a long time engaged in embracing, kissing, cocksucking, and body worship of the most passionate kind. All seemed to sense they should withhold their orgasms for the fucking which was to be the *piece-de-resistance* of their meeting.

And the *piece-de-resistance* was for each a joyous occasion.

Josh had never experienced a greater thrill than he knew when Dan impaled him on his matchless cock, and his joy was amplified further because his other friend lay on his back below him in "69," and the two boys sucked each other while Dan practiced his miraculous technique—a technique, they were soon to learn, that was developed and honed on that exact spot.

The veritable fountain of come that Dan exploded inside Josh would have put most men out of commission for several hours, but he was of such sexual precocity that within a half-hour after satisfying Josh's hunger, he sated his other friend with equal savagery and mastery, and the volume of his discharge was only very slightly less. In spite of two massive orgasms, Dan's level of enthusiasm was hardly diminished at all as he lay on his back, legs raised high and spread wide, and joyously got fucked in succession by both his handsome, exciting younger friends.

Dan had often had two, and even occasionally more, men fuck him in succession in this same room, but this time was special for two reasons: these two were boys around his own age, and neither of them fucked him with a condom, so he could fully appreciate the orgasms his enormous talent as a "bottom" inspired. Damon and two other high school classmates, and now Josh as well, were the only people who had ever fucked him without protection; all his other partners had been older men, sufficiently experienced in gay sex that protection was called for—and insisted on.

It was fortunate that Dan lived in a detached building. The cries of ecstasy the three boys uttered as they thrilled to the fucking and orgasms of the evening, further inspired by 'hits' from the popper bottle, would have drawn considerable attention otherwise. If they had been doing it in an apartment in the Castro, they would have drawn a crowd.

The break from sexual activity that two hours of such impassioned fucking necessitated provided Dan with the opportunity to explain things about the special bedroom, and about his father. He eased into the subject as they sat in the living room—Josh and Damon drinking Cokes, and he a beer—by playing a video tape for them.

"Where did you get this?" Josh asked.

"It's a tape I dubbed from a lot of different ones that belong to my dad, and before I explain why he has them, just watch for a while," Dan responded. "It's gonna explain a lot."

Although both Josh and Damon had seen parts of a few straight porn videos at friends' houses and at parties, neither had seen any male pornography. They were understandably impressed with, and excited by the physical attributes and the sexual magnetism of many of the performers on the video, especially Ryan Idol and Tom Steele and Jeff Stryker—not realizing that the dildo Josh and Damon had used to prepare themselves for this very night was molded on the latter's astonishing cock.

They decided that Steve Fox had to be the sexiest, most beautiful man they'd ever seen, although they also agreed that Tom Fox and Ryan Idol were close competition. There was no doubt that Matt Ramsey was the one who was most versatile. He was known as a savage, thrilling top with a beautiful, huge cock, and one who obviously adored having his perfect ass filled with big, hard meat. But considering that, in addition to his physical beauty, Tom Fox also had a bigger dick than even Jeff Stryker or Tom Steele, along with a body almost as awe-inspiring as Steve Fox's (and an appetite for getting fucked that seemed almost as voracious as Matt Ramsey's), they decided he was the one that they found, on balance, to be the most desirable. Tom's massive cock was also, like Jeff's, preserved for posterity in a commercially available facsimile dildo, but it would be a long time before one of them, Josh, learned that, and enjoyed its wonders.

Dan said he felt sure that Steve Fox and Tom Fox were probably not related, since he knew "Tom Fox" was really Tom Hunt.

Dan grinned and applauded when Josh and Damon settled on Tom Fox's supremacy, but refused to explain his special enthusiasm over their choice just yet.

The series of videos which followed that decision were different. They had no music, the sound track was muffled and the dialogue often indistinct, and all were filmed by a few fixed cameras with no close-up shots. What made them especially interesting to the two boys seeing them for the first time was that all had been shot in the special bedroom they had just temporarily abandoned.

"Holy shit, that's your bedroom!" Damon cried.

Another grin from their host. "Well, it's not really my bedroom. Mine is where we're gonna sleep tonight. Just keep watching. All this stuff was shot from three different video cameras hidden in the lights."

Josh and Damon were so astonished at the next succession of sexual pairings on the video that except for occasional interjections of amazement, they asked no questions of Dan.

Quite a few of the men who appeared in these scenes were among the same ones they had just seen in the excerpts from commercial videos. Dan's two guests had no way of knowing it, but several of them were known strictly as "tops"—claiming to be straight, "gay-for pay" porn stars, and were clearly revealed here as avid "bottoms" glorying in getting fucked, and so loudly affirming their enjoyment that even the muffled audio track did not disguise their happiness. There was also ample kissing, cocksucking, and rimming to balance the preponderance of joyous, athletic buttfucking which was obviously the principal delight of the participants.

Josh and Damon were disappointed that neither Ryan Idol, nor Tom Steele or Jeff Stryker appeared in this series (they did not yet know those actors by name), but they were gratified that two of those who had most impressed them most appeared again in these 'home video' pairings, including their favorite, Tom Fox. All those who appeared were enormously exciting, almost to a man well-endowed, and rather talented actors, but Tom Fox had them practically drooling with excitement—even though he was considerably older than the others.

By the fifth pairing on the new series, it became clear that the same man was appearing with a different partner in each scene. He had not been in the professional videos, and even though he was obviously quite a bit older than the others, he was well-built and very handsome—and as dedicated and capable as any of the others as either top or bottom.

Finally, Damon voiced the question which had been growing since the third scene, and which had been crystallizing in Josh's mind as well: "Jesus Christ, Dan, that's your father, isn't it!"

Dan laughed and grinned. "That's my pop! Is he hot, or what?"

"Yeah! Shit, he's hot as hell! You even look like him, but you ... well, I don't mean any disrespect, and he's obviously a good fucker, and he's got a good dick ... but it's not in the same league as yours!"

It was Josh's turn to laugh. "Hell, Damon, who else do you know that's got a dick in the same league as Dan's anyway?"

"Well we sure saw some other big league dicks in that video, but yeah, I sure don't know anybody else in that league! But how old are these movies, Dan? He sure as hell wasn't old enough to be your father when they were made."

Dan stood, walked to the VCR, and stopped the tape. He turned back and smiled at Josh and Damon. "Two of those scenes were shot less than six months ago, and one you're gonna see soon was filmed only last week." Dan explained that his father edited tape from the various concealed cameras into one final tape after the fact, and managed to set up certain camera angles as the filming progressed, without revealing that the action was being taped, by directing his partner of the moment to "play" for a given mirror in the ceiling or one of the walls, so they could watch each other having sex. He sat down and said, "Let me tell you about my dad before I show you the rest."

"My dad is a videographer, a cameraman for videos. He's started out as a cameraman working in movies, but he wound up shooting male porn because it's what really turns him on—and he's absolutely the best in the business. Everybody knows it. He's independent, and he gets hired by different video companies when he's available, and he's so good he can pick and choose which projects he wants to shoot. A lot of porn stars want him to shoot their videos, and a lot of the time they come here to visit him and try to persuade him to do it. If it's somebody who really turns Dad on, he let's 'em persuade him upstairs in the 'guest room.' One of those big names you saw in the commercial videos, but didn't see later with Dad in the guest room, persuaded Dad in his own bedroom in L.A., and Dad is sorry as hell he didn't get that on tape. He said they persuaded each other all night long, and it was maybe the best sex he ever had

"He looks so young because he takes care of himself, and because he's not quite thirty-eight years old yet."

Dan's father was only 20 when his son was born, but it was apparently a family thing; his own father had been the same age when he was born. At the time Dan was explaining all this to Josh and Damon, his paternal grandfather was not quite fifty-nine.

The elder Bliss had joined the Navy right after graduating from high school, since he had no plans to go on to college and wanted to avoid being drafted into the Army. In San Diego, where he was assigned (and settled after his military service), he met a girl he liked, and promptly impregnated her, and by doing the honorable thing he was a married father in his twentieth year.

Dan looked like his father, but he resembled his grandfather at the same age even more so. He also had other affinities with his grandfather that he did not share with his dad: grandfather was a high-school swimmer, and grandfather had a cock that was as large and hungry as the monster cock Dan had buried in his friends just shortly before beginning to tell them this story.

The grandfather, unlike Dan, reserved his supercock for employment with the ladies, except for a brief, semi-serious fling with a shipmate on an aircraft carrier, and one earlier, very passionate all-night sexual marathon in high school, when he and a similarly well-hung fellow swim-team member and his friend got together in the only 'threesome' he ever experienced. Bob, the swimmer, had sung the praises of his teammate's enormous cock to his best friend/fuckbuddy/lover John, at the very moment his own very considerable endowment was buried deep inside the latter. John hungered to see this magnificent tool, and both he and Bob longed at the very least to sample the delights such a wonder might provide if employed in satisfying their identical appetites—and so they engineered a night of sexual abandon that none of them ever forgot.

The later, semi-serious homosexual fling Grandfather Bliss enjoyed ensued because the shipmate was the self-same John who had shared the two gigantic cocks that night in Bob's bedroom back in Chicago—and who was not only insistent and persuasive, but who also offered welcome relief from sexual tension during the weeks they often spent at sea. Aboard the *Lexington* the elder Bliss was as 'married' to John as he was to his wife when he was ashore. Finding privacy for sex aboard ship was a constant challenge, but they somehow managed almost nightly to be together at least for a half-hour or so. John was the only fuckbuddy/lover he ever knew—and John's was the only cock he ever had in his mouth or up his ass except for Bob's gigantic tool that one night during high school days.

He always regarded himself as straight and, except for the one gay night back home in Chicago, and the shipboard romance, he was. Grandfather Bliss nonetheless obviously harbored some serious nostalgia for his brief forays into homosexuality, since he named his son Robert John, after his swim-team mate and his shipboard lover, respectively. The order of the initials was not arbitrary—R.J.'s father would have much preferred that his big-dicked teammate Bob had been the one to end up later as a shipmate.

From birth, young Robert John Bliss was known as "R.J."; his father insisted on it at first, and the name stuck—he was always simply "R.J."

R.J. wanted to live up to his father's expectation of heterosexuality, but he knew in his heart he was gay from the day he began to consider sexual expression. Still, he tried, and the upshot was that he, like his father before him, knocked up his girlfriend. Dan was the result—born in San Diego in '74.

Dan's parents stayed together less than a year before his mother disappeared—by then fully aware of the sexual appetites of her husband, but willing to keep that a secret if R.J. could convince his grandparents to unofficially adopt Dan and help raise him. Dan's mother, in leaving, said with the kind of bad grace only marginally excusable by the situation in which she found herself, "He's probably gonna turn out to be a faggot too, and I don't want any part of it!"

By the time Dan was fifteen, his father relocated to San Francisco from Los Angeles, where he had been working in movies, and then video. Most of his work was done either around L.A. or the Bay Area, and he much preferred San Francisco as a place to live. Dan was by then old enough to look after himself when R.J.'s work necessitated absences for a week or so of location shooting.

Dan's father discovered his son was also homosexual in a rather dramatic way—he found him in his own bedroom, fucking one of the porn stars R.J. himself had traded fucks with down the hall from there only a week or so earlier!

R.J. had not concealed his sexuality from his son once he thought Dan was old enough to deal with it. He remembered his own turmoil in trying to conceal his sexual orientation, and he told Dan that if he ever wanted to discuss sex with him, he would be there for him, and would support whatever kind of choices he might make. However, like most boys of fourteen (his age when this offer was made), Dan would talk about sex with anyone but his family.

It was only a year later that the porn star Dan was soon to be caught in bed with accosted him outside his house one afternoon. He had been introduced to him when he had visited

R.J. earlier, and had been mightily impressed with the youngster's good looks, but particularly impressed with the bulging crotch of his extremely tight and revealing Levi's!

The porn star was Joe Epps, who started out big in porn, but whose impressive endowment and very accommodating attitude quickly attracted the attention of a wealthy fan, who urged him to quit porn and share his bed on a permanent basis, and convinced him to do so by keeping him in the style to which he had hoped to become accustomed. Joe asked Dan if he knew what his dad had been doing with him a week earlier, and since Dan thought Joe was quite the most exciting thing he had ever seen, he readily admitted he not only knew what they had been doing, but brazenly added that he'd be happy to do the same thing with Joe himself any time he wanted.

Even though he was barely sixteen years old, Dan's sexual experience was already fairly extensive by that time. His outsized cock had attracted the notice of several of his friends, his scoutmaster, his church choir director, and a coach as well—and he had gratified the wishes of all of them. Dan was gratifying Joe Epps hard and fast and deep when his dad returned home unexpectedly.

The scene began very unpleasantly, with R.J. yelling at both Joe and Dan, and he only began to calm down when Dan told him, respectfully, but in no uncertain terms, that he not only knew what he was doing, he was doing it because he wanted to, and had done the same thing with quite a number of other guys. Without being insolent,which under the circumstances, was quite a trick, Dan told his father to either leave him and Joe alone to make love, or hang around and watch—or, if he wanted, to get naked and join them in bed. Though he was very, very liberal in sexual matters, R.J. was more-or-less shocked at the suggestion. Actually, Dan had offered most of his invitation without thinking, he had not seriously contemplated asking his father to watch him having sex, much less to join him in bed.

Joe, sitting there naked, and looking cute and sexy and needing to continue being serviced, offered, "Hell, R.J., the kid obviously knows what he's doing, and he sure-as-shit enjoys it! Come on and get with us! It's not like you're gonna knock him up and he's gonna have an idiot child!"

Dan sat there naked also, looking fully as cute and sexy and needy of the resumption of service as Joe. He was well aware that his father was handsome. He had himself thoroughly enjoyed sex with other men older than his dad (his coach and his choir director), and he thought Joe's argument was quite persuasive, so he smiled at his dad, and said "Come on, Pop, what the hell! It'll be fun!"

And in a sense, it *was* that simple. For the vast majority of people, R.J. and Dan, father and son, having sex together would be illegal, wrong, sinful, immoral, in poor taste, name your condemnation. Nonetheless, Dan welcomed their first coupling, and later encouraged his father to enter into another, and then further threesomes with other porn stars—who were at first somewhat shocked at the idea of sex with a father-and-son combination, but who warmed to the idea and eagerly participated after getting a look at the spectacular tool the son brought to the liaison.

Tom Hunt had often shared sex with R.J. He was seldom active any longer as a performer in porn, but he was an active producer who often wanted to secure R.J.'s services. He took the customary route to convince the videographer to work on one of his projects, but he also simply enjoyed sharing R.J.'s bed, especially after Dan began to appear there as well. Of the ensuing parade of porn people who shared the guest-room bed, Tom Hunt alone was not even initially ruffled by the idea of sex with Dan and R.J. together. He himself lived in an even stranger situation—a 3-way with identical twin men whose father had introduced them to sex and later all but sold them to Tom, who had loved them and treasured their same kinds of love for him ever since.

Like his father before him, Dan was of the opinion that Tom Hunt was the best—a nice man, a good person, and the most glorious stud he ever had sex with. Occasionally Tom would visit when R.J. was gone, for obvious reasons, and Dan found their one-on-one sex as deliriously exciting as anything he had ever experienced. Tom was also a wonderfully affectionate kisser and snuggler after they both had reached orgasm.

Within a few months of their threesome with Joe Epps, R.J. and Dan even began to express their sexual love for each other occasionally when no one else was present.

If Josh and Damon had been astonished at the video clips they had watched, and especially those of Dan's father fucking with porn stars, they had been virtually struck dumb by their friend's revelations. As he concluded that narrative, Dan said, "I guess you've probably got a good idea what you're gonna see on the rest of these videos."

His two guests indeed guessed, and the ensuing clips showed their friend locked in ecstatic sex with his own father and with some of the absolutely hottest men they had ever seen, including the awesome Tom Hunt. The video provided a transition for them from amazement to admiration to a return of the raging lust they had demonstrated in the guest room earlier that evening.

After an especially stimulating scene where a sexy Latino stud knelt on the bed and discharged a huge load all over R.J.'s body while Dan knelt behind him and buried his astonishing cock deep in his busy and appreciative ass, Dan proudly introduced the last one. He explained that the statuesque, heavy-hung, and drop-dead-gorgeous blond who appeared in it with him and his dad was one of the best known "gay-for-pay" actors in the porn business—generally thought to be completely straight, who fucked worshipping mouths and hot asses like a raging stallion, but never reciprocated.

In the scene Dan showed the boys, he not only sucked cock and kissed eagerly with both father and son, he whimpered with delight as he knelt on all fours and R.J. fucked his ass while Dan knelt in front of him to fuck his mouth. Later he actually shouted with joy as he rode frantically up and down the entire length of Dan's cock—fucking himself brutally, assisted with plenty of upward thrusting from the young stud below. Without even touching his wildly bobbing big cock, the 'straight' blond literally covered Dan with his trademark gusher of come as he continued to ride, then fell off the massive driving cock onto his side, and Dan knelt over him and masturbated, sending a very impressive load of his own into his open, hungry mouth.

All three boys were stroking their own cocks by then, and Dan said, "Let's go back upstairs! I'm horny as shit!"

The other two boys were equally anxious, but Josh wanted

Dan to assure them their session earlier that evening had not been taped. Dan did assure them, and promised further that any time they wanted to return there for sex, the cameras would not be filming their activities.

"Then let's fuck there and spend the night there. I want to sleep in the same bed where you fucked with Tom Fox!" Damon said, and the three boys headed back upstairs for a night of sexual abandon they all would treasure for years.

For the rest of the semester, Dan's final one in high school, Josh and Damon enjoyed unbridled and joyous sex with the older boy. If they could not meet as frequently as they wanted, they made up for it with the enthusiasm they brought to their exercises when they did get together. R.J. was well aware that Dan was sharing his bed with someone while he was gone, and after he finally met Josh and Damon, he liked them so much that he expressed the hope that they would feel free to visit his son any time, whether he was there or not.

Inevitably, R.J. expressed to his son that he thought Josh and Damon were not only nice young men, but they were also extremely attractive. "Hell, Dan, any gay man would have to be nuts not to want those two!"

Dan relayed his father's admiration to his friends, which caused mixed emotions in the boys, but discussing how sexy and accomplished R.J. had been in the videos they had watched, they decided to take him up on his apparent offer. Soon the two friends joined Dan and R.J. in the upstairs bedroom for a four-way sexual marathon that left all of them exhausted, but completely satisfied. Josh and Damon watched father and son make love, father and son watched the two guests do the same, and guests and hosts mixed it up in almost every conceivable combination of partners and positions before the evening was over. And although subsequent 'four-ways' were rare, they did occur. Both Josh and Damon enjoyed sex with Dan's father far more than they might have thought they would, and R.J. enjoyed sex with them exactly as he felt sure he would—enormously!

R.J. invariably used protection when he had sex with the boys, and urged them all to start doing the same if they began to branch out very far in their sexual contacts.

And they did branch out, sometimes together, sometimes in separate ways. Dan, Josh, and Damon often hiked down to North Baker Beach on warm days and walked around nude, for example, and their beauty and Dan's stupendous cock swinging as they walked always attracted a number of men who followed them into secluded places in the bushes and behind the rocks. The three boys, somewhat arrogant in their obvious sexual allure, it must be admitted, selected the most attractive from their temporary suitors and allowed them to suck them off (and those not selected frequently paired up to emulate the example being set, or brought themselves to climax while they watched). They invariably had condoms and lubricant with them, and on rare occasions an unusually attractive spectator might be selected to be granted the delight of receiving Dan's prodigious endowment up his butt—or perhaps even Josh and/or Damon as well! Only once was a spectator so attractive that he was granted special dispensation: Damon and Josh both took him up the ass—while Dan used his gigantic shaft to provide him with deep inspiration from behind!

Josh, of course, continued his sexual relationship with Kyle and alone with Damon. Even though Dan graduated that spring, he did not go to college, but stayed in the city, and Josh and Damon found that he seemed less interested in pursuing their sex play than he had been. They later found that Dan was running an ad in the "Models/Escorts" section of *The Golden Gate Nation*, advertising the availability of his sexual services on an 'out-call' basis only. The upfront (and accurate) advertisement of his endowment as "giant economy size" attracted a number of callers, and repeat business and word-of-mouth recommendation kept him quite busy, with considerably less need to express his lusty sex drive in non-commercial evenings of fucking-for-fun! While R. J. objected strongly, he had little moral high ground to stand on to preach, so he reluctantly tendered his blessing on his son and hoped for the best.

R.J. usually joined in when Josh and Damon revisited Dan in his special guest room, and on a few occasions the two visitors played with him even in the absence of his son. It was well over a year later that Josh and Damon discovered to their amusement that each had also been visiting Dan's father for occasional one-on-one private fuck sessions. And to Damon's surprise as much as anyone's, the private sessions between him and R.J. increased considerably in frequency and in satisfaction derived, to the point where by the time he graduated high school in the spring of '93, Damon was, for all practical purposes, involved in a real relationship with the older man.

Had Damon not gone off to college in Michigan that summer, it is likely the he and R.J. would have been exchanging vows of some kind soon. Dan and Josh had observed the increasing bonds of affection and serious attraction growing, and had even made good-natured jokes about it. Dan told Damon that no matter what he and his dad decided to do, he was not going to call him "Dad" too!

Still, Damon went to Michigan, and R.J. stayed behind, and, although they managed to meet occasionally for casual sex, the serious relationship that seemed to have been growing never became a long-term one.

As much as Josh enjoyed the feverish heat of three-way or four-way sex, he more and more found that he preferred the affection and intimacy of sex with only one partner, lying together in tender embrace, kissing and talking after sex, or, better yet, between sessions!

He shared these intimate sessions with Kyle almost weekly, and with Damon and R.J. ever more infrequently. Yet he maintained his friendship with Eric unabated, even though he seemed to be the one close friend Josh had whom he wasn't having sex with.

The fact that he was so occupied with sex kept Josh from being preoccupied with it as most high school boys are, and he found no difficulty in enjoying the completely non-sexual aspects of his life with a clear mind. And he, like Damon and Kyle, dated girls occasionally, but that was strictly one of his non-sexual activities.

His family life seemed somewhat less serene than it had before, although he tried to tell himself it was simply the way he was reacting to it as his own life changed. When his dad had returned from his trip back east for his prep school class's Twenty-Fifth Reunion, he seemed somewhat distracted. If his mother noted the same thing he would probably never learn, since he saw less and less of her all the time, given the increasing zeal she devoted to her editorial duties with *Bitch*.

Josh had somehow managed to keep his mother's professional position secret from his friends and classmates. He was proud of his mother's success in her field, but he also knew what teasing would be in store for him if the secret became widely known at school. Fortunately, she used her maiden name at the magazine, and few of his friends would have any way of knowing that editor Gwen Andrews was really Gwen Thornton, mother of high-school superstud Josh Thornton.

3.

It was not until he was 17 that Josh finally learned that Eric was gay, although he had suspected it for years, based on observation of his friend while he was looking at other guys, as well as comments he had made. Still, Josh was not sure, and Eric had provided no opening to pursue the subject.

Eric had been working as a life guard at the indoor pool of one of the city's larger hotels for over a year, and he regularly sneaked Josh and Kyle in. They frequently all played in the pool after closing hours, when Eric could leave his life guard's perch and join in the fun.

Since July and August in San Francisco can be very cold, and swimming in the ocean there is never very comfortable, pool swimming is usually the best option. In early August of 1994, just before he began his senior year in high school, Josh took advantage of an invitation from Eric to meet him at the hotel pool just before closing, and to stay and swim with him. Kyle had been invited as well, but for some reason could not avail himself of the opportunity to swim with his friends. By that time Eric and Kyle and Josh were like the Three Musketeers, the closest of friends, together a great deal of the time, and even thought of as a trio by their other friends and their families.

Kyle and Josh's joyous and active sexual relationship was based entirely on mutual attraction and close friendship. Romantic love did not enter into it, so in spite of the sex each occasionally found with others, they were not jealous as a result. They both wondered about Eric's sexual orientation, and often considered "testing the waters," so to speak, but Eric never went quite far enough in his comments to provide them with a comfortable opening. Had they found he was gay, they no doubt would have elevated a considerable part of their Three Musketeers relationship to the sexual level. Perhaps if Kyle had been able to accompany Josh to the pool that night, the revelations the night offered might not have crystallized.

Eric and Josh swam laps for a half-hour or so after the pool was secured for the night, and floated on rafts and talked for another half-hour before going to rinse off in the large shower area next to the men's locker room.

They continued to chat as they showered lengthily under adjacent shower heads in the wall. Eric stepped over to Josh and handed him the bar of soap he had been using and said, "How about getting my back?" He turned away from Josh, who began to soap him up. "Hmmm, that feels good. Keep it up!" After soaping and massaging Eric's back much longer than could possibly have been needed, Josh expanded the scope of his attentions to his sides, down the sides of his legs, his neck, and finally he reached around and soaped Eric's chest as well. Eric turned his head and smiled over his shoulder. "Better quit, it's gonna make me horny!"

Josh squeezed Eric's neck and smiled in return, "Can't have that, can we?" Eric turned around, and Josh was anxious to see if Eric already had an erection. He was pleased to note that the cock he had seen so many hundreds of times over the years in a flaccid state was now well on the way to full readiness.

Taking the soap from Josh's hand, Eric asked, "Want me to do your back for you?"

"Sure," Josh said, and turned his back to Eric. The situation was giving Josh an erection of his own, and the offer provided him with an excuse to turn his back to hide it—still not sure where things were headed.

Eric soaped at great length, slowly and methodically, often pausing to knead and rub Josh's flesh. As Josh had done, he began to soap his friend's sides, down the side of his legs, and reached around to soap and caress his chest and stomach. He gradually worked his hands down on Josh's front side until he was actually touching his pubes at times. "Eric ... " Josh began, the second time his friend's hand ventured into his pubic hair, but Eric quickly returned his attention to Josh's back and re-soaped it. His hands slowly moved lower again until he was now soaping and caressing Josh's buttocks. Unconsciously, Josh began to arch his back and press his ass backwards to meet Eric's busy hands.

Laughing, Josh said. "Now you'd better quit. You're getting me horny!" As he said that, the soap slipped from Eric's hand and hit the shower floor.

"Oops!" Eric said, and bent down to retrieve it.

Turning around, Josh observed Eric facing away from him

and bending over. His ass looked very tempting. "Man, don't you know dropping the soap is dangerous?"

Eric held the cake of soap in his hand as he stood and turned to face Josh. He stepped close and looked steadily into his eyes. "No real danger, is there?" Then he very pointedly looked down at Josh's cock, which was standing out at an angle of about 45 degrees from his body—very close to fully erect.

Eric looked for a full ten seconds at Josh's big cock, which began to grow and rise even as he watched. Neither boy said a word; Josh seemed to be holding his breath. Eric returned his gaze to Josh's eyes. Josh pointedly looked down at Eric's cock then, and was pleased to note that not only was it fully erect now, but Eric was lazily stroking its full length with his left hand! Josh looked up into Eric's eyes again, which were still fixed on his face. Eric gazed steadily for another ten seconds, and then slowly brought the cake of soap into their line of sight, holding it with only his thumb and forefinger. He held the soap there, continuing to search Josh's eyes without saying a word, and then with great ceremony he spread his thumb and forefinger wide so that the soap again fell to the floor. Very gradually, Eric's solemn gaze turned into a sly smile. After another silent, endless ten seconds he spoke one word quietly and about as slowly as one can say a one-syllable word.

"Oops!"

Still smiling, Eric turned slowly around; Josh was still, it seemed, holding his breath. Eric smiled back at Josh over his shoulder, and began to bend over slowly, and, with his hands on the floor, not even bothering with the soap, he not only made no move to rise, but actually backed up a step or so toward Josh, putting the tempting ass he almost surely was offering only a few inches from Josh's now-throbbing cock.

Without a word, Josh put his hands on Eric's waist and stepped forward, so that his balls rested in the crevice of Eric's ass, and his hard cock rested on Eric's back. Eric wiggled his ass gently, and Josh humped his cock up and down between his buttocks. Eric's hands came around behind him and pulled Josh's ass in tightly. Neither had yet said a word.

Dreamily, they continued their gentle play until Eric stood, reached behind, took hold of Josh's prick, and put it between his legs, under his balls, where Josh began to fuck deeper and deeper. Josh put his arms around Eric and caressed his chest with one hand and with the other formed a fist for Eric's raging hard-on to fuck. Eric turned and spoke finally, over his shoulder, "Do you want me, Josh?"

Josh turned Eric's body around, took his face in his hands, and with their lips only inches apart, he replied, "I've wanted you for a long time. I just wasn't sure you wanted me."

Their lips almost met as Eric whispered "I want you, Josh. I want your wonderful big prick inside of me. Please fuck me! I've been hungry for you to fuck me since ... since forever!" Their lips finally met, their arms went around each other to hold and caress, and the hot water continued to play on their magnificent young bodies as they expressed the love and desire they felt for each other—and which had been held in check for so long.

Eric took Josh by the hand and led him into the locker room. They dried off and Eric reached into his locker to take out a dispenser bottle of lubricant. "I've had this with me every time you've been here, just in case. At last I'll get to use it!" He lay the bottle down on a bench and sank to his knees in front of Josh. Josh took his head in his hands and as Eric opened his mouth wide, he gently and slowly inserted his throbbing erection as far into the hungry mouth as it would go. Eric's lips closed over the impressive tube of hard flesh, and he pressed his hands against Josh's ass and began to suck deeply. He could feel the muscles of Josh's ass playing under the velvet skin as it drove the engorged cock in and out.

Josh gripped Eric's head very tightly, and pulled his head in to meet each fierce thrust of his prick, then pushed it away each time he withdrew, allowing him maximum scope to drive his cock deep into his friend's throat. As Josh fucked his worshipping mouth savagely, Eric murmured his ecstasy, and he began to masturbate himself while he sucked.

Josh pulled him to his feet and kissed him passionately. "I want to suck you!" he said.

While Josh knelt in front of him and sucked, Eric began to fuck the eager mouth, but soon pulled away and knelt next to Josh. "Lie down on the floor so we can suck each other at the same time!" Their towels covered the tile floor where they lay on their sides in "69" position with their arms around each other, each feverishly caressing the other's undulating ass while he fucked his mouth joyously. They were so completely excited to be making love to each other at last, that nothing but orgasm would probably stop their impassioned sucking.

With a loud cry uttered around the bulk of Josh's driving cock, Eric began to ejaculate into the hot, moist heaven of his friend's eager mouth. As Eric's huge climax continued to spurt, Josh's cock drove faster and faster, until it was buried as deep as it could go, and spasms shook his body. He murmured his own loud cry, not only around a deep-driving hard cock, but with a mouth virtually filled with the delicious come that the plunging cock continued to supply. He began again to thrust in and out while explosive spurts of his scalding discharge filled Eric's mouth and throat.

The two boys continued to suck until their cocks were drained dry. They reversed their bodies and lay in each other's arms, kissing sweetly.

After a seemingly endless bliss of affectionate kissing and caressing, Eric whispered, "Will you fuck me in the ass?"

"You want me to?"

"Oh god, I've wanted to feel your cock up my butt since I was sixteen years old! Have you ever fucked anyone before? In the ass, I mean?"

Josh grinned. "Two guys."

Instinctively, Josh had decided he was not ready to reveal the details of his involvement with Dan and his father to Eric. Not yet, anyway—perhaps later. Had it only been Dan that he and Damon had shared sex with, he would no doubt have confessed to it. For some reason, though, the involvement of Dan's father made him feel something he himself did not yet understand. Damon had been there. They had watched each other fuck Dan's father, they had watched Dan and his father fucking each other, and the father had watched Dan fucking each of them and their fucking each other. He could (and did) discuss the experience with Damon. Maybe Eric would understand his confused feelings better than he did, after all, he wasn't a party to it! Yes, they'd probably talk about it, but not quite yet. Fuck each other tonight, see how it goes, and talk about fucking with other guys later.

"Do I know them?" Josh nodded. "Kyle is one of them,

right?"

Now Josh laughed. "Right! And we keep wondering about you, wondering if you'd want to join us. But you never picked up on any of the hints we gave you."

"So who's the other one?" Eric asked.

"It's Damon."

"Oh my god, he's so fuckin' cute and sexy! I'd love to fuck with him! He graduated last year. Do you still see him?"

Josh shook his head. "No, he went to Michigan for college, and the last time I heard from him he said he was in love with a guy there, and he still wanted to be friends, but he and the other guy aren't fucking with anybody else. He didn't even come home this summer. He went to Chicago to spend it with his new lover."

"You still haven't told me. Will you fuck my ass?"

Josh put his arms around Eric. "Yes, Eric, I will fuck you. I will fuck you so hard and so long you'll beg for mercy! And then I'll beg you to fuck me, if you want."

"Begging will not be necessary, I promise you!"

"Let me ask you about something I just don't get."

Eric grinned. "Ask me anything you want. But just remember, you're gonna fuck me after I answer!"

"Okay, why has it taken you such a long time to let me know you wanted to do this?" Josh asked.

"Because I've been dating someone seriously for over two years. He brought me out, and even as much as I've wanted you, I didn't want to break my promise to be with him only."

"Is it someone I know?"

Eric replied hesitatingly, "Yes, but ... I've never told anyone about it. I couldn't—I had to hide it from you and Kyle, and from anyone else. He could have got into so much trouble."

"You don't need to tell me if you don't want to, or if you don't feel you should. It doesn't make any difference. What made you decide to come on to me finally? Is it over with you and ... whoever?"

"Yeah. He's gone now," Eric said. "And he can't come back, and ... God, Josh, I've got to tell someone! Will you swear that this will only be between us?"

Josh kissed Eric and pulled him tight. "Eric, you don't have to tell me anything if you don't want to. It doesn't make any difference, but if you want to, I promise you no one will ever hear about it from me."

"Thanks, Josh ... you're a good friend. I want to tell you, especially since we finally ... well, you know." Josh smiled and told him to continue. "Okay. You know Mr. Rubich?"

"The history teacher?" Eric nodded. "Sure I know him. We were together in a class two years ago, remember? Wait. You don't mean that he's ... are you gonna tell me you and Mr. Rubich? ... that he's the one you've been screwing with?"

Eric nodded again. "He's really a wonderful guy, Josh."

"Well, sure, he seems like a really great guy, especially for a teacher, and he's really good-looking too. But shit, Eric, he's as old as my father!"

"How old is your father, Josh?"

"My dad? Dad is ... let's see, he just had his forty-fourth birthday a couple of months ago."

"Well, Mike, Mr. Rubich, is around three years older than your dad. And he's the sexiest man I've ever met. I know it sounds funny, Josh, but I love him very much, and not like he's an old man. He's sexy, and he's nice, and we had great times together."

"Wow! But it still seems strange. I'm trying to get used to the idea of your having sex with a guy, and then to find out it's someone older than my dad!"

"Josh! Have you ever looked at your dad? I mean really looked at him? He's one of the most handsome guys I've ever seen. And he's so sexy. I'd kill to go to bed with him!"

"My dad? I've never thought about that. I mean, yeah, he's an incredibly good-looking guy, but he *is* my dad!"

"I can understand how you never thought about sex when you thought about your dad, but believe me, he's unbelievably attractive—and just because he's older doesn't mean crap!"

Josh thought for a minute before he went on. "I'm gonna tell you something you've gotta keep strictly between us, okay? You remember Dan Bliss? He graduated last year?"

"Do I remember Dan Bliss? Shit, I used to drool thinking about Dan Bliss. Did you ever see his cock? I was in a swim class he helped out with, and I've never seen anything like it. Every time he got in the shower, I had to get out or I'd get a hard-on I couldn't hide. I used to lie in bed jacking off and thinking about his cock, playing with it, or sucking it off, or getting him to shoot his load on me—or in me! So what about Dan? You gonna tell me you and him did it?"

Grinning, Josh lay on his back with his hands under his neck, and told Eric all about him and Damon, and even decided to confess the whole thing about Dan and his father—what the hell, it shouldn't shock him now!

Eric was nothing short of astonished at Josh's narrative, and had been unable to avoid interjecting incredulous comments, which Josh turned aside with assurances of the truth of the torrid relationship.

After Eric had heard the end of the story, and had managed to begin digesting it, he said, "So you know how great sex with an older guy can be, then—and if you watched Dan and his father fucking each other, and Dan watched you and Damon fucking his dad, I don't see how my being hot for your dad seems strange to you. I just wish it had been you and your dad with Damon and me—I would have loved watching you and your dad fuck almost as much as I would have enjoyed fucking with him. Oh, and with Damon, too! God he was hot. You know, I suspected you and he were screwing around, but I was with Mike, and wasn't about to do anything to mess that up."

Josh let out a large breath of air. "Okay, I can see what you're saying. If my dad weren't my dad, yeah, I'd sure enjoy screwing with him!"

"Would you screw with him if you found out he was gay, and wanted to screw with you? That would be like Dan and his father, right? And that was okay, right again?"

"Jesus, Eric, I don't know. Maybe ... no, I just can't imagine."

"Well if you ever find out he is gay, fix me up with him at least, okay?

Josh laughed. "Deal. Maybe we can have a threesome! Eric, can you say *fat chance*?"

Eric laughed too. "Well, okay, but I never give up hope!"

"So anyway, what happened with you and Mr. Rubich—Mike?"

Frowning, Eric began to tell as much as he knew of Mike Rubich's history and his fall from grace at their school.

Mike Rubich had come to San Francisco to teach after a hitch in the Air Force following his college graduation in 1969, and he took his master's degree at the expense of the government following his separation. His first teaching position was the one he had just left—after nineteen years. He had discovered he was gay while in college. He had dated girls regularly all through high school, and continued to do so as a college student, but during his sophomore year a series of anonymous calls from a professor at the college opened new vistas to him.

The professor did not reveal his name to Mike, but told him he had seen him around campus frequently, and simply wanted to tell him how very, very handsome and attractive he thought he was! The professor's assessment was right on the mark, incidentally—Mike Rubich was an uncommonly handsome young man; gorgeous would not have been an inappropriate word to describe him.

Mike was somewhat nonplused by the conversation, but was also flattered, and he thanked his admirer for having shared his admiration. When the caller asked if he minded his calling him once in a great while, Mike could see no reason to object.

For the rest of that year, the anonymous professor called occasionally, and the two were soon discussing campus news and chatting like old friends, but at the same time he continued to tell Mike how handsome and attractive he found him, adding now how much he enjoyed talking with him. Shortly before the summer vacation began, Mike asked the still-anonymous professor if he didn't think they ought to meet, but his admirer said he would call him in the fall to see how his summer had been, and if he were still interested in a meeting, they would set it up then.

The meeting took place finally a few days after the opening of the fall semester. The professor turned out to be young (thirty-one years old), unmarried and unattached, reasonably well-built and handsome, and extremely pleasant to be with. His name was John, and he was an Assistant Professor of Music at the college. Mike had dinner with him a few times, and finally came out and asked him if he were interested in him sexually, if that was what this was all about. John admitted that sex with Mike was certainly something he would enjoy, but that if that was not something he could consider, he would understand, and although he would be disappointed, it would in no way diminish his admiration for him.

This was not unexplored territory for John, incidentally. During his three years at the college he had befriended several other very attractive young men who had turned him down when he finally approached them about sex. Finally he had approached yet another who became his lover for two years, and who had just graduated the preceding semester. It was this circumstance which had made it impractical for John to meet with Mike the spring just past.

Mike had for years known that he was more attracted to boys than he was supposed to be, but he had sublimated any urges he might have had to explore his possible homosexual leanings. He liked John, however, and found him sufficiently attractive that he decided this was a good opportunity to test the waters and see if he himself might be gay.

He was gay.

The first time John kissed him, he felt a warmth and an excitement his kissing with girls had only hinted at. The first time John sucked his cock he was so excited he ejaculated after only about thirty seconds, but with the pressure relieved and his nervousness abated, he relaxed sufficiently so that John was able to feast on him twice more that night at a reasonable pace. When he dropped to his knees before John to return the favor, he found he took to cocksucking as naturally as he had feared he might: that night of his very first gay encounter, he swallowed two loads of come, and slept all night in his suitor's arms—and woke to the thrill of his very first 69!

For the remainder of his college career, he and John were lovers. He still dated girls occasionally, to keep up appearances, and found that he had no trouble performing sexually with one when circumstances dictated, but he realized it was just that, a performance. He never knew it, but John was performing sexually with a series of other handsome young men at the same time.

During his hitch in the Air Force, Mike kept a very low profile. He did find that furtive sex with civilians on the prowl for military partners was relatively easy, sexual encounters with other servicemen were harder to arrange and probably more risky and, because of this, it seemed he found them much more satisfying. Airmen, sailors, soldiers, Marines—he sampled cock across inter-service lines, and enjoyed it all, but decided fucking Marines and getting fucked by sailors was the most satisfying! Cocksucking, on the other hand, seemed to be a talent practiced with equal excellence by civilians and the military as well.

Probably the very best cocksucker he encountered offered his only really "close call" while in the service. One night in Dallas, nearing the end of his enlistment, he picked up a stunningly handsome young man who was obviously offering himself for sex. He was even hotter in bed than he was handsome, and gave a better blowjob than Mike had ever experienced. Mike learned the next time they met that he was fifteen years old! Their 'affair' was the only extended liaison he developed while he was in the Air Force—and by all odds, the most dangerous—and it only ended with his discharge (his military discharge—the boy and he had shared endless numbers of the other kind). Mike missed the boy, but went off to graduate school breathing a sigh of relief that he had not found himself in trouble.

Mike's military father and his strong, domineering mother virtually pressured their son into getting married—they wanted grandchildren. He more-or-less convinced himself to fall in love with a girl when he was in graduate school, and she quite decidedly fell in love with this man.

He and Sharon liked each other, they enjoyed each other's company, and the sex they shared after six months of dating was okay for Mike and wonderful for Sharon. Aside from sex with her, Mike kept his dick in his pants.

Mike's parents liked Sharon, so they married, and Mike decided to put his homosexual life behind him and become a "normal" family man. He succeeded quite well, actually. Though they never produced the grandchildren both sets of parents wanted, they were reasonably happy—each busy with his or her own teaching career.

Although Mike knew he was gay, he limited his exercise of that side of his personality after he married to his imagination and the perusal of muscle magazines with some appearance of legitimacy. Later, as pornography became readily available, he watched porn movies and videos in 'quarter booths' in sex shops along both Folsom and Polk Streets.

Eric appeared in Mike's history class at the beginning of the '92-'93 school year, and Mike noted nothing special about the youngster, except that he was attractive, seemed more interested in his class than his other pupils, and was obviously more sensitive as well.

If his new history teacher thought he was attractive, it was nothing compared to the way Eric felt about him. He decided Mr. Rubich was amazingly good-looking and sexy. Eric had felt for some time that he was probably gay, and had often wanted to sound Josh out as a possible partner to help him explore his sexuality. He loved being around Josh. He thought he was the sexiest boy he knew, and he even suspected that Josh was doing something sexually, but he was afraid to say anything and risk being scorned as a homosexual. He liked being around Josh at his home even more, because he thought the father was as attractive as the son, and there was something about the maturity and stability of the older man that appealed to Eric.

Mr. Rubich was also a mature and apparently stable man who appealed to Eric enormously, and he was not only very friendly, but he seemed compassionate as well. Eric decided he was a good candidate to talk with about his sexual confusion. He could not discuss it with his family, and he was afraid to discuss it with his friends, but he needed to talk to someone. Whether he consciously realized it or not, when he sought that counsel he was probably hoping against hope that a sexual situation might develop with the handsome and very attractive Mr. Rubich.

Mike was flattered that Eric had sought his advice, and touched by the boy's fear and confusion—he knew it well. He neither actually wanted nor welcomed the strong attraction he soon began to feel for Eric as their meetings grew both more frequent, and increasingly intimate, but as it became plain to Mike that the boy was falling in love with him, he realized he was beginning to return that love.

One afternoon after school, talking as they walked in a secluded section of Lincoln Park, Mike put his arm around Eric's shoulder. Eric put his arm around Mike's waist in return, and they continued to walk for a few hundred yards before stopping to look out over the Golden Gate. Neither moved his arm for several minutes, and Eric turned to Mike and looked into his eyes. "Mr. Rubich, I ... " He stopped, and put both arms around the older man and hugged him. He pressed his face into his chest. Mike lifted Erik's face and studied him for several moments before bending his head to kiss the trembling boy's lips.

Nobody paid much attention to an older man kissing a younger one on that bluff. It was not an uncommon sight. In fact, at that very moment an older man had a younger man's cock buried in his throat less than fifty yards from where Eric and Mike were only sharing a kiss, and even that was not an uncommon sight, although it usually drew a bigger crowd of spectators.

Their kisses and embraces that afternoon were sweet and innocent, and on their next walk Eric confessed he was in love with Mike. When Mike admitted that he felt the same toward Eric, their kissing and caressing became much more passionate, and the feverish groping they shared led to exchanged blowjobs in the bushes.

A few days later, on an afternoon when Eric's parents were safely out of town, the two came together in Eric's bedroom. They were soon naked and painfully erect, trembling with both fear and desire.

Their sex proceeded slowly, but it grew inexorably. Eric, at sixteen, was a sensitive boy and, naturally, he fell profoundly in love with this handsome, caring man who obviously loved him so much. Unless one knew his sexual history, one might expect Mike to have been more restrained. But, since he had suppressed his true sexuality for seventeen years, the depth of his love for Eric was equally all-consuming.

Although their love-making remained strictly oral for six months or so, eventually Mike could no longer deny his appetite for the kind of love he had found most enjoyable during his military career. The first time Eric fucked Mike's ass he knew this was the romantic thrill he had been waiting for—and the first time Mike fucked Eric's ass, the boy *belonged* to him.

It was often extremely difficult to find a time or a place for

Mike and Eric to express their love for each other, but they managed all through that school year and the next.

Their world crumbled the day Mike's wife found a poem he had composed for Eric on the occasion of his seventeenth birthday. Mike had presented the smooth copy to his young lover, but had neglected to destroy the rough draft, which he carelessly left in the pocket of a seldom-used sport coat. His poetry—like his love-making with Eric—was passionate in the extreme.

Much poetry deals with oblique imagery, and indirect similes or metaphors, but Mike's wife had no difficulty comprehending the import of this particular verse. In no uncertain terms it hymned the joys her husband and a teenaged boy had found in each other's arms—to say nothing of in their mouths, in their asses, and with their cocks. She might have forgiven the sharing of their devotion had they limited it to their arms, but the uses to which Mike's poem clearly showed they had been putting their mouths and cocks and asses was more than she could tolerate.

Mike's wife did not even question him. She simply produced the copy of the poem she had found, and informed him he would resign his teaching position the next day and leave San Francisco at once. Further, she said she would begin divorce proceedings immediately. He could tell the school board or his family anything he wanted, but she still cared enough about him for the good years they had shared that she would not reveal his indiscretion to either the authorities or Eric's parents if he promised never to see the boy again. What he did after he left was of no concern to her.

She allowed Mike to write a terse note to Eric, explaining that everything was over, that his wife knew everything, and that he would never see him again. She allowed him to wish the boy well, but would not even permit him to express his love one final time, even with the traditional 'three little words.' She herself delivered the note to Eric at the hotel swimming pool where, had she known it, her husband and the boy had been having sex for almost a year.

Eric was crushed. Eric was young; he would get over it. On the other hand, he would always love Mike Rubich.

"That's really amazing," Josh said when Eric had finished his story. How did you manage to spend so much time with him, and still keep Kyle and I from being suspicious?"

"You mean to say, of course, Kyle and me," Eric laughed.

"Yeah, okay, smart ass. Kyle and me! How did you do it?"

"Well you gotta remember he was married, and had to make excuses to his wife all the time, so we couldn't be together that much. We just had to make every minute count. And besides, you and Kyle ... hey, you guys were fuckin' with each other all the time, and I had no idea. How did you work that?"

Josh laughed. "Well, I guess you had some idea about it—you sure guessed his name fast enough! But anyway, I guess you and I were both busy enough that we couldn't tell that the other one was spending so much time with his ..."

"With his lover," Eric volunteered.

"No, not really that, Eric. From what you say, obviously you and Mr. Rubich—Mike—were real lovers. But Kyle and I, well we're just friends, and we're ... Kyle says we're fuck buddies. I guess that describes it pretty well."

"We've been friends forever, Josh. How about fuck buddies for us too?"

"Do you want that, Eric?"

"More than anything, especially now that Mike and I can never be together again."

"Never's a long time, Eric. Things change. Don't give up. And hey! So far we're just suck buddies! Nothing wrong with that, but didn't I hear you say you wanted to be a fuck buddy? You better get on your knees and let me inside your hot ass! I've got another load I'm gonna give you!"

"Oh God, Josh, I'm looking forward to this so much!" They kissed again—much more passionately this time. "And fuck buddies. They fuck each other, right?"

Josh grinned and put the tip of his forefinger to the end of Eric's nose. "Until I feel that big cock of yours shooting another load, all the way up my ass this time! You aren't goin' anywhere!" He pulled Eric to his feet. "On your knees, hotshot! You're gonna get fucked hard tonight!"

Eric picked up a towel and spread it on the bench where the lubricant sat. He lay down on his back, spreading and raising his legs. Grinning up at the handsome blond who was now busily stroking his generous hard cock and squirting lubricant on it, he said, "This is the way I like it best!"

"Keep those legs high. You got it!" And Eric did indeed get it, and after that Josh took his place on the bench, and the friend who had just taken it from him demonstrated how adept he was at giving it!

Josh's senior year was his most sexually restrained one since his earliest high school days. He was a senior class officer, he was quite active with his soccer team and a couple of academic clubs. Damon was gone, Dan was busy selling his ass, and shortly after their senior year began, Kyle began "going steady."

Kyle started dating a classmate named Art Ling, half Chinese and half African-American, with the skin coloring of his black ancestry, and the fine features of his oriental ancestry. It was an alleged trait of the former that was predominant between his legs, apparently. He had a huge cock that Kyle described to his friends in rapturous terms! Kyle and Art apparently satisfied each other so well in the ways they wanted to be satisfied that they became a real couple, and Kyle enjoyed sex with Josh only rarely. When he learned Eric's recent sexual history, Kyle had sex with his other friend, of course, but only twice before his relationship with Art developed fully.

So sex during his senior year for Josh was with Eric, for the most part; given his busy schedule, that seemed to be about all he usually had time for. In addition, Josh planned to enter San Francisco State after graduation, and began studying extra diligently to prepare.

Eric was especially happy to have Josh's sexual friendship. It was considerably helpful in fostering his recovery from the affair with Mike Rubich, and he had always had something of a crush on Josh anyway. Eric had spent two years in a monogamous (for him) relationship, which had unnaturally repressed his somewhat adventurous sexual nature, and now when he wasn't actually practicing what was for him becoming more and more a real loving relationship with Josh, he went a little bit crazy. In addition to sex with Josh, Eric began frequenting video shops on Polk Street and Folsom Street, and often had sex with complete strangers there—and, on occasion, he walked the paths in Lincoln Park and shared anonymous sex in the bushes with men who accosted him.

The Three Musketeers, Josh and Eric and Kyle continued to meet socially. They often went to the Castro and flirted with other guys. They loved to do the same thing as they paraded their nudity on North Baker Beach, and only occasionally would they lead one or more of their admirers into the bushes or behind the rocks at the beach to offer samples of the delights they were showing, or to taste a few of the more toothsome samples they saw paraded there.

They watched male porn videos frequently, however. R.J. had given Josh quite a number, including some with their favorite stars, and soon Eric was able to rent the newer ones, having reached his majority before either of his other friends. Josh was the only one of the three who felt safe in keeping the videos in his room, so it was there they watched their old favorites and thrilled to the new ones. They almost cheered when Steve Fox finally showed his ability as a "top," and completely fell under the spell of the boyish (but incredibly sexy) Johan Paulik and his Czechoslovakian countryman Lukas Ridgeston. They agreed that Lukas was probably the sexiest and most beautiful guy they had ever seen, although Josh still held out for Tom Steele or Jeff Stryker as the sexiest, and Steve Fox or Ryan Idol as the most beautiful.

Josh's high school graduation was relatively uneventful. He had been accepted to San Francisco State, and planned to enter for Summer School. About that time he was surprised, but not shocked, when his parents told him they were divorcing; he had sensed they were growing apart for a couple of years now. Fortunately, the divorce was amicable. His mother rented an apartment and his father kept the house, so he still had his own room to come home to when life in the dorm got too hectic.

He had always been closer to his father than to his mother, and his mother's speedy remarriage following the divorce actually served to separate him further from her. He really did not care much for her new husband, Quentin Turley, whom he regarded only as his mother's new husband, not by any means his stepfather. Although he was close to his dad, and they talked almost daily, he actually saw little of him. He visited home only now and then, and even then his father was often gone. He didn't question where his father might be, thinking it none of his business.

His dorm life was tolerable; his roommate, sexually unattractive, spent little time in their quarters, and was almost always gone on weekends. The roommate was straight, and frequently spent some mid-week nights with his girlfriend in her apartment, allowing Josh to bring bed partners to their room with some frequency. Josh did not hide his sexual orientation from his roommate, and even had he been discovered screwing with another guy, there would have been no real problem.

And he did screw with other guys. Eric had gone off to Pepperdine, but was home for holidays and long weekends, when he invariably spent at least one night with Josh in bed. Kyle and Art were wrapped up in each other; he talked with Kyle occasionally, but there was no more sexual contact. There was an attractive sophomore down the hall in the dormitory, who shared Josh's bed two or three times a month. A fake I.D. allowed Josh admission to bars, where he occasionally found someone of interest to play with.

In all, he was so busy with his school work, that he didn't miss the intensely active sex life he had enjoyed in his first three years of high school. He was, as he so succinctly told Dan on one of his rare visits with him, "getting all the cock I have time for." At the very moment he said that, he was at Dan's house getting quite a lot of cock indeed.

It was half-way though his second year at State that he finally met someone whom he thought might prove to be more than just someone to have sex with. He was drinking a beer in a bar on Castro Street when he spotted a dark, very handsome guy with what had to be the cutest "bubble butt" he'd seen in a long time. He moved next to him at the bar and struck up a conversation. He learned the dark-haired, twenty-four year old beauty was called "Harp," and he told him his own name was "Jay Andrews", which was formed by using his first initial and his middle name. Josh never gave his real name in casual encounters with guys he didn't know, but hoped to have sex with. It wasn't necessary, and it just didn't seem like a good idea, anyway.

It was only a few minutes before each knew the other was interested in him sexually. Josh asked Harp if he wanted to come to his place, but Harp's apartment was much closer, so they went there for the best sex Josh could remember having had in a long time.

Harp was beautiful, versatile, and, as a bonus, he had the cutest ass Josh had ever seen, much less felt, kissed, licked, eaten out, or fucked—all of which he managed to do that night to his and his partner's mutual delight. All this passion Harp returned enthusiastically, wielding a cock which was impressive in size and almost as attractive as his ass.

Within six weeks, Jay and Harp were making love regularly, and Josh was aware that he was beginning to feel for Harp more than the comradely love he had for Damon or Kyle, Eric or Dan, or the more serious kind he had begun to feel stirring when he was with Dan's father, for that matter; he had not allowed that feeling for R.J. to develop, of course—as Damon had. He knew, however, he was beginning to fall in love with Harp!

Harp still knew little about Jay, except that he was a San Francisco native who was afraid his parents might discover he was gay. Harp had been fairly secretive too, not yet telling Jay what he did for a living. As Harp began to realize the younger man was falling in love with him, he wondered if he himself might not be feeling something of that nature toward Jay—even though he was at the same time beginning to feel mutual love growing between him and the older man he was also dating regularly. Finally Harp decided he had to confess his profession to Jay, and, although Jay was not shocked to learn that he was an escort, in fact, one of his friends was doing the same thing, he was a bit dismayed as to why Harp had to continue doing it. As the days wore on, Josh felt even more frustrated. As much love as he brought to their meetings, and as much love as he sensed on Harp's part, he also knew his lover was holding back—and he didn't think it was only because he was engaged in prostitution. Shortly after he realized he was falling in love, he had begun a campaign to convince Harp he should give up escorting, but he was making no headway, and more and more he resented having to share Harp's body with people who really cared nothing about it except as a glorious medium for a quick piece of ass.

By April of '97, Josh was actually angry about the escorting. Not so much angry at Harp, as he was angry at the situation. His lover continued to sell his precious body, his sacred cock.

Not completely sure why he decided to do it, Josh determined that he himself would try escorting. Probably it was a way to get back at Harp, but also he wanted to experience what Harp was engaged in, so that he himself might understand the situation somewhat better. He contacted Dan and told him what he wanted to do—asking him to help him get set up in the escorting business too. Even after Josh explained his situation and his reasoning, Dan thought it was a terrible idea, but Josh was determined to go through with it, so he agreed to help.

At Dan's request, R.J. took the photograph which Josh wound up using in *The Golden Gate Nation*, showing Josh's nude torso, with his cock splendidly hard, supporting a small towel that barely concealed it. He was actually surprised the paper agreed to run it. It was more graphic than any other picture. It showed his pubic hair, his balls were barely concealed, and it clearly delineated the outline of his cockhead under the clinging towel. Very likely it had passed muster because the clerk at the ad counter at the paper almost drooled when the gorgeous tall blond subject of the photograph brought it in. R.J. had also suggested the caption he wound up using with the picture: "Like the looks of this bat? You ought to see the balls! Let's play! I like to pitch, I like to catch! Andrew, 19 years old, drop-dead gorgeous, versatile, and horny as hell. This is a current picture, and it's exactly what $150 will get you. Out calls only."

The phone number which followed the sexy picture of "Andrew" was for his pager, which began ringing busily as soon as the ad appeared.

Balancing his class schedule with activities as an escort would not have been especially difficult, or coordinating those activities with Harp's own escorting activities would have been reasonably easy, but given the three factors he had to juggle, Josh's ingenuity was tested. He met the challenge somehow.

Josh found there proved to be quite a demand for his services as an escort. He stayed busy, but he was surprised to find how often his calls involved little more than allowing another man to play with him or suck him while he masturbated. Often, once the client had reached a climax, Josh was free to go, however short a time it had taken.

Josh made it clear to prospective clients that while he permitted body worship and allowed his clients to suck his cock, he promised no fucking or mutual sex play, in spite of claims to "versatility" in the printed ad. There were many occasions when a client was sufficiently attractive or seemed nice enough that Josh not only reciprocated orally, but fucked butt, and once in a while took it up the butt himself. What he especially found was that he was making a lot of money.

Understanding Harp's profession from first-hand experience did not in any way lessen Josh's eagerness that his lover abandon it. It did, however, make him realize that the sexual experiences Harp underwent as an escort were, as strange as it may seem, relatively impersonal. Still, he did not want to share Harp's love with someone else. Would Harp feel the same way about him if he knew he was escorting also?

Harp's escorting usually occupied only a few scattered hours on any given day or night, but in mid-May he was gone for four days on what he termed a "business trip," but which he would not discuss further. Harp was well aware of how upset "Jay" was about his going for such a long trip, presumably in his capacity as an escort, and he promised him they would get away for a few days very soon—away from everyone else.

Harp was especially loving after his return, and kept his promise about a trip for just the two of them. They went to a pricey, upscale resort along the Russian River, farther north in the state, and spent three days in a rustic cabin—part of the resort complex, but still quite secluded. Except for meals, and hikes in the area, they saw no one else—and on the porch at the back of the cabin, overlooking the river, they made love day and night.

Their last night there, lying on his back with his legs on Harp's shoulders and Harp's cock buried deep inside him, Josh looked up at his lover's face, framed by bright stars and scudding clouds, and said words he had never uttered with any of his past partners, no matter how much they had meant to him.

"I love you, Harp!"

Harp picked Josh's body up—keeping him joyously impaled—and kissed him long and tenderly. "I love you too, Jay."

There was complete honesty in Josh's expression—he was deeply in love with Harp. Harp's use of the name "Jay" when he replied to his expression of love jarred him. He had to tell him his real name and everything else about himself soon. After all, why not? Even if his family did find out about his affair with Harp, he didn't care any longer. He was an adult now—they would have to accept him for what he was, and accept whom he chose as a partner. If they couldn't ... well, like Scarlett O'Hara, he would think about that tomorrow.

There was honesty in Harp's expression of love too, but his reply did not say everything. He loved this sweet young boy, to be sure, and while he knew that love grew stronger all the time, he also knew he felt an even deeper attachment to his older lover back in the city. Harp knew that as long as he was escorting, he could not give himself completely to loving anyone, but he was sure that it was only a matter of time before he would give in to the pleadings of one of the two who both loved him and urged him to abandon the profession. Which one did he want to develop a real relationship with? What would he do if he stopped escorting? He had to decide something soon, in fairness to the sweet young man who lay there impaled on him, and to the equally treasured older man back in San Francisco.

Much to Josh's chagrin, when they returned to San Francisco, Harp resumed his escorting activities as though nothing significant had happened on the Russian River. Something significant had happened, in Josh's mind: they had declared their love for each other. On the trip back into the city, Josh had urged Harp to give up escorting right away, but he had only promised to consider it soon. Now, with his lover off again having sex with strangers, Josh vowed to resume his own activities as an escort with equal vigor.

Josh campaigned for a decision from Harp for almost a month, but small signs of Harp's irritation made him realize he was pressuring him for a determination he was not yet ready to make. He reluctantly backed away from urging a quick solution to the problem, which meant that he was giving his career as Andrew and his life as Jay extended leases on life.

It was after eight o'clock when a call came one night asking if "Andrew" would be agreeable to a threesome. The man was obviously speaking in an assumed, sexy voice (he himself invariably did the same thing when he talked with prospective clients), but he seemed very nice, and it sounded like it could be a lot of fun. God knows he had enjoyed sex with more than one other person any number of times in his own personal life, why not as "Andrew"? He agreed to meet with "Brad" and his friend at nine o'clock—still light out, since it was the longest day of the year.

About an hour later he was buzzed into the quite nice apartment building near the Embarcadero where "Brad" lived, and went upstairs to meet with him. He knocked on the door, and when it opened, he looked into the face of quite likely the last person he expected to see there.

His father opened the door to him.

. . .

Although the reader has seen them before, it seems appropriate to reprint here, *verbatim*, the final paragraphs of that section of this volume which detailed the story of Harp:

Neither could speak for a moment. Finally, Brad gasped, "Josh, what in hell is this? My God ... you're Andrew?"

"Dad? You're the Brad I'm here to meet?"

"Yes, I ... no! Oh shit, get in here! You've got a lot of explaining to do!

"I think maybe you've got a few things to explain to me, too, Dad!"

"Jesus Christ, I can't believe this! Come in here and ..." He took a deep breath. "Yes, you're right, Josh, I guess I owe you an explanation too. Come on in and let me get the door closed."

Josh came in to the room, looking around. "What is this place, Dad? What are you ... " He stopped short as Harp emerged from the bathroom.

Harp was totally naked, and he was holding his erect cock in his hand and grinning. "You guys ready for some of this?" He stopped, and his jaw dropped as surely as if he had been doing a vaudeville take. "Jay!"

It was Josh's turn to do the take. "Harp!"

The stunned silence which ensued was probably as fraught as a silence can be!

. . .

The first thing that happened then was that nothing happened. There was a stunned silence that probably lasted fifteen seconds, although it seemed like an eternity to all in the room—silent only because jaws dropping and necks swiveling back and forth produce no audible sensation. The second thing was that during the silence the impressive erection Harp had brought with him from the bathroom went South faster than a New York banker following his retirement.

Harp stared at Josh. Finally he blurted out, "What are you doing here?"

"Me? What are you doing here?"

Brad looked from one to the other. "You two know each other?"

Josh remained silent, but Harp finally turned his attention to Brad. "Let me ask you the same question. You two know each other?"

Answering Harp, but looking at Josh, Brad said quietly. "Harp, this is Josh. My son."

Josh looked at his father for a long time, and finally found his voice. "Dad, this is my lover!"

Harp looked at Josh, but addressed his lover's father. "Brad, this is Jay!"

Brad looked at Josh, but addressed Harp. "Jay? This is Josh! And Josh, he's my lover!"

"Your lover?" Josh couldn't decide where to look, so he divided his gaze equally between his father and his lover. "What in holy hell is going on?"

Had it not been for the sexual content, the situation would have done credit to a Marx Brothers movie, but as it stood, it better resembled a French or British bedroom farce. And this would have been the perfect time to ring down the curtain on Act Two; the only thing lacking was a curtain line, which Harp finally supplied.

"I think we'd all better sit down and talk!"

Coda: JOSH AND BRAD AND HARP

Harp Harper, Man-in-the-Middle, was more or less dumb-struck. If a similar incapacity had temporarily struck the father-and-son team he had just discovered book-ended his sex life, the situation that crystallized that night of June 21, 1997 might have been more speedily sorted out.

Neither Josh nor Brad could resist expressing astonishment at the discovery of each other's homosexuality, and Brad could no more resist expressing disapproval of his son's adoption of prostitution any more than Josh could resist condemning his father's patronization of a prostitute. Their astonishment and disapproval began to lead to rancor, and even threats ("I won't have you selling your body to strangers, Josh, no matter what you want to do in bed." "I'm an adult, dad, I'll do anything with my body I want!" "As long as I'm paying ... " etc., etc.) until Harp finally stepped in and calmed them down.

Harp had more or less kept out of the line of fire as father and son debated and argued. For one thing, he knew he was guilty of having led both men on—not confessing to Brad that he was as serious about "Jay" as he was, and not having told Josh about Brad at all—and at the same time telling both of them that he loved them.

"Look, both of you, arguing is not going to solve this problem! You both concealed things that maybe you should have told each other, " Harp said, "but I'm guilty of not being up-front with each of you, too. I know you love each other and ... "

Josh said. "You told me you loved me, Harp. You know I love you—what can I think when I find you here ... "

"Look, Jay ... Josh, I do love you. I told you that and I meant it ... and Brad, before you say anything, I love you too—you know that. And I know both of you love me, and ... well, if you want to beat anybody up about it, why not start on me? I love both of you, and I don't want to see either one of you hurt. How can I decide whom I love more. You're both wonderful guys. And look, Brad, did you ever tell your father you were gay?"

"No, I didn't, but ... "

"Okay," Harp continued. "I didn't think you would have,

and, in fact, you got married and had a family, and concealed the fact that you were gay, right?" Brad nodded. "So why be surprised that Josh hid his feelings from you? And Josh, why did you decide you wanted to have sex with guys, anyway?"

"I didn't decide to, Harp. I've always wanted sex with guys, I've always known it. What ..."

"Then don't you realize your dad is probably just expressing something that he's kept bottled up for years? Where do you suppose you would be if he hadn't done that? And do you object to your dad ... well, just really being himself, finally?"

Josh hesitated just a moment before replying. "No, of course not! But...."

"And look, both of you, you may think you have reasons to be mad at me because I told both of you I loved you. And you may be right. Hell, I don't know. But Josh, if you hadn't lied to me about your name. And Brad, if you had ever even so much as shown me a picture of your son, this wouldn't have happened! So maybe there's just blame all around, and besides, what difference does it make?" He looked at Brad. "I love you, Brad. More and more I've been thinking I wanted to stop screwing around and settle down—and to do that with you." He turned his attention to Josh. "And Josh, I love you too. I know if you were older I'd want to settle down with you too, but I don't know if you're ready to settle down yet. Maybe you are, and maybe I'd be the right one to do it with, and if that were the case, I just don't know what the hell I'd think. I can't very well settle down with two different husbands!"

In spite of himself, Josh began to cry. "Harp, I do love you, and I want to be with you always. I've never felt this way about anybody before!"

Harp stepped over to where Josh was sitting, knelt to him, and folded him in his arms. "I love you too, I really do, and I know what you're feeling."

Tears streaming down his face, Josh said, "What can we do?"

Harp said nothing, but kissed Josh's lips. He pressed the boy's body to him as they continued to kiss, and Josh held Harp's head in his hands. Josh's crying subsided, and their very long kiss finally broke. Harp turned his attention to Brad, who was looking at the floor, apparently intent on looking anywhere but at his son kissing a man who was at the same time his own lover.

Harp raised Josh to his feet, put one arm around his waist and led him across the room to where his father sat. He gazed steadily at Josh for a moment before turning his attention to his older lover, who was by now looking up at him. He held out a hand, and Brad took it and stood. Harp continued, "And I love you too, and I think I know what you're feeling." His hand went behind Brad's neck, pulled his head in, and their lips met for a long, tender kiss—with Josh watching soberly.

Brad's hands had held Harp's face as they kissed. Now, when their kiss ended, he put one hand on his son's face and looked at him for a long time before saying quietly. "I love you more than anything in the entire world, son. I can't do anything to hurt you. I love Harp too, but you're my son. Tell me what to do."

Josh's arm went around Brad and he pulled him close. "I don't know, Dad, I love both of you so much—in such different ways." He kissed Brad on the lips, affectionately, and then kissed Harp again, with equal gentleness.

Brad's arms went around the two young men, his lover and his son, and their arms encircled, and met behind him. It's not quite possible for three people to kiss, but they managed passably well for some time.

It is a mark of the freedom from modesty which had developed in Harp during his years as an escort and as a sexual performer that during this entire time he had been completely nude, and apparently oblivious to it. Josh was fully dressed, albeit skimpily, as befits an escort showing up for "work" on a warm night at the beginning of summer. Brad was wearing only loose trousers.

One of Josh's arms hugged his naked lover, and it was only natural that his hand sought the velvety smoothness of his lover's ass, generally understood by now to be an object of quintessential perfection. One of Brad's arms hugged his naked lover, and it was only natural that his hand sought the velvety smoothness of his lover's ass, generally understood by now to be an object of quintessential perfection! It must be remembered that each was seeking the velvety smoothness of the quintessentially perfect ass on the same young man.

Father and son's hands touched where they caressed Harp's buttocks. Each pulled his head back from the close proximity of foreheads and lips they had been sharing with the possessor of that magnificent ass to look into the other's eyes—somewhat startled. Neither said a word, and after a long time, their gazes gradually shifted from startled, to accepting, to amused. Brad's subtle smile, when it finally manifested itself, was matched by Josh's grin, and after the two hands met in a shared, affectionate squeeze, they parted. Father caressed and fondled the glory of Harp's rounded and heavenly right buttock as his son stroked and thrilled to the beauty of his left buttock—and their hands often touched as their embraces sought the sublime canyon between them.

Both father and son were now grinning, and their apparently-shared lover beamed an even broader grin at them. "I can see you two ... no, I can feel you two have met!" He wriggled his ass in delight as with his own hands he caressed the asses of his caressers.

Harp stepped back a bit and pointedly looked down at himself. His naked cock had returned to the condition it was in when he had emerged from the bathroom to confront 'Andrew' of the ultra-sexy escort ad—standing straight out from his body, and throbbing with excitement. "Now what, guys?"

Josh and Brad both instinctively reached for the tempting shaft they had found such pleasure with. Brad was somewhat slower than his son, for Josh's hand was already encircling it when he reached it. Josh grinned, "Beat you to it, Dad!"

Brad returned his son's grin, and saying "Plenty to go around!" he altered his goal, and took Harp's generous balls in his hand instead. Father and son were now caressing Harp's ass while at the same time they played with his cock and balls.

The object of their affection continued to fondle their asses and laughed, "Lord, now what do we do?"

Since neither of his admirers seemed to have a clue, Harp kissed one, then the other and said, "Okay guys, I'm naked, and you seem to think that's fine. So let's start by seeing some more hard cock here. Out of your clothes!"

The suggestion did not seem to bother Josh at all. He removed his hands from Harp, and began to pull his shirt off, then kicked out of his shoes.

Brad seemed hesitant. "Harp, I don't know if...."

Harp removed Brad's hands from his ass and his balls. "Now, I want to see you naked!" He tugged at the waistband of the loose trousers Brad was wearing, and with Brad's assistance, they dropped to the floor.

Brad's cock was not fully hard yet, but Harp knelt in front of him, looked up at Josh and smiled, and said, "I want you to watch this!" And with that he took Brad's cock in his mouth, and almost immediately it rose to full erection. Brad's hands held Harp's head, and he fucked his mouth slowly and deeply.

Brad avoided his son's gaze for a few minutes, feeling self-conscious about getting a blowjob while he watched, but when he did finally look over at Josh, he found him standing there completely nude, stroking his impressive cock, and smiling. "Looks hot, Dad!" he said quietly, as he stepped closer to his father and put a hand on his shoulder. He looked down at his lover sucking his father's cock and said, "God, it looks *really* hot!"

Harp stopped sucking Brad's cock and looked up at his two lovers. "How does this look?" he said as he turned his attention to Josh's fiercely erect prick and began to suck it as avidly as he had Brad's—at the same time fondling the father's ass with one hand, and the son's with the other.

While Josh moaned his pleasure and fucked deep, Brad watched for a while before turning his gaze to him. He reached out and took his son's chin in his hand. Josh opened his eyes and smiled as his father said, "Jesus, Josh, I can't believe this is happening!"

"But it is, Dad, and it's hot as hell, isn't it?" Brad's arm went around Josh's waist and hugged him as he agreed with his assessment of the situation. Without any ceremony, or apparent contemplation of the action, Josh reached down and briefly squeezed his father's throbbing cock while he said, "Harp is the greatest, isn't he?" Then he gave Brad a quick, impassionate son-to-father kind of kiss, but definitely on the lips, as he seized Harp's head with both hands and began to fuck harder; he closed his eyes, and murmured, "God, Harp ... suck my cock! Oh, Jesus ... "

Harp released Josh's cock, then pulled him close to Brad, and he held a cock in each hand. Without looking up, he murmured, "Two beautiful big cocks!" and took them both into his mouth at the same time while he shifted his hands so he could cup and fondle the two sets of balls as he sucked.

Harp had had two cocks in his mouth at the same time on any number of occasions. He was quite skilled at simultaneous sucking and licking in such a way that he could provide considerable gratification to both. He had had the cocks of guys he was at least to some degree in love with in his mouth thousands of times—Doug Truax, Dodge Venturi, Jeremy Lee, Steve Rommel, all had been been wonderful to make love to this way, and on any number of occasions two of those men had sought his oral services at the same time also. But, miracle of miracles, the two now invading him so delightfully he was actually in love with! Moreover, these were the plunging, ravening pricks of father-and-son—he had never had that experience before. The only father-son encounter he had experienced before had been back in Oconee, and on that occasion the "father" just watched while he fucked the "son".

Josh and Brad had each double-fucked a hot mouth many, many times, but except for his participation in such during his last year of prep school, Brad had not done this until very recently. Josh was fairly well-experienced—having begun doing it about a year before his father had resumed the pleasurable practice, and having done so with great frequency at Dan's house, at the beach, in his own room, etc. Needless to say, the two had never before double-fucked a mouth together—yet here they were, father and son, both fucking the mouth of a man each was in love with, and who, in turn, was in love with each of them! Together, Josh and Brad brought Harp new meaning to the term *father-son banquet*.

Brad was at first uncomfortable with the idea of his cock rubbing up against his son's while they double-fucked Harp's mouth. But Harp's expertise, his own love and passion for this adored younger man, along with Josh's beauty and obvious willingness lessened his discomfort enough that he was soon enjoying the experience fully. Not only did he share with his son an excited appreciation for the experience they were sharing, but when Josh began to caress his driving ass, he responded in kind, and he had to admit the ass he fondled was exciting him enormously. When his son seized his head and drove his tongue into his mouth, he returned the kiss as passionately as it was given.

Josh had often fucked and sucked with Dan and his father at the same time, so father-and-son making love with each other and even to each other was not new territory to him—although it was his father this time making love with him. His father was distinctly more handsome that Dan's, and he was obviously as hot and quite a bit better hung than R.J. as well. Moreover, they were both making love with a man whose love they shared. Given those circumstances, any uneasiness he felt about the situation evaporated quickly, and his father's hard cock felt wonderful next to his in his lover's mouth; his father's undulating ass felt divine as he fondled it feverishly, and his father's passionate kiss stimulated him much more than he would have imagined it would.

Harp quit sucking, stood, and walked over to a low table, where he lay down on his back and spread his legs wide, cupping his balls with one hand and with the other holding his beautiful big cock up for his lovers to admire. "Come on, you guys, eat this big hot dick!"

Neither father nor son needed further invitation. They bent over the body of their lover, and with one lunge, Brad soon had Harp's entire shaft buried in his throat, while his son sucked on Harp's big balls and eagerly fondled his own quite impressive set. The two spent quite a while in oral worship, sharing the wonder of Harp's profound thrusts between each other, and culminating in a lengthy shared suck—each with his lips pressed firmly above and below one side of Harp's cock and touching the other's lips in the middle, traveling up and down the entire impressive length together, and meeting at the end each time to share a kiss with the throbbing cock-head between their lips.

Harp moaned his delight at the tandem suck until he declared. "God, if you guys keep that up, I'm gonna come!"

Josh abandoned the sucking to his father as he kissed Harp and said, "What's wrong with that?"

"I want to get fucked before I come!" Harp panted.

Brad also stopped sucking to kiss his lover. "I hope you mean before you come the first time! I think we can work that out, who do you want first?"

"I don't care—I want both of you to fuck me!"

"You mean one at a time, I guess!" Brad said.

Harp grinned broadly. "Yeah, one at a time. For now! Who knows what'll happen? But I want both of you to fuck me, and I want you to watch each other do it. Then we'll see!" He spread his legs and raised them. "Fuck my ass!"

Josh put his arm around Brad. "Go ahead, Dad, I want to see you!"

With Harp's legs on his shoulders, Brad fucked his lover long and hard, and with maximum mutual enjoyment obviously evident. During this time, Josh often kissed his lover and sucked his cock, while Harp moaned his appreciation at the excellence of his older lover's service. Josh often caressed his father's well-formed ass and his muscular back while he watched him driving his generous cock deep into the ecstatic Harp.

Finally, Brad withdrew and frantically ripped off his condom at the last split second before climax, spurting an impressive amount of discharge on Harp's chest and stomach. Brad moaned his passion while Harp murmured his appreciation, and Josh exclaimed, "Wow! Great load, Dad!"

He stepped closer and spread his father's ejaculate around on Harp's stomach, then scooped it up and spread it all over his cock as he smiled at him and added. "Great fuck, too!"

Using his father's orgasm as lubricant, he rolled a condom on his prick and leaned down to kiss Harp. "Something to live up to, huh?"

Brad stood aside so that his son could take his place inside the hungry hole he reluctantly conceded to him. He kissed Harp while Josh was entering him, and then kissed Josh. "It's not a contest, son, just make love to him like I did."

Josh laughed as he began to plunge into the tight heat of Harp's already busy ass, "Funny, Dad, it looked just like you were fucking him!"

Brad caressed his son's ass, already humping and driving hard. "Then fuck him like I did—fuck his beautiful ass as hard as you can!"

If his delighted cries and exhortations to "Fuck me, hard!" were any indication, Harp obviously enjoyed Josh's fuck as much as he had Brad's rapturous love-making. While Josh had been somewhat more hesitant than his father as he began to lovingly drive his cock into his lover, by the time his orgasm approached it was clear to Brad that his son was fully as capable a fuckmaster as he himself. During the course of Josh's impressive fuck, Brad fondled, kissed, and sucked with both participants with the same eagerness Josh had accorded him and Harp while they had been fucking. Harp's cock was rock-hard while Josh fucked him, and Josh's muscular, driving ass felt wonderful.

Josh's orgasm, when it came was quite impressive in terms of both volume and velocity, even larger and more explosively delivered than his father's, and the puddle of semen on the smiling, satisfied Harp's chest and stomach was now enormous. Father, son, and shared lover all played in the hot, slimy pool for some time before Harp declared, laughing, "I'm gonna clean up, we're gonna have a drink, and then I get to fuck both of you!"

Initially, Brad objected to the beer Harp handed Josh when he mixed drinks, saying "He's too young to drink." Josh just rolled his eyes.

Harp laughed. "Brad! I met him in a bar! And don't you think if you've just been fucking me together with him, and kissing each other with the head of my cock inside your two mouths, you might figure he's man enough to drink a beer?"

Brad grinned. "Have a beer, son!"

Harp knelt and kissed Josh. "Yeah, have a beer son, you're gonna get fucked soon enough!"

"You might as well get this clear right now," Josh replied. "If you wind up marrying my dad, I'm not gonna call you Dad too! And in spite of where my Dad just had his cock, I'm not gonna call you 'Mom' either!"

All laughed at that, and Brad added, "Well Josh, if Harp winds up marrying you, I don't want him calling me 'Dad' too, you know?"

Harp went to Brad and kissed him. "Okay, I wouldn't call you Dad, but I would want you to love me like a son, and make love to me like a son, for sure!"

There was an awkward pause. Josh spoke quietly, "What happens now, Dad? I know you love me like a son, but ... is making love to me next?"

Brad began to speak, "Josh, I ..." but Josh cut him off.

"Do you want to make love to your son, now that you've made love to someone else with your son? Dad, we need to talk about this, I think. We're both gay, and we both just learned that about each other. We're both in love with the same guy!" He smiled at Harp. "Yes ... the same beautiful guy ... and we both just watched each other fuck him, and we sucked his cock together. But, what's next? Do you...?" He stood, then walked over to kneel in front of his father. "Dad, I've watched a good friend of mine fuck with his father, and ... "

"My God, Josh! Who...?"

"Never mind right now, Dad, we've both got a lot of catching up to do, and we'll get to it soon. But anyway, I'm not shocked at the idea of having sex with you! I guess you think I should be, but having been there with Dan and his dad ... "

"Dan Bliss? He's the one ... "

"Yeah, we'll talk about it. And I didn't just watch Dan and R.J. screwing each other, I've been with 'em when they did." Brad was dumbstruck. "But after that, and after what you and I just did with Harp ... hell, Dad, it's just not gonna shock me if you say you wanna do more with me than we've already done."

Brad placed his hands on Josh's shoulders. "Son, I have no idea what to think. This has already gone so much further than I would ever have thought it could, and if I had stopped to think ... Well, nothing I can do about it now."

Harp spoke up. "Shit, Brad, you've been thinking with your dick, just like we all do. You don't suppose Josh thought about this! Neither of you did—we all got carried away, and I for one thought it was ab-so-fuckin'-lutely terrific. Don't you guys even think about screwing each other, or sucking each other off right now! There's gonna be all the time in the world to sort out what we all think, and where we all are. I wanna fuck both of you. Then we can get something to eat, and you guys can fuck me again if you want. Then I'll fuck you both again if you want, and ... hell, tomorrow morning we may all think this is the worst thing we coulda done. I don't know. I only know I want to have sex with both of you tonight until we're too pooped to pop, and then I want to go to sleep right over there in that bed, with one of my lovers on one side, and one on the other. Then we can get up in the morning and try to sort it out by dawn's ugly light, okay?"

"Fair enough," Brad said. He kissed his son lightly. "Okay by you, Josh?"

"Okay by me, Dad" And he returned a similar short kiss, but after looking into his father's eyes for a moment, he kissed him again for a much longer time, and with considerably more passion than one might normally expect between father and son—unless, perhaps, one had just seen this father and son sucking a cock together.

Then Josh rose, walked to the bed and lay down on his back. He spread his legs wide and fingered himself as he raised his head to grin at Harp. "I wanna get fucked!"

Harp stood, and held out his hand to Brad, who stood and walked with him to the bed. Both grinned down while Harp knelt between Josh's legs and prepared himself and the eager young man. Josh raised his legs to rest his heels on Harp's shoulders as he massaged and applied the lubricant. With his eyes closed in pleasure, Josh murmured, "I want you to fuck me, Harp!" Then his eyes opened and he held out his hand to his father, smiling with genuine affection as he pulled him down on the bed with him; his expression turned to rapture as Harp's cock began to seek its target. Brad watched as his lover slowly, but without stopping, buried his cock deep inside his son. Josh smiled at his father and squeezed his hand, "Oh God, Dad, this feels incredible!"

Brad smiled back, "I know only too well! Enjoy yourself, you two, but you'd better save some for me, Harp!"

With Josh's ass high in the air and his calves on Harp's shoulders now, the handsome, dark-haired man with the perfect ass kissed the beautiful young blond and fucked with rapid, very long strokes—almost pulling out on each back stroke. Josh moaned in ecstasy and Brad played with Harp's balls and fingered his asshole from behind.

Harp finally slowed, saying, "I gotta rest or I'm gonna come!" Josh lowered his back to the mattress, keeping his lover deep inside him while his legs moved to circle Harp's waist.

Brad kissed Harp's ear and said, "Get over to the table again. I've got an idea."

With his young lover still impaled on his cock, Harp put his arms under Josh and began to lift him. Josh's arms were locked tightly around his neck, and his legs clasped his waist as Harp lifted his body and started toward the table. Just before putting his precious, sexy burden down, he started to laugh.

Josh said, "Jesus, I've never had anyone laugh while he was fucking me before!"

Harp stopped and grinned at the passenger riding his cock. "I just thought of a line I heard on a soap opera the other day." He turned to Brad. "I'm gonna tell you something I'll bet you never thought a man would say to you, Brad."

Brad put his arms around his lover's chest from behind and smiled at his son, who was grinning back at him. "What's that, baby?"

Harp turned his head and laughed over his shoulder, "I'm carrying your child!"

Brad laughed loudly and gave him a quick kiss. "God knows I fucked you enough to give you a child!"

Josh laughed with them. "Keep fucking me, Harp, maybe you can give him a grandchild, too!"

Harp lay Josh down on the table, and continued to work on a possible grandchild for a few minutes while Brad admired the perfection of his ass, and the supple musculature working beneath the velvet skin as it drove and undulated, sinking his cock deep inside the lucky young blond impaled on it—his own beloved, beautiful, unimaginably sexy son!

Brad grasped Harp's hips and held them immobile. "Stop for a minute, babe. Pull out."

Harp stepped backward, and his cock emerged from Josh with a little "Ploop!" Josh smiled dreamily up. "Don't be gone long, okay?"

Harp laughed. "Oh, I'll be back! Let's see what your dad has in mind."

Josh lay flat on his back on the table, with his legs hanging off the edge. Brad climbed on top of his body and knelt on all fours, with his knees straddling his son's waist and his ass pointing toward his lover. "Get your legs wrapped around me, Josh, and we'll give Harp a pair of asses to fuck!"

Josh and Harp both expressed their appreciation of Brad's idea, and Harp lost no time in lubricating his newly added target and finding it with his prick.

While Harp took turns savagely fucking Brad's ass above and Josh's below, and exclaiming his delight ever more enthusiastically, father and son shared kisses and whispered their appreciation of their lover's ardor and expertise—and their kisses were as impassioned as the fucking they were receiving! Both had raging, throbbing erections, and their hard cocks rubbed together as they got fucked.

Josh reached between them to make adjustments and apply some lubrication, but other than that neither he nor his father fondled the other's cock, although each humped the stomach of the other eagerly with his own. Had they not each delivered a massive orgasm an hour or so earlier, it is likely they would have discharged as they enjoyed the delightful frottage accompanying Harp's enthusiastic tandem fuck.

Inevitably, Harp could hold off no longer, and with a cry he pulled out of the ass he was fucking (Josh's, as it happened), tore the condom off his cock, and directed his cum equally over the two eager asses he had been servicing so magnificently. As the scalding offering hit them, Josh and Brad kissed and humped even more feverishly.

When Harp finished his copious orgasm and began to calm somewhat, he coated his hands with the ejaculate he had deposited, and reached between the still writhing asses of his two lovers to play with their balls and the two impressive cocks rubbing together there. Father and son looked into each other's eyes as their lover's slippery hand caressed them. Josh whispered, "God, I love him, Dad!" Brad returned his whisper with a smile, "So do I, son. He's quite a man, isn't he?"

Josh smiled at his father for a long time before replying. "He's man enough for us to share, if that's what you want, Dad!"

"I've always shared with you, Josh, haven't I?"

Josh barked a laugh. "Deal! Harp, I think you've got two lovers. You got enough to go around?"

Brad rolled off his son, and lay on his back next to him. "Two *demanding* lovers!"

"I'll do my best to keep you both satisfied. After all, I'm gonna get twice as much back, right?" His two lovers agreed to keep him well supplied, after which he first kissed them, then used his tongue to clean his own emission from their stomach, balls, and cocks—following which he alternated sucking the last-named with such diligence and practiced expertise that the two gushers which rewarded his efforts exploded onto his face at almost the same time. With a glistening, come-covered cock in each hand, and strings of come dripping from his face, he looked down and used words to convey his love to the two handsome men as his mouth and his hands had just conveyed his passion for them.

It was late, it had been a long and emotional evening of discovery, and after a quick shower, the three fell into bed—Harp in the middle, his arms cradling the heads of his father-and-son lovers, who reached across him both to hold each other and to caress him.

Harp had known he was falling in love the last month or two—a feeling his deep affection for Doug, Steve, Jeremy and the others had only suggested. At the same time, he had been torn between the competing objects of this growing love. It seemed it had finally flowered, and he knew he was in love. Unfortunately, he was in love with two men, but they loved each other as well as him—he thought it might not prove to be unfortunate at all. He knew he was happy, and he felt optimistic as he fell asleep between his two Adonises.

Harp and Josh slept soundly, but Brad awoke long before dawn, propped himself up against the wall, and studied his son and his lover sleeping so soundly and so innocently next to him. He was careful not to awaken them. He wanted time to think, and it was Sunday morning, so even though Josh was in Summer School, he had no classes to worry about getting to.

By the time the two men he loved most in the world began to stir, and waked each other, Brad had had ample time to consider some of the ramifications of last night's revelations and activities.

Josh went down to the grocery store/deli located in the apartment complex and brought back coffee and doughnuts. It is indicative of the seriousness of the conversation Brad wanted to have with Harp and Josh that Harp's impressive morning erection got only a caress as he kissed him during his son's absence, and told him to throw on some clothes so they could have a long talk without the distraction offered by such a tempting sight.

The three sat down with their coffee, and Brad asked them to let him get a lot off his chest before responding. They agreed, and he explained that as much as he loved Harp and wanted him as a partner, he knew that the greatest love in all his life was for his son. If his relationship with Harp was an insurmountable problem for Josh, he would have to give it up—very, very reluctantly. If that happened, and Josh and Harp became partners, he would give them his enthusiastic blessing and simply learn to live with the situation.

Whatever they decided to do, he continued, he earnestly hoped both of them would give up prostitution as not only dangerous, but also as something that would ultimately cheapen the love they all shared.

Josh broke in. "Dad, I only started to do it because I was mad at Harp. I don't want to continue running that ad now!"

"In a way I'm glad you ran it—at least for a little while," Brad responded. "It brought us together so we can sort this thing out."

Harp laughed. "Yeah, and it's also the absolutely hottest ad I've ever seen. I should have recognized that beautiful cock of yours—even under that towel!"

"I did hold it up pretty well in that picture, didn't I?" His father agreed he had indeed! "That was R.J.'s idea! He took the picture."

"Who the hell is R.J.?" Brad asked.

"He's Dan's father. He's really nice, and he's hot as hell, and he and Dan do a lot more together than we did together last night."

"I don't think I want to know!" Brad replied. "No, I take that back. I guess I do want to know. I want to know everything, son. I want to try to understand how we all arrived where we were last night."

"Fair enough, Dad. Where do you want me to start?"

Brad smiled and squeezed Josh's hand. "Plenty of time. I owe you a lot of explanation, I know. And Harp, I think we might sort this situation out better if you came clean!"

Harp laughed and kissed Brad quickly. "Hey, I'll come any way you want me to!" All laughed, and Harp added, "Seriously, I want to hear everything, and I want you to know where I'm coming from, too."

Josh squeezed Harp's crotch. "I know where you've been coming from!"

Brad had to laugh along with his son and his lover, but he tried to bring them back to the level of seriousness he felt was needed at that point. "Okay, later with the fun, and later with the life stories, okay?" He went on to suggest that Josh stop escorting, concentrate on his school work, and confine his sex life to a leisure-time activity—to be practiced with someone he loves, or at least cares about. He suggested that Harp give up selling his body and manage his sex life the same way he wanted Josh to, adding that he would be glad to finance his education to train himself for a more traditional career.

"Brad, I've got plenty of money. That's not the problem," Harp responded. "But what will I do?"

Brad put one hand on Harp's arm, and the other on Josh's. "There's a good program in Tourism and Travel at Golden Gate University, right here in the city. I hire graduates and even part-time interns from there in my business all the time. I'd like to see you go there and come into the business with me—and Josh ... "

"Dad, that's a wonderful idea! I could transfer there, as far as that goes. It would be great if we could all work together!"

Brad frowned slightly, " Well, I don't know how great it would work out with all three of us—too many cooks, probably—but if you two got trained and came aboard, I'd be happy to step aside and let you run things, assuming things work out as I believe they would."

Harp spoke up. "I think it's a great idea too, but that's the business side—what happens to the three of us personally?"

"I think that's up to you two. I love you, Harp. I want to be married to you, but I love Josh—and he feels pretty much the same way about you. Right, Josh?"

Josh nodded, "But Dad, last night we ... well, I thought it worked out pretty well. Is there any possibility ... why can't we both marry Harp?"

Harp laughed, "Would I have anything to say about it?"

"You have everything there is to say about it, Harp. You're the key." Brad took Harp's hand in both of his and looked at him very seriously. "Tell me where we stand, or at least where you see us going."

Harp matched his lover's seriousness. "I love you Brad, I want to be married to you." He turned his gaze to Josh, who looked stricken. "But I love you too, Josh, and being your partner would be fun and exciting, and would make me very, very happy. What you and Brad and I did last night was absolutely great, but it was pretty bizarre too—hell, I don't think the three of us deciding to get married would be any stranger."

Brad nodded. "You're right, of course, and the mechanics of the three of us sharing our lives shouldn't be any great problem. But what about sex? That's what brought us together here, and it's obviously pretty important to all of us. You two tell me, what sort of sexual arrangement do you think would work?"

Harp turned the question back to Brad, "I think you're the one in the middle, Brad. You tell us." Josh nodded his agreement.

"Okay. I thought about this a lot last night too." He went on to explain that having had sex with Harp at the same time as his son was exciting and satisfying, and something he had enjoyed, and, surprising himself, looked forward to repeating. On the other hand, he was in love with Harp, and certainly didn't want to give up having sex with just the two of them together, but he couldn't see himself having sex alone with just Josh. "He's my son, and I love him, and I can make love alongside him and enjoy his beauty and his sexuality just like I appreciate so many qualities about him, but ... " He turned to face his son. "well, I can't see myself fucking you or sucking your cock, Josh, and I can't imagine you doing the same to me, no matter what sort of relationship Dan and his father have. Do you understand?"

"Of course I do, Dad, and ... well, right now I'd feel funny about doing that too. I had great fun doing what we did do last night. I've enjoyed kissing with you all my life, but I sure never thought we'd be kissing like that! But it was great, and I enjoyed the feeling of you next to me, and holding you like we did. But right now I don't see us fucking each other or sucking each other off, the way Dan and R.J. do with each other." He grinned at his father slyly. "Right now, anyway!"

Brad looked a bit shocked. "Jesus, Josh!" Then he laughed

nervously. "Shit, who ever knows what will happen? Anyway, at this point we agree on that. And let me ask you, Harp, supposing we three became lovers. And if that sounded good to you, what if, for instance, Gundo Lopez or Richie Hassler walked in to our house and...."

Josh broke in. "Richie Hassler? *The* Richie Hassler?"

Harp grinned and nodded.

"Jesus, you fucked Richie Hassler?"

Harp laughed, "Hey, so did your father!"

"I am really looking forward to this telling-our-life-stories thing!" Josh said, a bit indignantly.

"You're gonna get your socks blown off!" Harp said. "Well anyway, Brad, if Richie, or especially Gundo walked in, I'd want to have sex with him, sure, wouldn't you? Would that be okay if we were married? Is that what you're asking?"

Brad nodded. "That's what I'm asking. I think if it were going to work, we'd have to have an open kind of arrangement. I wouldn't mind you fucking Gundo or Richie, or whomever, as long as it was Josh and me you're in love with. And Josh, if you wanted to have sex with Dan or ... yeah, with Dan's father—hell you're an adult, that's up to you. How would Harp fucking Gundo sit with you, Josh? Or how does Josh fucking Dan strike you, Harp?"

Harp agreed he would have no problem sharing Brad or Josh with someone outside their household if they were just having fun. Josh said he thought it would work out, "And I'd still like to be able to fool around with Damon or Kyle or Eric if they...."

Brad broke in. "So Eric did have sex with you!"

"Well, yes Dad, Eric and I ... oh my God! You fucked Eric! He told me he'd kill to go to bed with you if you were gay!"

Brad laughed. "He didn't have to kill. It was a lot easier than that. And for your information, we did it on a floor long before we managed to do it in a bed!"

"I can't wait for our life stories! Who else do you have to tell me about, Dad? Did you fuck Dan? Did you call his ad?"

"Dan Bliss is escorting too?" Brad asked.

Josh laughed. "I'll show you the ad! You can fuck Dan for a hundred bucks or so, Dad—and it might be the biggest, hardest cock you've ever had"

"Brad, where's the paper?" Harp said. "I've got a hundred bucks to spend!"

Josh laughed. "Sorry. Go on, Dad."

"So what I guess I'm saying is, shall we try to make it as a household? But with the understanding that we'll play around if we want to, but it's just play? I, for one, would like to try." Harp and Josh both agreed they thought the arrangement could work out—and they were more than willing to try it.

Harp said he thought that Brad and Josh needed to be more comfortable together than they had been during their sex the night before. "I'm not saying you need to suck each other off, or anything, but for God's sake, you're gonna be touching each other, and playing with each other more than you did while we were screwing around last night." He stood up. "Both of you stand up and get naked."

"Harp, I don't know if ... " Brad began.

"Look, before we plan anything too seriously, let's be sure you're both going to be comfortable when we're all having sex together. I think that's almost the key, don't you? Go along with me."

Brad and Josh stripped down, and faced one another rather shyly as Harp took his clothes off also. None of the three was, surprisingly, erect! "Okay, you guys, hold each other and kiss," Harp said. Reluctantly they approached each other; they smiled, embraced gently, and Brad kissed his son tenderly.

Harp said, "You know that's not what I mean—here let me get you in the mood!" He knelt beside them, and they turned their bodies to face him. He took their cocks in his mouth and sucked them together while he played with their asses. Very soon the two cocks in his mouth were too big and too busy with plunging in and out to be easily contained any longer. Stroking his own now very erect prick, Harp stood and said, "Now let's see you hold each other!"

Josh and Brad held each other tightly now, and their pelvises ground together avidly as they shared an extremely passionate kiss and, each began to explore the other's writhing ass with his busy hands. Harp grinned as he watched them. "That's more like it! Come on, grind those cocks together, and feel those hot asses! Shit, this is getting me horny as hell! I want to see each of you jack the other one off." He went to the bed and lay on his back. "C'mere, Brad, and let Josh beat you off while you blow your load on my face!"

Brad straddled Harp and Josh knelt behind him, reached around, and eagerly masturbated his father. Brad said nothing about it, but Josh's cock felt very exciting as he humped it between his legs and held him around the waist with one arm, while his other hand savagely stroked his cock, which felt even much better. Josh said nothing about it, but his father's body excited him too as he humped it, and pumping his dad's throbbing cock was really exciting.

Soon Brad's climax approached, and with a cry, his two hands went behind to pull his son's ass in tightly as his cock erupted and splattered the eager Harp's face. Josh continued to stroke and hump, Brad moaned his pleasure, and Harp complimented both on a job well done.

Brad kissed and licked Harp's face until it was clean, then stationed himself behind Josh to repeat the process, which was equally appreciated by all. Brad could not believe how very stimulating it was to press his cock against his own son's busy ass while he stroked his big and throbbing cock, and then felt the come gushing from it. After Josh had cleaned his own ejaculate from Harp's face, he and his father lay side-by-side on their backs as Harp stood over them and produced a veritable fountain of come, which he directed into their smiling faces.

The three lay together for some time, and all agreed they had taken an important step toward becoming comfortable about having sex as a threesome.

In lieu of lunch, the three decided to adjourn to the Thornton house for an impromptu early supper and a sharing of stories. "I should have had you out there long before this, Harp," Brad said.

Harp laughed. "You've had me here enough. Now you can have me out there too!"

By the end of that week, the three had not only openly shared the stories of their sexual lives, but had also approved the plan that Brad had suggested. Both Harp and Josh had canceled their Models/Escorts ads, and both had applied to Golden Gate University for admission to the program in Tourism and Travel. Josh's record at San Francisco State virtually assured him of entrance, and Brad made some calls to key people in the Program—with whom he had worked, and who owed him favors for his sponsorship of their intern program—and was assured that Harp's entrance would be approved speedily once his academic records were received from South Carolina.

Even though Brad's apartment near the Embarcadero was only a few blocks from the university where his son and his lover were to be attending classes in a short time, he decided it was no longer needed. Since Josh and Harp were going to be in residence in his house, he gave up both his apartment and Josh's room at State, and Harp moved from his apartment. The savings financed a large part of Harp's schooling.

Josh continued to live in his old room at home, Brad in his, and Harp nominally lived in the guest room, but almost never slept there. The pattern of their sexual life crystallized very quickly: Harp often slept alone with Brad, he often slept alone with Josh, and the three normally shared Brad's bed at least a few nights a week. If Harp tended to retire for the night with Josh somewhat more than he did with Brad, he often crept into Brad's bed in the early hours of the morning when he had been sleeping (and, of course, screwing) with Josh the night before.

Their lovemaking with others was mostly limited to visits with old friends and bedmates—and almost always in threesomes or foursomes. The lucky participants were normally happy to share the beds and the various orifices of all three residents during their visits.

Their recounting of their sexual stories had been both interesting and stimulating. Harp and Brad both expressed the hope for sex with Dan, if he were willing, anxious to sample the enormous cock Josh promised he would bring to the meeting. Josh and Brad were anxious to both meet and meat Steve Rommel if Harp could locate him. Josh and Harp hoped they would find Paul Stavros as beautiful and as good in bed as Brad had claimed. Josh was very anxious to meet Richie Hassler, and after seeing the autographed picture in Brad's apartment, he was very anxious to meet "Race Rivera" (Josh had not encountered any Race Rivera videos, strangely enough, but once he saw the gorgeous Latino's monster cock in action, he was dying to get together with him!). All those particular wishes eventually came true. A number of others resulting from their shared stories did not.

Dan continued to escort, but when he was not doing anything, he often dropped in to visit, and wound up fucking whomever was home with his magnificent shaft, and welcoming whatever hard cock or dildo anyone cared to bury inside him.

Paul Stavros proved to be as beautiful as Brad had described him, and he spent four entire days exploring and enjoying every sexual possibility the Thornton-Harper household offered. It seemed he did not want to repeat the experience, for he never returned, even though he had severed his relationship with Roy Saunders some time earlier. Privately, Brad thought Paul would have been happy to return permanently if he could live with him alone in a monogamous relationship.

Harp did locate Steve Rommel, who flew up to San Francisco to visit. Their reunion was joyous, and Steve shared his sexual favors with Brad and, especially, Josh, as enthusiastically as he renewed the intense sexual experiences he and Harp had shared. He was in a relationship with a wealthy older man, but he often found additional comfort in the arms of others. He was glad to re-establish communications with Harp, and enjoyed "communicating" additionally with Brad and, especially, Josh, so much that he visited with some regularity after that.

On the occasion of Gundo Lopez' next appearance at the Top 'n Bottom theatre, he managed to find time for several visits to the house, and while Harp and Brad delighted in renewing their sexual antics with him, Josh was ecstatic! 'Race Rivera' became his new favorite porn star, and Dan's monster cock had to take second place in Josh's estimation. Gundo promised Josh he would arrange for him to go to bed with his mentor, Tom Hunt. And he made sure Josh received a couple of Tom's "Tom Fox" videos to watch in anticipation of a bigger thrill than even he had been able to provide.

Gundo visited periodically, and he made good on his promise to introduce young Josh to the delights of his mentor's stupendous endowment—the very biggest living thing Josh had ever had in his mouth or up his ass. A few latex alternatives of even greater size had been employed to get ready for the encounter. Josh grinned and said he 'walked funny' for two days after getting fucked by Tom, but he declared it had been the hottest thing that had ever happened to him.

Gundo talked Harp into making a porn video for Tom's company, and the successful "Cal LaPidgin" series resulted, of course; the one which paired "Cal" with Richie Hassler was shot in Desert Springs, and Richie agreed to entertain Harp's two lovers there after the filming was done. Josh and Brad accompanied Harp when he flew down for the shoot, and Richie lived up to his promise.

Josh and Richie spent a lot of time together, and the ex-TV star was as enchanted by Josh's youth, beauty, and sexual prowess as Josh was with Richie's insatiable bubble butt! Josh delighted in the stories of Richie's sexual exploits with Monte Alvarez, and having his own cock where the super-hung Latino stud Monte's had been so often (and would be again soon) especially stimulated him.

Eric not only came to visit whenever he was home from school for vacation or holiday periods, he almost became a member of the household at those times. And, while he enjoyed sex with all three residents in every combination, it was clear to all that he was happiest when he was in bed alone with Brad. Josh and Brad both agreed they thought Eric had somehow re-established communication with Mike Rubich, and fully expected to hear some day that he had secretly gone to join his first lover.

After giving up the apartment near the water, Brad and Harp rarely saw the very well-equipped, sexy, sweet neighbor Louis, although they kept the friendship alive by telephone and the occasional shared meal.

One of the people in Harp's narrative who had sounded particularly interesting to Josh and Brad had been the blond, muscular Adonis Steve Adams, who had provided a wild sexual welcome on Harp's first night as a San Franciscan. Shortly before Christmas in '97, the three decided to go out to eat, and celebrate the one-half-year anniversary of their union. In the Castro district, trying to decide where to dine, Harp pointed out the restaurant on Market Street where Steve had been working, and where he had met him. They decided to try it, and found to their delight that Steve was still working there, was on duty that night, and was happy to serve as their waiter. Harp recalled his having thought that all Steves had at that time seemed to him to be gorgeous, tall, muscular blonds: Steve Rommel, porn star Steve Fox, and the magnificent specimen who brought him his menu and introduced himself.

It had only been a month or so before that night they all met Steve Adams that they had learned the sad news of Steve Fox's tragic suicide, but they knew that Steve Rommel was alive and exciting as hell, and this Steve was even more beautiful, built, and exciting than Harp had led them to believe—and the enormous bulge in the crotch of his skin-tight, faded jeans looked tempting beyond belief.

Steve Adams remembered Harp well, and had often hoped to renew their one experience together, so on learning the occasion of the evening's celebration, he offered to go home with them to help observe the occasion by participating in whatever rituals were appropriate! Steve's partner was not out of town that night, but he called him and told him he was spending the night with a visiting family member. Steve Adams proved to be as memorable as Harp had suggested; no one came even close to disappointment that night.

One of the dubious advantages of living in San Francisco is that one never lacks for out-of-town guests. None of Harp's family visited or communicated with him, but many of Harp's friends from his South Carolina youth came to visit. To a man, they were gay; to a man they understood the situation with Harp and his two lovers, and approved of it ; almost to a man they enthusiastically joined the sexual activities of the unique threesome during their visits.

Brad's family consisted of his parents back East. They never visited, and their health was such they would have been unable to had they so desired. They were Josh's paternal grandparents, of course, and his maternal grandparents limited their contact to Christmas and birthday cards or presents sent from the East Coast (they quietly disapproved of his apparent alignment with their daughter's deserter). Aside from his absent grandparents and his mother, Josh lived with his family every day.

Two days after Christmas, Gundo came to call and deliver a special holiday fuck to his friends in the Thornton-Harper household. Brad and Harp decided that as a special belated Christmas present to their handsome young son and lover, respectively, Gundo should present his 'Christmas present' to Josh alone, so he could re-live the ecstatic time he had spent in Los Angeles with his favorite porn star, and which, if his reminiscences about it were any indication, he obviously thought was the greatest sex of his life. Gundo didn't mind in the least, since the time he had spent alone with Josh had been memorable to him as well. Not only was the young blond adorable, he was "great in bed," as both a top and a bottom.

In truth, Brad and Harp weren't being completely altruistic. They had not had sex with each other alone in more than a week. They left the door to Brad's bedroom open while they made love there, and often laughed at some of the exuberant sounds that wafted down the hall when Josh and Gundo didn't have their mouths full of dick or tongue, or were plugging each other's asses with complete abandon and almost acrobatic ingenuity.

Late that night, too happy and too drained to get out of bed and clean up, Josh and Gundo lay next to each other, each with his cum drying on the other's body. They kissed and cuddled, and then talked long into the night. Josh mentioned that he was dreading a visit with his mother and stepfather the next week.

Josh had dutifully paid visits to his mother's house in Marin County, but the only thing he had truly enjoyed about them was the ferry ride to and from Sausalito.

Gwen had resigned her position at *Bitch Magazine* about the time her son and her ex-husband became, for all practical purposes, lovers. She had moved to the house that her new husband had purchased for them in Cuernavaca, outside Mexico City, and there Mr. And Mrs. Quentin Turley had become part of the large and socially active colony of retired *gringos*.

The All-American, but Mexican-by-heritage fuckmaster who had just exhaustively demonstrated his mastery to Josh, told him he envied him the visit. He said that Cuernavaca was a beautiful place he himself had enjoyed visiting when he had accompanied his father to a family reunion in Mexico. When Josh offered that if Gundo thought Cuernavaca was so wonderful, he would do well to accompany him on the trip.

Gundo surprised Josh by agreeing to go—an offer which added greatly to the euphoria the younger man already felt from having just fucked and been fucked by his very favorite porn star!

Brad gave his blessing to Gundo's going with Josh to Mexico, and he and Harp planned to enjoy some more quiet time together during their absence.

The night before the two flew to Mexico City was anything but quiet, however. The four had joyous and uproarious sex together in Brad's big bed for hours. Almost everyone sucked almost everyone else and fucked him at least once, but Brad and Josh limited their one-on-one love-making to holding each other's naked bodies while they kissed and caressed. Still, their kissing and fondling were much more passionate than usual: if they drove their tongues into each other's mouth deeper and more hungrily than they normally did, if each actually fucked the other's ass with his finger, instead of just caressing it as he usually did, and if they humped and ground their throbbing erections together longer and more eagerly than was their custom, it was a special night—a *Bon Voyage* party and early New Year's Eve celebration combined.

The first two nights Brad and Harp spent alone together were marked by the tender and sweet variety of love-making they too often found lacking in the ecstatic, but still gloriously fulfilling sex they so often shared when others were with them. And the last two nights they spent alone together before Gundo and Josh returned were similarly quiet and romantic. But those pairs of nights parenthesized a very exciting New Year's Eve 1998 night.

About six in the afternoon on December 31st Dan Bliss called and said he didn't expect any escort business that night, so he was hoping that Josh and company didn't have any big plans for the evening. If they didn't, he said he wanted to turn off his pager, pick up some champagne and a few porn videos he'd been wanting to see, and come over for a visit and a "whatever-you're-doing-at-midnight-on-New-Year's-Eve-you're-going-to-do-all-year-long" session of sex (a "cluster-fuck" was what he actually called it).

When Brad told him Josh had gone to Mexico with Race

Rivera, Dan first expressed envy, followed by a happy thought: "Hey, I've only got so many loads I can shoot in one night anyway, so there'll be more for you and Harp!"

Brad laughed, "Yeah, but there'll only be two of us to fuck you instead of three."

"Well," Dan said, "you guys are just gonna have to work extra hard then, okay?"

"Sure. Okay, we'll be waiting for you, and we promise to work extra hard if you promise to keep that extra-big cock of yours extra hard for us!"

"It's already extra hard just thinkin' about it," Dan laughed. "See you around eight o'clock."

A few minutes after eight, Dan breezed through the door carrying two bottles of champagne and three rental videos he had picked up. "I didn't bring any party hats—I don't plan for us to be wearing anything at midnight except big grins and even bigger hard-ons!"

They put the champagne in the refrigerator, and settled down in front of the TV with beers.

Dan put a cassette in the VCR, saying, "Here's a new Brenden Knight video—well, one I haven't seen, anyway. I've heard his scene is really romantic, and that should put us in the mood for some really sweet love. And then I've got a Jeff Palmer and a Tom Chase, and I figure those'll get us in the mood to fuck each other like demons."

The porn star Dan had most recently fallen 'in lust' with was the cute blond Brenden Knight. He had been voicing his desire to fuck him ever since he first saw the adorable K.C. Hart plowing his gorgeous ass on a boat in *Malibu Beach Hunks*. Brenden had bottomed in every video Dan had seen so far, but as this one began, Dan said, "With that big dick of his—and it stays hard every fuckin' minute—he's gotta be an incredible top. I wish to hell I'd be the first one he fucks in a video."

Harp laughed, "Hell, you just wanna be one he fucks however you can work it out!"

"You got that right," Dan replied.

The Brenden Knight scene at the end of the first video was very satisfyingly hot and sexy, with plenty of steamy fucking and sucking, but a single red rose, sheer curtains blowing in the breeze, and gentle kissing gave it an aura of romance that engendered plenty of sweet kissing and cuddling on the part of the three viewers.

The performance of the mega-studs Tom Chase and Jeff Palmer put them in quite a different mood. Tom Chase had a great body and an astonishing cock, which combined enormous dimensions with an unfailingly steel-hard rigidity extremely rare in porn. Jeff Palmer was gorgeous. He, too, had a wonderful physique, and his impressive cock stayed as hard as Tom Chase's. What set Jeff apart was that he was perhaps the most savage, most *ferocious* buttfucker any of them had ever seen. As a special endearing characteristic, both Jeff and Tom always blew huge, explosive loads.

The mood these last videos put the three in was clearly shown when Dan stood and said, "Let's get in bed. If I don't get some ass to fuck, I'm gonna blow a gasket."

"Well, we don't want you to blow a gasket," Brad said as he and Harp rose. "But after watching those guys you're sure gonna have to blow a couple of hard pricks!"

Within a record-breaking short period of time, all three were naked and rolling on Brad's bed. Their collective two-plus feet of raging hard cock got enough exercise to observe several New Year's Eve celebrations.

As midnight began to strike, Harp had his prick buried deep inside Brad's ass while the enormous bulk of Dan's was plunging in and out of his own ass with nine-inch piston-strokes. Dan pulled his raging cock out of Harp and ripped the condom off, telling the two men kneeling before him, "Lay down on the bed, I'm gonna shoot all over you both!"

By the time the clock tolled its twelfth stroke, Dan shouted "Happy New Year!" and began bathing Harp and Brad in a hot white shower—much appreciated and admired, as the two voiced their enthusiastic encouragement. Dan fell on top of them both, and the three rolled together, embracing and kissing lustily, lubricated by the copious orgasm.

Brad and Harp made Dan use his tongue to clean up after himself, which he did with great pleasure. Dan then knelt on all fours at the side of the bed while his two lovers-for-the-night stood behind him and alternated fucking his hungry ass with the same kind of dedication he had brought to servicing them. Rather than spraying Dan's body with the liquid salute he had given them, each blew his load deep inside the appreciative young man's ass. With their cocks sheathed in condoms and buried inside, the mighty discharge each delivered was not palpable, nor was its impressive volume observed, but the fervor and artistry involved in producing it was apparent to all—especially to the eager recipient.

They continued to "ring in the New Year" in similar fashion over about two more time-zones before falling asleep—exhausted, satisfied, and happily wrapped all around each other.

The first day of 1998 began for Brad and Harp and Dan with a three-man shower, which consumed an inordinate amount of time, since their attention to personal cleanliness was constantly interrupted by sexual horseplay and some joyous cocksucking and buttfucking as well. Three orgasms later, they dried off and had breakfast. Brad didn't even feel he had to apologize for his having only contributed one to the total produced during the shower—he had matched Harp's three the night before, which was close enough to the total of four the raging stud Dan had delivered. And besides, he thought, I'm old enough to be these guys' fathers.

And Brad was about the same age as the father whom Dan soon went to visit, and with whom Dan later that day demonstrated the same talents he had shown Brad and Harp that very morning.

And Brad was the father of the young man who was waking about the same time in the arms of Gundo Lopez, some 1,750 miles to the Southeast. The matchless cock Josh felt poking into his stomach was even larger and more nearly irresistible than the leviathan Dan Bliss was then using to service his father, and his father's lover, and his own lover—two people with three descriptions! Neither Josh nor Gundo could delay making love until they got in the shower, however, and they didn't!

Gwen had been delighted to learn that one of Josh's friends was going to accompany him to Cuernavaca, and promised the two could stay in a separate guest house by the pool. Gundo was made to feel welcome at the Turley house, and few questions were asked about his relationship to the considerably younger Josh—and those were easily answered with mutually agreed-upon lies. The guest house proved to be especially advantageous, as Josh and Gundo spent many, many hours every day and night in athletic and fairly noisy sex there!

Returning home, Gundo told Josh a secret he had waited to reveal until they left Mexico. Quentin Turley had not only recognized him as "Race Rivera," but on three separate occasions when Josh and his mother had been absent on short shopping trips, he had paid $500 for the privilege of administering an expert, obviously practiced blowjob to Gundo's monster cock. Gundo added, laughing, that Francisco, the supernaturally beautiful Mexican pool boy whom he and Josh had spent an entire night fucking with, had told him after giving him a surreptitious 'good-bye blowjob' while Josh had been taking leave of his mother and stepfather, that it was his own lovely, ample Mexican cock that *El Senor* Turley usually serviced.

. . .

In March '98, San Francisco mayor Willie Brown conducted an unofficial mass wedding ceremony for gay couples at City Hall, pronouncing about fifty couples "domestic partners for life." There was no legal paperwork involved, so the fact that one of the men participating in the ceremony married two different men at the same time was not remarked.

At that moment, Mark David "Harp" Harper, former Model/Escort, became a partner in a three way marriage that ultimately allowed him to become something of a Model Stepfather to one of his partners, and at same time a Model Stepson to his other partner.

And they all lived happily ever after. At least for quite a while—longer than anyone would have predicted.

Really!

Acknowledgements

The coverboy, Luke, and Roy, featured on the frontispiece and above, appear through the courtesy of the celebrated English photographer David Butt. Mr. Butt's photographs may be purchased through Suntown, Post Office Box 151, Danbury, Oxfordshire, OX16 8QN, United Kingdom. Ask for a full catalogue. A collection of Mr. Butts's photos, *English Country Lad*, was recently released by Gay Men's Press, and is available from STARbooks Press and at fine bookstores worldwide.

The photograph on page 213 was supplied by the model and is used with his permission.

The author is deeply indebted to John Patrick and Don James for their assistance.

About the Author

The author, shown with the two men to whom "Model/Escort" is dedicated.

During his professional career, John Butler wrote music and scholarly articles in his role as a professor, and unthinkable mountains of correspondence in the capacity of administrator at a major American university. Following his retirement he decided to write about his personal interests—not matters of the heart, but matters of a different body organ (his favorite one), located a bit South of his heart.

"Model/Escort" is the first of his novels to be published.